Return to Turand

Praise for
Return to Turand
Echo Sonata
Legends from Turand

This is a story of loss, mystery, treachery, faith, courage, compassion, and above all, great love in all its forms. With her tremendous, thoroughly descriptive story-telling ability, Ms. Valencia develops her characters fully, and leaves the reader feeling that they have known Gregor, Alexa, Victor, and others for years. She draws the reader into the story on every page, and in a way makes it easy to lose sight of the fact that the story is fiction. This is a must read!

—Janice Thompson, Ohio

By the time I finished a few pages, I was hooked all over again. When I finished, I couldn't believe I already reached its end. Days passed by and I couldn't help thinking about the book. There were ideas and concepts that haunted me. So, I read it again. Ms. Valencia has created characters so real that I can close my eyes and see them. Their triumphs and challenges take my breath away. What I also see is a sort of wisdom I never expected from a book like this.

—Songbird

Return to Turand

Echo Sonata
Legends from Turand

Sandra Valencia

Book Design & Production:
Columbus Publishing Lab
www.ColumbusPublishingLab.com

Copyright © 2022 by
Sandra Valencia
LCCN: 2022920190

Hardcover ISBN: 978-1-63337-699-1
Paperback ISBN: 978-1-63337-700-4
E-Book ISBN: 978-1-63337-701-1

Printed in the United States of America
1 3 5 7 9 10 8 6 4 2

Take comfort in the faith you have been given.
Guard it well.
Love is your strength.
Faith is your shield.

I received encouragement from many people, especially the readers of Song of Turand, who sent messages urging me to complete this return journey. I sincerely appreciate their dedication to this unusual story.

I dedicate this book to the memory of Geneva Jackson: woman, teacher, and guide. By transcending social and racial barriers, she courageously reached out to change many lives. She believed in me when no one else did. In doing so, she taught me to believe in myself.

True love is honest, real beyond our imaginations,
Powerful enough to span the ages and the universe,
If only we open our souls to believe.
And though we believe, trials will surely come.
Sorrow and despair will test our spirits.
We must learn to summon courage and faith to our hearts,
So that all we have been may continue to be.
In doing so, we discover eternity is possible only through love.

Author's Note

Our world changed dramatically three days before the initial release of Song of Turand. Within weeks, readers were approaching me with questions. Was Song of Turand a collection of premonitions? Did the book contain messages related to events that coincided with the book's release? Some referred to eerie similarities to those events and pointed out specific book details that substantiated their observations.

The questions and observations left me startled and, more than ever, mystified. My connection to the story of Turand is one that had already perplexed me when it began nearly twenty-five years before the book was published. I was overtaken by a series of dreams more vivid than any motion picture. At first, the images and words were disjointed. No thread of consistency bound together words and pictures in a way I could comprehend when I awoke. However, I remained haunted by the people whose faces and voices I had come to know so well.

After years of my scribbling page after page of dreams, the night images abruptly stopped. Then, more than a year later, just as suddenly, they began again. A significant difference in the dream pattern was obvious. This time, the events held distinct chronological order. Quite honestly, I don't know if I succumbed to inspiration or obsession. I only knew I had to write down what I had seen and felt.

Nearly three-quarters of Return to Turand was already written when Song of Turand was published. A close friend had already begun reading Echo Sonata when readers' questions cast stunning light upon new, inexplicable events that held fresh mystery. Her calls and observations left me bewildered. Since then, I have cried more than I care to admit.

Are these books simple adventures from some faraway, fictional world? Are they the author's attempt to write down a story that disturbed years upon years of sleep? Is it possible that inspired messages have been delivered in an unusually mysterious form? Do cautionary words reach out to us from the nation of Turand? Then, I could not say with absolute certainty. With new images invading my dreamtime, I awoke and asked myself those same questions.

Introduction

Turandans have resurrected their faith in Val. In doing so, they have revitalized their nation. Prosperity abounds. Artistic endeavors flourish anew. In peace, the glories of the past have returned as blessings to the people.

As King Gregor assesses the successful accomplishment of treasured dreams for his nation, sorrow fills his heart. His people, friends, children, and even his one-time enemy, Lord Victor Garogan, share his grief. For months, all have struggled to unravel the mystery of Alexa's disappearance. No trace lingers as clue to his wife's fate. Turandans are left only to cling to their adored Valkana's memory and the faith she extolled.

Lord Victor Garogan relentlessly pursues resolution of questions connected to Alexa's strange absence. Years have failed to dim his feelings for her. Despite her intense love for Gregor, time itself has not severed the connection binding Victor to her. Assaulted by dreams, he refuses to accept that she simply vanished.

All the while, Gregor continues his life's journey while haunting memories repeatedly transport him into the past. How rich those times past when Alexa's presence graced his life. How empty his future without her love. Contemplating overwhelming loss, Gregor aches in both body and spirit.

And—beyond the pressing desire to know what fate befell his beloved Alexa— Gregor voices the question asked by all of Turand.

When will Val return to Turand the blessing of Valkana?

Part 1

My Lord, my God,
My eyes do I cast toward Your heavens,
Yet my tears Your sun cannot dry.
My heart feels frozen; it knows no warmth.
My body, racked with pain, aches to die.

My Lord, my God,
My ears recoil, rejecting agonized cries.
My mind retreats, stunned and terrified.
Frightful screams torn from a tortured soul.
Silence again. My God, it was I who cried.

And cry out did she,
"My Lord, my God!
Forgive me my greed!
Look not on my selfish heart!
My love for You
Remains ever true,
But my heart, in tatters, does not forget."

Return to Turand

My Lord, my God,
Your message came from light and love.
Your servant child You sent to me
With hand so delicate wrapped 'round mine,
From darkness she led me and set me free.

My Lord, My God,
Her image appears within my mind.
Her smile so glorious, her eyes so bright,
Her voice a song, her touch a balm,
As my life of despair she turned to Your light.

And cry out did he,
"My Lord, my God!
Forgive me my greed!
Look not on my selfish heart!
My love for You
Remains ever true,
But my heart, in tatters, cannot forget."

My Lord, my God,
I hope, I pray, Your will to comprehend,
So dark is this place where You did send me.
My promises, my vows, I struggle to keep.
Oh! Help Your child live faithfully.

My mind seeks escape, my heart yearns for home.
His arms, I'm so sure, long to hold me again.
Our lives tightly bound, our souls as one,
My life the journey. His love, my destination.

And cry out did she, "My Lord, my God!
Forgive me my greed!
Look not on my selfish heart!
My love for You
Remains ever true,
But my heart, in tatters, does not forget."

My Lord, my God,
Cherished blessing You sent to be mine.
Through our love came children so dear.
Now, to my chest, I clutch them tightly,
Through their angelic voices, hers I still hear.

My body revolts. Her touch it demands.
Through nights long and lonely, I do not sleep.
I think on years, now gone, when slumber escaped
And her song so sweet took my weariness to keep.

And cry out did he, "My Lord, my God!
Forgive me my greed!
Look not on my selfish heart! My love for You
Remains ever true,
But my heart, in tatters, cannot forget."

My Lord, my God,
The blows they strike slash my flesh.
My screams resound! Louder than before.
The pain into my body sharply pierces.
That body, so weak, can take no more.

Blackness, so welcome; the void becomes all.
Their fury, their hatred, they cast at me.
My blood drawn forth, my life they steal.
Fall, I do; will sweet death now set me free?

And cry out did she, "My Lord, my God!
Forgive me my greed!
Look not on my selfish heart!
My love for You
Remains ever true,
But my heart, in tatters, does not forget."

My Lord, my God,
Recalling those sacred promises I made,
My pledges I kept as we fought for peace.
With her by my side, I was no longer afraid.
But dread has returned. Will grief never cease?

My Lord, My God,
Sounding in my soul, a canyon wide:
Memories, wealth of life, voices from long ago.
Across soaring peaks and valleys broad,
Ring now lost treasures, forever to echo.

And cry out did he, "My Lord, my God!
Forgive me my greed!
Look not on my selfish heart!
My love for You
Remains ever true,
But my heart, in tatters, cannot forget."

My children, my children, beloved are you.
Sojourn you must through the canyon of grief.
Turn your ears to the breeze; listen for echoes.
Great comfort memories bring.
Let your songs not lament,
Love's wings can carry you from sorrow's throes.

My children, my children, beloved are you.
Think not of greed when so much you have given.
Your hearts filled with love are all that I see
As my love for you remains ever true
My children, my children, beloved are you.
Valleys stretch wide. Mountains sweep high.
Love is my gift. In my hands, you I hold.

Lift high your voices. Send forth your songs,
With melodies sweet, their return is foretold.
Throughout the ages you are destined to go.
Greater than memories, more than an echo,
As forever and longer, I shall be with you,
As my love and yours remain ever true.

Echo Sonata

Chapter 1

S unlight cast brilliant, arrow-straight rays in a glorious circle bursting through puffs of clouds that drifted across the morning sky. The fresh scent of rain-washed soil hung in the air. Barely audible, yet there for any choosing to listen, was the sound of thirsty ground drinking in life-renewing waters poured down from heaven the night before.

Gregor stood, a solitary figure, by the forest's edge near Lindaval's great hot springs. He gazed pensively toward the sky. Golden shafts of sun. Turquoise heavens. Clouds blushing with rosy hues. His dark brown eyes absorbed every delicate color in the natural masterpiece stretching before him.

He sighed heavily. His longish hair, now liberally streaked with silver, rippled in the fragrant breeze. His tall body, still elegant and powerfully built, carved a striking profile against shining sky. Breathing in deeply and smiling, he recalled how she had constantly reminded him to savor with all his senses the majesty nature so generously shared.

Slowly, he began trudging across sodden ground and through thick, wet foliage, feeling glad he had decided to take a few days to come alone to Lindaval. Only now was he beginning to realize how much he had needed time to himself—time away from the kind intentions of friends and even his children.

Nearly six months had passed since she had disappeared during a mission of mercy to the north of Turand. Six months. He squeezed his eyes tightly shut. Six months of agony since he had journeyed to Kisana to join her party. The desolation and destruction wrought by nature following a severe ground-quake and subsequent flooding. Disconcerting quiet. Mushrooming anxiety as he and his Royal Guard searched for miles around, finding few signs of life and not even a single vestige of his wife, her personal guards, or the four Valiria priestesses who had accompanied her.

Gregor paused a moment, then crouched down. Long fingers picked up a broken lilac branch still clinging to its cone of delicate lavender flowerets. He held the tiny blossoms close to his nose, savoring the soft fragrance that never failed to evoke her memory. "Alexa. My beloved Alexa," he whispered reverently. He closed his eyes, pondering yet again the mystery that continued to ravage his soul.

Faint breezes rustled leaves in the trees, and he felt convinced that, for fleeting seconds, they carried with them sweet notes of her laughter. Shaking his head against the impossible, he rose again to resume his hike.

Penetrating deeper and deeper into the forest, he began to perspire heavily from the exertion of climbing over fallen timbers and jumping across broad, muddy puddles. His heart beat powerfully inside his chest, and his lungs drew in clean, invigorating air. How desperately he had needed this afternoon! As he carefully climbed over a huge, moss-slick tree that had fallen across his path, he realized he was smiling despite the weight of his sorrow.

"Gregor, my love, always remember. Together, we weathered storms of history. We faced the fury of the Sifiq, and we met the tempest of civil war. We spent years sailing winds of change as we rebuilt Turand, both materially and spiritually. No matter how dark the storm or how heavy the winds, calm always returned. The sun always conquered."

Her words echoed throughout every corner of his being. Her fascination with storms had always perplexed him, especially considering that her character was usually so calm, so steady, and so serene. Still, injustice or the need to defend those she loved could provoke her own storms of temper. Wistfully, he recalled her expression as she drew comparisons of calm and tempest to life itself.

Gregor soon found a clearing where an enormous sun-dried boulder provided a wide, flat surface where he could sit and consume the lunch he carried inside a canvas knapsack. Thick slices of smoked meat and smooth, yellow cheese between a sliced, crusty, freshly baked baguette provided satisfying sustenance. To wash down his food, he had brought a flask of red wine.

Having eaten, he pulled a rolled-up mat from his knapsack and laid it flat next to the stone. Sitting on the mat, he leaned back against the rock. Closing his eyes, he rested his head against hands clasped together behind his neck. As the sun warmed his cheeks, he grew drowsy from the combination of exercise and wine. Within minutes, he drifted off to sleep.

Dreamlike memories paraded through his mind. He was a little boy again, running capriciously through palace gardens. Stumbling on an uneven stone, he tumbled to the ground. With hands scraped, pants torn, and knees bleeding, he cried loudly.

Taking only seconds to reach him, his mother lifted him from the ground and into her arms. He had buried his tear-stained face against her shoulder, the stinging of his scrapes and cuts nothing compared to his humiliation. He had ignored his father's admonition to be careful, only to fall and hurt himself.

His body still recalled the rhythm of his mother's steps as she carried him to a stone bench, where she put him down before sitting close beside him. The love in her expression was like a glow driving away his shame and his hurt. He had concentrated on his mother's dark, beautiful features, scarcely noticing how her hands floated back and forth above little hands and knees. All that mattered was the soothing serenity of her smile as her hands melted away his pain and closed cut and scraped skin. Soon, he was running again, although much more mindful of his father's affectionate reminder to watch where he was going.

A hint of a smile curved sensuously full lips framed by his full beard. He lowered a hand from over his shoulder, sliding it down to his chest and allowing his palm to rest above the miniature crystal pyramid beneath his shirt. The treasured memento had belonged to his mother. Until Alexa had found it and given it to him just before he rode off to war, he had never known his mother was a Valiria priestess. Ever since then—for nearly twenty years—he never allowed it to be far away from him.

Now, that pyramid began to vibrate gently with a life of its own. He felt the odd sensation beneath his fingertips. Part of him wanted to awaken. His heart resisted. His spirit welcomed the rest while his soul responded to the tingling seeping throughout his body.

"Gregor, my son." Her voice sounded so close—so real.

"Yes, Mother?" His mouth formed words spoken only inside his head.

"My son, Alexa was right those many years ago when she told you that you, too, are blessed. I love you, Gregor. Your father and I are so proud of all you have done. Our spirits rejoice in you, our son, and in your family. Stay faithful, Gregor. Remain strong. Always remember what your father and I taught you. Gregor, never forget Alexa's words to you."

Gregor's head rolled from side to side. The expression on his face clouded with pleading. "Mother, please! Don't go! Mother, please! I need you! I'm that little boy you held so long ago. I hurt, Mother—like I've never hurt before. Help me, Mother. Please don't leave me alone again."

The sensation of loving fingers caressed his face, soothing away his distress. "Your father and I are always near, my son. They murdered our bodies, but never could they destroy our souls. Do not forget. Part of us dwells forever within you. You are our physical immortality, my son, as are your children. Live, Gregor. Remember what Alexa always told you about storms."

Again, words sounded so close inside his weary, sleep-drugged mind. "Gregor, my love, the calm always returned. The sun always conquered."

It was late when Gregor returned to Lindaval's manor house. The nearly impenetrable Lindaval darkness hardly slowed his pace across a terrain he knew by heart. Once back, he bathed and dined alone. The manor's caretakers, an elderly couple, observed his mood and respected his desire for solitude. They noted that lines of grief remained etched around his eyes; however, there also existed a sense of change in him. Not reluctant surrender to the idea that Alexa would never return to him. Not inevitable acceptance of her death. Instead, it appeared he had met his terrible sorrow and discovered inner strength to manage it.

That night, Gregor stretched out his long, nude body between the coolness of smooth sheets and blankets covering the bed he had shared with her so many times throughout the years. Instead of his recent tossing and turning, he fell asleep almost instantly. For the first time in many months, dreams did not invade to torment him with all he had lost. Instead, deep within his being, her presence lingered. As always, that presence fortified him—comforted him—encouraged him. Her love continued to saturate every fiber of his body, every color in his soul.

In his sleep, he smiled tenderly. "No, Alexa," he whispered. "Not the sun. Our love always conquered."

⌣

Three days later, Gregor returned to his capital city of Toraval. Riding through streets toward the palace, he still felt amazed by how much the city had changed during the years since the Sifiq occupation had ended. Toraval, the heart of Turand, throbbed with its own zesty rhythm and vitality. Buildings constructed centuries earlier had been restored to their original architectural beauty following years of abuse and neglect under Sifiq rule. Creativity, so deeply ingrained in Turandans, had once again blossomed. Toraval's many parks boasted lanes and squares dotted with dozens of easels as artists sketched, drew, and painted. Lavishly costumed mimes pranced and danced through their silent mimicry of everyday events, intent on evoking humor or thoughtful contemplation. Music enlivened the air as summer's warmth inspired minstrels to sing of legends, hope, and love.

The commercial center bustled, its shops bursting with daily necessities and luxuries now reaching a level of abundance in a thriving Turand. Artfully arranged seascapes crafted from driftwood, seashells, and other treasures yielded by the oceans arrived from coastal provinces. From the western regions came intricately designed gold and silver jewelry, often set with rainbows of brilliantly cut and polished stones. From eastern provinces originated many finely crafted musical instruments. Richly grained woods from the south were displayed in beautiful furniture styles ranging from simple lines to ornately carved designs.

Yet, despite all the wealth flowing throughout Turand's twenty provinces, the material items yielded by a prospering nation only hinted at the true riches the people had reclaimed. Intellectual pursuits flourished, and Turandans once again embraced Val's teachings. Gregor's people had learned a bitter, valuable lesson. They had listened carefully to their Valkana, paying heed to her wisdom. They had studied her example and striven to renew the faith she demonstrated. They enjoyed the fruits of their labors but had learned better than to covet them.

Friendship. Devotion. Loyalty. As she had often reminded them, the greatest of Val's treasured gifts were love, peace, and fidelity. Turandans had returned to this concept upon which their society had been founded and now guarded it ferociously. As a people, they had vowed never to allow history to repeat itself, thus avoiding the despair of the previous century.

Arriving at the square in front of the palace, it seemed all six of Gregor's children must have been watching for him as they hurried to greet him even before he could dismount. As a groom led his horse away, he was assaulted by two little girls with waist-length ebony curls bouncing in the air. Gregor knelt and laughed as their little arms circled his neck. Then, with one strong arm around each child, he hugged them close and kissed them both. "Marina! Karina! How I've missed you!"

He then rose to embrace DiMarco and Thikos, his middle sons. Both laughed when their father declared they had each surely grown taller since he had left just a week ago. The boys, thirteen and eleven, hugged their father tightly, glad to have him home. Both had struggled since their mother's disappearance. Each harbored secret fears about losing their father.

His oldest daughter assumed control of her four younger siblings. After admonishing them to calm down since their father must certainly be tired from his long trip, she moved straight into Gregor's arms and kissed his cheek. "Welcome home, Father. We've missed you, too."

Anlía. Sometimes, he found it almost heartbreaking to look at her, so much was she like Alexa. She moved with the same quiet grace. Her delicate features reminded him of her mother. And though her dark hair and skin tones were obviously inherited from her father, she was the only one of his and Alexa's children to inherit her mother's stunningly beautiful emerald eyes.

"Father!" Nikolai's voice sounded strong above the continuing bubbling chatter from his brothers and sisters. "It's so good to have you home again."

As Gregor reached above bobbing heads to embrace his oldest son, he felt exceedingly grateful for the blessings of his large family. Many had thought him nearly crazy when Thikos, his fourth child, had been born. Few Turandans ever had more than two children. With three children considered a huge family, a fourth child was extremely rare. Then, when Gregor had announced Alexa's fifth and final pregnancy, waves of good-natured twitters had erupted over the very evident nature of his relationship with his wife and the prolific results. He had laughed heartily, readily admitting enslavement to his wife's attractions and fascination with their children.

Now, those same children provided him with both focus and purpose. For Gregor, they had become his anchor as he so often felt lost and alone in uncertain seas since Alexa's disappearance. He smiled at his children's happy faces, acknowledging that, ironically, he truly needed them more than they needed him.

Home again, Gregor quickly immersed himself in the daily routines of governing his nation and parenting his children. He rose early every morning, going to the palace chapel to pray alone. His faith in Val had flourished in the years following his marriage to Alexa. Even now, tormented as he was by her mysterious fate, his love for Val comforted him. The serenity and solitude in that sacred space were an essential beginning to his days. In the peaceful hour just after dawn, he reinforced through prayer the faith that had carried him through years of turmoil and challenge.

After prayers, Gregor leisurely took tea in his office and reviewed his schedule for the day ahead. He then returned upstairs to awaken each of his children personally with a hug and a kiss. Even Nikolai, who would soon turn eighteen, welcomed his father's ritual. Alexa had instilled in her family a deep and abiding appreciation for the physical demonstrations of affection. She had shown them how to respect one another and how to love. As a result, Nikolai felt no shame or embarrassment that his father embraced him and kissed him daily. Instead, he considered his father's open show of affection a sign of loving security.

Gregor's days were spent in meetings and planning sessions, all orchestrated by Stefan Sidano, who continued his role as Gregor's most trusted adviser and best friend. The two men had matured their boyhood friendship into a powerful force that had led their nation out of occupation and rebellion. They had then stood at the forefront during the early years of reorganizing Turand's government and subsequent rebuilding of a country nearly decimated by the scourge of a cruel enemy. Now married to Alexa's best friend and enjoying his own prolific family of three, Stefan continuously offered dedicated service and supportive friendship to Turand's king.

Gregor rarely missed midday with his children. He took an active interest in their education, their ideas, and individual talents. He found that a meal with all of them gathered together provided him opportunities for lively interaction and insight into each one. Gregor had also developed a master's touch at drawing each of them into revealing discussions. Afterward, he never failed to feel stimulated and refreshed.

Just as he rarely missed midday with them, he jealously guarded most evenings to reserve time with his family. Following Alexa's example, he had assigned each child a special evening, spending a full hour in private to discuss anything that came to mind. Those hours he considered sacred. His children cherished those special nights when Father's time was exclusively theirs. The bonds already forged with his sons and daughters grew even stronger.

Following what they called "Father's Private Hour," the entire family gathered in the library or the family sitting room. Most often, they continued a beloved tradition Alexa had initiated by reading aloud. Some nights, they invited musicians so the family could listen to music or participate in lively sing-a-longs. Once the little ones tired, Gregor ushered his brood into the chapel for night prayers. As a family, they prayed for continued good health and offered thanks for the many blessings bestowed upon them and their nation. And, without fail, they prayed that Val would keep their mother safe in His loving care.

Chapter 2

Two weeks following his return from Lindaval, Gregor sat quietly in his office. He leaned back in his tall leather chair with hands clasped together, thoughtfully considering Stefan's review of plans for Nikolai's eighteenth birthday celebration. Tradition called for the king to formally announce his son's transition to manhood. Then, with elaborate ceremony, Gregor would also proclaim Nikolai as the official heir to the throne of Turand.

"Stefan, it seems only yesterday that I carried Nikolai downstairs to introduce him to you, Adrina, and Victor. Where have the years gone? How is it possible that he is already grown into manhood?"

Stefan smiled and nodded. "I see my own family and feel awed by how quickly they've grown. I can only imagine how you must feel."

Gregor sighed. "I keep thinking of that little boy who was such a hero when Anlía was born. Or the little imp who sneaked the snake inside the palace that Victor helped him catch in Garogan. I will never forget how hard I laughed when Lady Manaran fainted that day. She was always such a nuisance. Now, my little boy is taller than I am!"

"Well, Turand has finally grown accustomed to its giant king. So why not start a tradition?"

Chuckling, Gregor stood and walked around his desk to clasp Stefan's shoulder. "As always, you have organized an excellent program. I can't imagine better plans for the celebration." As soon as the words were spoken, his eyes darkened, and his expression turned somber.

Stefan instantly recognized the pain reflecting from Gregor's deeply wounded soul. "Don't, Gregor. She wouldn't want you to continue suffering this way. You know that."

"You know it won't be the same without her. If only I knew what happened. If only I hadn't agreed to her leaving ahead of me. My children might still have their mother, and I would still have my wife. Victor warned me years ago, but I didn't listen."

"Gregor, stop it. You cannot change what happened. If there's one thing I learned from Alexa, it is that life is a gift despite all its challenges and sorrows. What was it she always used to say? You must continuously expect blessings in life. If you do, you will surely find them."

Gregor's face dropped, and he stared at the floor. "I know you're right." He answered, then looked back up at Stefan. "Too many unanswered questions creep into my mind that are just too damned difficult to dismiss. What could have happened to her? When will Val present us with a new Valkana? Why hasn't he done so already?" Gregor stroked his beard thoughtfully. "So many unanswered questions, Stefan."

"You must concentrate your thoughts elsewhere. Try to enjoy the preparations for the fete in Nikolai's honor. He idolizes you. Your personal involvement will make it all the more special. Not only that, your efforts will help him, too. You know how close he was to Alexa. Her absence will be hard for him."

Gregor nodded. "I remember how hard it was not having my mother with me. You're right, Stefan. You may need to nudge me or remind me from time to time, but I promise. I will do everything possible to make this occasion as special for Nikolai as he deserves."

The following day, Gregor summoned Nikolai to his office. Victor, who had arrived in Toraval the previous afternoon, and Stefan both attended. Nikolai appeared somewhat puzzled as he lowered himself into one of the chairs in front of his father's enormous desk. He rarely had occasion to interrupt his father during the course of daily business and, upon entering, was surprised to find both godfathers waiting with his father.

"Nikolai," Gregor began thoughtfully, "Stefan, Victor, and I have been discussing plans for furthering your education after your coronation as Crown Prince. However, I think it is only fair that you participate in those plans since this is your life we're discussing."

Nikolai's left eyebrow arched, making him resemble Gregor more than ever. "Father, I trust both your wisdom and your judgment. Is this really a matter with which to trouble Stefan and Victor?"

Gregor suppressed a smile. Although he would be heartbroken if his son chose to forsake his heritage, Gregor was also determined to allow Nikolai the right to decide his own future. "Nikolai, more than just the matter of your education, I want to be certain you understand the responsibilities that come with monarchy. Quite honestly, there have been times in my life when I nearly cursed my birthright. I am grateful to Val that Turand has nearly recovered all that once was lost. You should come to the throne under much better circumstances than I did. However, there is tremendous work involved. The sacrifices can be staggering. I want you to carefully consider that, knowing that I offer you a choice."

Nikolai glanced first at Stefan, whose daily presence at the palace had allowed the young prince to serve as a protégé since his early teens. History, politics, and all the related skills of negotiation had fascinated the prince. Stefan had patiently explained intricate traditions and diplomatic techniques required for the successful management of Turand's government.

Nikolai had proven himself an astute student from the beginning, earning both praise and admiration from his mentor and his father alike.

Nikolai then met Victor's penetrating hazel eyes. As always, he felt unique closeness and camaraderie with Victor that often puzzled him. Throughout the years, the royal family had returned to Toraval from Garogan, occasionally leaving Nikolai with Victor. Other times, Victor had come to Toraval, and the two had ridden together to Garogan Province. While Victor instilled a great respect for nature in his godson, he also taught Nikolai how to survive in the wild. Victor had instructed his godson to use the sword, bow and arrow, and every other sort of weaponry known to Turandans. Victor had stressed the critical importance of resolving conflicts peacefully. Life was too precious to endanger with violence if any other option was available. However, circumstances might dictate another war someday. Victor considered it essential that Nikolai be prepared to serve as soldier-king should the need ever arise.

Nikolai's brain whirled with questions. Did this meeting hold a hidden agenda? Did his father harbor doubts about his commitment? Had one of his godfathers expressed concern about some shortcoming? Why were they offering this opportunity to back away from a future that would make him king?

Nikolai drew in a deep, sustaining breath. With sudden insight, he believed he understood. He certainly had earned respect from his father as well as his godfathers. Having been more than a good student wanting to please them, the prince had worked hard, understanding that challenges and hardships lay ahead in a life dedicated to serving his nation. He also recognized that there remained much for him to learn. Still, youthful confidence filled him; however, that confidence was not marred by arrogance. His father truly meant to offer him alternatives. His godfathers stood ready to encourage and support him, whichever path he might choose.

"Father," Nikolai began, "I sincerely appreciate the fact that you care enough to offer options for my future. I know that your reign began under the harshest of circumstances. You then led our people to overcome the worst Turand has ever faced. I take my heritage very seriously. I consider it more than mere birthright as your firstborn child. I acknowledge that I have the unique opportunity to continue what you, Mother, Stefan, and Victor fought for so long ago. I harbor no uncertainties regarding my path to the future. I wish to serve Val first, then our people."

The three older men exchanged satisfied looks. Nikolai had spoken simply, firmly, and for one so inexperienced, eloquently. Confidence clearly reflected in his eyes and in his posture. His voice held no quavers born of indecision. On the contrary, he was focused, secure, and determined. He would become king for all the right reasons.

Gregor rose and, walking around from behind his desk, stopped close in front of his son. "Nikolai, we needed to be positive that this is the path you choose, not one that has been chosen for you. My son, I am proud of you."

Nikolai rose and embraced his father. Smiles and solid pats on the back followed. His godfathers expressed in words as well as actions their own immense pride in the young man they were preparing to assume stewardship of their beloved Turand.

⌐

"Come in," Gregor responded to the light rap on the door to his suite and, looking up from the settee, closed the old, private journal on his lap.

"Father?" Nikolai's voice was tentative as he slipped through the door and quietly closed it behind him. "Am I disturbing you?"

Gregor shook his head sideways. "Come, sit with me. I was only looking through some old books. Is something troubling you?"

Nikolai sat quietly at his father's side for a long moment, a slight smile lighting his face. "Not now. I do admit to being quite shaken for a while this morning when I went to your office. I hadn't expected Stefan and Victor to be there. Now? I just want to thank you."

Gregor's left eyebrow lifted questioningly. "For what?"

"For caring enough to offer me options. Beyond that, I want you to understand that I always thought I had a choice if I wanted."

"I imagine you remember too many of your mother's presentations and lectures. She always reminded us that we're gifted with many possible choices."

"And she was always determined that we make the right ones." Nikolai fell quiet, his youthful face growing thoughtful. "Mother made many of her choices when she was very young, did she not?"

Gregor nodded. "She decided to become Valiria when she was only ten and had already taken her vows into the Order of Val before she turned sixteen."

"Tira once told me that Mother was one of the youngest ever to become avowed Valiria and the last to be anointed before the Sifiq persecution began."

"That's all true. Now, explain how all that relates to this late-night visit." When Nikolai did not answer for several long moments, Gregor patiently waited for his son to speak.

"Father," he began at last, "I want you to feel secure in the knowledge that I do know what I want for the future despite the fact I'm only seventeen. I have no idea how I'll accomplish everything. I certainly know I can never fill your footsteps. On the other hand, I am determined to prepare myself in every way possible to become a good king someday. I consider it imperative that you understand my commitment to continuing and preserving Toscano family traditions. I intend to serve our people to the best of my abilities."

Gregor studied his son's face and proudly acknowledged the intense dedication and sincerity evident in eyes mirroring the depths of Nikolai's young soul. There existed no doubt of the youthful idealism he saw as he placed a hand on his son's shoulder. "I believed you earlier, my son. Just now, I feel you more committed than ever. You can be certain that I shall rest easy knowing Turand's future will be left in your hands."

Nikolai did not reply. Instead, he smiled his appreciation for his father's approval. Anxious to change the subject, Nikolai pointed at the dog-eared book lying in his father's lap. "So, what were you reading when I interrupted?"

Gregor glanced down at his journal and rested his hands on top of it. "An old personal diary. I was reading some entries I made just after the Civil War ended."

"Really? What was it like then?"

Gregor closed his eyes and sighed. Memories swam before his mind's eye. Somehow, he wished to avoid discussion of those days long past. Still, he could appreciate his son's natural curiosity. He also dreaded a past that held disturbing truths he knew he must one day share with Nikolai. Reluctantly, Gregor allowed himself to slip into that past. He began by relating some of the initial events in Turand's recovery period in a quiet voice.

"Nikolai, those days were exhilarating in many ways. While Turand mourned those lost during the occupation and then to war, a kind of euphoria simultaneously infused the entire populace."

Memories ushered Gregor back in time. In this very room, sitting in a rocking chair transported from Garogan, Alexa had held tiny Nikolai. Watching as she gazed into her baby's face, Gregor had been unable to restrain a smile at the sweet tenderness she lavished on their son. Feeling his eyes upon her, she had lifted sparkling eyes to his. "Is it time?"

"Yes. Stefan and Adrina are waiting with Victor in the library. I also believe that nearly half of Turand is standing outside between the palace and the temple."

Alexa chuckled as she rose from the rocker and handed her infant son to her husband. She walked to the bed and smoothed fluffy white blankets edged with embroidered lavender ribbons. Gently laying the baby on the blankets so Alexa could wrap him snugly against the cold outside, Gregor then lifted his bundled son from the bed and carefully cradled Nikolai against his chest. Alexa slipped her hand beneath her husband's arm, and they left the suite and descended the stairs.

Outside, throngs of Turandan citizens from every part of the country had braved Toraval's wintry temperatures. Each face in the sea of people shone with anticipation. Children sat high upon their parents' shoulders. Adults stretched or stood on tiptoe. All wished to glimpse the royal family as it crossed the square to the Great Temple of Val. Their king was now vindicated, declared courageous hero instead of treacherous villain. His queen was blessed Valkana. They now carried their firstborn child, heir apparent to the throne of Turand, into the nation's most holy center of worship. In a country that had suffered decades of privations and violence, all felt honored to witness such a joyous event.

Inside the temple, Thero stood by the altar where he would celebrate the Ceremony of Naming for the young prince. As the officiating priest, he waited patiently, a serene smile curving his lips, a warm glow lighting old eyes. Watching Gregor and Alexa as they walked down the center aisle, Thero still marveled at the incredible transformations Val had wrought over these past two years. How two people could come together as they had was simply miraculous.

Gregor had decreed the celebration be opened to all who could enter. In the long rows of pews, Turandans packed themselves close together. People crammed themselves into the vast temple, quickly filling every available corner. Children sat on laps. There existed no disorder, no competition for better position or seating. Citizens of Turand were quiet and respectful, desiring only to be part of this blessed event.

When the enormous double doors of the temple closed, Thero raised his arms high above his head. A distinct hum, soft and sweet, began to emanate from the crystal pyramid suspended above the altar. Subdued light started to glow around the golden sun embedded within the pyramid's center, prompting Thero to begin the chant of welcome and the initial, meditative prayer. He then paused to allow time for private contemplation. When his voice sounded again, he instructed Gregor and Alexa to approach the altar with their child.

The king and queen presented a stunning image for all who looked on. Gregor was attired in a solid white uniform, his tunic jacket falling to midthigh with a wide, black leather belt at his waist. A purple sash, edged in gold trim, dropped from a narrow strap at the shoulder to just above the hem of his jacket in the back and front. White leggings hugged his muscular legs and slid neatly into the tops of shining, knee-high, black boots. Standing tall beside her husband, Alexa wore a simply designed white gown of finely woven wool. The lavender shawl wrapped around her shoulders was secured in front by an antique amethyst brooch that once belonged to Gregor's mother. Her glossy brown hair was tamed into a knot of springy curls at the back of her head. Both monarchs wore bejeweled crowns. Both faces shone with peace and joy.

"King Gregor and Queen Alexa, you bring a child before the altar of Val. For what purpose do you come?"

Gregor answered the priest's question. "We bring our son so that we may request Val's blessings upon his most precious gift to us."

"In doing so, do you acknowledge the commitment you undertake in requesting such blessing?"

"We are committed to teaching our son to live his life in accordance with Val's ways." Alexa's firm response was clearly heard, even in the farthest corner of the crowded temple.

The light that ringed the sun began to dance and shimmer, expanding its boundaries to the inside edges of its encompassing pyramid. Alexa's head tilted backward for several moments as she absorbed invisible energy radiating from above the altar. As Priestess Valkana, she was exceedingly sensitive to any physical manifestation of Val's presence. Thero and Gregor watched and waited, understanding her reaction.

"Have you honored Val's law of abstinence to prepare yourselves to receive his blessings that you, too, will need as you assume responsibility for guiding this young child?"

Alexa and Gregor glanced at each other and smiled. Though it had not been easy, they had honored ancient tradition requiring them to abstain from sexual intimacies for the first two months of their child's life. They wanted the best for little Nikolai and sincerely believed that Val's laws were intended for the health and well-being of all his creation. "We have," they stated in unison.

When Thero spoke again, his words reminded the new parents of the many joys and the great work inherent in bringing up a child. He described the responsibilities to teach and to guide. He emphasized to them that all would be best accomplished through love and respect. Thero then counseled that they should avail themselves of the wisdom and advice they would find in the Great Book of Val.

Thero's comments lasted no more than five minutes. He then paused, giving time to absorb the content of his oration before addressing the royal couple once again. "King Gregor and Queen Alexa, tradition allows you to name godparents for this baby. Will you do so?"

"We will," Gregor stated. He and Alexa turned to face each other before taking several steps backward. Gregor held Nikolai in front of him, and Alexa placed her hand over the sleeping baby's heart.

"I name Lady Adrina Garogan as godmother to our son," Alexa announced.

"King Gregor, do you agree?"

"I do."

"Lady Adrina Garogan, please step forward." Thero continued, "Lady Adrina, if you understand and accept the responsibilities that come with being godmother to this child, so state now."

"I do understand and accept these responsibilities with a loving heart."

Thero approached Adrina and, dipping his finger into a gold cup of fragrant, perfumed oil, traced triangular lines across her forehead and beneath her eyes. He then touched a drop of the oil to her lips. "This oil bears the blessing of Val. May it penetrate your mind, your vision, and your words so you may help guide this child in the ways of Val."

He returned his attention to Gregor and Alexa. "Do you name another godparent?"

Gregor answered. "We name Sir Stefan Sidano and Lord Victor Garogan as godfathers to our son." The fact that Gregor's voice remained strong and steady was not lost on those who knew of the intense enmity that had once existed between him and Lord Garogan.

Thero displayed no reaction. Instead, he concentrated on the elaborate ceremony and asked Stefan to step forward before repeating the essence of his question to Adrina.

Stefan responded with his usual solemnity, "I undertake responsibility as godfather to this child with the intent of being a loving guide and of providing by example the actions of a man blessed by Val."

Once Thero anointed Stefan with the holy oil, he invited Victor forward. A great hush descended upon the gathering. "Do you, Lord Victor Garogan, understand and accept the responsibilities of being godfather to this child?"

Victor lifted his head and gazed momentarily into the crystal pyramid. Deep within his soul, he buried the sharp ache of having lost one of his most coveted dreams, that of sharing with Alexa the presentation of their own child. With emotions under tight rein, his voice echoed clearly and powerfully. "I accept my role as godfather to this child. I vow to love him, to teach him, and to guide him as if he were my own son."

Alexa glanced sideways as Victor was anointed with the oil. She smiled upon perceiving a faint spark of happiness in him. At the same time, she expected he would never again be completely happy. Glancing back into Gregor's eyes, her love for her husband deepened with gratitude for his understanding and willingness to allow Victor to remain an integral part of their lives.

Thero's voice called her from momentary reflection. "Parents, what name do you give this child?"

Gregor smiled at his wife. "We declare this child to be Nikolai Maxim Toscano, firstborn child of Gregor and Alexa, and prince to the royal throne of Turand."

Thero proceeded to anoint mother and father, after which parents and godparents each anointed the child and prayed blessings over him. The entire gathering then raised voices to Val in an ancient hymn of thanksgiving for the blessing of new life. Then, to sounds of joyous song, Gregor and Alexa donned warm capes and, followed by beaming godparents, strode from the temple, bearing with them the son considered by all of Turand the symbol of everything Val would restore to them.

The quiet in Gregor's suite was broken only by the occasional call of a night bird outside. He looked up into Nikolai's face. "Your birth coincided with what was truly a rebirth for Turand. Foreign invaders were banished. Civil strife ended. For the first time in memory, there was real cause for hope. In that sense, you still remain a symbol of hope for our people—and for me."

Nikolai's smile was humble. "I can only hope never to fail as that symbol."

Gregor shook his head. "There can be no failure so long as you hold faithful to our beliefs."

"Father, what happened after the Ceremony of Naming? Didn't the National Tribunal occur immediately afterward? I know the basic history, but I'm curious about what it was really like."

Gregor remained silent for several long moments. "Midwinter was approaching. As a matter of practicality, we decided to convene the tribunal one week after your official presentation. So many provincial representatives had already come to Toraval for the celebration. Besides, it seemed wise to proceed with trials to address all the bitterness and wrongdoing so we could put it behind us. There could be no moving forward until we reconciled ourselves with those who had tried to destroy us."

Again, Gregor regressed into the past, describing details of events that began reshaping the newly freed nation of Turand. "Each province sent two representatives for the tribunal. We met first to establish standards of conduct. You cannot imagine all of the conflicts and arguments that ensued.

"Some demanded severe and immediate punishment for the prisoners. Others advocated a more moderate approach. Everyone there had suffered in some way or another. Rational discussion disintegrated in the face of unbridled anger. I had to adjourn several sessions early in order to negotiate the settlement of disputes among members of the tribunal. As a result, our most daunting challenge became one of achieving a less volatile environment in which to discuss upcoming proceedings.

"Your mother said little during those first few days. Instead, she watched and listened as many of the tribunal judges argued or shouted to convey their personal viewpoints. Instinctively, she understood the need to exorcise demons of anger and even hatred seeking to dwell in so many of us.

"When she finally spoke out, her words provided thoughtful insight. Her presence alone delivered a calming tone to the conferences. She firmly demanded that there be no tolerance of indiscriminate hatred. No one had suffered more than she at the hands of the Sifiq and Lord Anderon, yet she was the one who argued that all decisions regarding justice needed to be based on truths and compassion. Your mother insisted that much more was at stake than the fates of rebel and Sifiq prisoners. The tribunal would establish precedents that could have enduring effect on how Turand would deal with all future injustices. Closing my eyes, I can still see her standing before the tribunal. One day remains especially vivid in my mind because I truly believe that day steered this nation onto the road of recovery."

Gregor sat upon the throne. His back was stiffly straight, his expression grave. Rectangular tables stretched out from each side of the throne and then turned to form long sides, leaving an open area in the middle. The king's closest advisers sat on each side at the front. From the corners to the ends of the lines of tables, twenty provincial representatives on either side faced each other. The open center held chairs for prisoners and a large area where speakers could be seen and heard by all.

Alexa, standing in the center, dominated the tribunal chamber. She had chosen a lavender gown, trimmed in dark purple velvet. She wore little jewelry, only her wedding ring and a gold chain from which hung a crystal pyramid. Her presence exuded calm resolution and regal command. Confidence and determination shone from magnificent emerald eyes. Her expression was stern, allowing no tolerance for nonsense.

"Esteemed members of this tribunal, I remind you that justice for one signifies justice for all. As well as anyone here, I know the horrors brought upon us by years of brutal violence. However, my past sufferings represent but a mere fragment of the total tragedy Turand endured at the hands of Sifiq conquerors and power-hungry, Turandan rebels. Still, it is essential that we judge each individual based not only on past transgressions but also on what exists now within his soul. Val has already shown us that even Sifiq soldiers are capable of learning to love him. In our midst, Sifiq have turned away from evil and now strive with full hearts to serve Val and his people.

"I implore you. Heed my counsel as channeled from Val himself. Do not close your hearts to the power of forgiveness. Forgiveness is a unique power unto itself and possesses potent healing capabilities. I do not suggest that you disregard those who remain contemptuous of our God and his ways. However, do not seek retribution for the sake of retribution. Seek justice. Seek Val's wisdom and counsel."

Gregor stood, obviously agitated by his own years of emotional outrage. "Lady Valkana, you are well aware that many of these prisoners refuse to denounce their evil ways. Others will most assuredly attempt to deceive us into thinking they wish to change. How do you propose we deal with such issues?"

Even with general standards established, bitter arguments had continued over methods of punishment. There existed widespread accord that immediate execution was necessary for anyone convicted. Gregor himself struggled with perplexing uncertainty regarding the issue of imposing penalties of death. He harbored no great pride in the part of him that craved revenge for the many lives destroyed, especially those of his own parents. Still, the very idea of inflicting more death made him cringe.

Alexa sensed his conflict and met her husband's direct gaze without flinching. Instead, green eyes reflected profound personal conviction. "We have already been forced to march into battle. The precious lives of too many good Turandans were sacrificed in our struggle to regain peace. If we choose to impose punishment by execution as revenge for those deaths, our only accomplishment will be to stain our hands with more blood. That is when we will become little different from those we seek to punish."

The tribunal judges expelled a unified gasp of shock as her words echoed throughout the court. Heavy, uncomfortable silence instantly pervaded the chamber. Alexa chose not to move. Instead, she gazed directly into her husband's dark eyes. Her aura had begun to pulsate and glimmer. The silence intensified as no man or woman present could escape the terrifying concept their High Priestess Valkana had expressed aloud. Long, agonizing minutes ticked by as she awaited reaction.

"I agree with our Lady Valkana."

Abruptly rising to his feet, Victor added his voice for the first time during the weeks since tribunal members had begun to meet. He had spent hours with Alexa the day before. They had discussed the tumultuous emotions churning inside him. Comfortable with her as he could be with no one else, he had expressed intense sorrow, regret, and guilt for what he considered reprehensible and unforgivable actions as a leader of the failed rebellion. In return, Victor had received a sense of hope, a chance for renewal—all possible through the forgiveness of their loving God.

Gregor shifted his gaze toward Victor. What he observed stunned him. Tears created glistening tracks running down Victor's cheeks. Respectfully, Gregor responded, "Lord Garogan, state your reasons."

Victor backed away from his chair. Very slowly, he walked the length of the tables on his side of the chamber until he approached the spot where Alexa stood, stopping only a few feet from her side. His eyes sought hers and received the encouragement he so desperately needed. Speaking from the depths of a troubled soul, his voice quavered.

"Your Majesty and honorable tribunal judges, with all my heart, I express absolute agreement with our Valkana. We must not seek to inflict the punishment of death on any prisoner. These past two years have taught me many painful lessons. For years, I personally witnessed the worst of what the Sifiq perpetrated on innocent victims. I smelled the sickening stench of death left in their wake. With my own hands, I wrapped the bodies of Turandans who had been brutally murdered. I then labored to dig their graves. Some of those bodies were nameless strangers. Others belonged to cherished family members and friends. I watched the misery. I comforted those who lost loved ones to that violence. As you surely understand, my grief remains constant.

"It took very little time until outrage took root and surged within me. I then embarked on my fight against the Sifiq in every way possible. What I never expected was to get so entangled in the drama and fight to affect change that I would lose myself to the very violence I had sworn to end. Inside me existed no concept of the contagion violence becomes. As a result, I began rationalizing my actions, convincing myself that the only way to stop the bloodshed and death was to become an active participant. The final result was that I suffered losses so grievous that I will never fully recover."

Victor's shaking voice steadied as he continued. Unspoken approval from Alexa fortified him, enabling him to express the darkness he had only begun to escape. "Personal loss transformed into anger that grew like cancer, eating its way through the essence of my soul. Engulfed by anger, I allowed sheer hatred to overcome me and every shred of honor I ever possessed.

"How my life has changed. How different is my perspective. I pray each day that Val will truly forgive me for the blood that stains my hands. Blindly, I killed our own people. I believed my way was the only way and that any who disagreed with me were bent on the total destruction of Turand and our way of life. In nearly losing my own life, I finally faced how easily I had been deceived. My own slide into the darkness of selfish ambition and hatred had been fueled by the violence that surrounded me. What I now comprehend is this: If we sink into a renewed pattern of violence, that same violence will guide us straight back onto the path of decline and destruction."

Victor walked in a deliberately slow circle. His posture commanded attention from every judge. "Should this honorable court choose execution for any one of these prisoners, then, rightfully, I hereby declare that I must be the first to die. Val offers reconciliation and forgiveness. As such, I do not fear death. However, I ask you each to carefully consider what execution by Turandans means. I implore you to consider words of wisdom that I will regret for a lifetime that I once ignored. Do not become that which you hate most."

Victor turned and gazed intently into Alexa's eyes. His heart reacted to the sheen of tears that glazed those beloved emerald mirrors to her soul. Once again, the unique bond existing between them connected them, even though they did not touch. She bowed her head in a gesture of respect and profound gratitude. When she lifted her face again, his heart basked in the glory of her approval.

Alexa once again faced her husband. "Your Majesty, just punishment must be exacted. Furthermore, we must act decisively to avoid the risk of future repetitions of such violence by those who refuse to denounce their evil actions. Following hours of meditation, I believe we must place ultimate decisions of life and death into Val's own hands."

Gregor cocked his head to one side, his expression questioning and perplexed. "And how, Lady Valkana, will Val manifest his judgment before a people righteously outraged by the deeds wrought by these prisoners?"

"I propose that judges divide into committees to interview prisoners individually. Later, each committee must summarize its assigned cases. Prisoners will then be allowed to speak directly to the entire Tribunal Council. As a group, we will decide the severity of each prisoner's transgressions. All will be offered opportunities to study and follow Val's ways. Those who honestly seek forgiveness and accept Val's path will be forgiven.

"However, knowing many will not renounce their past, I recommend that we consider different levels of punishment. Those we believe to be guilty of following orders because they are conditioned to do so, without regard to conscience, will be taken to an isolated island where there is no chance for escape. They will be provided regular, basic means to sustain life. However, they will sacrifice their freedom and be forced to toil for their own survival. For those guilty of wanton murder and destruction, final judgment will be exacted by Val himself."

Alexa suddenly grew very quiet. Her eyelids had dropped, and ethereal light once again surrounded her entire presence. Speaking after several long moments, even her voice sounded different. "There are those who even now consider the realities of serving Val. Unfortunately, there are also those whose souls are mired in darkness and destruction. This tribunal bears responsibility for differentiating between these prisoners. The most blatant offenders or those suspected of continued deception will be taken to the Holy Temple of Val. There, they will be allowed to make personal statements. Val will judge their actions and, most importantly, the truth in their souls. Val is the giver of life. If life is to be taken, then Val must be the ultimate judge and allowed to reclaim that which is his."

"Father?" Nikolai interrupted his father's lapse into silence.

Gregor cast an apologetic look toward his son. "It's still so easy to lose myself in remembered images. Your mother and Victor brought intense wisdom to the tribunal that still lingers in our judicial system. Thankfully, we have never needed to return to such harsh realities."

"Father, the history books state only that Val exacted justice upon the guilty. There is never any mention of how."

Gregor rose to his feet and walked across the room to pour a glass of brandy. "Detailed journals are kept at the temple. Few have complete access and only with special authorization. I think it's better that way." He sighed. "Val is not a vengeful God, so he inflicted no further suffering. However…"

Nikolai saw a different kind of sadness cross his father's face. "Do you not wish to discuss it further?"

"It isn't that." Gregor returned to sit beside his son. "You have the right to know. Although I fervently hope not, you may have to face similar events someday. As you're aware, prisoners still live on Cálaza Island. They were primarily followers, both Sifiq and Turandan. Those prisoners not incarcerated on Cálaza were taken in groups of five to the temple.

"Your mother had gone early to the temple to enter a deep state of trance. By the time I arrived, the temple's pyramid glowed fiery red. Never had there been such a phenomenon, and we all believed it to be the result of Val's anger. With each group's arrival, your mother—from her state of trance— spoke individually to the prisoners, allowing each an opportunity to make a statement. Surprisingly, a few requested forgiveness and were granted the chance to study Val's ways and make amends. Some were arrogant enough to believe they could deceive Val and asked forgiveness. Red-hot light shot out from the pyramid, striking them. They instantly fell dead to the floor. Others obstinately defended their right to take whatever they wanted by any means possible. They, too, fell dead after being struck by the red light."

"Were you there the entire time?" Nikolai asked, intrigued by a piece of history he had never even imagined.

"I considered it my responsibility. From a personal perspective, my most difficult moment was when Lord Anderon was escorted to the altar. He had schemed with the Sifiq in hopes of seizing the throne for himself. I held personal animosity toward him not only for that but even more so for other despicable deeds he had committed. I had never forgiven him for having your mother beaten while threatening her with execution. Before Val's altar, I watched him whine and beg for mercy until it made me sick to my stomach. His pleading was in his own self-interest. There was no shred of remorse in him for his part in all that happened."

"How did Val punish him?"

Gregor closed his eyes. "Words echoed within the temple that came not from your mother but from the voice of Val himself. He declared death was too easy a punishment for someone as evil as Lord Anderon. Although well aware of Val's laws, Lord Anderon had defied Val in search of personal power. As such, Val decreed that Anderon should spend the rest of his life on Cálaza as a servant to the other prisoners."

"But why? I don't understand." Nikolai's dark eyes reflected confusion. "Your mother explained later. Val wanted Anderon to stand as a living example of what could easily happen again in Turand if we turned away from our faith. Val's decision was that Anderon should live the life he had intended to inflict upon Turand. There could be no better punishment."

Nikolai shook his head. "I cannot imagine living through such times. For normal citizens, it must have been horrible. Knowing you as I do, it must have been agony."

Gregor smiled thoughtfully. "In some ways, it was. So many of us were forced to contend with the same kind of personal battles Victor so eloquently described. We also had to examine and acknowledge traces of the ugliness that had tainted our own lives. The trials brought us face to face with the horrors we had all lived through. We finally realized that we needed to confront those difficult and painful horrors before we could ever move beyond them. Thankfully, the tribunal lasted barely six weeks. I still thank Val that I had you and your mother as daily reminders of just how precious life could be."

The two sat in contemplative silence for several minutes before Nikolai left for bed. Gregor sat for a while longer, stroking his fingers back and forth across the worn leather cover of his journal. Finally, with a heavy sigh, he got up and placed the book on a shelf, then closed the glass doors of the wooden bookcase. Slowly, he walked inside his bedchamber, removed his robe, and climbed into bed.

Lying on his back, he stared up at the ceiling with eyes that were far from sightless. Instead of the darkness of night, his vision filled with her image from that long ago evening following the Ceremony of Naming.

She had worn a gossamer nightgown that did little to conceal the feminine curves of her body. Her smile had been shy, almost virginal. When he raised his hands to cradle her face, he realized that her entire body quivered. She was as excited as he that they would be able to make love to each other for the first time since he had sent her home from Garogan.

He recalled how he had kissed her slowly, carefully controlling himself as her lips parted in invitation. His fingers glided through the thick tresses of her hair before sliding down to remove the straps of her gown from her shoulders. His heart hammered furiously, sending blood throbbing through his veins. Passion surged powerfully as he pulled her satiny smooth body against his.

Alexa had whimpered, her hands moving to his buttocks and pulling him firmly against her. She whispered his name again and again as her lips tracked their own blazing paths across his shoulders and chest. Her need for him was as great as his for her. Their bodies communicated in an unspoken language, moving slowly and sensually together. He covered her with sweeping caresses and hot, moist kisses, wanting her to be ready to receive him at the first moment of their coming together.

What then followed was a night filled with indescribable love. Their bodies had connected in long-missed, searing passion. Their souls spoke to each other through words of love and precious intimacy that could only be expressed through such complete union. He had known nothing of the hours ticking by as he indulged himself in the sweetness of her body.

Restlessly, Gregor turned over and pulled the covers higher around him. Such nights were now no more than cherished memories. No woman could ever inspire him as she had. No woman would ever know the love he had given her. With her name on his lips, he drifted into sleep.

Chapter 3

"Father! Father! Hurry! Papino Victor! He's back!" Anlía's excited voice echoed through the corridors outside Gregor's office.

Raising his head in surprise, Gregor silently questioned the unusual tone in his daughter's voice. Then, just as he rose from his chair, she burst through the doorway of his office, breathless from running. Her eyes were wide and somber as his own dark eyes questioned her.

"Father, you must hurry. Papino Victor has returned from Tolura Province. He's leading a procession—several wagons—all draped in black."

Gregor's head fell backward. His heart thudded heavily inside his chest. His lungs refused to fill with air as he fought rising nausea. Victor had insisted on traveling northward for one final attempt to solve the mystery of Alexa's disappearance. Gregor had clung to the faintest glimmer of hope that, since no bodies had ever been found, maybe—just maybe—his wife might be alive somewhere. But, if Victor had brought bodies home, no such hope could remain.

Nikolai appeared behind Anlía, his face solemn and fearful. "Father, Victor has almost reached the square. I asked Silina to take the other children upstairs until we learn what has happened."

Gregor forced a deep breath into his constricted chest. Nikolai approached his father and embraced him. Anlía looked on worriedly, feeling the terrible distress so clearly etched on her father's face.

Leaving his son's embrace, Gregor stepped toward Anlía. She offered both her hands to him. "Father, I promise you. Victor isn't bringing Mother home. You must believe me. Mother isn't with him."

Gregor and Nikolai exchanged glances. Anlía alone dealt peacefully with her mother's absence. Assuming the role of surrogate mother, she guided her younger brothers and sisters with a firm, loving hand. She also concentrated on her studies with unparalleled earnestness, intent on becoming a Valiria priestess as Alexa had been. Daily prayers and meditation were as important to her as eating and breathing. Words of comfort and reassurance flowed from her. Anlía remained steadfast in believing she would live to see her mother again. Gregor dreaded the day when she could no longer deny the reality of her mother's death. He ached with the idea that today might very well be that day.

Moments later, in silence, the three proceeded together from the wing of palace offices. Uneasy quiet was shockingly apparent in a place typically filled with bustling activity. The palace's entire staff had gathered in the grand entrance hall, waiting for the king to appear. Gregor's mouth was a taut line as he quietly acknowledged all who stood in solemn respect while he walked with his two oldest children toward the impressive doorway.

Across the square, Victor headed a somber procession winding past swelling crowds. Those who had accompanied him to Tolura now formed an escort for five wagons bearing black bunting, a clear indication that no ordinary cargo lay within. Victor's face revealed excessive weariness. Halting his horse in front of the palace, he glanced toward Nikolai and Anlía, his eyes briefly shining with affection for the two teens standing by their father's side. Finally dismounting, he dropped to one knee before Gregor.

"Your Majesty, I return from Tolura Province with the bodies of seven of Queen Alexa's private guards. I regret to inform you that I found none of the four priestesses who accompanied the queen. Neither was there any trace of Alexa—except for this." From inside his coat, he pulled Alexa's crystal pyramid pendant. "I found it among the rocks on the cliff where we discovered these soldiers."

Slowly, tentatively, Gregor reached toward Alexa's pendant. His breath caught painfully, and he stopped just short of touching it with trembling fingers. Finally, he forced himself to take it, clutching it tightly in his hand. "Please, Victor, rise."

Gregor stepped down to ground level, where Victor now stood. He saw anew the sorrow that continued to fill his old adversary. Both men stared at each other with hands trembling and hearts grieving. Gregor was the first to move, wrapping his arms around Victor's shoulders as the two men embraced. Banished were past animosity and rivalry. Buried, at least for this moment, were memories of bitter violence. Shared between them was the excruciating anguish of losing the one woman they each loved more than their own lives.

When they parted, Gregor and Victor walked with Nikolai toward the wagons. Gregor called for members of his Royal Guard to come and transfer the tightly wrapped corpses. Then, while the bodies moved past them for burial preparation, Gregor and his son stood stiffly at attention and saluted.

After the last body disappeared from sight, Gregor turned to Stefan, who had arrived just as Victor had dismounted. "Stefan, I must go inside to talk with Victor. Meanwhile, would you please announce that our queen was not found? We can only presume she is dead. I will come to the square and speak to everyone tomorrow morning at ten o'clock. When you finish, please join us in my office."

When Gregor looked around, he saw that Anlía, having silently left his side, had almost arrived at the temple entrance. He would allow her time to compose herself until he could talk with her later. For now, he needed to learn the details of Victor's grisly discovery.

Reaching his office, Gregor felt much too nervous to sit. He had paced back and forth until he finally turned to stare out a window with unseeing eyes. No one uttered a word. Nikolai sat on the edge of a table. Stefan arrived quickly and leaned back against the closed office door. Victor alone sat in a chair, his eyes as distant as Gregor's presence seemed.

At long last, Gregor swallowed hard. "Tell me how you found them, Victor."

"I thought for a long time how we had located absolutely no evidence of their arrival at the disaster site at Kisana. Something haunted me until I awoke from a dream one night. You know how we combed the area when we first went there. My dream made me realize that not only did they never arrive, they never got close. If they had, there would have been some sign. If nothing else, we would have found traces of campfires or discarded food. Something."

Gregor never moved. "So?"

"We decided to backtrack to the most likely road they would have taken to Kisana City. I'm certain you recall how badly damaged the area was from flooding following the quake. We met many Kisanan residents who have now returned. The aid sent by the Interior Ministry has helped the rebuilding process. Anyway, no one with whom we spoke had seen Alexa or any of her party. Some older gentlemen suggested they might have approached Kisana from another less frequently used road, closer to the ocean. The terrain was more rugged but higher. They would have been able to travel more easily than over wet, muddy ground."

Gregor turned and settled uncomfortably on his chair, leaning forward. "Then what?"

Victor shut his eyes and expelled a heavy breath. "We left Kisana and located the road through the mountains. When it carried us near the shore, the road stopped at the edge of a cliff. We peered over the edge of a steep canyon. That was when we saw the ruins of the bridge. It appeared to have collapsed at the far end. We never reached the canyon's bottom. However, we climbed down far enough to retrieve the bodies we brought back. I have tried to understand why we couldn't find Alexa or the other priestesses. I can only assume they were riding near the front with the guards who are still missing. They must have plummeted all the way to the bottom of the gorge."

Nikolai interrupted the heavy silence that followed. "Papino Victor, where did you find mother's pendant? Are you certain it belongs to her?"

Victor rose and walked toward Nikolai, resting his hand on his godson's shoulder. "I'm sure, Niko. Only Valkana wear pyramids with the corners edged in gold."

Gregor's hushed voice interrupted the prolonged, uneasy silence that followed. "Victor, you must be exhausted. Why don't you get something to eat and then get some sleep? We can discuss this later. Right now, if no one objects, I think I could use some time alone."

With everyone dispatched from his office, Gregor opened his hand to reveal the single remaining link to Alexa's disappearance. He studied the tiny object as if he had never seen it before and noticed how the golden shank that had once secured it to its chain was missing. He then remembered how he had come to find it for her.

Chapter 4

"Gregor, what are you reading?" Alexa's face glowed with health and vitality as her presence filled the library where he relaxed.

"Just a book of poetry," he responded with a smile when she came to sit beside him on the wide, comfortable sofa upholstered in soft leather.

"Poetry? In the middle of the day? That's not like you." Laughter brightened her voice as she leaned forward to kiss his cheek.

"And what are you doing here in the middle of the day? Don't you normally teach classes at this hour?"

She nodded, her eyes turning thoughtful. "I was looking for you. I wondered if I might talk to you for a few minutes."

"Of course, you may. What do you have on your mind?" Sparkling eyes invited her to move closer as he carefully placed his book on the side table.

"I wanted to discuss the wedding. You know Adrina leaves tomorrow for Garogan." She settled herself close to him, sitting sideways so she could gaze into his face.

Gregor gazed back into his wife's eyes and saw what he could only describe as uncertainty. "Yes, I know. She's leaving to attend to final wedding arrangements. Then we leave with Stefan in three weeks to travel to Garogan for the wedding."

"Well," Alexa began thoughtfully, "Adrina and I've spent a lot of time discussing details and final arrangements. I've been helping her with the planning, especially considering that I'll be her matron of honor."

Gregor felt uneasy with the tone of her voice. "And?"

Alexa leaned forward and kissed him lightly on the lips. "Adrina needs my help. I don't want you to be upset with me, but, as her closest friend…"

Studying her face, he thought about how the mobility of her features enhanced her expressiveness. "Exactly what is it you're trying to tell me?"

She chewed her lip, looking more like a nervous schoolgirl than queen and high priestess. He might have laughed had it not been for the unpleasant turn he expected in their conversation.

"My love, please don't be angry. I want to take Nikolai and go on ahead to Garogan with Adrina." She noted immediate, intense disapproval on his face.

"Alexa, how can you even suggest such a thing? You have responsibilities here. Besides, you certainly don't need to go to Garogan with Adrina. She has a full staff there, and I'm quite sure she has other friends who'll be more than happy to help her."

"Gregor," Alexa pressed on, "I want to go. Please try to understand. Adrina is more like a sister than a friend. We always dreamed of helping each other get ready for our weddings. She wasn't here with me when you and I were married. I want to go. I want to help her. Please?"

Gregor stood up abruptly and began to pace. "Alexa, I need you and Nikolai here. With me. You are not to go."

Alexa rose to her feet. "Tell me truthfully. Is it that you need us here so much, or is it that you don't want me to go because Victor is there?"

Gregor stiffened and spun to face her. His jaw twitched from side to side before he spoke. "Alexa…" He hesitated, unwilling to give voice to the jealous feelings he wanted to conceal from her.

Alexa clearly felt what he sought to hide. She approached him and reached out to caress his cheek. "Sometimes, Gregor, you disappoint me. You alone are the love of my life. What Victor and I once shared will never be again. What we did share has never once approached what you and I have. Why do you not trust me?"

The expression in her eyes stung him almost as much as her words. He shook his head. "I trust you completely. However, as I said, you are not to go. I wish to discuss the matter no further."

Alexa's lips pursed together as her expression grew mutinous. "Gregor, I love you. I suppose only time will reassure any insecurities you still have. However, I am decided. Although I much prefer going with your approval, I will leave tomorrow for Garogan."

He watched her spin on her heel to stride from the library. Her entire posture was a portrait of defiance. Gregor wanted to reach out, to mend the rift, but an unwelcome force inside him had already taken control. "Alexa, listen to me. You are not to leave tomorrow. I forbid it."

Alexa stopped for an instant, breathing in deeply. Although she had no desire to argue with him, she was also determined to depart the following morning. Without a single word, she left the library.

The next day, Alexa rose at dawn to go to the palace chapel for meditations. Returning to the suite she shared with her husband, she found him sitting up in bed, holding their cooing, six-month-old son on his lap. It was impossible to hide the smile borne from her heart at the sight of them together.

Once she reached the side of the bed, she dropped to her knees and tenderly stroked Nikolai's chubby cheek. She then drew her index finger along the length of Gregor's hand. "The two of you are awake early this morning."

When Gregor met her gaze, shadows lurked in the depths of his reproachful brown eyes. His face grew accusingly somber. "I wanted some private time with my son. Especially since you insist on taking him away from me."

A gentle smile was her only response as she rose to her feet and lifted Nikolai from his father's arms. Then, settling herself in her old rocker, she prepared to nurse their baby.

"Well?" Gregor tensed, praying she would relent and stay.

As her infant son suckled contentedly at her breast, she lifted emerald eyes to the man she loved more than anyone else. "I love you, Gregor," she began tenderly. "I love you more than you may ever know. Remember that."

Morosely, he stared at her. "But?"

"But," she said firmly, "Nikolai's things and mine are already packed, and we shall leave in a few hours. For me, Garogan is still my home in many ways. I need to go."

"Alexa, please. Don't leave me." He choked on swelling, unreasonable fear.

"Gregor, I must go. In a few weeks, you'll come to Garogan with Stefan for the wedding. Nikolai and I will be waiting for you."

Gregor pressed his lips tightly together. "Why? Why must you go? Are you sure it isn't to see Victor?" As soon as the words had escaped, he wished he could take them back.

Green eyes grew stormy. "How dare you even suggest such a thing? What does it take for you to trust in my love for you, Gregor?"

He sighed in exasperation, closing his eyes for a brief moment. "Forgive me, Alexa. Please. I just don't know how to face your leaving. Especially to Garogan. Stay. Please."

Silently, she waited until the baby finished nursing. She then handed him to Gregor so that she could adjust her clothing. Then, rising to her feet, she lifted her gaze to his. "There are reasons I must go. Besides, I promised to help Adrina, and I cannot fail her."

Gregor shook his head and backed away from her. "So you choose to fail me instead?"

Sadness, mingled with determined purpose, crept into Alexa's eyes. "How I wish you had more faith in me."

Later that morning, Gregor carried Nikolai from the palace to the coach waiting to transport Adrina, Alexa, and his son from Toraval to Garogan City. His expression was stony, his eyes withdrawn. There were none of his usual displays of close affection for his wife. He had not even offered her his arm as they walked down the front steps of the palace. Instead, his manner remained remote.

In contrast, Alexa smiled and chatted with Stefan and Adrina as if nothing at all were amiss. Vibrant energy was like a cloak around her. Life, even with its occasional troubles, had become a joy. Confident happiness formed its own glow around her.

She stood back as Stefan kissed Adrina in a tearful farewell and helped her into the carriage. Meanwhile, Alexa turned and gently removed a wiggling Nikolai from Gregor's unresisting arms. She walked to the carriage and handed him inside to Dina, the baby's nurse. Alexa turned around and stepped back to Gregor. Then, smiling lovingly into his tightly controlled face, she stood on tiptoe to touch his lips with a brief kiss. Then, softly, she whispered, "Remember, Gregor Toscano. I love you. We'll be waiting for you."

With not another word, she went back to the coach and climbed in without assistance. She didn't bother to look out the window. She clearly felt her husband's unmoving, brooding presence just beyond.

"Perhaps you should stay, Alexa. I don't think he's managing this very well."

Adrina's suggestion came just as the carriage lurched into forward motion. "We can still stop."

Alexa was touched by the genuine concern and compassion reflected in Adrina's eyes. When she replied, her expression was both serene and knowing. "Adrina, I have my reasons for going—not the least of which is the promise I made to you. Besides, Gregor must learn that my path will likely separate us many times in the years to come. He must understand that no matter how far away that path leads me or for how long, Val's will is that we shall always be reunited."

⌒

Five days later, the travel party passed through the gates of Garogan Castle and rolled to a stop. Although the trip had been calm and uneventful, everyone was glad when it ended. Adrina was the first to alight from the carriage. "Victor!" she exclaimed, happily rushing into her brother's arms.

Brother and sister hugged tightly. Now that the dark days preceding the war were successfully behind them, their closeness once again became apparent to all who saw them together. When their embrace ended, they still held hands as they backed away to appraise each other's appearance.

Victor started to say something when movement caught his eye, causing him to glance toward the carriage. Alexa had just stepped down from the coach. Surprise widened his eyes and softened his smile. "Alexa…"

She walked toward him with arms extended, took his hands into hers, and kissed him on each cheek. Looking into his hazel eyes, she smiled before hugging him. "It's so good to see you again."

His hands grasped her upper arms and held her away from him. "What a surprise to see you! Did you bring my godson?"

Alexa laughed, early afternoon sunshine sparkling in her eyes. "How can you even imagine I would leave my baby behind?" She then returned to the carriage, where Dina passed the baby outside into his mother's waiting arms.

Victor hurried toward them and took Nikolai into his arms. He lifted the chubby little boy high into the air and laughed aloud at the jolly baby laugh he received in response. "It's been barely a month since I last saw him, and look how much he's grown!" Refusing to relinquish the baby to Alexa, Victor then carried Nikolai inside the castle while asking one question after another about ongoing events at the capital.

A little later, they all sat at the dining room table to share midday. There was much discussion about what Victor had accomplished in anticipation of the wedding and what still needed attention. With Adrina home, progress should be much faster since she knew exactly what she wanted for her special day and could direct the effort. Alexa's presence would also be invaluable, considering her organizational and artistic skills.

When they finished their meal, the three lingered at the table over frosty glasses of fruit drinks. A slightly more serious tone entered the conversation when Adrina asked, "Victor, would you mind escorting Alexa to talk with Mrs. Tarandá?"

Victor glanced up in surprise. "Why?"

Alexa and Adrina exchanged glances, and for once, Alexa was glad to allow Adrina to speak on her behalf. "She needs to discuss the possibility of staying there for the next few weeks."

Victor shook his head in complete lack of comprehension. "I don't understand. Alexa, you still have your rooms here. Why would you want to stay with the Tarandás?"

Adrina responded while Alexa remained silent. "Victor, things are different. Alexa is married now. It wouldn't appear right."

Victor resisted. "I don't understand what that has to do with where she stays. No one could ever question her moral integrity. They never did before. Why would they now?"

"Victor," Alexa spoke up, "circumstances were completely different. You know that I never cared much for what people might say about me. I knew my own actions. More importantly, so did Val. My concern now is out of respect for my husband. He trusts me, but he is still uncomfortable with the relationship you and I share. I can walk to the Tarandá home in twenty minutes. It will be easy to come here every morning and go back for the night."

Victor sighed. Her closeness never failed to ease his loneliness. Not a day passed that he didn't awaken to thoughts of her, and not a night fell that he didn't miss her. Not only that, he had come to love little Nikolai as his own son. That tiny, happy cherub allowed him moments of escape from the drab world in which he now dwelled. He wanted so much for them to stay at the castle. Slowly, Victor nodded his head. "All right. Give me half an hour to finish something outside, and we'll go."

Later, Victor carried Nikolai as he and Alexa walked along the brick-paved road leading to the Tarandá house. Tirstan, now named lieutenant of Alexa's private guard, followed at a discreet distance. "Doesn't it bother you having someone follow you everywhere you go?"

Alexa chuckled softly. "Over the years, I've grown accustomed to it. As I recall, you used to do the same thing."

Victor looked sideways at her, grinning wryly. "That was different."

"Gregor worries about me. He trusts Tirstan to watch over the baby and me. I trust Tirstan. Besides, if I really want to get away…" A mischievous glint lit her eyes.

"Ah, yes. Our mysterious and mystic Valkana. I nearly forgot. I almost feel sorry for your husband."

"Victor!"

"Well, it's true. Sometimes, you can be absolutely impossible!"

"Now you even sound like my husband!" She grew quiet instantly, realizing she had inadvertently struck a raw nerve. "Victor, I'm sorry."

He shook his head, dodging as short, plump fingers grabbed at a fallen lock of hair. In his mind, he felt grateful that Nikolai provided a welcome distraction.

"It's all right. Alexa, I don't want you worrying about every little thing you might say. At least allow me to enjoy something of the spontaneity that we've enjoyed through the years."

The remaining five minutes of their walk continued in relative silence. Later, after enjoying refreshments and making arrangements with DiLeno's mother, they returned to the castle. Adrina had already separated things Alexa could leave behind. Servants then went outside to load a wagon with baggage to take later to the Tarandá house.

❧

Days passed in a flurry of activity. Alexa, who was excellent at embroidery, added exquisite finishing details to Adrina's wedding gown. Adrina had already prepared menu plans in Toraval. She started working with her kitchen staff to prepare for the days of shopping and meal preparations for the upcoming wedding celebration. The castle was cleaned from top to bottom in anticipation of the many expected guests, including Turand's king. Victor supervised carpentry work for the dance floor under construction outside and the many decorative arches that would bear festive floral garlands.

Despite all the work, Alexa reserved time to play with Nikolai. While the baby was nursing or falling asleep, she often sang to him. Occasionally, Victor stopped to observe her from a distance. He had always admired so much about her. However, in her role as mother, he considered her exceptional. A unique bond existed between mother and son that Victor felt positive he had never seen before. Some of his regrets temporarily receded as he contemplated how happy she looked.

One evening, nearly two weeks after Alexa and Adrina had arrived in Garogan, a violent thunderstorm crashed through the heavens. Black skies flashed vividly white with jagged bolts of lightning. Roaring thunder sent shock waves reverberating through the air. Rain pounded the ground and stone walkways around the castle. Typically, Alexa stood outside, eyes cast skyward, lost in thought.

When the storm finally began to wear itself out, Victor went to see if she was ready to leave for the Tarandá home. As he approached, he sensed uneasiness in her posture. When she glanced around upon hearing his footsteps, desolation plainly showed on her face. Without a word, she moved into his arms and hid her face against his shoulder. For long minutes, she made not a single sound. Victor held her close, worried by whatever had troubled eyes that had looked at him with such sadness.

Finally, she moved away slightly and breathed deeply in and out. "Victor, I need your help."

"Alexa, whatever it is, you know I'm here. What's wrong?" His voice, gentle and low, failed to conceal the love he would forever feel for her.

"It's one of the reasons I needed to come back. I needed to talk to you. You're the only one who would understand."

Victor took her by the hand and led her to sit at a table beneath the covered veranda. "Talk to me, Sweetest. You look like you're hurting."

She lifted her eyes to him, and he saw intense pain in those emerald depths. Her lips quivered as, unsuccessfully, she attempted to smile. "Victor, I want to go to Zinzan. I want to go home."

Victor was stunned. "Alexa. Sweetest, no. I have taken you back there three times over the years. Each and every time, I had to carry you away before we made it even halfway through what's left of the village. Don't do this to yourself. It's torture."

"Oh, Victor, I don't expect it to be easy, but I have to go. I need to go," she insisted. "I'm much stronger now. My faith fortifies me as it never did before. Gregor's love makes me stronger than I ever believed I could be. I must make peace with what happened there." She paused. "It's time for me to bid final goodbye to my family."

"Why? Why now? Wait, Alexa. Give yourself a few more months. You've had so little time to be happy."

"Victor, there's a place inside me that doesn't rest. I know it's because of how I left things there. Please? If you don't understand, no one ever will. Turmoil lingers there. Spirits remain in confusion—without reconciliation or peace. I must go, but I want you to go with me. No one else alive knows the terrible sights and sounds we experienced there. Please, Victor. Try to understand."

Victor gazed out into the night. His troubled eyes watched as cooling breezes pushed aside clouds, revealing first a hazy light and then the silvery-white moon. Ironically, he realized that was precisely what she was trying to do. Winds of change had blown through her life, yet clouds still blocked the promise of light in the night. To allow that light to shine forth—to cast away all the shadows from the past—she would have to face this challenge that had so far defeated her.

"Victor?" His name was like a plea.

"Alexa, it's late, and I need to escort you to DiLeno's. Mistress Tarandá will be worried. We can discuss this further tomorrow. Just let me think about it."

She nodded before rising to go inside for Nikolai. "Just let me think about it" had always meant he would give in to her when he really would rather not.

Two days later, Victor busied himself with adding finishing touches to the wide, latticed arch beneath which Stefan and Adrina would exchange their wedding vows. The clatter of dozens of horses' hooves entering the gate and approaching the castle heralded the unexpected and early arrival of the groom's party, including the king. Victor handed his tools to an assistant and wiped sweaty hands on a rag dangling from his pocket before hurrying to greet the new arrivals. He stopped just an instant, laughing aloud as he watched Adrina nearly fly through the castle's main entrance and into Stefan's waiting arms. It warmed his heart to see his sister so joyful.

"King Gregor, once again, I welcome you to Garogan Castle," Victor greeted. "I didn't expect to see you so soon."

Gregor dismounted and acknowledged Victor by extending his arm to shake hands. "Thank you, Victor. You look well but exceptionally busy."

Victor chuckled. "My sister has become something of a slave driver. It seems everything has to be just so, and I get to do most of the work." Victor then turned his attention to Stefan, greeting him with a brotherly hug. "Welcome back, Stefan."

"It's good to be here," Stefan answered, glancing lovingly into Adrina's dancing, light brown eyes. "I apologize for the early arrival. We were facing daunting issues at home in Toraval. The palace quickly grew much too small for two irritable, lovesick men. If you know what I mean."

Adrina glanced up at Gregor's face, noting immediately that his eyes were searching for Alexa. "Gregor, she's not here yet."

He looked at her with concerned puzzlement. "Not here? Where is she?"

"Come inside. We'll have something cool to drink," Victor invited. "We can talk there."

The men settled themselves at a table inside a parlor that felt at least ten degrees cooler than outside. Adrina requested a refreshing, lemony punch and cakes be served before she sat, where Stefan draped his arm around her shoulder to keep her close by his side.

"Tell me, Victor, where is Alexa? Is she all right? And Nikolai?" Gregor was noticeably concerned, even though no indication had been given that anything was amiss. Ever since Alexa had left, he had grappled with guilt over how he had behaved. The separation had made him more than anxious to make amends.

Victor sipped from the glass of punch he had just taken from a tray that a servant had placed in the center of the table. "We received word early this morning that she probably wouldn't arrive until after midday. Nikolai is apparently teething and kept her awake most of the night."

"Pardon me if I still don't understand. Where is she?" Dark eyes questioned Victor.

"She comes here in the mornings to spend her days. We then take her every evening to spend nights with DiLeno's parents." Victor stared at Gregor as if the explanation should make perfect sense, but comprehension still eluded the king.

"Gregor," Adrina addressed the king calmly, "she didn't want to spend nights here until you arrived."

When Gregor recognized the near admonition in Adrina's eyes, he sighed and shook his head in embarrassment. "Only my Alexa. How far away is she?"

Victor stood up and stretched. "It's barely a twenty-minute walk from here. We can ride, but I would prefer to walk. I have something important to discuss with you. It's hot outside. I suggest you leave your uniform jacket here."

Victor and Gregor got up and left together. The first several minutes of their short trip were quiet before Gregor interrupted the silence. "It seems my wife has caused you a fair amount of extra effort and trouble."

Victor shook his head and shrugged broad shoulders. "I told you a long time ago. What makes her happy makes me happy. There is nothing I wouldn't do for her."

Gregor only smiled his admiration. He knew his own character well enough, and he seriously doubted he could ever face a reality without her the way Victor did.

Hesitantly, Victor spoke again. "Two nights ago, Alexa and I had a long talk. To be honest with you, I am more than a little worried. I'm glad you've come early."

"Why? Something is wrong, isn't it?" Gregor saw dread in Victor's eyes and waited.

Victor faced downward and watched his feet moving forward on the dusty road. "She asked me to take her to Zinzan."

It was Gregor's turn to feel first surprise, then dread. "To Zinzan? In the name of Val, why?"

Victor remained quiet a minute or two. "I've taken her there three times in the past. The first two times, she collapsed before we barely entered the town. The last time, we were almost halfway through Zinzan before she begged me to bring her home. Now, she insists she must go back. She told me that she needs to pray for the spirits remaining there and to bid farewells that she never could before."

Both men stopped, and Gregor gazed at Victor, whose face was shadowed with somber memories. "This is one time when I must rely on the wisdom of your advice, Victor. You were there. You know what she lived through—then and afterward. Can she do it? Is she ready?"

Victor blinked his eyes several times and began walking again. He breathed out several long sighs. "She does need to go. Alexa needs to put final perspective on what happened there and to say goodbyes that were never said. She asked me to go with her. I will because, as you said, I understand what happened there. I believe she can finally do it now. As Valkana, she possesses the mystical capabilities that will enable her to do what she must so she can satisfy unresolved spiritual aspects. If she has you by her side, I believe she'll find the emotional strength to face and reconcile the terrible grief she has borne these many years."

Gregor glanced ahead and saw that they were quickly approaching the Tarandá house. DiLeno, who had been outside, was already hurrying toward the visitors. Just before DiLeno reached them, Gregor said quietly, "I'll discuss it with her later. I trust your judgment. If she tells me she wants to go, we'll take her."

Inside, Gregor stood behind the wide column of an archway leading to a small inner courtyard. The smile on his face reflected the loving fullness in his heart. Alexa sat on a blanket beneath the shade of a tree. Nikolai sat on her lap, intently gazing at his mother's face.

"I know, I know, my little one. You miss your father almost as much as I do. Father should be leaving home soon. I do fear Mother will need your help, though. Father wasn't very pleased with me when we left. In fact, I think he was downright angry."

Nikolai gurgled at her, and she kissed ebony curls atop his head. "Yes, I know, but Mother needed to come. I just wish Father had tried to understand a little. I love him so much, and I miss him terribly. You must promise to help me when he finally gets here. Will you?"

At that moment, motion caught Nikolai's attention, and he squealed in delight as his father crouched down, resting one knee on the edge of the blanket. Nikolai practically jumped from his mother's lap toward his father's outstretched arms. Alexa looked around in total astonishment and gasped. "Gregor!"

Her husband didn't reply. Instead, he lavished undivided attention on his son. "Nikolai! Father heard you weren't feeling well. You certainly look fine to me! Especially when I've missed you so much!"

Alexa's features glowed beneath a proud smile. Tentatively, she took the index finger of her husband's right hand and rubbed the tip along Nikolai's lower gums. "He woke up this morning with his first tooth. He feels much better now."

Gregor continued to talk and coo at his little boy before he finally looked directly at Alexa. Leaning forward, he covered her smiling lips with his mouth. Just kissing her filled him with heady intoxication. Then, reluctantly parting from her, his eyes caressed her lovingly. "Dare I admit how sorely I've missed you?"

Her eyelids slid closed at whispered words that returned gladness to her heart. Smiling, she opened her eyes and lost herself for a moment within the adoring brown richness of his. "I told you we would be waiting for you."

He laughed silently and nodded his head. "Only my Alexa," he thought. "Only my Alexa."

Chapter 5

Vast, velvet skies twinkled with jewel-like stars. Midsummer's moon shone brightly white. Soft, fragrant breezes rustled leaves in trees standing like sentinels across the countryside. Rippling waters flowing over stones could be heard coming from a not-so-distant river. Night birds sang, calling out in search of mates.

Victor sat silently on a fallen log. Ordinarily, he loved being out at night and far from civilization. For years, falling asleep beneath the stars had provided a welcome retreat from intrigue, strategic planning, and, more recently, painful memories.

Now he couldn't keep himself from gazing toward the fire. Stretched out on thickly padded mats placed close together, Alexa lay asleep with Gregor's arm holding her tucked close against his body. Her expression in sleep was more peaceful than he had ever seen before. Grinding his back teeth together for a moment, Victor fended off the onslaught of emptiness that struck at the mere sight of her. Silently, he reminded himself yet again that, at long last, she was truly happy.

Finally, Victor forced himself to walk over to where his own sleeping mat lay undisturbed. Stretching out and then waiting for sleep to come, he prayed. "Dearest Val, please let me rest. Help me find strength enough to help her tomorrow. You know better than I the guilt and sorrow she has carried these many years. Help her, oh, Val, and, please help me, too."

The following day, they reached the outskirts of Zinzan by midmorning. Before the Sifiq massacre, Zinzan had been a quaint village a little more than two days from Garogan City. The population of nearly one hundred had enjoyed the prosperity of a farming community that took care of itself before transporting its abundant produce to nearby cities. Many families could trace their presence in Zinzan back for more than six generations. Alexa's was no different.

Since its destruction, Zinzan had gained an almost mythical reputation. Few dared to walk its streets. Those who did most often returned white with fright, fearfully avoiding discussion of what had driven them away. Rumors arose, transforming into frightening legends. Some swore that the screams of women and children still echoed throughout the area. Others insisted they had seen and smelled smoke when they traveled too close to the devastated village. Some only shook their heads sadly, convinced that, forevermore, Zinzan would be home only to lost spirits.

Alexa stopped her horse and dismounted as they turned onto what had been Zinzan's main street. Her face was taut, her eyes grim. On each side of the street stood charred remnants of what had been a colorful town that once resembled something spirited away from a fairy tale. In her mind, she noted where the baker's shop had been. She could almost taste the creamy, filled pastries the baker's wife topped with colorful icings and sweet, edible flowers. Glancing to her right, she clicked off in her mind where the cheese shop, butcher, and cobbler had maintained brisk businesses.

Slowly, she began to walk toward the village square. Beautifully carved granite balusters had once surrounded it but were now overturned and either cracked or broken. In the square's center stood the intricately sculpted statue of a Valiria priestess. Her right hand stretched skyward.

Upon it sat a crystal pyramid. Jagged chips had been hacked out of her stone robes. Rotting ropes lingered as grim testament to Sifiq efforts to topple the statue. In mute defiance, the Valiria priestess had stood her ground and had resisted the enemy. She had prevailed.

Alexa stretched out her hand and stroked a rippled fold sculpted into the priestess's gown. The stone was cool to the touch and unyielding. The face she saw when she looked up was serene as its eyes stared toward the heavens. During her childhood, Alexa had spent many hours beneath the shadow of this ancient guardian of Zinzan. She had often talked to the guardian in the childlike belief that some special spirit resided within.

Huge hands came to rest around her waist as Gregor's lips whispered against her ear. "Beloved, are you all right? What are you thinking?"

She remained motionless. "I never got this far into town. I didn't know the statue had survived." A tiny sob escaped her. "Finding her is like meeting an old friend you thought lost forever."

"Alexa, come. You need to eat. Let's find some shade and sit for a while."

Alexa allowed Gregor to lead her by the hand to where an enormous tree cast protective shade over the elevated stone walkway where villagers had once strolled back and forth, visiting with one another or attending their daily business. Victor joined them, and the three consumed their meal without any conversation. Even the six soldiers who had accompanied them remained silent. Their horses seemed skittish. Nerves were tense. There could be no denial that an eerie atmosphere pervaded their surroundings.

Alexa slowly nibbled her lunch and drank at Gregor's urging. As she finished, her eyes closed. Her body began to sway in gentle rhythm from side to side, then back and forth. Gregor exchanged a fleeting, worried glance with Victor. Victor shook his head, silently signaling they should remain still.

When Alexa opened her eyes once more, a strange expression transformed her face. "Do you hear that?"

Gregor looked once again at Victor before turning his attention back to Alexa. "Beloved, I don't hear anything. What are you talking about?"

Her lips almost formed a smile. "Silence. Nothing but silence. It's the middle of summer. We should hear buzzing insects and breezes rustling through the leaves. Zinzan was always a haven for dozens of species of birds. Listen carefully. There are no sounds whatsoever except for the ones we make."

Victor cocked his head to one side. He knew exactly what she meant. He had heard it before but had never been able to define what it actually was. Now he understood. There were absolutely no signs of any kind of life. His voice sounded uncharacteristically nervous. "Alexa, what does it mean?"

She slid her feet from the sidewalk and onto the street. Rising, she turned slowly in a circle. "It seems as if all that was life in Zinzan is frozen in time. I feel them. They are here. For some strange reason, they never returned to Val."

"Alexa?" Gregor's voice was subdued.

Abruptly, Alexa strode purposefully toward her horse. Then, lifting her foot into the stirrup, she quickly mounted. "It's time! I must go home!" she called out as she leaned into her horse and galloped off.

When they rode up behind her, she already knelt in front of the ruins of her childhood home. Strewn all around were tarnished copper pots, cooking utensils, tools, and other items the Sifiq had discarded as useless to their way of life. To the left, the stone foundation and a tall, two-sided stone fireplace remained as guardians for the burned remnants of the newer section of the Maraná home built by Alexa's grandfather. To the right, centuries-old stone walls of the original residence showed signs of weathering.

Gregor and Victor both swiftly dismounted and ran to her side. She reached upward and placed her hand into her husband's, letting him help her to her feet. He was relieved to see that, so far, she remained calm.

Pointing toward the left, she began to speak. "We had a summer kitchen on that side of the house. The day the Sifiq attacked was warm, so we were making fruit preserves there." She slowly approached the floor, now covered with dirt and all sorts of debris. Thoughtfully, she drew her fingertips across the gritty, rusted hulk of the enormous wood-burning stove before returning to where Gregor and Victor quietly waited.

Gripping Gregor's hand tightly, she swallowed against a lump in her throat and started toward the back of her parents' house. Her eyes roved over every remaining detail of the structure. Often, she reached out to stroke a charred timber or knelt to touch something in the dirt that caught her eye. Not once did she release the lifeline her husband's hand had become.

Arriving at the far end of the house that had been constructed from quarried stones, she leaned against walls where traces of sooty smoke still lingered. "Amazing," she commented. "This happened days before my eighteenth birthday. I can hardly believe there are still smoke stains after six years."

Again, she walked until she reached a tall oak tree at the end of the house. She planted her free hand against its great trunk and leaned into its strength. "Those branches stretch out over where the roof of the newer part of the house connected to the original walls. Victor pulled me out through my bedroom window, and we jumped off that roof into the branches of this tree. Few leaves had fallen, so, combined with all the smoke, this tree hid us from the Sifiq."

Reluctantly, she removed her hand from Gregor's grasp. Moving away, she began stepping carefully as if she were testing the ground. Several feet from the house, she discovered what she had been seeking. With the toe of her boot, she pushed aside years of dirt that had accumulated over the cellar door. "Victor, please. Help me with this. I never could open it by myself."

Victor shot a quick look at Gregor and saw him nod. Then, quickly moving to her side, Victor leaned forward and grasped the rusted iron handle, pulling up. With a creak and a cloud of dust, the door raised, and Victor let it fall open. For the first time in nearly six years, sunshine peeked into the shadowy interior that had saved his life and Alexa's.

"Gregor, come with me," she requested, beckoning to him with hands outstretched. With physical contact re-established with her husband, Alexa sat on the edge of the cellar opening and stomped on the steps leading down. Fearful that the old wood might crumble and break, she moved sideways and, letting go of Gregor's hand, dropped inside without warning.

Instantly, Gregor followed her. Inside, she was able to stand; however, he was much too tall and needed to hunch over to move around. Shelves lining the walls still held neat rows of glass jars that had been filled with preserved fruits and vegetables, their rusty lids now covered with years of undisturbed dust. Gregor could not restrain the thought that, with the door above closed, this cellar must have seemed more like a tomb for the two days and nights Victor had kept her there. The idea sent a shudder up his spine, and he immediately reached for her, pulling her body tightly into the curve of his.

His closeness was precisely what she had needed. For long moments, she pressed against him, eternally grateful for his love that now shielded her from the past and gave her courage to be here in this dark place. Speaking softly, Gregor suggested they leave the cellar now that Victor had dropped in a rope to help them climb out safely.

Once outside, Alexa slapped dust and cobwebs from her riding skirt and resolutely headed toward the inside of the house. Climbing over scorched timbers and fallen beams, she reached the stone staircase that led upstairs. Before Gregor or Victor could stop her, she started up the steps, stopping only long enough to push debris aside and leave a narrow path for the men to follow.

"My room was here," she called out as she entered the now doorless chamber. Stark skeletons were all that remained of her furniture. Surprised, she found a tiny round table wrought in solid brass. "I had forgotten all about this table!" she exclaimed as she unsuccessfully rubbed at thick layers of sooty dust and tarnish.

Gregor carefully crossed over to the window frame to which a few shards of glass still clung. He leaned forward and gazed out. The view from this room was spectacular. Glancing downward, his eye caught a reflection of light. He peered more closely, unable to discern what he had seen. Mentally, he noted to investigate later.

Alexa rummaged around and, amazingly, found two unbroken porcelain figurines. A small, satisfied smile curved her mouth as she clutched the tiny treasures close to her breast and allowed Gregor, carrying her table, to guide her from the desolate room and back downstairs. Once outside, she went to sit on a dusty, wrought iron bench placed beneath one of the many trees that surrounded her childhood home.

Pulling a handkerchief from her skirt pocket, she carefully began to wipe away greasy soot and dirt covering the figurines, one a lady of the royal court, the other a Valiria priestess. Her concentration was intense, the meticulous action of cleaning heirlooms from her past drawing a curious parallel to the spiritual cleansing she had undertaken upon returning home.

Finally satisfied at having done the best she could for the moment, she retrieved a towel from her saddlebag and carefully wrapped the figurines to protect them for the journey home. Smiling, she then looked up at Gregor and Victor. "I think we're safe if we set up camp here for the night."

"Alexa, are you sure?" Victor asked, unable to shake continuing concerns for her.

Walking over to him, she gently touched his cheek. "You need not worry anymore, Victor. Now. Now is the right time for me to be here. I promise. I'll be fine."

Eerie, unnatural silence descended that evening, encompassing the ruins of the Maraná home and unnerving everyone except Alexa. They all knew that dozens of Zinzan's villagers had been brutally slain on the very ground upon which they walked. Following uncomfortable discussion about the placement of fires and sleeping mats, soldiers built huge bonfires to ward off the uneasy darkness that settled over the grounds. Surprising everyone, Alexa fell deeply asleep almost the instant she lay down after Gregor had covered her with a light blanket.

As she slept, Gregor and Victor sat before one of the bonfires and quietly talked. "I can't believe she's asleep already," Gregor remarked, casting a glance in his wife's direction.

"Neither can I. She has done unbelievably well this time. After all we faced here..." Victor's voice trailed off, his eyes retreating into the tragic past. Then, suddenly, he began to describe the event that had occurred here those long years ago—something he had also kept buried deep inside himself.

"I don't know how much Alexa has told you about the massacre. I was visiting because we were getting ready for her birthday celebration. We also planned to use that occasion to announce our betrothal and the date for our wedding. I went hunting early that morning, but I had a sudden premonition that something was terribly wrong. Returning, I saw Sifiq soldiers chasing a group of villagers toward the house. Alexa's father saw me and shouted at me to go inside and get her to safety. I knew about the hidden closet and went straight to her.

"Smoke was already billowing up the stairs when I reached her room. I often think the fire was really started by Alexa's parents to keep the Sifiq from finding her. Anyway, the lock on the door jammed. I think only desperation gave me the strength to open it. Alexa was so terrified that I had to drag her to her feet and out the window. I still have no idea how we managed to get down from that tree and into the cellar without the Sifiq seeing us."

Gregor gazed compassionately at Victor's pain-stricken face. That day must have scarred his soul almost as dreadfully as it had Alexa's. "I firmly believe Val meant for the two of you to survive. There can be no other explanation."

"Survive... There were so many times when I was terrified Alexa wouldn't. When we finally emerged from that cellar..." He sighed heavily and squeezed his eyes tightly shut against hideous memories forever etched into his memory.

"If you thought carnage on the battlefields was bad..." He shook his head against ghastly images that refused to go away. "At least during the war, we were all there by our own will. Here, it was different. I swear to you, Gregor. The ground was stained red with all the blood that was spattered around. Women had been raped and then butchered. Children had been slashed to death. And when we found Alexa's parents..." Victor choked on a sob.

Without thinking, Gregor reached out and placed a hand on his shoulder. "Victor, it's over. You don't have to do this."

Victor swallowed several times. His hands shook violently, and his jaw twitched uncontrollably. "It still hurts when I think of it because I loved them, too. Gregor, they left her parents, side by side, in front of the house, as if they wanted to leave a sign. They had chopped off their heads, legs and arms. Then they left her mother's head and limbs with her father's body and put her father's parts with her mother's body. The whole massacre occurred because they were searching for Zinzan's Valiria priestess. Although the Sifiq knew she was here somewhere, not a soul in town betrayed her."

Gregor's grip on Victor's shoulders tightened, and he watched rivers of silent tears track down Victor's face. "Does Alexa know that?"

Victor nodded, choking out his response. "From the very beginning. Even when we were inside that cellar, I held her while she sobbed about it being all her fault. It wasn't. It was never her fault. I think she understands that now. Evil always seeks to destroy good, and she always represented good."

Gregor didn't bother trying to stem the tears swimming in his own eyes. Victor's revelations were nothing less than heartrending to anyone with a sense of love and respect for life. The reality was staggering. There also existed touching irony that he was coming to understand more of his wife's past and her character—that he was learning through the painful memories and confidences shared by a man who made no effort to deny how much he loved Alexa.

Gregor awoke abruptly. Dawn had not yet come, and the only light shone from the bonfires beginning to burn down. Something struck him as wrong. He turned on his mat, sat up, and looked around. "Alexa? Alexa, where are you? Alexa!"

Victor sat up instantly, shaking himself awake. "Gregor, what's wrong?"

"Alexa! She's gone!"

Both men scrambled to their feet and began to scan the camp. As soldiers began to awaken, aroused by the sounds of anxious voices, Victor grabbed Gregor's arm and pointed toward the right of the house. A slight, heavily wooded rise leveled off and stretched far into the distance. Shimmering clouds of light seemed to dance as far as the eye could see. In the center glowed a well-defined, blue-white orb.

"She's there, Gregor. Only Valkana produce such light. That's where we buried her parents and the others who died here."

Without hesitation, Gregor and Victor immediately ran toward the ethereal display of lights. They slowed as they approached, carefully advancing through thick brush. Simultaneously, they both stopped and stared.

Alexa hovered in a kneeling position, perhaps four feet above her parents' graves. The clouds that had drawn their attention appeared as many separate, slightly undulating puffs of light. Two of the glowing puffs were elongated and barely touched the edge of Alexa's aura.

"Alexa, remember, sweet child. This land is now sacred. It has been washed with the blood of many who refused to surrender their faith. We have long awaited your return, daughter. You needed to know. Our souls cried when you blamed yourself. Still, we trusted in your strength. We believed in your faith."

"Mama, Papa, I still miss you so much. Please forgive me for not coming home sooner."

"We understand, Alexa. We, too, have missed you. We all have. You meant so much to us all. We wanted you to live—for yourself and for us."

"Oh, Papa, my life is so different. I have a baby of my own now. And a husband who loves me so much. Mama, I am happy in so many ways. I just wish you could be with me." Emotion shook Alexa's voice.

"Shush, Alexa, shush. We know. You are now Queen and Valkana. You help guide our people back to faith and peace. Daughter, we always believed in you as much as we always loved you. Our spirits are forever with you. Your husband comes for you now. Remember the message we have waited to give you. Do not forget. This land is now sacred, washed with the blood of the faithful. Our spirits can finally return in peace to Val. We leave with you our love."

Alexa's body began to lower to the spot where Gregor now knelt to steady her. Sparkling clouds of light that had started to recede paused momentarily. Inside his head, Gregor heard unfamiliar voices.

"King Gregor, we leave our beloved daughter in your care. Love her well. As she loves you."

Aloud, Gregor responded. "You have my promise—my vow—to love her eternally—forever and beyond."

⌒

Gregor now rolled the crystal pyramid around and around between his fingers. He remembered how he had led her from her parents' graves. Although she had been physically exhausted, her grief had been purged, her spirit finally healed. None of the party had been able to go back to sleep. Instead, they extinguished fires and began to break camp for the return to Garogan City.

Just before they left, something prompted Gregor to recall the day before when he saw the reflection of light in the tree outside her bedroom. Asking everyone to wait, he hurried to the far side of the house. After several minutes of peering into branches laden with broad, green leaves, he again saw the bright glint. He reached high up into the tree. There, snared by a branch, hung the heavy gold chain that still bore the pyramid Alexa had received the day she was anointed into the Order of Val.

As plainly as if she stood before him this very minute, he could see the joyous smile that had transformed her face. Yet again, he felt against his lips the heated, crystalline tears of happiness that he had kissed from her cheeks. Emerald eyes had sparkled with loving appreciation for what he had found and returned to her—the symbol of her faith that she had lost years earlier.

Reverently, Gregor lifted the pyramid and, holding it against trembling lips, surrendered to sobs that racked his body.

Chapter 6

"Nikolai, I just said goodnight to your brothers and the twins. I haven't seen Anlía since supper, and she isn't in her room. Do you know where she is?"

Nikolai sat up in bed, his youthful face illuminated by moonlight streaming in through multi-paned windows. "She said something earlier about going to the temple. You know how she is sometimes. Do you want me to go with you to look for her?"

Gregor solemnly shook his head. "No," he replied. "Try to get some rest. I imagine tomorrow's funerals will be draining for us all. I'm glad Victor and Adrina are leaving early to take the little ones to Garogan for a short holiday. Good night."

Gregor closed Nikolai's bedroom door and, with heavy footsteps, descended the marble staircase and slipped out the front entrance of the palace. Autumn's evening air carried with it sounds of vibrant life and scents of lush plant life that flourished around Toraval. Gregor paused by the edge of the Fountain of the Valkana. Cold, clean waters lapped up against the fountain walls. For just a moment, he dangled his fingertips into the chill wetness. Then, sighing heavily, he proceeded toward the front steps of the temple.

Slowly, he edged open a door. Candles burned on steps leading up to the dais. He smiled to himself at the sight of Anlía, sitting cross-legged in front of the altar, her head bowed. As quietly as possible, he walked the length of the aisle and stopped a short distance behind her.

"Father, you needn't worry about me." She spoke without ever moving.

He knelt down, wrapped his arms around the front of her shoulders, and pulled her closer to him. "There's nothing a loving father does better than worry about his children." He kissed her temple. "Anlía, it's time to go home. I want you to rest. I am going to need you tomorrow. All of us may need you."

She rose gracefully from the floor and turned around. Already taller than her mother had been, she stretched her arms out to encircle her father. "You have so many things to worry you, Father. Don't let me be one of them. My faith sustains me."

Gregor gazed adoringly upon this daughter who meant so much to him. Holding her close, he praised and thanked Val for this child who continuously brought him such a sense of solace since Alexa's disappearance. "Come. Let's go. I wish to discuss something I want you to do for me."

Hand in hand, they strolled unhurriedly back to the palace. Gregor relished the peacefulness of such a beautiful night and the calm he absorbed from his daughter's presence. Often, she rested the side of her face against his arm as they walked. The gesture was bittersweet, reminiscent of one of Alexa's habits that he had always dearly cherished.

After entering the palace, he sent her upstairs to get ready for bed. He made a quick trip to his office and waited long enough for Anlía to change before going up. When he knocked and entered her room, she was still stroking a brush through the length of her waving hair. He took the brush from her, passing it through her hair several times before reaching over her shoulder to place it on her dressing table.

"Mother always loved for you to brush her hair, didn't she?"

Gregor smiled at echoing memories. "She did. She accused me of spoiling her, and I readily admit that I loved doing it."

Anlía moved away from him and sat on the side of her canopied bed. "What was it you wanted to discuss with me?"

Gregor joined her on the edge of the bed. "You saw that Victor brought me your mother's crystal pendant."

Anlía responded with a nod, her eyes alone questioning him.

Gregor reached into the pocket of the gray woolen sweater he wore and pulled out an intricately carved wooden box. Snapping it open, he revealed Alexa's pendant. He had ordered the piece cleaned and polished. A new gold shank had been attached and connected to a simple brooch. "I can't bear to see it worn again as a necklace. However, I know she would want you to have it. Using the pin, you can wear it as a brooch or secure it inside a jacket or a pocket. I only ask that you guard it carefully."

Anlía removed the box from her father's hand, closely observing the shining piece resting inside. With delicate fingers, she carefully lifted the pyramid from its velvet niche and held it up. For no more than a split second, she saw the fluctuation of light from the center sun. An incredibly beautiful smile crossed her face. She turned toward her father and lightly touched his lips with hers.

"Thank you, Father, for trusting me with this. I promise to guard it well. Someday, I plan to have my own. This one I intend to keep until we can return it to Mother."

Tears welled in his eyes as he wrapped his arm around her and held her close. "Anlía, Anlía. Darling, please, you must accept that Mother isn't coming back. We've lost her." Following several long moments, he released her.

Tenderly, she wiped away tears that had rolled down his cheeks and stopped to shine at the edge of his beard. "Father, you need to get some sleep. Tomorrow will not be an easy day."

"Anlía, you're avoiding the subject," he said, trying unsuccessfully to sound stern.

She rose and opened her door. "No, Father, I'm not. But I do love you very much. And, since Mother asked me to watch over everyone until her return, I'm telling you to go to bed. You're exhausted."

He could have laughed except for how much she reminded him of Alexa. Realizing he had lost the battle, he rose to his feet and walked to the door. "Good night, my darling daughter. And always remember. I love you, too."

Anlía closed the door behind her and immediately extinguished the lamp on her bedside table. Earlier, she had opened the draperies at her window to allow moonlight to enter. Placing a pillow behind her shoulders, she sat back to concentrate on the precious pyramid that her father had entrusted to her care. With the tip of her index finger, she traced golden lines forming the edges of the pyramid. She concentrated on the gold sun embedded in the crystal's center. This time, the fluctuating light lasted several seconds, its blue-white hue unmistakable. Anlía kissed the precious object and, placing it back into its niche in the wooden box, set it on her nightstand and settled into bed. As she drifted off to sleep, she murmured into the darkness. "Just let me know how, and I'll help you. I love you, too, Mother."

⊷

The faces of Turand's elite Royal Guard solemnly reflected respect directed toward their lost comrades. Their gray uniform jackets all bore mourning bands of black satin. The soldiers formed the sides of an enormous triangle. The triangle's base was created by a row of seven wooden caskets arranged side by side, each resting on an ornately carved cart. Each coffin was draped with Turand's white flag with its central purple and gold emblem.

At the tip of the triangle, with Nikolai directly behind him, Gregor stood in full dress uniform. His mourning sash draped straight down from its shoulder strap and fluttered in the cool breeze. His shoulders were squared, his back straight, his salute firm in honor of men who had sacrificed their lives while in service to their queen.

Nikolai wore the dark gray uniform that belonged only to princes of Turand. As Crown Prince, he wore a mourning sash identical to his father's. At Gregor's signal, Nikolai stepped to his father's right. A second signal was given. Gregor and Nikolai each headed an opposite side of guards to open the triangle into parallel lines.

With elegant military precision, guards waiting at the base of the triangle, behind the carts, divided into groups of four to flank each funeral cart. Each guard then folded bronze handles outward and began the solemn task of rolling the coffins through the center of the honor guard. Families followed as the carts bore the caskets into Toraval's main cemetery. Gregor and Nikolai, facing each other, began to march toward each other. The remaining guards followed in carefully synchronized steps. As each pair met at the center, they turned and marched into the cemetery.

Behind a podium built on a raised platform, Gregor assumed his position for the ceremony. Stefan and Anlía already waited. With them were Tira, Valiria and retired lady-in-waiting to the queen, and her daughter, Lady Tirani Tarandá. Once Nikolai arrived to stand by his father's right side, mourners took seats lining the large garden area provided for outdoor services.

Gregor drew in a deep breath. He felt his daughter's eyes upon him and glanced into her face. The encouragement shining back gave him strength to continue this most sorrowful duty as king. In a voice that had mellowed and grown more resonant over the years, he addressed friends and families of the dead soldiers. His words offered comfort as he praised the dedicated, unselfish efforts of men who had gone with their queen to aid fellow Turandans in dire need. He reminded everyone to recall the words of their Valkana. Faith would always sustain them through sorrow if only they opened their hearts and souls to Val. And, though mourning was an emotion through which all must pass at some time in their lives, they must never allow that mourning to dictate the direction of their paths. Life was a gift too precious to waste.

Two hours passed as each soldier was named and his family allowed to deliver a brief eulogy dedicated to the person they had loved. Then, after each casket was carried to its grave and lowered into the ground, Lady Tirani led the gathering in prayers that Val's blessings might be bestowed upon the spirit of the fallen soldier and that Val would provide loving comfort for surviving family members. After the close of the ceremony, Gregor asked Nikolai, Stefan, the priestesses, and Anlía to escort mourners from the cemetery to the palace's assembly hall, where a hot meal awaited.

Gregor remained behind, exercising his right as king to partake of private time at each gravesite. Calling each soldier by name, he personally offered thanks for the dedication shown to Alexa. By the time he reached the last grave, tears coursed down his cheeks. These men had been with her during the final moments of her life. He prayed their spirits would accept his gratitude.

Turning to leave, he saw a lone, uniformed figure hunched over in a chair in the last row of seats. The body shook violently. The soldier, an officer, was obviously overcome with grief. Summoning what emotional control remained to him, Gregor approached the man. When he recognized the solitary mourner as Tirstan Fratino, Captain of the Queen's Royal Guard, Gregor sat beside him and draped an arm around the man's shoulders.

When Tirstan looked up and saw who had come to him, he started to rise to attention. Gregor restrained him. Tirstan dropped his face back into his hands and tried to stop the sobs shaking him. "Sire, I don't know how to face you. I should have been there with her. Ever since I rode with her to Garogan Province—when she was pregnant with Prince Nikolai—this was the first and only time I didn't accompany her on an expedition. Instead, I was away visiting my parents. While I was enjoying myself at home, I let my comrades and my queen die."

Gregor had no idea how to console Tirstan or to help him cope with undeserved guilt tearing at his core of honor. He searched for words and silently prayed to Val for guidance. "Captain, I believe even you have no idea how much faith my wife placed in you. You cannot blame yourself for what happened. I wrestle with my own guilt whenever I remember how I allowed her to convince me that she could leave ahead on her own. Still, her words always come back to me. She always reminded me that she followed the path Val set before her. You must believe that. You are too valuable and experienced an officer for me to risk losing."

"Sire, I failed my queen! I requested leave when I should have attended my duties! She never once failed me. She saved my brother when he was wounded during the rebellion. Later, she healed my son when he was thrown from a horse. She believed in me when no one else did! And now I've failed her!"

"You know she would tell you that Val is the one who did all of the healing."

"Yes, but she allowed herself to be Val's instrument of healing," Tirstan countered, lost to guilt and inner turmoil.

"Captain, you must remember that we all have responsibilities to our families as well as duties to our people. You weren't wrong to visit your family. Besides, your king still needs you. Anlía is becoming a most lovely young woman. You also know that she can be as headstrong as her mother. Soon, I'll need to assign a detachment to keep her safe when she goes to study at the Zinzan Spiritual Center. I need assurance that the unit

I assign will be loyal to her. Tirstan, I can think of no one I trust more than you to command that detachment. Furthermore, I know that Alexa would insist that you be in charge."

Tirstan lifted his face, blotched red and wet with tears, to look at his king. "Your Majesty, I don't know if I can."

"Captain, unless you plan to resign your commission immediately, I believe you have no choice. Now, breathe in deeply and control yourself. I want you to take a one-week leave and report directly to me when you return. I will accept your final decision then."

Years of military service and command took over as Tirstan wiped his face and straightened in his chair.

Gregor nodded in satisfaction. "Captain, my presence is required inside the palace. I wish for you to act as my escort."

Chapter 7

The funeral ceremony for Alexa's guards drained Gregor physically and emotionally. That night, he went to bed early. Even though he expected it to take hours to fall asleep, he craved privacy. Inside his private suite, he felt her essence more intensely. He sought refuge in the place where they had expressed their love most intimately. There, the faint scent of lilac always lingered. There, they had discussed and planned so many aspects of their lives. Within those rooms, they had conceived their children. Inside those chambers, he had laid aside the mantle of monarchy and lived as a man in love.

From one of several bookcases, he removed a journal. Sitting against a mountain of pillows on the bed, he opened the cover and leafed through yellow-edged pages. Smiling, he settled back and read a few of the entries. It wasn't long before his eyes closed, and sleep ushered him backward into years past.

"In Val's great name! What happened?" Gregor shouted as he raced outside. In his arms, Victor Garogan carried Alexa's limp body toward the front steps of the palace. Before Victor could answer, Gregor led the way to a sitting room where Garogan could gently lay Alexa on a sofa.

"I have no idea. We were walking outside in the garden when suddenly, with absolutely no warning, she fainted." Victor's face had drained of blood, and he was clearly frightened. "I sent a guard for the physician."

Gregor knelt by Alexa's side and rubbed her hands between his own. "Is the doctor on his way? Someone hurry and find out what's keeping him!" Then, in a softer voice, he pleaded with his unconscious wife. "Alexa? Beloved, wake up. I'm here, Alexa. Please. Wake up, my love."

The new palace physician arrived within moments and, ordering Gregor aside, immediately began to check her heart and pulse. As he examined her, he questioned Gregor and Victor about what she had eaten or done before the fainting episode. Neither could think of anything that even hinted at possible illness.

Finally, the physician solemnly rose to his feet and faced the king. "Sire, except for the fact that she has fainted, there seems to be nothing else wrong with her. Has this ever happened before?"

Gregor stared at the doctor before a dumbfounded expression caused him to blink several times. Suddenly, a broad smile broke across his face. "Once," he answered with a sudden laugh. "Only once."

Victor stared at Gregor as if the king had lost his mind. "Gregor, excuse me if I find nothing humorous in this situation. Alexa is lying here unconscious, and you're laughing?"

Gregor shook his head and quietly laughed again before he knelt back on the floor, lifting Alexa's hand to his lips. Kissing her fingers, he used his free hand to stroke loose strands of hair that had fallen across her face. "Alexa, my love, wake up. Alexa?"

She began to stir, turning her head toward the sound of her husband's voice. With eyelids so heavy she could barely open them, she gazed into his grinning face and smiled. "I know what it is now," she mumbled, too quietly for Victor or the physician to hear. "It's the first time our spirits connect."

Gregor leaned forward to kiss her forehead. "Are you all right?"

"I will be," she whispered as she encircled his neck with her arms and pulled his lips against hers. After kissing him lightly, she pulled his ear against her lips. "She's the daughter you've wanted so much."

"My little girl?" Gregor again laughed aloud, a sound replete with the relieved happiness flooding his great body from head to toe.

"Gregor! What in the world? Have you lost your senses?" Victor demanded, increasingly irritated by the king's levity when it seemed he should be more worried about Alexa.

Alexa turned her head on the sofa to look at Victor. "I'm so sorry I frightened you, Victor. I wasn't expecting this."

"Expecting what, Alexa? Just tell me you're all right!"

Gregor answered for her. "Victor, I'm going to take her upstairs. She'll be fine."

"Excuse me, Sire," the physician interrupted, "I'm the doctor, and I still have no idea what's happening here."

Gregor grinned as he stood and clapped the doctor on the back. "Very simple. My wife just informed me she's carrying our second child, and this time, we're having a daughter."

Pregnancy suited Alexa. Her eyes shone more brightly than ever, and she positively glowed, even when she wasn't in meditative prayers in the chapel or at the temple. Her energy level increased, spurring everyone into motion to maintain her pace.

With this second pregnancy, Gregor resolved from the beginning to enjoy every minute since he had been away almost the entire time she had carried Nikolai. His excitement bubbled over the day he was first able to feel his baby move. Gripped with fascination at the changes in her figure, he frequently fell asleep with his hand moving in circles over her swelling abdomen.

Little Nikolai would be three years old when his sister arrived. Neither Gregor nor Alexa excluded him from discussions regarding the baby. They included him in family planning sessions as they discussed names and decided on patterns and fabrics for baby clothes for the little princess. With Nikolai's valuable help, not to mention a few secret conversations with his mother, they decided to name the new baby Anlía in honor of Gregor's mother.

Gregor turned in his sleep. As he did, his journal slid from the bed and thudded to the floor. The noise awakened him. Groggy, he reached down and picked up the book. His grasp was weak, and the book nearly fell a second time. He sat up and closed the book before placing it on the nightstand and extinguishing the light. Lying barely awake in the darkness, he could almost hear Alexa's voice.

"Gregor, please, let me stay home. I really don't want to travel all the way to Nipala. You have no idea what six days of travel is like for me right now." Her eyes pleaded with him for understanding.

"Alexa, I know it must be difficult, but these strange explosions in Nipala have terrified people there. More than anyone else, you can calm them while we investigate. And, no matter what you say, you aren't that big yet."

She glanced at him sideways, using her most piteous expression. "I am so. Besides, you aren't the one who'll be stuck in that coach with a three-year-old and a stomach that is three months away from bursting!"

Grinning, Gregor tugged her into his arms. "I promise to become a contortionist and travel the entire way with you inside the carriage if only you'll agree to accompany me."

She stuck out her lower lip in what she hoped was her best pout, finally expelling a heavy sigh. Emerald eyes glittered with teasing humor. "Watching you that long in a coach might be worth the trip."

Gregor chuckled, bent his head down, and kissed her soundly, satisfied that, for once, he had won an argument with her.

Two weeks later, at the weekend home of Nipala Province's governor, Gregor sat beside Nikolai and tucked him into bed. "I won't see you in the morning because I must leave very early. I want you to take care of your mother until I return tomorrow night. Can I trust you?"

Nikolai nodded his little head emphatically. "I'll take care of Mother. Promise."

The next evening, supper was finished, and the sun had set. Gregor, Stefan, and a group of provincial officials had not yet returned from their trip to investigate the most recent explosion to rock Nipala. Over several months, more than fourteen explosions had split open the ground, causing long-lasting fires that had burned forests and, in six cases, destroyed homes. The random eruptions had killed almost twenty people.

Mentally, Alexa distanced herself from the household activities around her. She smiled to herself. Sensing that her husband was well, she excused herself to the governor's wife and went upstairs to wish Nikolai goodnight before retiring for the night.

Quietly entering the room where Nikolai was supposed to be in bed, she grinned when she saw him with his face pressed against a window facing the back of the house. "And why aren't you in bed, my little one?"

He spun around for only a moment before returning his full attention to the night sky. "Look, Mother! Flying lights in the sky!"

With none of the clumsiness she claimed to suffer, she knelt at her son's side and gazed upward at the sky. "I believe those are meteors, Nikolai! A whole cluster of them!"

"Meteors?" he repeated excitedly. "Beautiful, Mother! I like them!"

Seized by his enthusiasm, Alexa snatched up his robe and urged him to put it on quickly. She grabbed the blanket from his bed and, leading him down the back stairwell, took him outside. Several yards behind the house, a small, wooded hill gently sloped downward. Mother and son hurried down the gentle knoll and found a perfect spot to spread their blanket.

For more than half an hour, they watched the meteor shower and discussed the constellations when the force of an enormous boom knocked them both over. Dazed for several moments, Alexa drunkenly dragged herself into a sitting position before pulling a terrified Nikolai into her arms. Far above them, a towering column of flames completely engulfed the manor house where they had been staying. Trees around the house and at the top of the hill were already glowing from blazes threatening to consume everything in sight.

Sucking in a deep breath, Alexa recognized that she and her small son were in the direct path of the firestorm. Staring into Nikolai's eyes, she concentrated on calming him. "Nikolai, that fire is very dangerous. I need your help right now."

His dark brown eyes were wide with fear, but he listened attentively and nodded.

"Dear one, I want you to think of your father and be brave just like him. We must hurry as fast as we can to escape that fire. Mother really needs you to help me. Will you?"

"I promised Father to take care of you. I can be brave. I can!" he insisted, trying very hard to look courageous and manly.

"All right, Nikolai. Hold my hand. Tightly, little one! And hurry!" Every step deeper into the woods brought more difficulties in their efforts to escape rapidly spreading flames. Heavy smoke filled the air, burning their noses and throats and causing them to cough. Alexa frequently had to stop to lift Nikolai over fallen logs before clumsily clambering over them herself. Their desperate flight finally led them to an outcropping of rocks overhanging a broad stream. Scanning the immediate area, Alexa spied a steep, rocky path where she thought she could get her child to the safety of the water. Slipping and sliding on loose, gray, flat stones, she finally got them to the water's edge with only minor bumps and bruises.

Finding momentary shelter beneath a protruding rock shelf, Alexa concentrated on controlling her breathing. She clutched Nikolai close while she considered how best to continue. Her last backward glance left her with the terrible acknowledgment that there was no way they could backtrack toward the direction from where they had come.

Finally, she knelt and embraced her small son. In a voice as calm as if she were home in her own bed, she began talking to him encouragingly. "Dear Nikolai, I'm so proud of you! Father will be, too, when I tell him how brave you've been. We're going to take a minute to pray for Val's help. Then I'll pull the ruffle off my gown and tear it into two pieces. We'll dip the pieces in water and tie them around our faces so we can breathe better. After that, we need to get farther away before the fire gets here. Can you do that?"

"I can, Mother. Don't worry. I'm strong, just like Father. We'll be fine. Val will help us."

Following brief moments of intense prayer, Alexa and Nikolai splashed across the stream and followed its course toward the west. After ten minutes that seemed to have lasted a lifetime, they neared a road where a narrow bridge crossed above the stream. Fires continued to rage, sweeping out of control.

A smile lit Alexa's face, and she pointed up. "Look, Nikolai! Val sent help!" On the bridge, snorting nervously and stomping her hooves, Alexa's horse Vela seemed to be urging them to hurry. Alexa prayed aloud as she rushed toward Vela. "Dearest Val, thank you for giving me the idea to bring Vela for Nikolai to ride, and thank you for sending her to help us."

"Vela, you wonderful, wonderful creature!" she exclaimed, climbing onto the bridge and hugging the horse's neck. Breathlessly and with some effort, Alexa lifted Nikolai and seated him on Vela's back. Instructing the boy to hold tightly to Vela's mane, Alexa used the railings alongside the bridge to climb high enough so she could mount. Glancing one last time over her shoulder at the approaching flames, she pressed her knees into her horse's sides, and together they escaped on the road through the forest.

⤳

Less than two miles from the governor's house, Gregor and Stefan were astounded by the magnitude of the blast that literally shook the ground beneath them. Stunned for only seconds, the riding party raced toward the site of the explosion. Passing through an arched, brick gateway, they yanked back hard on the reins of their horses. The sight before them was horrifying.

Gregor leapt from his horse, running without hesitation toward raging flames that fully engulfed the manor. Stefan and several Royal Guards raced after him and fought with him to keep him from charging blindly into the fire. A second explosion, almost as powerful as the first, rumbled the ground and knocked them off their feet. Struggling mightily against men who refused to release him, Gregor dragged himself to his knees.

"Alexa! Nikolai! No!" He shouted their names at the top of his voice until, in shock, he began to weave drunkenly before covering his face with his hands and pitching forward to the ground.

Stefan barked orders at other guards to help grooms leading horses from their stalls where embers had landed on the roof and set the stables on fire. He watched as Vela reared and bolted from the groom guiding her to safety. He then saw the governor and several aides running to help two people lying on the ground, their bodies hurled away from the fire by the explosion. Stefan then turned his undivided attention to Gregor.

With two guards remaining to help him, Stefan pulled Gregor into a sitting position and firmly restrained him. Muddy tears streaked Gregor's face. His eyes reflected eerily flickering, undulating lights cast by the fearsome blaze. He tried to speak, halting between words and choking on sobs. "She didn't want to come, Stefan. She only came because I insisted. Now I've lost her. I've lost them all. My little Nikolai. My baby girl. In Val's name, what have I done? What have I done?"

Stefan drew Gregor's head against his own chest and held it there. Stefan's gray eyes closed as he prayed in thanks that Adrina had remained in Toraval with their three-month-old daughter. He then prayed for strength, both for Gregor and for himself. Without Alexa and Nikolai, he expected it would be nearly impossible to convince Gregor that life would be worth living.

⤚

Raindrops bounced off the heavily compacted dirt road. Dawn was approaching. The sun would be concealed for hours yet by heavy cloud cover that carried rains to tame the forest fire that had blazed through the night. Exhausted, Alexa kept shifting her weight to prevent little Nikolai from falling after he had finally collapsed into the kind of sleep known only by small children. She had seen the top of a chimney in the distance, and blue smoke drifted from it in lazy swirls. Vela sensed her intentions and wearily plodded in that direction.

When they finally arrived, yellow light already shone through small windows at the front of the house. Soaked by the now steady downpour and too tired to try dismounting with a sleeping child in her arms, Alexa called out as loudly as she could. "Please! Someone! Please help me."

Within moments, the door opened, and an elderly man peeked out. His lined face jerked in surprise as he hurried out. "What in the world? Here, careful! Let me take your little one." With sturdy arms, he pulled

Nikolai down and cradled him against his chest. "Wait here. I'll only be a minute to carry him inside."

Emerging once again, he guided Vela toward the side of the wide porch in front of his house and carefully helped Alexa down. Staggering slightly, Alexa gripped his arm for support until she regained her balance. "Sir, I thank you so much."

"Mistress, go inside where it's dry. I'll put your horse in my barn and out of the rain. I'll be right back."

Inside and with arms pressed tightly to her chest against chilling wetness, Alexa stepped close to the roaring fire. In front of the screened fireplace, the man had laid Nikolai on a brightly woven rug and draped a cover over his little body. Alexa tucked the blanket around his ears before standing up and moving closer to the fire to warm herself.

She heard the door close and turned around. The gentleman pulled a chair around for her to sit and immediately poured a cup of tea from the steaming pot whistling merrily on the stove. "Here, Mistress, drink this while I look for something dry for you and your little one to wear. You'll be deathly ill if we don't get you dried out and warm in a hurry."

An hour later, she snuggled into the fluffy depths of a featherbed heated by hot, glowing coals passed beneath thick, quilted covers. With Nikolai snuggled close to her side, she prayed to Val in thanksgiving for delivering them safely from the fire and for her husband, whom she was sure must be frantic.

⌒

"Drink this. Now." Stefan ordered sternly, placing a mug of hot milk in Gregor's hands. "Drink, I said."

Stefan ached as he looked into Gregor's eyes, so glazed and so bleak. Gregor had eaten nothing for a day and a half. Having accepted hospitality in the house of the mayor in the nearby town, he had occasionally shuffled from one room to another to find a place to sit and stare at nothing in particular. Stefan or Tirstan had followed him everywhere, fearful of leaving him alone.

Eventually, Gregor drained the cup, and Stefan removed it from fingers that seemed to have forgotten how to function. Stefan requested Tirstan's help, and the two men led their unresisting king into a small breakfast room. With a great deal of prodding, pleading, and demanding, they finally managed to get him to consume a bowl of stew and a slice of bread. The intense effort tired both of them, more mentally than physically.

Only two people, the governor's teenage son and daughter, had survived the explosion. They had been outside at the time and had been hurled several yards away. Both had suffered burns and broken bones, but they would live. The local doctor who had attended the children suggested to Stefan that they get Gregor into bed so that a sedative could be administered.

Half an hour later, Stefan and Tirstan wrestled with a resisting Gregor while the doctor forced him to drink the potion that would induce sleep. As the medicine began to take effect, silent tears began to slide down the king's face as he clutched the sleeve of Stefan's jacket. "It's my fault, Stefan. I brought them here to die. I brought my wife and babies here to die. Don't make me sleep. Please don't make…"

His eyelids, heavy and swollen, succumbed to the effects of exhaustion combined with medication. Stefan glanced up at the doctor's face. "How long do you think he'll sleep?"

The physician, a distinguished man with graying hair and bespectacled blue eyes, shook his head. "I gave him enough that he should sleep through the night. However, it's hard to be certain, considering how he's fighting the sedative. In his present state of mind, I recommend that someone stay near him until morning."

Stefan nodded in somber agreement. When the doctor left, Stefan instructed Tirstan to have guards posted at the king's side throughout the night. Instinctively, Stefan knew Gregor well enough to know that he would do nothing intentionally to harm himself. However, considering the devastating blow he had just suffered, Stefan feared the king might accidentally hurt himself. Whatever the case, prudence seemed the logical course of action.

By the following morning, the rains had diminished only slightly when Gregor finally sat up in bed. He pressed long fingers against throbbing pain in his temples. His eyes felt dry and full of sand. His throat was sore, and his stomach ached. Looking around, he was puzzled by unfamiliar surroundings and how he had come to be there.

"Your Majesty?" The guard who had pulled the last shift of duty stood and spoke quietly.

Gregor glanced up. "Where am I?"

"You are in the home of Mayor Lomarán. The local physician gave you a sleeping potion last night."

Gregor's eyes closed, and the expression of total devastation returned to cloud his face. "Now I remember."

The guard began to pull hangers from a closet with the clothes Gregor had worn two days in a row. "Sire, after we put you to bed, we removed your clothing so they could be measured and laundered. Sir Sidano summoned some local seamstresses to make new clothes for you. Unfortunately, yours were all destroyed, and you're too tall for us to borrow anything clean for you to wear."

Very slowly, Gregor forced himself to rise from bed. The simple act sent searing flashes of pain through his tortured brain. "Thank you, Sergeant. I think I can manage to get dressed now."

The young sergeant knew he was being dismissed. "Sire, forgive me. I have orders not to leave you alone."

Gregor cast him a baleful look of anger that quickly faded. He sighed in resignation, feeling too empty to muster even a weak protest. After attending ablutions in the adjoining bath, he returned to the modest bedroom. Almost mechanically, he began to dress, fumbling with the links on his cuffs and resisting a dizzying wave of nausea. With tears swimming in his eyes, he realized how rarely he now performed the task of fastening his own cuffs. Alexa had seemed forever at his side, affectionately closing buttons and smoothing the fabric of his shirts. Swallowing against a lump in his throat, dread flooded him with the realization that even the most simple of tasks would only remind him of her.

With the soldier at his heels, Gregor found his way downstairs. Sympathetic glances accompanied hushed greetings within a house of mourning. The governor's wife, who was the mayor's sister, had also died in the fire. The governor's entire household staff, several visitors, and Nikolai's nurse had all perished in the explosion. The two injured teens suffered severe burns and broken bones. People moved about quietly, aware that Turand would now enter a prolonged period of national mourning.

Stefan awaited the king at the bottom of the stairs. Their eyes met, reflecting shared grief, and they embraced each other. The trembling in Gregor's body shook Stefan to the core of his being.

"The sergeant sent word that you would be coming down," Stefan said as he pulled away from his friend. "Breakfast is ready."

"I'm not hungry," Gregor muttered.

"Your Majesty," Stefan responded formally, "I prefer not to repeat yesterday's episode, but if you insist on making things difficult for me, I will have you held down and see that you're force-fed."

Gregor glared at him for several seconds. He saw that his old friend's threat was completely serious. Again, he lacked any will to resist. His lips briefly tightened into a thin line. He didn't speak. Instead, he meekly allowed Stefan to guide him to the breakfast table.

"It looks like the rain might finally stop," Alexa remarked as she stuck her head out the door for what seemed like the hundredth time that morning.

Master Budrino chuckled. "You must be quite anxious to get back to that husband of yours."

Alexa turned and grinned sheepishly. "You have no idea how he worries about me. He can be difficult at times. By now, he must be impossible to live with."

Master Budrino's face wrinkled with a kindly smile. "I know how I was with my dear Endra. A good man should worry about a pretty lady like you."

"Father says Mother is the most beautiful woman in all Turand," Nikolai piped up proudly.

"Master Niko, I could never doubt the word of your father," the old gentleman responded as he pulled Nikolai up into his lap and gave him an affectionate hug.

Alexa shook her head in amusement, although her eyes reflected distress. She knew that Gregor must be convinced they had been in the house when it had exploded. Yesterday and this morning, she had gone out and watched traces of smoke still rising from the intense fire. Knowing how devastated her husband must be, Alexa was anxious to return.

"Mistress, I've already packed some food and drink for you, and I even found a saddle for your horse. I won't deny how much I've enjoyed your company, but I understand your need to leave. Your husband must be suffering terribly. I imagine no one escaped that explosion with their lives."

Alexa's smile revealed her appreciation for his understanding. "Master Budrino, I expect you will have another visit in the next day or two. I know my husband well. He will not allow your kindness to go unacknowledged."

Again, the old gentleman chuckled. "Although I never turn away visitors, there is no need for him to come. Your thanks are more than enough; however, if he does come, perhaps he'll agree to allow me to visit this delightful young man when I visit my son and daughter near Toraval in two months when I go to sell some of those statues that fascinate this young boy of yours so much."

"Oh, Mother, say yes. Can Master Budrino visit us? Please?" Nikolai pleaded with all the fervor of a small child.

Alexa laughed at the plaintive expressions on both their faces. "I have no doubt that Father will welcome a visit from Master Budrino."

"Now, young Master Niko, before you go, I have something for you. Remember that statue I showed you yesterday? The one you liked so much?"

Nikolai's brown eyes grew wide. "The tall one that you made? Of the king?" Master Budrino nodded seriously. "That's exactly right. The one of good King Gregor. Since you liked it so much, I'm going to give it to you as a gift. And, if it is Val's will, I will go to Toraval. Hopefully, I will get to see our Valkana this time. If I do, I will carve a statue of her to go with your king."

"Really! Promise?" Niko's eyes sparkled with delight as little arms wrapped around his newfound friend. Peeking up at his mother, their conspiracy unbroken, he carefully took the intricately carved piece of wood into his hands. "I've seen King Gregor. This looks just like him."

Alexa barely contained herself. She was so proud of her son for not revealing the secret of their identities. She had not wanted their host to feel uncomfortable knowing that he had taken Turand's Crown Prince and his pregnant mother under roof. She had carefully coached Nikolai before they had gotten up from bed the day before. He had thought the game exciting, especially with the added suggestion that they use Papino Victor's pet name of Niko.

A little later, with rain barely a drizzle, she donned the raincoat loaned to her by Master Budrino. They all hugged, and Alexa promised that her husband would undoubtedly arrange for Master Budrino to visit them in Toraval. Then, with their host's assistance, she climbed onto Vela's back and settled Nikolai on the saddle in front of her.

After little more than an hour of riding, Alexa felt desperate to get down from her horse. She searched until she found a spot high enough to climb down safely. With feet planted firmly on the ground, she stretched and twisted. Her back ached, and her muscles complained painfully. Even though it would surely cost her an unwelcome delay, she decided to let Nikolai ride while she led Vela the rest of the way to Nipala's Cosaná Hamlet.

Late afternoon was gray and overcast when she finally reached the outskirts of the village. With her eyes closed, she stopped a moment. The all-day drizzle was growing heavier. Nikolai was shivering in the chilly dampness. She glanced up into his sweet face and saw him smile.

A sensitive child, he anticipated her question. "I'm cold, Mother. You keep going. Father must be close. He's waiting. I know."

"My little Nikolai," she praised. "Just wait until Father hears how brave you've been. I want you to snuggle as best you can inside that coat and blanket. Mother is going to concentrate. Don't be afraid if you see my eyes closed."

Allowing herself to slip into a light trance, her feet followed the path laid out before her by another hand. After half an hour, she stopped outside the stone entrance of a rambling, two-story house about thirty yards back from the road. She breathed yet another prayer of gratitude. She clearly felt her husband's presence beyond those walls.

Her steps dragged as she passed through the front gate and headed toward the house. She saw two uniformed soldiers walking from a stable toward the main house. One of them looked up and stopped abruptly. Suddenly, both men broke into a dead run in her direction.

Tirstan reached her first. "Blessed be our Lord Val!" he exclaimed. "Your Majesty, we thought you lost in the fire!"

Alexa affectionately reached out to embrace Tirstan. "Only by the grace of Val are we alive. Tirstan, please help me get Nikolai inside. He's freezing with this rain, and I know he's hungry. And have someone take good care of Vela. She saved our lives."

"Private, tend to the horse," Tirstan ordered as he lifted Nikolai out of the saddle. With Alexa clinging to Tirstan's arm for support, Tirstan then carried Nikolai toward the house.

Stefan, who had been staring broodingly out the window, saw the three approaching and ran to meet them at the front door. "Alexa!" he shouted joyfully. "Dearest Val be praised! I can't believe my eyes!"

Alexa welcomed Stefan's embrace. "Oh, Stefan, it's been terrible. I can't tell you how glad I am to see you!"

Nikolai reached for Stefan. "Papino Stefan, I'm hungry!"

Stefan took the little boy into his arms and kissed both plump cheeks before sending Tirstan to the kitchen to see that the prince would have whatever he wanted to eat, reminding Tirstan to have someone bring warm blankets to wrap around Nikolai.

Stefan then helped Alexa remove her dripping raincoat before tucking his own jacket tightly around her shoulders. Then, grasping both of Alexa's hands with his own, he held them tightly. "It looks like you need to go upstairs to dry off and change. Besides, I know someone who will be extremely happy to see you."

Alexa looked at him with a tired smile. "I suppose he's been somewhat difficult?"

Wrapping his arm around her shoulder, Stefan turned to guide her upstairs, where Gregor had spent most of the day in gloomy silence. "Your

Majesty, sometimes you have an incredible talent for understatement." His voice turned very serious. "He needs you, Alexa. He needs you so much."

Standing outside the bedroom door, Alexa paused to take a deep breath. She could feel waves of despair emanating from within. Pushing against the door, she knocked lightly as it opened.

"Go away!" There, on the edge of the bed, sat her husband. His elbows were on his knees, and his face was buried in his hands.

"Must you send me away when it has been such a hard trip back to you?"

At first, he didn't move a muscle. She started to wonder if he had even heard her until he lifted his head and turned to look in her direction. His face, ravaged with grief, was a mask of utter disbelief.

Smiling tenderly, she quickly crossed the room and dropped to her knees between his legs. With gentle fingers, she caressed from his face locks of uncombed hair. She then raised herself enough to lightly kiss his lips. "Please say I don't have to go away again."

With sudden shock, Gregor realized he wasn't dreaming. Instantly, he wrapped both arms around her shoulders. Long fingers almost frantically tangled into the damp waves of her hair as he clutched her face tightly against his chest. He rocked back and forth as a violent sob shook his body. "Alexa! My sweet, darling Alexa! You're alive! Dearest Val, you're alive!"

With her arms around his waist, she let him cry. When his sobs finally subsided, she listened as he repeated her name time and again. After a long while, she pulled back and gazed up into dark eyes that, minutes before, had reflected sheer devastation. Placing her hand against his cheek, she smiled. "I love you, Gregor. I love you so much. Hold me again."

With his heart overcome by joyful relief, he embraced her almost desperately. She had seemingly come back from the dead. Alexa had again returned to where she belonged—where he needed her most. Val had restored to him the wife he loved more than anything else in all the world.

ᗧ

Gregor awoke. The midnight toll of the temple carillons reminded him yet again that she was gone. The mournful sound had begun the night before he left Toraval to meet her in Tolura Province. Since then, not a night had passed that the bells had not rung out their sorrowful melody.

Lying in bed, he remembered the joy that had inundated him those many years ago when she had come back to him. How fervently he wished he might know that joy again. He turned on his side and adjusted the pillow under his neck. This time, Alexa had been gone too long. He closed his eyes, summoning vivid memories of her. Resignation was his unrelenting companion.

ᗧ

When Gregor practically burst into the kitchen of Mayor Lomarán's home, Stefan and Tirstan were busy offering sweet treats that both knew were only occasionally given to the little boy. When Nikolai looked up and saw his father, little arms flew into the air. Rapid steps carried Gregor to his son's side, and he picked up his baby, clutching him tightly. He didn't even try to hide the tears in his eyes.

"Father?" Nikolai asked almost hesitantly. "Father, you hurt? Are you all right?"

Gregor laughed softly. "I'm better than all right! I missed you so! My little boy is back, and I am so proud! Your mother told me how brave you were! And I love you so much!"

Nikolai tightly hugged his father's neck. He was puzzled by his father's reaction but excited by his father's praise. "Oh, Father, I have so much to tell you. We saw meteors in the sky, and Mother took me outside to watch. And then there was a big boom! We fell over and saw the big fire. And then Vela came. We rode in the dark woods, and then we met Master Budrino!"

Gregor laughed heartily at the non-stop string of chatter from his son. Suddenly, he was surprised when Nikolai demanded to be put down. Hurrying toward the enormous tiled fireplace where the coat and blanket were now hanging to dry, Nikolai fumbled with the coat until he pulled a small, well-wrapped package from a deep pocket.

Alexa, wearing a thick, warm robe borrowed from the lady of the house, entered the kitchen without a word. With her arms tucked tightly over her pregnant abdomen, she leaned against the wall. Affectionately, she watched as her husband crouched down to inspect the object that Nikolai's chubby fingers carefully unwrapped. The detailing of the intricately carved statuette was impressive. Stained wood that glowed warmly in the firelight revealed an incredibly striking resemblance to King Gregor.

Gregor straightened. Holding the figurine against the light so he could better study the curves and lines carved into his own likeness, he felt honored to have been the model for such an exquisitely crafted piece of art. He knelt once again, placed the statuette back into Nikolai's waiting hands, and tightly hugged his son. Glancing upward, Gregor looked into his wife's tranquil face. Tears glistened in his eyes. More than ever before, he cherished the presence of treasures more precious than he could have imagined.

⌐

"What are you thinking?"

Stefan's voice drew Gregor from reflection on the dreams that had filled his night. Gregor shook his head slightly sideways. "I was just thinking about the year Anlía was born. I just watched her enter the chapel for meditations. She is quite a young woman now, yet it seems like only yesterday that I held her in my hands the day she was born."

Stefan recognized that Gregor had arisen to face the day in a pensive mood. The king's closest friend felt relieved that there was little outward sign of strain brought on by the previous day's funerals. Instead, the appearance of a nostalgic expression in his friend's eyes revealed the comforting memories of happier times.

"I think I'll never forget Nikolai's entrance to your office that day. Or the expression on the faces of your generals when Nikolai excused himself while insisting he had a 'mergency' to discuss with his father."

Gregor chuckled at the memory. "I was so surprised when he strode into my office, looking for all the world like he was in complete command of all of Turand. That little face was so serious."

Stefan also laughed. "Even when you ordered him to wait until you finished with your meeting, he refused to be dissuaded or intimidated."

Gregor laughed again. That day had begun with the small family's customary prayer session. Gregor had then gone to his office for meetings regarding plans to augment Turand's defenses. Following three years of peace and steady progress in the restructuring of Turand, the country's king had vowed to do all in his power to prevent any new invasion through a carefully planned readiness program.

Alexa and their son had spent much of the morning upstairs reading. In the final month of her pregnancy, Alexa contentedly enjoyed time with her first child. A new nurse had not yet been chosen to fill the void left by the one who died in Nipala. Following the loss of that well-loved nanny, Alexa devoted hours to Nikolai, especially knowing that soon he would no longer be the sole center of his parents' universe. Instead, he would have to share with his new sister.

Gregor had not known that, shortly before midday, Alexa had left Nikolai in her sitting room while she went to the bathroom. Inside, she had felt the first of several powerful contractions that began without warning and hit in rapid succession. Alexa quickly pulled several towels from a wall shelf before sinking to the floor. She could hardly believe that she was unable to walk even as far as the adjoining bedroom.

Nikolai quickly missed his mother and peeked his head around the open bathroom door. Seeing Alexa's flushed face as she grasped the side of the bathtub, he grew instantly alarmed. He rushed to her side and, with fluttering fingers, petted his mother's hair. "Mother, you all right?"

Alexa forced a smile meant to encourage him. "Nikolai, Mother needs your help. I need you to be brave the same way you were when we were in Nipala. Do you remember?"

He nodded seriously, concern shadowing his face when he saw his mother's features tighten as she sought to control her breathing.

"Nikolai, your father is in his office with his generals. You know he may be cross when you interrupt, but you mustn't worry. Once he knows why, he won't be upset with you. I want you to go to him and talk to him very quietly. Tell Father where I am and tell him I need his help. Tell him your baby sister..."

Another contraction overwhelmed her, and she quickly puffed breaths of air out. Not wanting to frighten the young child, she spoke very quickly. "Nikolai, tell Father that Anlía is coming. Tell him to hurry. Can you do that?"

Nikolai shook his head vigorously up and down. "I can, Mother. Really! I can!"

Alexa smiled her encouragement. "Then go, my little one. Hurry, but be careful on the stairs."

Nikolai turned to leave but stopped for an instant. Turning back around for just a moment, he smiled. "Don't be afraid, Mother. You'll see. I'll bring Father fast." He then rushed from the bathroom, leaving his mother panting through yet another contraction.

Minutes later, Nikolai sucked in a deep breath and knocked on the door to his father's office. He didn't wait for a response. Instead, proudly confident, he slowly opened the door and stood as tall and straight as he could while awaiting his father's acknowledgment.

Gregor glanced up and frowned sternly. He spoke to Stefan and the three generals seated in front of his desk. "Excuse me a moment, gentlemen. Nikolai, Father is in a meeting. Please go outside. We can talk when I finish."

Nikolai faced his father boldly. "Excuse me, Father. I have to talk to you. Now. It's very important."

Gregor stifled a grin before responding in a more stern tone. "Nikolai, go now. I said we could talk later." He then watched as his son approached the broad desk in a most regal and commanding manner.

"Father, it's a 'mergency.' I have to talk to you now." Nikolai enunciated each word distinctly and with as much dignity as a boy of three could manage. Stopping just in front of his father's knees, he signaled with his index finger for his father to bend forward.

Indulgently, Gregor surrendered to his son's unusual insistence. Leaning forward, he felt little hands come to rest against each side of his face. Nikolai then placed his mouth close to his father's ear.

"Father, I told you. It's important. You have to hurry. Mother needs you."

Gregor straightened slightly and looked into his son's intense, dark eyes. His own brown eyes revealed suspicious doubt. "Mother sent you? Are you sure?"

Nikolai nodded before pulling his father's face closer again. "Father," his whisper was more demanding this time, "you have to come. And you have to hurry. Mother sent me to tell you the baby is coming."

This time, Gregor straightened immediately in his chair. "Nikolai, are you sure? Where is Mother now?"

Nikolai inhaled deeply, growing impatient with his father's questions. "She's in her bathroom. On the floor. She didn't look very good, and she was breathing funny."

Leaping to his feet, Gregor started to run from the office. As he did, he called over his shoulder. "Stefan, send for the physician. And have someone watch Nikolai!"

Bursting into their suite, Gregor heard the sounds of Alexa's panting from inside their bathroom. He rushed through the door, finding her leaning forward, her knees bent and her arms locked around her legs. Her skirts were pulled up into a tangle of fabric around her hips. Beside her lay the pile of towels she had dragged from the shelf on the wall.

Relief filled her eyes when she saw her husband. "I—I thought you'd never come," she gasped.

Crouching down, Gregor encircled her shoulders comfortingly. "Let me help you into the birthing room."

She shook her head quickly. "No time! Bring a pillow for my back. Hurry! Then wash your hands." Another contraction overpowered her, and she launched into a fresh round of rapid, panting breaths.

Gregor disappeared for a matter of seconds before returning with two large pillows that he carefully placed between her back and the wall of their enormous enameled tub. He then hurriedly washed his hands. Then, kneeling again at his wife's side, he gazed at her helplessly. "What now, Alexa? What do I do now?"

Rolling her eyes slightly, she forced herself to speak. "Get a towel. A big one! Hurry! Gregor, hurry! She's coming!"

Alexa gave him no time to think or to be afraid. Her need for help was too urgent. Instead, with curt, clipped orders, she told him what to do. Within minutes of his arrival, his huge hands gently grasped and turned his new baby's head as she made her abrupt entrance into his world. Securely, he held onto the slippery body that emerged so quickly and then wrapped the infant in a large towel. Taking care with her umbilical cord until the doctor could arrive to free her from her mother, Gregor stared with utter enchantment at his little girl's face.

The baby had cried out only a few brief seconds, quieting immediately as her mother's fingers caressed the side of her tiny face. She appeared perfect in every way. Her head was crowned with swirls of damp, dark hair. Her eyes already showed promise of the wide, almond shape of her mother's eyes. Gregor inhaled sharply. In his hands, he held a tiny beauty so incredible that she caused his heart to throb loudly within his chest.

He glanced up into his wife's perspiration-streaked face. Now relieved from the powerful contractions that had brought their daughter forth into the light of day, his wife's smile was joyous. "She's more beautiful than I imagined," Alexa whispered.

Her husband nodded, unable to speak. His smile spread and then shakily faded before lighting his face again and again. When the physician arrived with Stefan and Adrina at his heels, Gregor could barely move in response to firm instructions to let the doctor take Anlía. Gregor was reluctant to allow any distance that might separate him from his wife and newborn daughter.

Once the doctor had assured himself all was in order, he carefully passed the newborn infant to Adrina. With Anlía safely in Adrina's care, the physician requested assistance getting Alexa up from the floor. Gregor stubbornly refused to allow her even to stand. Instead, he lifted her into his arms and carried her to the birthing room, where she could rest comfortably. While they awaited Adrina's arrival with the new addition to the royal family, Gregor whispered a continual flow of loving praise to the wife he adored.

Once baby Anlía was delivered to her parents, Gregor and Alexa both examined every inch of her. Tiny fingers received sweet kisses. Silken smooth cheeks received delicate caresses. Velvety thick baby hair was stroked into a smooth cap. This baby, a full pound lighter than her brother had been at birth, seemed already responsive to the subdued voices of her parents. Father and mother were ecstatic with Val's newest gift to them.

Recognizing Alexa's need to rest, Gregor leaned forward and tenderly kissed her forehead, her eyelids, her nose, and her lips. Each kiss manifested a husband's loving tribute. With the warmth of his lips caressing her face, Alexa's eyelids grew heavy. As she fell asleep, he tucked a blanket beneath her chin. With Anlía cradled close against his chest, he smiled with quiet bliss as he left to introduce his baby girl to brother Nikolai, now the palace's youngest hero.

"Gregor?" Stefan's voice yet again drew his friend's attention back to the present.

Gregor glanced around sheepishly. Memories had claimed his complete attention to the point he had nearly forgotten his friend's presence. "Please, Stefan, accept my apology. I didn't intend to drift off."

Stefan's blue-gray eyes reflected understanding. "That was such a beautiful time in our lives. We were both still relatively new at being happy, as well as deeply in love. Sometimes it's much too easy to drift away into those memories."

Gregor responded with a nod. For just a moment, he had felt the strangest sensation—as if Alexa's voice were whispering into his mind. "Life is such a wonder, my husband. Cherish forever all we have shared."

Glancing upward, he smiled warmly at Stefan. "I praise Val that memories are not all that's left to me. Alexa gave me six wonderful children and enough love every single day to sustain me for a lifetime."

Stefan breathed in a sigh, grateful that his friend's face showed little trace of the pain and sorrow he had wrestled with the day before. Instead, despite the hint of sadness lingering in his dark eyes, Gregor appeared more tranquil than any day since Alexa's disappearance. As both men turned their focus to the daily routine of governing a nation, Stefan offered a brief, silent prayer of thanks that Gregor was finally regaining his perspective.

Chapter 8

DiLeno's fair hair showed signs of silvering, although his bright blue eyes still shone with youthful exuberance. The years had been kind to him while he applied his energies to the operational management of the Zinzan Spiritual Center. Less than a year after Turand's civil war ended, DiLeno had married Tirani, the queen's lady-in-waiting. Previously, he had sometimes been indifferent to the teachings of Val despite his close friendship with Alexa Maraná and her fiancé, Victor Garogan. However, his petite wife had taught him in a very big way how much faith could enrich life.

Following his wedding, DiLeno had delved deep into studies of the Great Book of Val. Much of what he found in those voluminous writings echoed his parents' beliefs and mirrored principles he had never consciously recognized as being tied to dormant faith. With Tirani's encouragement, DiLeno had recommitted himself to the teachings of his childhood and then sought ways to serve Val and the people of Turand. He discovered the perfect vehicle for that service when the king and queen announced that Zinzan would become the consecrated site of a center dedicated to education and preparation for those seeking to become priests and priestesses. That center would also serve as a retreat for any Turandan wishing to explore and nurture personal faith and spirituality.

DiLeno spent an entire year helping Victor, his cousin and closest friend, draft plans for the revitalization of Zinzan. Both men possessed strong organizational skills, and DiLeno enhanced the team with his architectural training. They spent days inspecting Zinzan's ruins, deciding what needed to be razed and what, if anything, should be preserved. Their collaboration resulted in the design of an expansive central square where broad rays of flowering trees and colorful gardens would radiate from the Valiria statue that had remained intact despite Sifiq efforts to destroy it.

DiLeno and Victor paid particular attention to developing a sanctuary in which portions of Alexa's ancestral home would be preserved as part of an enormous temple dedicated to the memory of Zinzan's massacred citizenry. Initially, Alexa had resisted the idea, worrying that such a shrine might be misconstrued as an effort to draw personal honors toward herself and subsequently focus attention away from the site's actual purpose. However, after listening to appeals from relatives and friends of victims of the Zinzan massacre, she finally relented.

The installation of a curving wall bearing the engraved names of those killed at Zinzan created a touching memorial to the sacrifice of Alexa's family and neighbors. The wall swiftly developed a haunting mystique even before its dedication. Almost immediately upon its completion, workers and visitors insisted that voices whispered reminders never to forget the magnitude of Val's blessings. With increasing testimony of mystic incidents occurring at the memorial, the monument soon gained its unofficial title: The Whispering Wall of Zinzan.

Hard work won generous praises from Turand's people. After six years, the Zinzan Spiritual Center bustled with activity. Although not all buildings were completed, the logistics had been planned well enough to provide sufficient classroom space for students and faculty and room for many from the burgeoning list of Turandans wanting to visit the center.

DiLeno and Victor also earned their king's praise and respect. The center quickly became a symbol of their nation's struggle to revitalize its infrastructure and restore its sovereignty based on the foundation of faith. King Gregor frequently traveled throughout Turand, giving generously of his time and energies while encouraging his citizens during the reconstruction period. He often extolled the activities at Zinzan as an example for the entire kingdom. That which had experienced complete devastation was being brought back to vibrant, blessed life. He freely acknowledged the accomplishments of Victor and DiLeno, and he urged all Turandans to follow suit.

DiLeno was taking a brief sabbatical from his responsibilities as rector at the center. Sensing a pressing need for her presence, Tirani had explained her desire to spend time in Toraval. He had held his wife in his arms and given his blessing for her to pursue her instincts. He had told her he would take their son to Garogan City to visit his parents and later join her in the capital. His timing had been such that he was preparing to leave with Victor and Adrina the following day as they traveled back to Toraval with Adrina's three children and the king's four youngest children in tow.

"What time do you plan to leave in the morning?" DiLeno asked, lounging back against a deeply padded rocker on the covered veranda.

Victor sat on a stone balustrade and leaned against one of several tall columns lining the open corridor. "I thought nine o'clock would be good. That way, all the children can eat breakfast early and have a little time to work off some of their energy."

DiLeno chuckled. "A five-day journey with eight children ranging from fifteen to six. We'll be lucky to reach Toraval with our sanity intact."

Victor laughed despite his heavy mood. The trip to Garogan had indeed been challenging enough. Still, he had such a knack for dealing with Alexa's children that he had almost enjoyed the barrage of constant questions, even the too frequently asked, "When will we get there?"

DiLeno studied Victor's face. Tanned skin showed little sign of aging even though Victor had recently turned fifty. Little lines were just beginning to form at the corners of his eyes. Shiny chestnut hair bore only a few white strands. Because of constant physical activities, he had gained very little weight over the years, and his body still retained its muscular physique. DiLeno sighed. If only those hazel eyes didn't reflect such sadness.

"And what are you thinking?" Victor asked, noticing DiLeno's appraising expression.

"Nothing, really. Just wondering if I'll live long enough to see my best friend happy again."

Victor's eyes darkened. "I've had more good, productive years than most people ever dream of. I have the satisfaction of having made more than a cursory contribution to healing and rebuilding this nation. I also have my faith. There's little more I could want."

"I wasn't intending to lecture. You know how much I value our friendship—cousin. I just wish you could have had someone to love and share in your accomplishments."

Victor straightened his legs and slid off the balustrade, standing up and turning to face distant mountains. "I have had someone to love. Alexa never stopped encouraging me and caring about every aspect of my life."

"Victor, don't be angry. With all the years that have passed, I can't help but wish things had been better for you. You don't deserve the loneliness you've suffered."

Victor breathed heavily in and out. His voice was subdued when he answered, "DiLeno, I gave my heart only once, and I gave it completely. When Alexa was alive, I could always go to her and talk about anything that weighed on my mind. We never lost that part of our connection despite how much she loved Gregor. Still, you're right. I have suffered all these years, especially knowing full well that I was the catalyst for what drove us apart. I also know that, in her own way, she never stopped loving me. All I have left is to thank Val that I have her children as my godchildren and that they give me so much happiness."

"You still deserve better," DiLeno said, approaching Victor and resting his hand on his shoulder. "You deserve more."

Victor dropped his face and shook his head. "Gregor made her happier than I ever could have, no matter how hard I might have tried. I accept that because she was so happy." He shook his head. "If only I could accept that she's gone."

DiLeno's eyes closed a moment, and he inhaled deeply. "Even I have difficulties believing we've lost her. I can't begin to imagine how you must feel."

Victor stood very still, imagining that the cooling autumn breeze bore whispers from the woman he would forever love. "If only we could have reached the bottom of that chasm to retrieve the rest of the dead. She sacrificed so much of herself for all of us, and we can't even give her a decent resting place. You don't know how that eats away at me."

"Victor, she was Valkana. No matter where she died, she was assured of holy rest with Val. How much more dare we ask?"

Victor turned around, a single tear sliding from the corner of his eye. His voice trembled. "I wish only a place to go where I can talk to her again. DiLeno, I still love her with all my heart."

DiLeno led his friend from the veranda and out of the castle compound. Fresh air and exercise would do more than any words to dull the sharpness of Victor's pain. That much he had learned quickly almost twenty years earlier.

That night, Victor made his rounds, tucking into bed his two nieces, his nephew, and four youngest godchildren, wishing goodnight last to DiMarco. At thirteen, DiMarco had entered an awkward stage where he was neither child nor man. Losing his mother had been a terrible blow. At times, he coped by withdrawing into himself. Victor had spent hours hiking through the woods with DiMarco during this visit. He had listened as the boy revealed his thoughts, insecurities, and his grief. Much like Nikolai and Anlía, DiMarco wanted to comfort his family. However, he was too absorbed in his own sorrow to know how. Victor had helped him work his way through those feelings. When DiMarco shyly hugged Victor that night, he had thanked his godfather. That expression of appreciation had provided unexpected balm to Victor's weary spirit.

Returning downstairs, Victor, Adrina, and DiLeno sat quietly for a while, relaxing before a fire. Beginning tomorrow, they would spend five days on the road. Each one knew the challenges of traveling with so many children at one time. DiLeno was the first to go upstairs, leaving Victor and Adrina alone.

"You look tired," Adrina observed.

"I'm really not."

"Victor, you know you did your best to find her. Will you never stop punishing yourself?"

Victor stared straight into the fire. "Whether you believe me or not, I'm not punishing myself."

"Then what are you doing?" Adrina asked gently.

Victor turned his head slightly and glanced quickly in her direction. "I don't know exactly. Remembering, I suppose. Trying to understand. Wondering about the strangeness I feel inside."

"What kind of strangeness?" his sister asked, puzzled by the look on his face.

"The first time I saw her, Adrina, she was only three months old. She was the most beautiful baby I had ever seen. That is quite a lot to say, considering I was almost eleven at the time. I still can't believe I'll never see her again."

Adrina rose from her chair and came to sit on the arm of the sofa by her brother's side. "We all miss her terribly. She was the best friend I ever had. When I think of her and realize she's gone, I find myself saying a prayer thanking Val for the years I did have to enjoy her. You should do the same."

Victor dropped his face into his hands. His eyes burned with tears that refused to fall. His voice was hushed. "I miss her, Adrina. I hurt knowing that I can never again see her smile or hear her laugh. Even when it hurt so abominably seeing her with Gregor, a part of me was satisfied just being close to her. Why? Why did someone so good have to die so young?"

Adrina swallowed against the lump in her throat. So many times had Alexa been hurt yet conquered her grief and pain. She had labored tirelessly in her role as Valkana, offering kindness, healing, and wisdom to those in need. She always carefully managed her time to fulfill her roles as devoted mother and loving wife. Neither had her friends ever lacked for her attention or her affection.

"Victor, we all relied on her strength. I don't have the answer to your questions, but surely she gave us enough of that strength to carry us through this."

When Victor raised his face and looked up into his sister's eyes, he saw that Adrina wept. Wrapping his arms around his sister, he finally surrendered to his grief.

↝

"Alexa! What in Val's name are you doing up there?" Victor demanded. Gregor entered just behind him and echoed the fearful exclamation.

Twenty feet above them, Alexa balanced on long, sturdy planks stretched across the foyer. As a precaution, sturdy ropes were looped around her waist and tied securely to each side of the balcony railings of the castle's upper floor. Two of her guards stood on either side, holding the ropes while letting them in or out as she directed. She looked down into two ghostly white faces and laughed. "Almost finished! I'm adding these garlands to the chandelier. You weren't here, and you know everyone else is afraid of heights. Besides, I like the way I hang the decorations. Men just don't have the right touch."

"Alexa, come down! Right now!" Gregor ordered, his hands visibly shaking.

Alexa laughed again. "Of course, my love. Whatever you say." She winked mischievously at the guards and signaled them to start releasing the ropes, lowering her rapidly to the ground floor.

As soon as she was low enough, Gregor reached up and grabbed her around the waist. She placed both hands on his shoulders as he pulled her safely down.

"Don't say anything. I hate climbing up and down ladders. Besides, the ropes keep me safe."

Victor stared into Gregor's blanched face and suddenly began laughing. "Get used to it. If you can. I've known her practically her entire life, but I never did."

Gregor glanced briefly at Victor before turning his full attention to his wife's flushed and grinning face. "If you don't want to become a very young widow, I suggest you never let me see you do something like that again," he scolded sternly. His heart still thudded heavily inside his chest, and his hands were clammy with fright.

Giggling, Alexa rose onto her toes and kissed him. "I'm Valkana. Remember? Being high in the air suits me very well."

The following morning dawned bright and sunny. Already summer, the temperature was comfortable and velvety warm but far different from the scorching heat of the previous year. Birds sang in the gardens around the castle walls. Lively conversation and enticingly rich aromas drifted from white-draped tables lining the castle's covered veranda. A small orchestra performed an array of traditional ballads and songs of love.

Gowned in ivory satin glistening with pastel silk embroidery, Adrina glowed. Stefan held her hand securely, keeping her close at his side now that she had become his bride. They had married in a courtyard outside Garogan City's chapel. Tirani had presided over the ceremony so Alexa could honor the promise made years earlier to be Adrina's matron of honor. The ceremony had been relatively simple, with minstrels providing sweet music on dulcimer-like instruments.

The King of Turand had read passages from the Great Book of Val before reciting a poem favored by his lifelong friend. Then, in the company of friends and family, Adrina and Stefan had exchanged wedding vows within sight of Garogan's own pyramid symbol of Val.

A lavish reception had been prepared at the castle, and everyone shared in the high spirits of the day. Even Victor showed exceptional enjoyment, sincerely delighted by the love shining on his sister's face. After everyone had partaken of the bountiful repast and enjoyed sparkling punches and fine wines, music grew louder and livelier.

Turandans typically loved dance, and the people of Garogan were no exception. Victor and Adrina started the first dance before Victor passed his sister's hand into Stefan's. The newly wedded couple glided across the floor to a romantic ballad composed more than a hundred years earlier.

Afterward, guests moved onto the floor, enjoying transitions from quick rhythms to slower pieces and then back again to the more energetic dances favored in Garogan Province. Before very long, many began clamoring for demonstrations of Garogan folk dances. In the past, on occasions when people had sought refuge in tradition, Victor and Alexa had often paired together. Caught up in the excitement of her own special day, Adrina begged Alexa to dance just once with Victor. The dance she wanted to see was one performed only at weddings, one she had never seen done better than when Victor and Alexa danced together.

Alexa resisted at first, but she finally relented with Gregor smiling and nodding approval. She joined Victor in the center of the floor while everyone else drew back to allow enough space for the vigorous dance ahead. Victor, eyes shining, knelt on one knee in the center of the floor. Standing six feet away, Alexa began the intricate steps that slowly carried her toward Victor and then in a circle around him. As the rhythm quickened, Victor took her hand and rose to his feet. The dance assumed a life and vitality of its own, demanding intricate footwork, vigorous shifts in rhythm, and nearly acrobatic movements as it depicted rituals of romance and courtship. The dance ended when Victor lowered back onto one knee while supporting Alexa as she gracefully arched backward over his thigh until his face came to rest against her neck.

Wedding guests erupted into thunderous applause and excited cheers as the two dancers, flushed and breathless, rose to their feet. Adrina ran and hugged them both. Alexa smiled brilliantly, expressing disbelief that she could still perform the exacting steps. She quickly hugged Victor and kissed his cheek before turning to look for Gregor. Standing beside Stefan, her husband smiled, his expression concealing possessive jealousy from everyone except his wife.

She hurried to his side, intent on reminding him through her presence that her love was his alone. Linking her arm with his, she laughingly led him to a buffet table to get a much-needed glass of punch. "Gregor," she whispered softly, "it was only a dance."

He gazed down into her rosy face, perturbed by her immediate assessment of his inner battle. He forced a smile. "That dance was perfectly executed, Alexa, as if you were meant to dance with him forever," he remarked, glad that no one had been close enough to hear his comment.

She smiled, her eyes alight with gentle admonition. "Let me drink this punch and catch my breath. Then I promise to show everyone, especially you, the man I am forever meant to dance with."

Minutes later, musicians initiated a slow, steady drumbeat as deft fingers coaxed intricate chords from stringed instruments. This time, Alexa led her husband to the center of the floor. Her body began to sway sensually as tantalizingly evocative music filled the air. Conversation ceased as everyone watched, their fascination swelling as their king and queen began moving together in unison to the sultry, heavily romantic music of an ancient, Toravalian love song.

As the beat gradually intensified, so did the requirement for Alexa to tap her heels against the floor, accenting the drum rhythms as she slipped teasingly close to her husband's body before gliding smoothly away. Following her, Gregor matched her steps and her graceful undulations. Their bodies moved together in synchronized perfection, almost as if they were connected as one being. The provocative sensuality of the dance grew passionately intense, requiring extreme concentration and coordination from each dancer.

The music gradually grew more impassioned, the intensifying, throbbing beat of the drums mimicking the quickening pounding of lovers' hearts. Onlookers found themselves involuntarily breathing faster and faster, drawn into fiery, erotic overtones as they watched Alexa's eyes respond to smoldering flames burning within the darkening depths of her husband's. Emerald sparks flared in her eyes as, nearing the dance's climax, Gregor snaked a long arm around her, his hand sliding sensually downward along the curve in her back until his long fingers flared just above the fullness of her hips. Slowly—provocatively, he pulled her tightly against him, their bodies never ceasing to sway with the music. Holding her firmly against his body, yet without losing the beat of the music, his free hand caught her wrist and glided up her arm until only his fingertips rested against her cheek. As the music softly receded, her head fell backward, and he leaned forward to press opened lips against the fullness of her mouth.

Abruptly, Victor sat up in solitary darkness. Instead of the familiar confines of his bedchamber, his eyes saw yet again the passion ablaze on Alexa's features as that single dance so clearly displayed the intensity of the unifying love she shared with her husband. Before or since, he had never seen that dance performed as beautifully or passionately as Gregor and Alexa had done on the day of Adrina's wedding. No room for doubt existed. Theirs was a unique love, rare and extraordinary.

Victor remembered that precise moment when Gregor's lips had claimed hers for all the world to see. He had felt searing pain rip through his soul before swiftly hiding his heartbreak behind a congenial smile. Sitting in the solitude of his room, he knew he would willingly relive that excruciating heartbreak a thousand times if only Alexa could be returned to the people who would forever love her.

Chapter 9

ollowing a long day of meticulously planned and flawlessly executed events, Gregor retired to welcome privacy in the palace library. He settled himself into the corner of a comfortable sofa where he frequently spent many sleepless nights. This night, however, was different: a time for reflection—a time for savoring the satisfaction of a uniquely special day that had begun early that morning.

"Prince Nikolai, you make your father proud beyond words." Gregor adjusted the sash that draped from his son's broad shoulder down to the hem of his long, formal, uniform tunic. The king's expressive black-brown eyes glistened. "Step back, my son."

Nikolai, holding himself tall and straight, did as his father requested. Today, on his eighteenth birthday, he would be officially proclaimed Crown Prince, heir to the throne of Turand. His excitement was intense, but it could not compare with the happiness he derived from his father's obvious pride and approval. He could think of nothing that could make this day better—nothing except his mother's presence. How he wished she were with them to share such a momentous day of ceremony and celebration.

Gregor gazed into the young face that was almost a mirror image of himself as a young man. Sharp eyes glimpsed the fleeting shadows in his son's eyes. He lifted his arms and rested them on his son's shoulders. "Remember, Nikolai. Always remember. Your mother's spirit will live forever within you and your brothers and sisters. Part of her is here with us—not only today but always."

Only the suggestion of a smile softened the line of Nikolai's mouth as he breathed out a sigh. "I know, Father. Still, it's just not the same."

Gregor turned away and crossed the sitting room that still bore traces of her very essence. No one could possibly feel the truth of Nikolai's heartfelt lament any more than the father. No one could possibly miss Alexa more than Gregor did.

Nikolai approached his father and placed a long hand against the back of Gregor's shoulder. "Forgive me, Father. My intention was not to upset you."

Gregor shook his head and turned back to his son. A single tear glistened on his cheek. His voice was thick with emotion when he spoke. "There's nothing to forgive. You can't know how much I want her back. I know she would be very proud of you."

The two men embraced with the intensity of shared joy tinged with sadness. Upon parting, father and son were distinctly aware of bonds far more vital than just blood unifying them. Their shared love was a permanent, ever-precious gift—Alexa's living legacy.

Later, on a morning that had dawned cold and bright, Gregor ceremoniously led his three sons and three daughters in a solemn procession to the Holy Temple of Val. People had traveled from all over Turand to participate in the celebration of Prince Nikolai's coming of age. Many had lined Toraval's central square before sunrise, hoping for a chance to see Turand's beloved royal family as they began their day in private worship.

Once inside the temple, Gregor and his children knelt for fully half an hour in earnest, meditative prayer. After all had centered, they arose and joined hands. The warm resonance of Gregor's voice carried words of his final prayer throughout the temple.

"All praises to you, our great and loving Val. We stand before you, united in our love as a family. We ask your blessings on each of us and, today especially, for our Nikolai. Today marks a milestone in his lifetime. Not only do we acknowledge his transition to manhood, we also acclaim his commitment to his destiny to one day become king. We pray for your blessings of patience, wisdom, and strength. Our prayers are that you will guide him through the years to come. Oh, Val, we ask you to help each of us give him the loving support that will enable him one day to lead your people and this nation."

Gregor paused, his voice catching. "Dearest Lord Val, we also pray, wherever you have taken Alexa, my beloved wife and mother of these precious children, that she rests peacefully. Her legacy to Turand's people, her children, and especially to me is one of love, faith, and constancy. We ask that you bless her with your most gentle love, just as we lovingly cherish her memory. Be with us, Lord Val, today and always."

Following the intimacy shared inside the temple, the royal family quickly became the focus of a full day of festivities. The first was a grand parade that began at the front steps of the Royal Palace, crossed the central square, and finally wound through the main streets of Toraval. Musicians in gray uniforms trimmed with bright purple stripes led the procession and trumpeted the king's approach.

Gregor and Nikolai rode side by side on matching white stallions. The image they presented was stately and dignified. Each wore tall, polished, black leather riding boots into which black, form-fitting leggings were tucked. They wore identical tunic jackets of gray and white tweed that buttoned across the right shoulder and down the front right side. Wide, black leather belts accentuated trim waistlines on both men. Over their right shoulders hung royal sashes that matched the fabric of the jackets. The hem of each sash was trimmed with a broad band of black silk adorned with five rows of silver studs and edged with fringe.

King Gregor wore the jeweled crown of Turand over hair enlivened with steaks of invading silver highlighting his ebony locks. Nikolai's hair was the same glossy black his father's had always been and flowed backward in shining waves. The most striking difference was that the prince was clean-shaven, while his father appeared more breathtakingly distinguished than ever in his full, immaculately trimmed beard.

Behind Gregor and Nikolai rode Anlía. Golden sunshine highlighted Anlía's delicately sculpted features that were the same exotic shade as her father's. Glancing backward, Gregor's heart skipped a beat upon seeing his daughter's beautiful face, especially her eyes that were wide and the same almond shape as her mother's. And, just like Alexa's, her eyes glittered with that distinct, glittering shade of emerald green.

White horses, stepping high and in unison behind Anlía's, bore the younger Princes DiMarco and Thikos. Between the two boys rode Marina and Karina, now seven and as full of life as all four of the other children combined. The children's faces were bright, intelligent, and thoroughly charming as they cast youthfully exuberant smiles at people lining the parade's route.

Other members of the king's court, including Stefan, Adrina, and Victor, rode on beautiful horses or in decorated coaches behind the princes and princesses. Leaders from all twenty of Turand's provinces followed. Brilliantly hued garments, fluttering flags, and waving banners splashed the streets with color. Majestically prancing horses tossed brushed manes and tails as if they believed they alone commanded the attention and admiration of parade onlookers. Toraval vibrated with the exciting display and pageantry. Turand's citizens were inspired to joyous cheers. "Long life to King Gregor! Long life to Prince Nikolai!"

Once the long parade wound back to the front of the palace, uniformed honor guards escorted the royal family to the top of the palace steps. Gregor faced the sea of humanity that swelled far past the edges of the central square. He patiently waited until jubilant cheers subsided.

His voice, as powerful as ever, projected far through crisp, clean air. "My dear people, I face you today with the pride of a father whose son has given him years of joy and more than a few intellectual and physical challenges. As we celebrate Nikolai's official entry to manhood, I cannot begin to describe the love and respect my son has earned. I will forever rest easily knowing that he possesses the strengths and capabilities to lead this nation in accordance with Val's will when Val chooses to complete my path in this world. I ask for your prayers for my son. I also ask that you join me in wishing a very happy birthday to our Prince Nikolai."

The crowd burst into a renewed frenzy of wild cheering and applause. The noise exploded into an almost deafening roar until Nikolai stepped forward. He paused long enough to embrace his father. The prince, who now stood slightly taller than his father, waved and smiled at the excited gathering.

Gregor changed positions on the sofa. A log had shifted in the fireplace, and a crackling shower of sparks bounced off the mesh screen. Lost in thought, Gregor reviewed all that had followed the exultant scene just outside the palace.

He smiled to himself, recalling formalities that followed in the vast hall that served as the assembly site for the throne of Turand. Lord Victor Garogan and Sir Stefan Sidano, Nikolai's godfathers, had presented the elegant prince to the king. Each godfather had stepped forth to name talents and virtues that would count Nikolai worthy of being declared Crown Prince of Turand. Each man had responded with a resounding *yes* when King Gregor had asked if they believed Nikolai should be confirmed as the next leader of the Royal House of Toscano and, thus, heir to Turand's throne.

Gregor had smiled and bowed to the godfathers before they took several steps backward, leaving Nikolai alone before the imposing figure of Turand's reigning king. Gregor addressed his son, administering the sacred oath that would bind his son's destiny to that of Turand. He then completed the ceremony by placing a gleaming crown of gold on his son's head.

Gregor had then raised proud eyes to those guests privileged enough to witness the historic event. "Ladies and gentlemen, in accordance with the treasured traditions of Turand, I present to you my beloved son, Crown Prince Nikolai. May Val bless his life with wisdom, good health, and longevity that he may serve Turand well in the years ahead."

Nikolai bowed before his father and then turned to face enthusiastically applauding celebrants. He lifted his arms in a gesture that requested silence. His voice carried throughout the hall when he spoke. "I cannot begin to express my confidence and delight in the presence of such warm acceptance. As you may know, the palace ballroom is festooned with more garlands, banners, and streamers than I have seen in my entire eighteen years combined. I believe the menu to be even more expansive. I am also quite certain all of you are as hungry as I. As such, my speech will be short."

His eyes sparkled at the spontaneous laughter and applause that erupted. When the crowd quieted, he continued, "My promises are made to serve the people of Turand and to do all I can to preserve our peaceful state. This is my future, which I accept wholeheartedly, although I expect many challenges will surely come. However, the commitments to which I pledged today are made with great confidence because of those who have provided me with a solid foundation. Even now, they continue to teach and guide me as they have since my childhood. Therefore, I wish to acknowledge them before we partake of the banquet awaiting us.

"First, I thank my godmother, Adrina Garogan Sidano. She has always been quick to disguise a delightful snack with lessons of profound wisdom. Her skills at soothing a child's anger and frustration have helped me grow into a better person." Nikolai executed an elegant bow toward his beaming godmother.

"Next, I honor Stefan Sidano. Papino Stefan has been an incredible teacher throughout the years. I can only hope that someday I will be as quick-witted and adept with words as he. I also hope to develop some of the masterful diplomatic prowess he demonstrates so well as my father's Chief Royal Adviser."

Nikolai stopped a moment, gazed at Stefan's smiling face, and bowed respectfully to his godfather. When he straightened, he turned slightly. His gaze met the proud hazel eyes of Lord Victor Garogan.

"To Papino Victor, I offer gratitude for all the sore, aching limbs, cuts, and bruises I suffered through the years as he taught me how to have fun and how to survive in the more rugged regions of Turand. He has shown me how to use my intellect as well as my body. With these long arms and legs of mine, I can assure you that his was no easy task." Again, laughter filled the hall as Nikolai saluted a grinning Victor with another smartly executed bow.

Nikolai walked to the right side of the throne, where his brothers and sisters stood in a straight line. He paused, smiled, and then embraced each one. "To my brothers and sisters, I'm thankful for the rivalries, games, and even the pranks that have kept me humble and grounded. Despite our occasional disagreements, I love each of you dearly."

Nikolai slowly returned to where his father stood beside the intricately carved throne that would one day be Nikolai's inheritance. He again addressed his guests. "Words escape me when I wish to thank my father. He has always provided inspiring examples of what a king should do and be. Beyond that, he has instilled a sense of responsibility, practicality, and determination. Father always demonstrated exceptional love, not only in matters of discipline but in a sense of fun and humor that many might not realize he possesses."

The prince turned to face Gregor. "Father, before Val and all assembled here, I want to tell you how much I love you and how much I respect you."

To renewed applause, Gregor stepped down and embraced his son. For Nikolai, his father's embrace offered security and confidence. To Gregor, his son's tribute deeply touched a soul that cherished the young man's life for not only all he was but as a living testament to a love Turand would never see again.

Nikolai smiled at his father before turning one last time to face his audience. The prince's face had grown wistfully reflective. Silence ensued as everyone awaited his final comments.

Nikolai swallowed against tightening in his throat before voicing his final thoughts. "This morning, while Father made a final inspection of my uniform, a thought crossed my mind as I considered the day's coming events. I thought that the only thing that could make this day better would be my mother's presence. These past months have been unspeakably difficult without her."

Nikolai faced his father once again. "Father, this morning, you said her spirit would always live within her children. I tell you now that my mother was so much a part of you that I am absolutely certain that she lives within you, too." Nikolai sucked in a deep, audible breath as he sought to sustain the flow of his thoughts.

Closing his eyes, he lifted his face upward. "Mother, though we never found you, I believe you're with us now—this very minute. We shall feast in celebration of my birthday. I just want you to know that, wherever Val has taken you, I celebrate this gift of life that you and Father gave me. And, Mother, wherever you are, I love you."

Nikolai's voice had cracked at the last. Within seconds, his father's arms wrapped around him, and the two were engulfed in a sea of tears and the embrace of family and friends.

"Father?" Anlía's voice startled Gregor from his profound state of reflection. When he turned to acknowledge her presence, silent tears soaked his face. He stretched out an arm and pulled his eldest daughter down onto his lap.

"Father, you need to get some sleep," she admonished, gently wiping away his tears with the cuffed edge of the sleeve on her robe.

He smiled into her tender features and those hauntingly beautiful eyes. "I know, my darling. I just wanted some time to myself."

Anlía settled more comfortably in his lap and rested the side of her face against his shoulder. "Everyone else has long been in bed and asleep. Even Nikolai. You should be, too."

"You sound more like your mother every day," he remarked, swallowing hard against invading sadness as he spoke of Alexa.

"Father, you know I love you, and I would never say anything to hurt you. Still, Mother would be very unhappy with you right now. You know she would insist that you go upstairs and get some rest."

"All right. All right. I surrender. If you go up to bed right now, I promise I'll do my best to get some sleep. Just let me stay here a little while longer. I need to calm myself after all the excitement today." He arched his dark eyebrows and grinned at his daughter.

She slid from his lap and stood up to stare down at him. Her stern expression evoked even more memories.

"Are you sure?" she demanded.

"Positive," he declared. "Now, kiss me goodnight and go back to bed."

Alone once again, Gregor stretched out his long limbs on the sofa. How many memories filled this room. Some were sad, tinged with shame and regret. Most were joyful, filled with love and laughter. Fatigue seeped through his muscles and into the very core of his bones. As weariness overtook him and he began to drift off, he imagined the sweetness of her voice calling his name.

Into the velvety dark invasion of sleep, he whispered. "I love you, Alexa. Forever and beyond."

Chapter 10

Less than a month after Nikolai's eighteenth birthday, Gregor turned over in the enormous bed he had once shared with Alexa. His soul still ached with loneliness. Swirling mists concealed faint images before his mind's eye, and faraway noises sounded painfully like her voice crying out his name. Feather soft and as brief as a sigh, the gentle stroke lifted his hair and ruffled through its layered mass.

Of its own volition, his hand reached out for the beloved source of that well-remembered caress. Abruptly, he bolted upright in bed. The dream was gone, leaving only emptiness in its wake. Yet—most assuredly—something real had awakened him. Of that, he was certain as he swiped a stray tear from his cheek.

Faint tapping crept into his consciousness, and he glanced toward the door. "Father? Father?"

Gregor swallowed against the swelling tightness in his throat. He had to force himself to climb out of bed to respond to the urgent beckoning in his daughter's voice. With a quiet click, he opened the door to his suite.

Surprise registered on his face the moment he glanced into Anlía's eyes. Especially beneath soft lights burning through the night in the palace corridors, she appeared more than ever like her mother. The tumbling mass of curls hugging her face and shoulders. Her high cheekbones and sensuously shaped lips. And, most of all, those heavily lashed emerald eyes that held tears tonight for the first time since Alexa's disappearance.

"Anlía? Darling, what's wrong?" he asked, enfolding her in a father's protective embrace. Her entire body shook in his arms as he turned and led her inside.

He sat on the edge of the settee in the sitting room, guiding her to his side. Instead, she pulled away, going to stand in the center of the room. He observed as, wordless, she turned from one side to the other, then in a full circle. A strange expression haunted her delicately defined features. She took several steps toward the bedchamber and stood motionless, eyes closed, slender arms outstretched. Following a prolonged silence, she turned back to him. Tears slid down her face. A wobbly smile touched her mouth.

"Anlía?"

"Father! It was no dream! She came here, too, didn't she?"

Gregor rose to his feet, only to be quickly captured within his daughter's embrace. "Anlía, what are you talking about?"

"Mother! She was here! Tonight! I felt her in my room. She spoke to me, Father! At first, I thought it was a dream. Now I know it was real!"

Gregor placed his hands on her shoulders in a solemn gesture and pushed her slightly away from him. Moonlight shone brightly through a window he could not remember opening. "Anlía, you must have been dreaming. Dear one, Mother has been gone almost a year now."

Anlía smiled confidently into her father's face. She thought briefly of the light that occasionally appeared in the center of her mother's pyramid pendant. A wistful expression crossed her face, only to be replaced by one of renewed assurance. "Father, can't you smell it?"

"Smell what?" he asked in surprise, automatically drawing in a deep breath. Instantly, his heart throbbed heavily within his chest. The fragrance was unmistakable as it floated around him. Still, he had resolved to accept his bitter loss. He refused to torture himself with any more fruitless hopes.

"Anlía, your mother and I shared this suite for many years. It should be no surprise that traces of lilac linger in the air."

"But, Father, this is fresh lilac. And the same lilac fragrance fills my room, too. Father, she was here!" Anlía insisted.

Gregor closed the window against invading cold air before sitting back down and pulling Anlía close beside him. Just as he found words he hoped would console her, another knock sounded at his door. "Yes?"

"Father? May we come in?" Before Gregor could respond, the door swung open, revealing DiMarco and Thikos. Both boys were wide-eyed and anxious.

"Is something wrong?" Gregor asked, stretching his arms out in invitation.

"Father!" Thikos, the more extroverted of the two boys, spoke first. "Mother came! She spoke to both of us. She told us that she loves us and misses us both! I think she even kissed me!"

Both boys then moved closer to their father, seeking reassurance in being near him.

"It seems you boys and your sister were all dreaming about Mother. I'm glad it was a happy dream."

DiMarco, usually quiet and reserved, shook his head. "Father, you don't understand. It was no dream. Dreams don't leave behind the scent of fresh lilacs."

"Lilacs? Again? Look, we all know how much Mother loved lilacs. So if you dreamed of her, it seems only natural that you would dream of how sweet she always sm…"

Before he could finish, two dark-haired beauties burst into the room in an exhilarated rush. They ran to their father, flinging their arms around him in unabashed excitement. "Father! Father!" they cried out in unison.

Gregor released a resigned laugh. "Don't tell me. Mother visited you, too?" His eyes shone with loving indulgence.

Both little girls rapidly nodded their heads up and down. "Oh, Father, she felt so beautiful! We told her we love her and that we pray for her every day!"

Gregor shook his head. He had always known Alexa's spirit to be incredibly strong. That she could touch her children all in one night should not surprise him. At the same time he wanted to share in their euphoria, he forced himself to retain self-control. He knew he would rise in the morning and, yet again, face life without Alexa.

"I have a suggestion," he finally managed, desperately needing to shift his children's attention in a different direction. "My bed is so big and so lonesome. Why don't we all go inside and try to get back to sleep?"

"Together? All of us—in your bed?" Karina's sweet voice echoed the excitement of her other siblings as the younger ones all scrambled up and raced to jump into their parents' bed.

Gregor chuckled to himself, unable to contain the briefest moment of levity as he watched Anlía put order into four wiggling bodies squirming around in competition for pillow space in the wide bed. He finally joined them and, as they quieted, luxuriated in the simple pleasure of listening to them breathe softly as they fell asleep. Beginning to relax, he could have sworn the scent of lilac wafted over him just before another knock sounded along with the opening of his door.

Gregor lifted his head slightly. He should have been surprised. "You, too?"

Nikolai came and sat on the edge of the bed by his father's side. "At first, I thought it was a dream. But, Father, she has been everywhere. I checked every room. Father, they all smell like lilac."

Gregor gazed thoughtfully at his oldest son's grave expression. Perplexed. Stunned. Skeptical. Hopeful. Looking at Nikolai's face illuminated only by the moonlight filtering through filmy curtains, Gregor could almost believe that she had come to them. He nodded slightly. "I believe there may be room for just one more."

Nikolai readily accepted his father's invitation and quickly settled his tall frame into the crowded bed.

Once again, Gregor began to drift off to sleep. For no more than a second, he could have sworn he felt a tender warmth brush against his mouth. His lips moved silently into the night as they had every night for many months. "I love you, Alexa."

⌇

Stefan leaned heavily back against the edge of his enormous desk. His head ached abominably, and his expression grew more frustrated by the complete impossibility of concentrating on the sheaf of documents in his hands. He glanced upward as Gregor entered the office from the corridor.

"Good morning," Stefan greeted, hoping he had succeeded in concealing his tension.

"I intended to wish you the same, but it seems I may already be too late." Noting unusual strain drawing Stefan's face, Gregor looked puzzled. "Are you all right this morning? You look uneasy." Sighing, he then settled himself into one of the comfortable side chairs in front of Stefan's desk. Gregor's expression was one of concern. Stefan rarely displayed such obvious distress.

Stefan set aside his stack of paperwork and straightened before moving forward to sit in the chair beside Gregor. He sighed heavily. "Tired, I suppose. I have a terrible headache. I was awake half the night."

Gregor's eyebrows quickly arched in question. "The children aren't ill, are they?"

Stefan shook his head. "No, they're all fine. I just couldn't sleep." Stefan carefully avoided sharing with Gregor the disturbing, sleepless night he and Adrina had spent with Victor.

Gregor read uncertainty in his friend's eyes and instantly struggled to subdue the gentle wave threatening to give rise to fresh and furtive hope. "I do hope you had no ghosts visiting during the night."

Involuntarily, Stefan's eyes widened as he studied Gregor's speculative expression. He breathed in deeply before trusting himself to speak. "Unless I'm sadly mistaken, it appears as though you may have spent a sleepless night."

Gregor shrugged broad shoulders. "I awoke this morning to Thikos' snoring, Karina's knees in my back, and DiMarco's legs pinning down my ankles. Marina's elbow was poking me in the side, and considering how much room Nikolai takes to spread out, I still haven't figured out where Anlía was beneath the mountain of Toscano children. Yet, despite all that, I actually managed to sleep a few hours."

Stefan chuckled aloud. "You and all six children in one bed? Why do I think the night in the palace might have been as eventful as the night we had at home?"

Gregor suddenly leaned forward, his expression intensifying as tension tautened every muscle. "Tell me, Stefan. What happened?"

Stefan sought elusive words. He resisted the very idea of causing Gregor any more grief than he had already suffered since Alexa's disappearance. How could he even begin to explain last night? Blue-gray eyes assessed the look on his friend's face. He breathed in again, trying to steady vibrating nerves. "Gregor, spring is months away, but we all awoke in the middle of the night to the fragrance of lilacs. I still find it difficult to believe. It was especially hard for Victor. We actually smelled the lilacs on his hands."

Gregor closed his eyes and sat without moving. "What else?" he asked reluctantly, still surprised that twenty years had not entirely erased his jealousy.

"I got up with Adrina while she tried everything she knew to calm Victor down. He was sobbing uncontrollably."

"Sobbing? Why?" Gregor sat stiffly straight. Sudden fear mingled with apprehension and creased his brow. Alexa had never ceased being able to communicate with Victor on a level of intimacy far beyond Gregor's comprehension. The very thought of Victor so overcome was one of frightening proportion.

"Gregor…" Stefan's voice grew quiet and more subdued as he attempted to withdraw from the question.

Gregor's long arm snaked out across the short distance between the chairs, and his hand tightly grasped Stefan's wrist. "You must tell me."

Stefan wanted to pull away but realized he was trapped. "Victor was inconsolable. When Adrina finally calmed him to the point we could understand him, he said that Alexa had come to him. He told us he felt nearly unbearable weakness and excruciating pain emanating from her. Victor was convinced she was in dire need of help, but he was lost to have any idea where she was or how to reach her. He was thoroughly distraught—nearly out of his mind. He seemed intent on tormenting himself, trying to understand what he called a most perplexing request she had made of him."

Stefan's eyes sparkled with teardrops that he refused to let fall. Better than anyone, he knew how much sorrow Gregor kept locked away, borne of sheer determination to ease his children's loss of their mother. Indeed, as king, he strived daily to alleviate the mourning all of Turand had endured since their beloved Valkana had disappeared. Stefan could not bear to add burden to that inner battle.

"Stefan?"

Stefan looked directly into Gregor's dark eyes that could be so expressive one moment and, the next, hide all the burning passions that were so significant to his character. "Victor said that Alexa's request was so simple yet so earnest. She asked him to listen to her children."

Gregor's head dropped, successfully hiding the expression of despair that ravaged his face. Still, Stefan had been as close as a brother for too many years not to be keenly aware of the grievous wound that had never begun to heal.

Stefan earnestly addressed his friend. "You know Alexa's gone. We must learn to accept that she will never return. I think these things happen because we all refuse to let go."

Gregor sat motionless, fingers still tightly gripping Stefan's wrist. When he finally spoke, his voice sounded far away. "DiMarco told me that ghosts don't leave lilac-scented trails. Could it be, Stefan? Is it possible she really was here in Toraval last night?"

Stefan breathed in a sustaining breath, saddened by fresh tears sliding down Gregor's now upraised face. Stefan bit at the inside of his cheek, his own loss of a dear friend obvious. Uncomfortable silence hovered between them as both continued to contemplate the truth of their reality without Alexa.

A knock interrupted the ponderous silence inside the office, and Stefan turned to face the door. It opened, gradually revealing Anlía, her face radiating fresh confidence. Even her eyes glowed brightly, though she carefully drew her features into a calm façade.

"Good morning, Papino. I was looking for Father." Gliding gracefully into the room, her every movement was reminiscent of Alexa. "I see he's here."

She quickly approached the chair where her father sat and rested her hands on his broad shoulders. Intuitively, she knew he was crying and preferred that she not see. Her grip tightened and relaxed as she lightly massaged his shoulders and neck.

"Father, the children have all eaten breakfast. We're all going for a walk in the woods with Papino Victor. I just wanted to let you know."

Gregor nodded, struggling to neither choke nor sob as he replied. "Be careful, Anlía, and watch the little ones."

She leaned forward and planted a kiss on the top of his head. "I will, Father. And, Father, please don't worry. Everything will be right again. I promise."

Gregor turned around just in time to catch a glimpse of her face as she left the office. "I often believe that child is a complete enigma."

The corner of Stefan's mouth lifted into a hesitant smile. "Victor always says she's undeniably her mother's daughter. She was always so close to Alexa, even though you're her absolute hero."

A wry smile touched Gregor's tear-stained face. "A role I guard jealously, even though I know that, sooner or later, some young man will come along to steal her away from me."

Stefan gladly picked up the diversion, guiding the subject away from Alexa in order to discuss strategies of how both men could keep their daughters safe from predatory suitors seeking beautiful brides.

⮑

Victor perched on a boulder that rested deep in the woods near the palace. He could not have known that once, many years earlier, Alexa had hidden behind that same rock while hoping to avoid Sifiq soldiers. Now surrounded by her children, he allowed himself the momentary fantasy of thinking of them as his own. Having stood as godfather to each of them, they had indeed become a part of his life. Victor had expended massive amounts of time and energy playing integral roles in their lives by lavishing them with affection and attention. Those children, in turn, had delivered meaning to his life.

As he gazed at their excited faces, Victor couldn't help but smile. No matter Alexa's fate, her immortality was virtually assured. Bundled up in warm coats and knitted hats against wintry cold, their cheeks were bright and rosy. Youthful energy kept them in motion. Enthusiasm made it nearly impossible for them to cease constant chatter. Both physically and spiritually, Alexa would continue to live through these children and the generations to follow.

Upon speaking to them, Victor's voice revealed none of the turbulent emotions that had overwhelmed him in the early morning hours. "So, we all agree. We must keep our secret from everyone, most especially your father. He has so many responsibilities, and we don't want to make him more worried or unhappy than he already is. Am I right?"

Four shining faces bobbed up and down. Anlía leaned back against Nikolai. Both nodded, signifying their alliance with the conspiracy. Unable to squelch the excited chatter about their mother's visit, Victor had sought direction for the children that should minimize risks for future disappointment. He had successfully convinced the younger children and, perhaps even Nikolai, that Alexa might come again for another midnight visit if they all prayed hard enough.

Expectations were bright. Victor also believed that Alexa would indeed return. What perplexed him most was the different light shining in Anlía's eyes, a light that he had first come to know very well many years earlier. That light gleamed almost identically to the one he had often observed in Alexa's eyes. Anlía had long been convinced that Alexa was not dead. As of yet, she had refused to confide in him why she felt so sure. He chose not to prod. When the time was right, she would share her reasons.

After the night before, he, too, was convinced. Victor was positive that Alexa's spirit had come to Toraval. Valiria, as a whole, and especially Valkana, possessed spiritual prowess far exceeding ordinary people's imaginations. Victor had known and loved Alexa too long and too well. Her presence the night before had been too powerful for a mere dream. She needed help. He had no doubt. Despite that knowledge, he also knew there was no choice but to remain patient—especially since he had to help the children cope with whatever time remained to wait. Deep inside, he was sure she would find her way home. For the first time since learning of her disappearance, Victor felt alive again.

Seated on top of cold, gray stone, Victor watched Nikolai and Anlía herd the younger children back to the palace for the day's classes. He ignored the rumbling in his stomach and the chill air stinging his cheeks. His thoughts turned exclusively to his cherished Alexa.

Years of watching her build a happy marriage with Gregor had never diminished his absolute adoration. Acknowledging his role in losing her, he contented himself with the loving friendship and indescribable bonds that allowed him to continue participating in her life. He had frequently voiced concerns regarding the undeniable difficulties Gregor wrestled with when faced with her unyielding position that Victor remain as part of her life and her children's lives. She had addressed Victor's concerns with her usual strong determination gentled by inherent empathy for the powerful emotions of both men. She declared that once she loved a person, she was incapable of turning her back on that person.

Never once had Victor considered marriage. To become involved with another woman would have been utterly unfair. He feared he could never avoid drawing unkind comparisons to Alexa. Instead, he allowed his days to become consumed with managing many ongoing projects vital to the rebuilding of Turand and establishing provisions for his nation's defense. Never again would outsiders be permitted to launch a full-scale invasion of Turand without staunch resistance.

Gregor's recognition of his exceptional organizational skills provided Victor far-reaching authority over public works and gave him reasons to spend weeks at a stretch in Toraval. Carefully utilizing that opportunity enabled Victor to dedicate ample time throughout the years to his nieces, his nephew, and Alexa's children in Turand's capital.

When summertime created greater demands for Victor at home in Garogan Province, Gregor and Alexa regularly entrusted their sons to his care. Alexa insisted that her children experience the robust outdoor life typically enjoyed by most Garogans. Whenever her duties as Valkana and queen permitted, she took her daughters to Garogan with Adrina, where they took adventurous camping excursions into some of the province's remote forest regions.

Victor's thoughts returned to the present. Smiling to himself, he touched precious memories and tucked them safely back into his heart. He must think. He must prepare his mind. Too clearly and without question, he believed Alexa was in terrible trouble. He must be ready, open to the sign she would surely send. Victor had heeded her trembling request to listen to her children, accepting reassurance that she would come again. Once she called out to him, he would go to her, even if it meant sacrificing his own life. Not even for a fraction of a second would he hesitate. There was no danger too great if only he could see her once more.

Two days later, Victor returned to Garogan. With a heavy heart, he hugged his sister and kissed his nieces and nephew goodbye. Earlier, he had said farewells to his godchildren. Responsibilities at Garogan Castle had arisen, demanding his attention. He also needed to fulfill a promise to meet DiLeno there to work on plans to expand facilities in Zinzan and prepare for the upcoming General Council of the Order of Val. He grappled with anxiety. If she called out to him, would he hear? If her children received her message, how would they communicate it to him? Still, he could not neglect other critical commitments. With a forced smile on his face and a prayer in his heart, he departed for home.

⤻

The winter in Toraval had been unusually mild. Whipping winds were infrequent. Temperatures were not nearly so cold. Occasionally, the ground sparkled as if covered by millions of tiny diamonds when a dusting of snow greeted early morning risers. Those glistening crystals disappeared quickly as morning sun coaxed temperatures above freezing. The heavens boasted brilliant, golden sunshine and cotton-puff clouds against azure heavens.

Gregor glanced out the door where DiMarco and Thikos awaited him. Tugging on lined leather gloves, he laughed as their voices called out challenges. Having promised the night before to play field ball with them, he headed down the front steps and jogged unhurriedly to where they awaited him. The three then strode off toward the open meadow covered with crunchy brown grass, where they would practice.

Between classes, Nikolai joined them for a while. Hearty laughter marked the rollicking good fun all four enjoyed as they practiced their skills chasing each other and stealing the ball away. Not one remained clean for long as headlong chases led to body-jarring slides across damp ground. They had not bothered dividing into teams. Individual competition was far more exciting until the younger boys launched a joint attack against their father.

Anlía had decided to take a long, leisurely walk outside and found herself drawn toward the sound of laughter. Arriving at the edge of the field, she delighted at the now rare sound of her father's laughter. One of the great treasures of her childhood was the sound of laughing inside the palace. Her parents always made a habit of playful teasing that sparked frequent gleeful outbursts that, for Anlía, sounded especially musical and lighthearted when coming from her father. Smiling at pleasant memories, she watched the spirited competition carrying her father and brothers from one end of the expansive field to the other.

Suddenly, against her chest, Anlía felt faint vibration. Removing a glove, she slipped her hand inside her heavy woolen cape and rested it atop the crystal pyramid she carried everywhere. Her eyelids dropped, and her expression grew solemn. Her head turned from side to side, almost as if in slow motion. She then lifted her face heavenward, allowing winter sunshine to bathe delicate features. A trace of a smile touched her mouth as her lips moved almost imperceptibly. "Mother?"

Gregor glanced up just as Anlía's head had tilted backward. More than ever, the very image of his eldest daughter evoked memories of Alexa. For several seconds, he suppressed a powerful urge to go to her, wondering what thought had so transformed her face. Although he quickly returned his full attention to his sons, he found it impossible to dismiss from his mind the unusual glow he had just observed on his daughter's face.

Early that evening, Gregor quietly entered the palace chapel where he had married Alexa. Only steps inside the doors, he stopped. In front, Anlía knelt, her youthfully slender figure radiating unusual solemnity combined with a sense of something else—something impossible to define.

Transfixed, he studied his daughter intently. Gregor watched as her head moved slightly but almost constantly as if she were talking with someone. Her hair cascaded down her back, flowing like gentle waves kissed by soft summer breezes. Observing her, he would have sworn she was immersed in conversation, except that he was the only other living soul inside the chapel. Gregor suddenly shivered, touched by a whispering presence that momentarily captured his breath.

Anlía slowly rose to her feet. Her face was serene. Although her eyes were cast in his direction, she seemed far removed from the room where they stood. "Father." Even her voice sounded especially reserved and distant.

"Anlía?"

Gracefully, she seemingly glided from the front of the chapel straight into his embrace. Her arms encircled his waist, and she rested her face against the firmness of his chest. Almost hesitantly, he wrapped his arms tightly around her, and they stood for long moments, sharing the unique bond between father and daughter. Anlía finally backed away from him. Emerald eyes glowed, reflecting from their depths unexpected joy. She raised her hand and placed her palm against her father's cheek. Full lips, tender yet promising future sensuality, gradually spread into a smile.

"Anlía, is everything all right?"

Her eyelids fluttered before her gaze steadied. Her head nodded slightly. "I feel tired, Father. If you don't mind, I'd like to go up to bed early."

"Anlía, tell me truthfully. Are you sure nothing is troubling you?"

She shook her head firmly and smiled again. "Honestly, Father, I'm fine. Good night."

Slowly, she moved past him, grazing his hand lightly with her fingertips. He stared after her as she walked through the corridor away from him. His sweet Anlía. She really was almost as much an enigma as her mother had been.

Two weeks later, Victor's firm stride carried him toward the library. He had listened intently as Gregor described concern for Anlía that had grown ever since that evening in the chapel. Although her outward presence was as serene as ever, Gregor was convinced that she had inexplicably withdrawn. Hesitating to press her, her father understood that she led her siblings in a conspiracy to protect his feelings. Victor, who had arrived unexpectedly, was most definitely a godsend since the children were usually so willing to confide in their godfather.

When Victor grasped polished brass handles and opened the library doors, Anlía's image stunned him. Except for her dark coloring, she could so easily have been mistaken for Alexa. The erect posture. The angle at which she held her head. The way she held the book in her hand. Sensing his presence, she lifted her face to him.

"Papino Victor? I've been waiting for you," she greeted, her voice unusually subdued. "How glad I am that you've finally come." Rising to her feet, she approached Victor and hugged him tightly. Then, grasping his hand, she led him across the room to the leather sofa where she had been sitting.

Victor should have been puzzled by her comment. Somehow, he wasn't. She demonstrated sensitivities so similar to Alexa's. He felt more anxious than curious to know why she had expected his arrival. In silence, he waited for her to speak.

Anlía shifted and leaned sideways, retrieving a book from the table beside the sofa. With the volume lying open on her lap, she leafed through the pages until she reached a section near the center. She pointed at a detailed drawing depicting a lighthouse standing sentinel above a rocky beach. When she spoke, her voice was steady yet very hushed. "I saw this lighthouse last night. In a dream. Today, I searched for a long time until I found it."

Victor leaned forward to examine the picture more closely. "Is that not the Timeri Lighthouse?"

Anlía nodded and, faintly smiling, traced the outline of the drawing with the tip of her index finger. "You will go, won't you?"

Victor turned on the sofa so he could better study his goddaughter's face. He was keenly aware of her anxiety. Still, even more evident was the excitement gleaming in her eyes. He chose a cautious approach. "Anlía, your father is terribly worried about you. He said you haven't slept well this past week and that you have been extremely tired. Tell me what's happening inside that lovely head of yours."

She continued staring at the picture, almost as if her heart and mind were worlds away from the palace library. "Papino Victor, I've done my best to help her. She's so weak and sick. We need your help. You once promised you'd never fail her. Please don't fail us now."

Victor blinked against a long ago, very private memory. Dismissing the dreamlike image from the past, he worriedly noted the peculiar switch in Anlía's speech from "I" to "us" and "we." Stretching out his hand and, with gentle fingertips, he turned her face toward his. "Tell me, Anlía. You must explain more specifically what you're talking about."

Her eyebrows knit together in surprised reaction, revealing that she had clearly expected him to already understand.

"Anlía?" he prompted again. Appraising the gravity of her expression, Victor felt a sudden hollowness in the pit of his stomach.

"You did promise her, didn't you? I thought you knew already. Isn't that why you came?"

Gazing into expressive green eyes, Victor finally began to comprehend the confusing dreams that had awakened him every night for the past two weeks. How right he had been to heed the feeling of urgency that had prompted him to leave Garogan for an unusual winter trip to Toraval.

She read dawning comprehension in his eyes and sighed her relief. "Then you'll go?"

"Anlía, why haven't you told your father about this?"

She shook her head emphatically. "Father already worries too much that I've been deceiving myself. Besides, maybe I am wrong. If that's true, it will be much easier to beg your forgiveness than for me to try to explain to him."

It was Victor's turn to shake his head. "I know you well, Anlía, and I trust in your good sense. Tell me what makes you so certain."

Anlía lifted her hand, sliding it inside her sweater. With respectful reverence, she revealed her mother's crystal pendant. "For a while, when I first started hearing Mother's voice, I thought Father might be right. I missed her so much. I thought—maybe I didn't want to believe she was gone. Then, when you brought this back, Father gave it to me to keep. When she faces her greatest trials, the pyramid vibrates. I feel it, and I go to the chapel or to the Temple of Val to meditate on it. Papino Victor, sometimes, it starts glowing. I know it's Mother because I see blue-white light, just like her aura."

Forcing himself to remain calm, Victor studied Anlía's face thoughtfully. "Are you absolutely sure?"

With the pendant resting on her open palm, she gazed into the gold sun set within the crystal's depths. She whispered in response. "See for yourself."

When Victor glanced down, his breath caught in his throat. For brief seconds, he glimpsed the misty glow he had first seen more than twenty-five years earlier. Without conscious thought, he extended the index finger of his left hand and just barely touched the crystal's smooth surface. Faint vibrations tickled the end of his sensitive fingertip. He lifted astonished hazel eyes to Anlía. The certainty he had felt earlier that winter returned. Part of him wanted to cry out for joy. Another part reeled in fear.

"She's coming home, Papino. I think soon."

"Where is she, Anlía?"

Anlía drew in a deep breath and stared into nothingness. Even her voice sounded hushed—distant. "I'm not really sure. Far away from Turand. That's all I know."

"And you believe we'll find her in Timerion Province?" Victor's voice remained firm, although his tone lowered.

She nodded slowly before responding in a near whisper, "I saw the Timeri Lighthouse last night. Somewhere nearby, I saw an old cabin and a triangular formation of rocks. She needs us there. Father would never let me go. Besides, I cannot shake the feeling that you must be the one to go. It makes no sense at all."

When she looked up at him again, Victor felt momentarily awe-struck. For a brief moment—so brief that he almost questioned the reality—Victor saw Anlía's face obscured by eerie, swimming light that fleetingly settled into Alexa's image. The vision vanished as quickly as it had appeared, leaving his heartbeat rapid, his breathing ragged. His soul lurched in response to the desolation he had seen on her face.

Swallowing against choking thickness in his throat, Victor drew his goddaughter into his arms. There, for the first time since Alexa's disappearance, he saw Anlía weep. Holding her for a long time, Victor was unaware that, observing in silent anguish from just beyond the library doors, Gregor stood watching.

⮌

"I find it hard to believe you actually have business in Timeri." Stefan crossed the spacious sitting room of his house and handed Victor a snifter of golden brandy.

Victor inhaled the rich aroma of fine liquor before indulging in its fiery warmth. "You should know me by now, Stefan. I can still produce a surprise or two." He forced himself to smile, knowing that Stefan's astute eyes might easily see things best hidden for the time being.

"Well, I'm glad you plan to see Lord and Lady Karanan. Gregor frets enough about them as it is but most especially when they winter at Timeri. Winter weather there can be so harsh and blustery. At their ages…"

"I'll remind you of this conversation when you approach your eighties." Victor's retort was a humorous jab at his brother-in-law.

Having said goodnight to her three children, Adrina joined the two men in the sitting room and immediately went to sit beside her brother. Smiling affectionately at her, he was struck anew by how lovely she had grown through the years. Life in Turand's capital had been good to her, especially considering the loving marriage she shared with Stefan.

"Is it my turn?" Stefan inquired of his wife, fondly gazing into her light brown eyes. When she nodded, he excused himself to go upstairs for his own nightly ritual.

Once Stefan left the room, Adrina turned her attention to her brother. Her voice sounded skeptical. "Timeri? Business?"

Victor avoided her eyes and tipped the snifter once again to his lips. He allowed the liquid to roll smoothly over his tongue before swallowing. Then, leaning forward, he set the glass on the table in front of the sofa. "And what is so strange about that?"

Adrina glanced at the set of his jaw. "Nothing, I suppose—except you're my brother, and I learned a long time ago to recognize when you were holding back from me."

"Sister," he said, almost too firmly, "do you never trust me?"

She grinned at him. "Always, but saying that, I also know that business isn't your real reason for going to Timeri in the middle of winter."

He stared at her, barely able to hide his amusement. "What makes you think that?"

"Victor," she responded solemnly, "I see it in your eyes. I won't pry, but whatever you have in mind, I want you to be careful."

Victor smiled, somewhat sheepishly, at her perception of hidden motives. Then, suddenly, his smile faded. "Sister, just pray. Pray like you've never prayed before."

"Pray? Whatever for?" she asked, perplexed by the desperate light that flashed into her brother's eyes.

He took her hand, held it tightly, and gazed intensely into her face. "Pray, Adrina, that all will again be right in Turand." He then kissed his sister's cheek. Saying goodnight, he left her to gaze questioningly at his retreating figure.

Part 2

Unto my maker my soul I direct.
Into His care, my woes I dispatch.
Unto his heart, my faith I deliver.
Into his hands, my life I return.
No more blessings for me to expect,
In loneliness traveling my forlorn path,
Lamenting memories, my lips do quiver
Within my heart, love continues to burn.

To this place, my Lord, my self You sent.
All that I am, you have set to task.
In this place, my Lord, their pain to see,
My faith, my heart, my soul, you ask,
You wished of me, their guide to be,
With all I am, their hopes to waken.

Behind me, Oh! Sings the sweet past.
His loving heart, mine does call.
Fingers so strong desire to caress.
Voice so rich beckons me home.

Memories again, Oh! My grief so vast.
To unyielding ground, tired, I fall,
Unheard, unnoticed, my utter distress,
Without him, fearing darkness to come.

Morning sun, no warmth does it bring,
Yet its blinding light my skin does sear.
My ears their cries cannot ignore
My toil, my blood, for them I give
Silver stars to night skies cling,
My faith a refuge to harbor their fear,
Giving to them 'til I have no more,
For strangers, how long must I live?

But, to this place, my Lord my self did send.
All that I was, he set to noble strife,
In this place, he said, their hope to restore,
With my faith, my heart, and even my life.
With all that I am, his will do I honor,
Praying my Lord this sorrow will end.

Alexa's Lament

Chapter 11

A lexa lay sprawled on the stone floor where she fell. Quickly, she gulped in several breaths of air as she forced herself to ignore the pain from the blow struck across her shoulders. Valiantly, she fought rising anger in the knowledge that, next to God, self-control would be her strongest ally.

On unsteady legs, she managed to stand. Emerald eyes momentarily flashed fury before taking on a cool, shuttered appearance. The face she finally presented to King Bin-Lot was a portrait of tranquility. Straightening, she refused to reveal any discomfort to this newest Sifiq tormentor.

"So unusual for a mere woman," Bin-Lot drawled in an acid voice. "Still, you must learn your place among men."

Alexa remained silent, offering no comment. She had spent the past half hour being subjected to a stream of ugly, deprecating remarks regarding the essential uselessness of females. The king obviously harbored intense contempt for women. He had baited her incessantly until a sharp retort had sprung forth. She would not weaken again before his tactics.

He studied her with immense curiosity as he mentally clicked off a note to reward the naval commander who had been foresighted enough to bring him this woman and her four companions. Blue eyes glittered with anticipation as thin lips spread into a cynical smile. This woman was proud to the point of arrogance, and her self-confidence fascinated him. He saw tantalizing promise for great entertainment at her expense.

Breathing out a heavy sigh, his paunchy middle rose and fell. He took several steps toward Alexa and then reached out, taking a thick strand of her hair into his hand. When she not so much as glanced at him, he jerked hard on the thick tress, forcing her to look into his face. "Remember the most important rule of all, woman. Never! Never ignore my presence."

"To ignore you, sir, is impossible," Alexa replied calmly, having directed her thoughts to Val, receiving in return his reassurances.

Releasing her, he paced a deliberately slow circle around the other four Valiria and then once again around Alexa. As he leered at them, Alexa sensed disgustingly lewd thoughts running through his mind. With her own mind, she reached out to her sister priestesses. "Sisters, gather your faith as a cloak around you. Val certainly will protect and preserve our virtue."

Bin-Lot emitted a crude laugh when he finally stopped and faced Alexa once more. "I believe you women will serve quite well once you are tamed."

Alexa's eyebrows lifted; however, she said nothing.

"You. Again. What name do you have?"

Alexa felt her Valiria sisters issue united advice. They must conceal her identity as Queen of Turand. "I am Alexa Maraná."

"Alexa Maraná," he repeated, twitching his lips from side to side in a vulgar expression. "What is your purpose in Turand?"

"My purpose?" she asked, unsure what he really meant.

"Yes, your purpose. What use do you serve?"

Alexa maintained tight control over her expression. "I serve many roles. I am a teacher and guide to my people. I am wife to my husband and mother to our children."

Bin-Lot's face transformed a moment, and Alexa felt sickened by the lascivious nature she read in his life force.

"You say you have a husband?" he demanded.

"I do."

"What work does this husband perform? And how is it that he allows you to roam the countryside with a band of soldiers?"

Alexa breathed in deeply to steady herself. "My husband administers affairs within our government. We were captured while on a mission to help victims of a massive ground-quake and subsequent flood."

"Hmmm. Yes. I do recall my father saying that Turandans are a weak-hearted lot. You would send aid instead of allowing survivors to develop character by facing and resolving their own troubles."

When Alexa offered no comment, he continued, "You are stubborn and argumentative. I assume your husband must be a very weak-natured man."

Despite rising danger, a part of her almost laughed. "Sir, you assume incorrectly. My husband is a very strong man, both physically and in character."

"Obviously not strong enough to tame you into submission."

"Sir, that is not our way in Turand. My husband and I combine efforts based on our unique capabilities. I offer him support, love, and respect. He does the same for me."

"Nonsense!" Bin-Lot's florid features grew more vividly red. "The only respect a woman understands is force! By nature, you are contemptuous creatures, incapable of more than deceit and treachery!"

She waited quietly as he paced rapidly back and forth in front of her. His outburst had been brief and venomous. His life force revealed that his comments were not the result of personal experience. Instead, his ideas resulted from a deeply engrained cultural philosophy.

Suddenly, he seemed to calm. "You say you have children. I presume all to be useless females. How many?"

"Sir, again, you presume incorrectly. My firstborn is a son, as are my third and fourth children."

"You have four children?"

"No. I have six, three sons and three daughters."

"Three daughters! And your husband allows all to live?"

For a fleeting moment, Alexa's face registered uncomfortable questions. Quickly, she recovered her calm façade. "He does. My husband cherishes his daughters and his sons alike."

The king snorted his contempt. "Incredible that you consider such a man to be strong. And what about these women with you?" He turned his attention to the four priestesses who had formed a straight line just behind Alexa. "What are your names?"

"I am Lisana Faradón," responded the Valiria furthest to his left.

"Step forward," Bin-Lot commanded, appraising her blonde features and finding them pleasing. Then, once she moved forward, he spoke directly to her. "Are you, too, married?"

"I am, sir, for five years."

"Have you any children?"

"Not yet. My husband and I planned to begin our family after my return from our mission to Tolura."

Rudely dismissing her, he turned his attention to the next. "You?"

Gracefully, despite her fear, the next priestess stepped forward. "I am Marlí Gotrano. I am married now for only a year."

Bin-Lot studied her from head to toe, so far finding himself impressed with the physical attractiveness of these Turandan bitches. "Next?"

The next Valiria to step forth showed no more weakness than the others. "My name is Kiralí Seraná. I am not yet wed, although I am betrothed."

"Betrothed? What is this?"

She responded smoothly, "I have promised myself in marriage to the man I love."

"Love!" Bin-Lot rolled his eyes in disgust. "Love is nothing but a meaningless, poisonous deception plotted by the minds of women. Now. You." He quickly turned his attention to the final member of Alexa's group.

"I am Sulía Kohira. I am neither wed nor betrothed." Dark brown eyes held steady, as did smooth, cinnamon-colored features.

"So, we have quite an interesting collection of Turand's females. You, Sulía whatever. Why does this one, Alexa, take the lead? Why do you all appear subservient to her?"

Sulía, lifting sparkling eyes to Bin-Lot, presented a commanding image inherited from her father, who served as Gregor's most trusted general. "We are not subservient to our sister. We merely show respect for her experience and wisdom, which far exceed our own."

"Then she is your leader?" Bin-Lot directed his question to Marlí, carefully observing individual reactions while seeking a weak link.

Marlí's voice was as firm and confident as Sulía's had been. "If you wish to see it that way, sir. We always listen to her, just as she listens to us. Through discussion, we reach consensus. If uncertainty prevails, we defer to her judgment based on her knowledge and longer years of service."

"Service. I keep hearing this word. Service. Serve your people. What do you mean by this?"

Lisana answered. "We are teachers and healers for our people. We serve our people in this way so we may please our Lord Val."

"Val? He is your king?"

Kiralí answered. "Our king is Gregor. Val is our God."

"God? Ah, yes. I remember. You Turandans foolishly believe in some invisible spirit who supposedly created this world and all that is in it. Idiots." He shook his shaved head condescendingly.

None of the priestesses moved, maintaining their unity in an unbreakable bond. When he saw no reaction, he swept his eyes around his court. High-ranking officers lounged negligently in padded chaises or on chairs as they observed their king in amusement. Few Sifiq women were present, and those who were moved silently, serving the men from trays heavily laden with food and drink.

"My subjects, these women actually believe in some invisible god!" He basked in the raucous laughter he received in response. "What say you to such nonsense?" Hisses and all sorts of disgusting sounds spewed forth, satisfying their king very well.

He returned his attention to the Turandan prisoners. "Let's forget about this ridiculous god of yours. I now recall hearing years ago about this Gregor. If memory serves me well, he was a greedy, selfish traitor who was all too happy to work with our army. How is it you speak of him with respect when he willingly supported us for his own good?"

Alexa drew from the calm she felt in her Valiria sisters. "King Gregor was not what he appeared to be. It was he who built the secret army that defeated your occupation force."

Bin-Lot sneered at her. "Defeated them? Turandans actually bore arms against the Sifiq army? I find that highly unlikely. I have little doubt another reason exists for their failure to return home."

"This is our history. Our people grew tired of being prisoners in their own land. While we much preferred peace, our people were determined to end the death and destruction inflicted by your army. Our king lured your military leadership into unsuspecting complacency. He then led us to victory."

"You speak proudly, woman. Too proudly. Why?"

Alexa chose her words carefully, realizing she had come perilously close to revealing herself. "We are all proud of our people's efforts to restore our nation's freedom."

Bin-Lot emitted a detestable grunt. "I tire of this. You will be taken away while I decide what to do with you."

Days later, the iron door to their small cell opened. Three Sifiq women entered, and the door clanked shut with a loud, echoing bang. The Turandan prisoners, who were sitting together in a semi-circle, glanced upward. Alexa was first to stand. Her expression revealed no emotion; her eyes questioned the women's presence.

One of the women, blonde and slender, stepped forward. Her features were lovely, accented by azure eyes beneath widely curving brows. Her lips were generously full, and her oval face appeared sculpted from fine alabaster. When she lifted her gaze to meet Alexa's, multiple sensations flooded the high priestess. She felt smoldering fires within this woman's soul, partially born of anger grown out of grief. Over and above the sense of sorrow existed what Alexa could only identify as resistance. To what or to whom, Alexa could not discern. Her own initial reaction was one of wary precognition. Surging certainty filled Alexa that this Sifiq woman would play an essential role in whatever destiny awaited them in the Sifiq Kingdom.

Following several moments of quiet assessment, the young woman addressed the Turandans in a voice that was clear and emotionless. "I am Oui-lest Var."

Without a word, Alexa bade her priestesses rise. "I am Alexa Maraná," she replied. "These are my sisters, Kiralí, Marlí, Lisana, and Sulía."

Oui-lest lifted her eyes in surprise. "You have four living sisters?"

Again, Alexa felt that disconcerting perception of something terrible in the unspoken portion of Oui-lest's inquiry. "We are spiritual sisters. That does not mean we share parents."

Oui-lest shook her head once, unsure of the explanation yet unprepared to discuss the matter further. "We come to escort you for preparations before you are again presented to our king."

"Preparations?" Alexa asked, uncomfortable with her perception of the word's implications.

"Yes. Guards will escort us to the women's quarters. There, you will prepare to return to the palace."

Alexa exchanged looks with her companions and then drew in a deep breath. "You will explain as we go?"

Oui-lest's head drew back in surprise. "Oh, no! We must not speak in the presence of the guards. It is not permitted. To do so invites punishment. Once we arrive at our quarters and the men leave, I shall explain all." She studied Alexa's direct countenance momentarily. "Please, I ask of you. Do not look at the guards as you look at me. Such boldness is not permissible."

"Then where are we to look?" Alexa asked curiously.

"Down, of course. Come now. Quietly, please."

Kiralí and Lisana assumed places behind Oui-lest. Alexa followed. Marlí, Sulía, and the remaining Sifiq women walked behind her. After a fifteen-minute walk in silence, the men waited until the females entered the brownstone building that served as housing for those assigned duties within the palace. The Turandan women had quietly relished being outside, which had provided them sustaining relief beneath open skies and golden sunshine.

Upon entering the building, they were more grateful than ever for the brief exposure outdoors. The interior of the women's quarters was bright and scrupulously clean. However, no trace existed of the kind of inviting style in which Turandans preferred to surround themselves. The rooms they passed through were austere. Furnishings were sparse, utilized solely for function, not comfort. Those women not on duty at the palace moved quietly through the rooms and corridors. The atmosphere struck the priestesses as one of hopelessness and somber dejection.

Alexa remained silent, observing the foreign environment and opening herself to the subdued emotional nuances filling the rooms. Sadness was pervasive, pride nearly non-existent. Voices cried out, yet not a single person spoke. These women existed to serve—their sole purpose was to provide comfort and amusement to Sifiq men assigned to the palace.

Oui-lest led the women, single file, through a narrow hallway and proceeded to what appeared to be a communal bath. On long, rectangular tables lay clean clothing. Alexa immediately noticed that some of the clothes had been cut and refashioned from the few things they had carried with them.

Oui-lest closed the door firmly before she finally spoke again. "King Bin-Lot has ordered you to return before him at court in three weeks. First, you must be made presentable and instructed in proper behavior."

Sulía, the most outspoken Valiria, immediately responded. "What was not presentable the last time we were dragged before your king?"

The two women accompanying Oui-lest looked at each other in nervous apprehension. Oui-lest, however, maintained her composure. "First, you must remove your garments. They are considered too extravagant for women. You will be provided clothing more appropriate for women assigned to palace service."

Alexa closely observed the three Sifiq women and realized that each one she had seen since her arrival used the same basic attire. All wore straight sheaths with long sleeves and rounded necklines. Slits at the ankles were only high enough to allow sufficient freedom to walk. None wore belts or any other kind of adornment.

"Then we are to dress as Sifiq women?" Sulía asked, unimpressed with the stark, uniform appearance of the clothing.

"Yes," Oui-lest answered. "First, you must attend to matters of personal hygiene. Who will go first?"

Alexa stepped forward, although somewhat anxiously. "I will."

Oui-lest guided her to a chair. "You may discard your clothing, except for your undergarments, of course. We will cut your hair before you are permitted to bathe."

Alexa jerked her head backward. "Cut my hair? I do not wish to have my hair cut."

Oui-lest showed no sign of impatience other than a sigh. "It seems long hair is a luxury permitted in Turand. Here, it is considered a nuisance. It requires too much time to wash and dry. Besides, most Sifiq men consider long hair a sign of vain pride to which women have no right."

Alexa's eyes grew distant as she reached up, resolutely beginning to undo thick braids that had kept her long hair relatively tidy these past weeks. As her fingers slipped through the wavy mass, she thought only of Gregor. How he had always loved to comb his fingers through the length of her hair. How often had she closed her eyes and luxuriated in the delightful sensations of him brushing her hair in an intimate display of affection? She had always relished the tingling tremors that danced along her spine when his hands brushed against her neck as his long fingers stroked through flowing tresses.

Finally returning from retreat into cherished memories, she reached around to her side and undid the buttons of her split skirt. After stepping out of it, she stripped away her sweater and blouse, glad to discard garments she had worn now for far too long. She then glanced at the unpadded chair, breathed in slowly, and sat down.

Closing her eyes, she tried not to cringe as she felt one of the women lift her hair to cut away its length. She felt her face involuntarily draw into grimaces with each snip of the sharp scissors. Feeling almost lightheaded, Alexa cringed when the Sifiq woman's fingers combed through the very short locks that remained, ensuring an even length overall.

At last, the deed completed, Alexa opened her eyes and looked at the swirling lengths of golden brown hair heaped high on the floor. Immediately, she suppressed a jab of anger rising from the feeling of personal violation. Instinct made her well aware that this was most likely only a portent of worse yet to come.

Each Valiria was subjected to the same treatment until all were shorn of the long tresses scorned by Sifiq men. All then finished undressing and took whatever comfort they could from a warm bath and being allowed to dress in clean clothing. They were then led to a large kitchen, deserted for the moment, where resident women dined at plank tables while sitting on backless benches.

Oui-lest invited them to sit at one of the tables. She then called for bowls of hearty soup accompanied by baskets of crusty rolls and earthenware mugs filled with fresh water to be set before them. Grateful for their most generous meal since arriving in the Sifiq Kingdom, the priestesses joined hands and prayed together before sitting down to eat.

Oui-lest Var curiously studied her charges. She had never seen anything like the ritual these foreign women had performed before partaking of their meal. Watching them eat, she recognized the deeply ingrained interpersonal commitment that existed among them. They obviously cared about each other, and although they did not speak, she was convinced they managed to communicate among themselves.

Once the meal was finished and the table cleared, Alexa faced Oui-lest. "We appreciate the kindness of this meal. May we now ask what comes next?"

The Sifiq woman controlled her surprise. A Sifiq woman would have waited in silence until told what to do. However, the continuing direct questions from her charges prompted immediate realization that she might not be equal to her designated task. She shuddered at the thought of what might happen should she fail in her assignment.

Her tremors did not go unnoticed by the Turandans. Instead of questioning her further, they waited for Oui-lest to speak.

Oui-lest Var addressed the foreigners in a voice far more confident than she felt. "I am to teach you behavior that is acceptable when in the presence of Sifiq men. If you misbehave, you will be punished. Our men tolerate no insolence from females. We are inferior and must show respect to our superiors."

Alexa's eyebrows shot up, clearly reflecting her dismay. "Do you honestly believe what you just said?"

Oui-lest's blue eyes clouded, and she ignored the question. "You must understand. You are never to look directly into a man's face unless he instructs you to do so. You must always request permission to speak unless asked a direct question. Remember that…"

Alexa threw her hands up into the air. "Stop! Please!"

Oui-lest's eyes widened, the interruption unexpected and beginning to test her nerves. "Please…"

Alexa rose from the table and approached the Sifiq woman. Without conscious thought, she reached out and grasped hands that were cool and trembling. Alexa closed her eyes in order to touch the young woman's life force. What she perceived spawned a torrent of dread. When her eyelids slowly lifted, Alexa smiled reassuringly and led Oui-lest to the table. When both were seated, Alexa assumed leadership of the group.

"Oui-lest Var," she began in a soothing tone, "our wish is not to cause you discomfort or difficulties with your men. Please explain to us how we are to proceed."

Over the course of the next week, the priestesses of Val learned much about the hardships and heartbreaks of a woman's life in the Sifiq Kingdom. Oui-lest Var found herself irresistibly drawn to the foreign women and, when alone in the priestesses' presence, began opening her very soul. Not only did she do her best to teach them the very real restrictions on the behavior of Sifiq women, she also began to reveal much more than the rigid standard of conduct imposed by Sifiq men.

Nearly two hundred years earlier, a Sifiq king had decreed all women be relegated to a state of subservience. Their designation as inferiors was instated by a man sworn to vengeance for the humiliation he experienced at the hands of an unfaithful wife. With pride wounded and ego suffering, he declared all women to be contemptible creatures. He pushed Sifiq society into an era of change, and women became little more than objects of convenience.

Strict rules developed into harsh standards. Women were required to keep their hair cut short to discourage vanity. Unless given permission to speak, they were required to remain silent in the presence of men. Feminine clothing styles became stark and plain to emphasize their undesirable station in life. Meanwhile, their men wore elaborate frock coats, flowing trousers, and jewel-adorned turban headpieces.

As Sifiq societal attitudes shifted, so did the severity of women's treatment at the hands of men already renowned for ferocious natures. Women could be selected as mates to fulfill rigid, well-defined roles in the management of households according to their husband's desires, to satisfy their husband's sexual appetites, and to bear and rear children.

Alexa and her priestesses were horrified to learn how extreme Sifiq men had become in their domination. Women were expected to produce sons. A woman who produced sons earned some assurance of a more comfortable existence. The birth of a daughter could be tolerated; one daughter promised working hands and potential bargaining value in securing advantageous alliances. A woman who produced a second daughter risked alienation and banishment from her mate's household. The shame she bore could not begin to compare with the heartbreak she would undoubtedly face as Sifiq men practiced their most terrible punishment—the slaughter of undesirable, newborn, female infants.

Oui-lest had personally suffered such tragedy. At an early age, she had been mated to a highly egotistical officer in the king's army. Her first-born child, a daughter, had infuriated a man who considered the baby an intentional insult. Refusing to accept the infant, he killed her immediately. Afterward, Oui-lest had been promptly divorced.

Unlike many such women in her circumstances, Oui-lest escaped exile to slave away as a field laborer. Talented as a seamstress and clothing designer, she was summoned to direct the staff responsible for the king's wardrobe. As her organizational talents surfaced, she was assigned additional responsibilities until she assumed full supervision of the women assigned to palace service. There, she did her best to ensure that those under her met all their duties to the satisfaction of the men they served. In doing so, she found solace in helping them avoid cruel punishment while immersing herself in constant work to ease the grief carried in her heart.

Before the Turandan women's second presentation at the palace, Alexa lay awake long into the night. She had meditated and prayed, knowing the next day would likely bring challenges that would test her mettle. In quiet darkness, her thoughts drifted home. Even though he was half a world away, she could feel the ache within her husband's heart. Her memories were vivid, and she smiled, recalling the way his eyes sparkled whenever he looked at her. Closing her eyes, she could almost imagine the tantalizing warmth of his fingers stroking across her bare skin. She swallowed hard, fearful that she would never again know the sheer joy of his arms wrapped tightly around her as his body pressed firmly against hers.

Nearly asleep, she heard a shuffling sound in the corridor beyond the room she shared with her sister priestesses. Sensing Oui-lest's presence, she decided to rise. Leaving the bedchamber, she saw the younger woman standing in front of a window at the end of the hallway, gazing out into the star-studded sky. Silently, Alexa approached Oui-lest and rested her hands on the other woman's shoulders.

"Your thoughts are so sorrowful, Oui-lest Var."

The younger woman turned around. The light of the moon caused streams of tears to shine silver. "I will always wonder what it would have been like to hold my daughter to my breast. I never even had the chance to hold her in my arms." She then found herself leaning her face against the shoulder of the prisoner, seeking comfort from a stranger considered enemy to the Sifiq.

Alexa held her, allowing her time to weep. She then led her downstairs to the deserted kitchen, where they both took cups of water and sipped quietly.

"I have no doubt your daughter's soul would have been as lovely as her mother's."

Oui-lest gazed at the serene countenance of her charge. "Is it really so different in your country? Do men really cherish their daughters?"

Alexa smiled, tears welling in her eyes. "I have three beautiful daughters. Their father loves them dearly. In fact, he was very excited when I became pregnant the second time because he hoped we might have a little girl."

Oui-lest dropped her face and shook her head. "It is impossible for me to comprehend such a notion. Still, every time you speak of your husband, I hear something in your voice I have never heard before. And your eyes—they drift far away and actually seem to glow. What is he like?"

Alexa closed her eyes and breathed in softly. "He is a very tall man, more than two heads higher than I. His eyes are so dark brown they often look almost black. He has very dark hair and a beard."

"Beard? You mean hair on his face?"

Alexa laughed quietly. "Yes, hair on his face. Beyond the fact that he is so handsome to look at, he is a brilliant man. Strong, thoughtful, determined. He is faithful to our God Val. For me, he is the greatest gift Val could have given me. He loves me in ways I could never express in words. He is gentle and kind. He makes me laugh. We do so many things together." Alexa paused, a sad expression creeping into her eyes. "We love to touch one another. I miss him so much it hurts. I have no doubt that he feels very much the same right now."

The two women sat for a long time, quietly discussing striking differences that existed for women in Turand. Oui-lest questioned Alexa extensively regarding the relationships between men and women there. She asked about the freedoms women enjoyed in Turand, obviously fascinated by the fact that the foreign women in her charge held highly respected positions in their own nation. When Alexa informed her that Turandan women even held key government posts, Oui-lest felt nearly as stunned as she had upon learning that women were not forced into marriages to satisfy political alliances or serve as housekeepers and breeding stock.

Oui-lest had already heard how the soldiers with the priestesses were forced off a bridge before the bridge was collapsed into a steep ravine. Only the women captives had been permitted to live. The naval officer who had captured them had decided they might provide a fresh diversion for his king back home. Nearly gasping in disbelief, Oui-lest then learned that the murdered soldiers had actually been assigned in service to these women.

When Alexa finally crawled back into bed, she wearily closed her eyes. She had left the Sifiq woman in a more tranquil state of mind. Now she would attempt to rest this night, fully expecting the following day to set the tone for whatever time she would spend in the Sifiq Kingdom. Slumber came as a welcome visitor on a velvet wave, carrying home her mind, her thoughts, and her heart.

～

"Alexa, I see no future anymore. The past holds me prisoner. Sometimes, especially at night, it seems that if I sleep at all, ghosts haunt me no matter which way I go." Victor's voice held a slight tremor as he turned his back to the museum's painting of Garogan to face her. "I feel lucky when my dreams retreat to times before I ever left for Toraval. Even though I feel so empty when I wake, at least for a little while, I escape to when you were there, and I was happy. Mostly though, I see their faces. I wonder about their families—the lives they left behind. Then, inevitably, I see my hands covered with their blood. Alexa, how do I ever move beyond what I did? How?"

Victor's hazel eyes brimmed with tears as he gazed into her face that held such serenity, such compassion. As she took his hands into hers, he could not avoid wondering how she faced him without even a hint of revulsion for all he had done when he betrayed the dreams and ideals they once shared. Gazing into the emerald depths of her eyes, he asked himself how she could continue to provide such a vital source of comfort and encouragement.

Alexa's smile reflected gentle inspiration. "Victor," she began thoughtfully, "knowing you as I do, I realize the impossibility of your ever forgetting what happened. Still, you must seek a different perspective. Despite your lingering pain and sorrow, you cannot deny the good that already rises from the nightmare. For the first time in my memory, Turand is free of Sifiq brutality. Who can say how many lives are now saved because they were defeated? Think, Victor. Turand's children no longer live in shadows of fear."

Watching him, feeling herself flooded by the intensity of his remorse, her voice grew more earnest. "As a people, we're now free to build our nation and our future based on a foundation of faith and peace. Victor, no matter what happened—no matter the misguided deeds committed—you emerged a leader. A hero! You demonstrated for us all a rare courage by admitting grievous wrongs. You then redirected your efforts to goals that were most true to who you were.

"You suffered as much as any of us. Try to understand that Val sees more than the darkness that sometimes prevails. Believe me, Victor. He also sees when we open our souls to restore the light. That is exactly what you did. You seized the light of faith and used it to drive out the darkness. Your image—your strength—your devotion… All those aspects of your character are essential to what we only begin to accomplish."

His eyelids dropped, and he breathed in deeply. Always before, her words had carried conviction and determination. Now he perceived the change he had often anticipated. Newfound confidence swelled and flowed from her being. Valkana. The transition had already woven itself into the complex fabric of her nature. Energy almost crackled around her. Words poured forth with forcefulness and wisdom.

Gazing back at her, he grasped both her hands tightly. Swallowing hard, he forced a pleading whisper. "Sweetest, are you sure? Do you really believe Val can forgive me for everything I did?"

Pulling one hand free, she lifted it to stroke his cheek. "Victor, Val's love is so immense that it is incomprehensible. I promise. He has already forgiven you."

Relief flooded him. For brief moments, he felt the surge inside him and understood its source had been Val's own love. Victor silently renewed his promises to their god. Fresh doubts then assailed him. "Alexa," he whispered again, "can you also forgive me? I mean, can you really forgive me?"

She smiled and embraced him. "Had I not already forgiven you, do you think I would have convinced Gregor to allow you to be Nikolai's godfather?" Receiving what could almost be called a smile for her effort, she encouraged him again. "Victor, I am going to need your strength and support tomorrow. People don't yet understand the way you and I do. Go. Rest now."

After he left, Alexa went upstairs to her suite. Inside, Gregor was patiently contending with a fussy, hungry infant. After taking the baby, nursing him, and rocking him to sleep, she placed the baby inside his crib.

Getting into bed and nestling close to her husband, she kissed his cheek and laid her head against his shoulder.

"Is he better now?" Gregor inquired. His voice, quiet and solemn, revealed only concern, although deep inside lingered unresolved anger and cautious resentment. He feared he would always struggle to conceal his true feelings concerning Victor.

"He will be once he can escape all his self-recriminations." She sighed, pressing her cheek against the brushed flannel of Gregor's night-shirt. "Right now, all I want is to concentrate on you, my love. Hold me?"

Her husband's lips curved into a smile as he turned and drew her into his embrace. The tribunal would open in the morning. For tonight, he would fortify himself with her love. Slowly, he brought his mouth to hers, partaking freely of the open invitation she offered. With warm hands, he began to explore enticing curves that quickly ignited his passions.

"Gregor."

Her voice caressed his name in an ardent whisper. Abruptly, she sat up. Her breath shuddered within her breast as wakefulness brought the anguished realization that her heart beating so rapidly resulted from nothing more than a dream—a vital, throbbing memory. Her body trembled, its need for him apparent and almost painful. Her throat constricted; her stomach twisted. Tears scalded the backs of her closed eyelids. Finally, she managed to calm herself.

To fall asleep again, she escaped into prayer. Her mission to Tolura Province had been undertaken with Val never expecting its completion. Instead, she and her Valiria sisters had been led to assume a different task, one that Alexa feared would test her strength, her capacity to love, and even her faith to the very limits of endurance.

Chapter 12

When the Turandan priestesses were next brought before King Bin-Lot, only a few silent guards stood by doorways while the king initiated his quest to assert domination over his prisoners. Reclining negligently against his throne's thick, upholstered back, Bin-Lot's posture made his generous belly look larger than ever as it bounced and shook with vulgar laughter. Intent on trying to bait the Turandan women into a show of resistance, he hurled crude insults at them. Disappointed when his taunts failed to elicit any reaction, he grew agitated to the brink of belligerence. Finally, he rose from his chair and approached silent prisoners.

Reaching out, he grasped Sulía's wrist and jerked her against him. Sulía stiffened as he rubbed his body against hers. Her lips tightened as she glared at him, totally disgusted by his unwelcome advance. His lips were drawn into an ugly sneer, his eyes glittering in self-assurance that physical domination over these women would break their silence and their spirits.

"So, bitch," he growled in a low voice, aroused by the voluptuous curves of the youngest Turandan, "you do not know what it is to provide pleasure to a man. Or are you like the rest of your kind?"

Sulía, refusing to respond, received a stinging slap against her cheek. Still, she carefully held her temper.

"Speak, woman, when your king asks a question of you!"

Sulía glanced into Bin-Lot's ruddy face and buried the initial retort that would have surely earned her a second punishing blow. "Sir, I am a Valiria priestess. As such, I have undertaken vows of virtue to which I must adhere."

"Virtue?" Bin-Lot snarled, deriving wicked excitement from the sport of verbally tormenting his prisoners. "Women know nothing of virtue. The very idea is only a weapon used to deceive men until opportunities arise to prove their unfaithful natures."

Abruptly, Bin-Lot shoved Sulía away. He snickered obscenely at her failed attempt to hide her contempt. Behind his lewd smile hovered thoughts of perverse pleasure as he anticipated prolonging his enjoyment of slowly destroying their undeserved pride.

Next, he turned his attention to Kiralí. "You are the one who is... How did you put it? Betrothed to the man you love?" Sarcasm was delivered in a voice deliberately lowered to a mock tone of seduction. Again, Bin-Lot's eyes glittered with ugly delight.

"I am," Kiralí responded quietly. She determinedly clung to her Valkana's assurance that Val would protect the oath of virtue to which each was sworn. For a fraction of a second, she feared her conviction might waver as the king's pudgy hand touched her cheek before sliding down to cup the firm roundness of her left breast. However, just as her senses wavered, her sisters' voices sounded clearly in her mind. With confidence restored, she stared at Bin-Lot without revealing her innermost thoughts.

"You are as cold as the ice mountains moving past the coast after winter," the king sneered at her. "I believe the Turandan male you left behind should be glad to be rid of you."

Intent on humiliating each, he proceeded to bestow rough and unwelcome caresses on both Marlí and Lisana. Neither of the two reacted, causing the king's expression to shift from mocking to surly. Dismissing the four younger women from his mind, he turned his attention to Alexa. Instinctively, he knew that if he could break her resolve, he would conquer them all.

Alexa observed the king carefully from beneath discreetly lowered eyelids. With complete certainty, she sensed his intent to intimidate her into submission in order to subdue the others. Instant understanding filled her that her faith and strength were ready for the first test.

"You, Alexa Maraná, must be well accustomed to satisfying male appetites if you have borne six children. I am suitably impressed that your body is still in such fine condition after so many children." He studied her unyielding posture and decided he would not begin with her. Instead, he would enjoy great satisfaction in watching her while the others were forced into submission. "For now, I choose to make you wait to discover what it is to give pleasure to a real man. I choose this one—Lisana—to be the first to perform the duty of satisfying a Sifiq man."

He glanced toward the court's main entrance and signaled one of the guards. "Summon Lieutenant Tal-Mon." Only a few minutes passed before the lieutenant entered through the doorway and approached his king. He immediately bowed low. Upon straightening, the man, in his late twenties, revealed a face that might have been called handsome had it not been so twisted with arrogant malevolence.

"Lieutenant, you recently performed great service to your king by uncovering an intended revolt against guards in the farming district. As a reward, you will be permitted to be the first to show this female how women are expected to treat Sifiq officers." Bin-lot then grabbed Lisana's arm and swung her around into the officer's waiting arms.

"Lisana, hold tight to your faith," Alexa's voice sounded firmly inside her companion's mind. "Val will protect you so long as you believe."

Lisana responded instantly to the spiritual support delivered by words meant for her mind only. Her body relaxed as the muscular lieutenant dragged her toward the privacy of a suite just beyond the king's court. Deliberately, she slowed her heartbeat and focused her mind on her god. Yes, she did believe. He would not fail her. She was convinced that Val would not allow violation of sacred oaths made to him and to her husband.

Inside the suite, Lisana gasped as Tal-Mon shoved her toward the bed. Moving with deliberate slowness, he undid his belt and began to remove his knee-length uniform tunic. He then commanded her to get up and approach him.

Cautiously, she obeyed. Refusing to allow Tal-Mon to see her nervousness, she followed his order to unbutton his shirt and remove the flowing trousers that matched his discarded jacket. When he stood naked before her, he was disappointed that she observed his aroused state with no more than aloof disdain.

"I will now remove your clothing for you," he sneered, grabbing her arm. Quickly sidestepping, she moved beyond his reach. Her reaction infuriated him. "Come here, bitch."

The whispered voice of Val filled her being with promises of protection. Defiance sparked in Lisana's blue eyes, and she smiled. "I warn you, sir. You are not to touch me. To do so will surely invite the wrath of my god."

"Your god? Your imaginary creator of this world? Some invisible spirit no one has ever seen? Woman, you and your kind exist for one purpose. You are to do the bidding of men who are your superiors." He lunged toward her. Again, she stepped quickly aside, causing him to lose his balance. He stumbled heavily against a table. His anger boiled. "Now I will show you!"

"Do not touch me!" she cried out in warning. "If you do so with evil intent, I will not be responsible for whatever price you pay!"

Disregarding Lisana's warning, Tal-Mon advanced again, driving her into a corner. Viciously, he grabbed her by the arms and crushed his mouth against hers. Then, abruptly, she felt his fingers fall away from the bruising grasp with which he held her. Stunned, she watched as he stumbled backward, crossing his arms tightly over his chest.

"What evil…?" His disbelieving question died as his knees buckled before he collapsed, face first, onto the floor.

Lisana's chest heaved a sigh heavy with relief and gratitude. She gratefully accepted the lesson this test had brought her. Val had not abandoned her. His protection was assured. Even faced with the certainty that the Sifiq would try to drive her and the others to despair, she had learned a most powerful truth. Val was with them.

Almost an hour later, Bin-Lot waited impatiently for the lieutenant to return with details of his mastery over the Turandan priestess. The four priestesses who remained with him had been allowed to sit on the cold tile floor. Finally, unable to tolerate his curiosity, the king sent a guard to summon Tal-Mon.

The guard's face was tense when he finally reappeared and bowed before his king. "Your Majesty, I bring ill tidings."

"Ill tidings?" Bin-Lot demanded angrily. "What sort of ill tidings?"

"Excellency, when I found Lieutenant Tal-Mon, he lay dead on the floor." The young guard avoided facing his king.

"What? Dead? How dare that Turandan bitch kill him?" Bin-Lot bellowed furiously.

"Sire, I found her sitting on the floor. The lieutenant does not appear to have been struck in any way. Instead, it seems his heart failed."

Bin-Lot jumped from his throne and angrily stalked from the court and into the suite reserved for the pleasure of his best officers. A doctor and several other officers had arrived before the king and already knelt over Tal-Mon's nude body. The doctor glanced up. "It appears he suffered an unknown heart condition, Excellency. I believe his heart burst inside his chest."

Bin-Lot's eyes spewed fury toward Lisana, who waited with face downcast and eyes closed. The king gestured at one of the officers and ordered that she be dragged back to court. Once there, the officer held Lisana firmly as Bin-Lot paced in front of her. "What did you do to my officer?"

"Sir, I did nothing to harm him."

"Liar!" he shouted, striking her full in the face with his open hand.

She would have fallen had she not been held firmly by the officer. "Sir," she responded shakily, "I am Valiria. I dare not lie lest I face the anger of my god."

"God! This god of yours makes me sick!" Again, he struck her.

With Lisana struggling not to cry, Alexa's voice broke through the tension.

"Excellency, I request permission to speak."

Bin-Lot's attention diverted from the target of his anger. "And what have you to say about this?"

"Sir," Alexa pronounced respectfully, "we tried earlier to explain to you. Our god protects the integrity of our vows of virtue. Your officer has died because he intended to violate my sister."

Bin-Lot shoved Lisana out of the officer's grasp and onto the floor. He then pointed at Alexa. "Bring her to me."

The officer obediently approached Alexa and, grabbing her arm, yanked her to her feet and dragged her to face the king. Alexa's calm demeanor only served to fuel the king's rising temper.

"I want to see how well this god of yours protects you!" he shouted furiously. "Your companion will be stripped and lashed."

Alexa's eyes sparked with fury not to be suppressed. "Sir, with due respect, I suggest you reconsider your order to punish Lisana. She has done nothing more than remain faithful to her beliefs and to her husband. Even your own physician informed you that your officer died from heart failure."

"Bitch! You dare to suggest that I not have her lashed? Perhaps you prefer to stand in her stead!"

Emerald eyes, revealing no hint of weakness, met his. "I will gladly stand in her place."

Bin-Lot tilted his head with renewed interest, his anger abating. This one was undeniably their leader, even if the others refused to acknowledge such truth. "Are you sure?"

"Are you certain you are prepared for the consequences?"

Bin-Lot laughed, the dead officer forgotten and his humor restored. He glanced at the officer who restrained her. "Prepare her."

That night, Alexa lay quietly, face downward, on a bed inside the priestesses' bedroom. Her Valiria sisters prayed fervently to Val that he might dispatch his Healing Graces to aid them. When the brilliant sparkles of light finally hovered above their Valkana, each offered thanks for the relief Val would grant his high priestess.

Earlier, she had entered a state of trance just before the first brutal lash had been struck against her bare back. Leaning forward over a wooden bench, she had not cried out a single time as the strap snapped against her flesh, drawing narrow strips of blood. When women servants lifted her to her feet, she clutched her sheath over her breasts and forced herself to stand and walk without assistance. Although she would collapse upon reaching her bed, she had demonstrated for the first time the fortitude the Sifiq would now face in their own land.

Just after midnight, Alexa awoke to the sounds of driving winds and deafening explosions of thunder. Jagged lightning flashed brightly through shades covering the window. She glanced around the room, seeing the others also waking to the furious blast of nature's violence. Lisana sat up first and turned her gaze toward Alexa. The others quickly rose. All came to sit by their Valkana's bedside.

"My sisters," Alexa whispered, sensing their questions. "Do not fear. We are safe for now. The storm is Val's theater while he demonstrates his displeasure. It is a warning—a promise of all he will bring upon this land if its king refuses to turn from his dark path."

"Do you think Bin-Lot will understand the message?" Kiralí asked in a hushed voice.

Alexa smiled thoughtfully. She felt grateful that, for this time at least, the only remnants of yesterday's beating were bruises and uncomfortable tenderness. "I think not, Kiralí. Bin-Lot is a stubborn, arrogant man. He will require many difficult lessons. We must prepare ourselves for much worse than we faced yesterday."

Sulía chewed thoughtfully at her full, lower lip. "Milady, why? What I do not understand is why our Lord Val brought us here to endure such a fate. Have we failed him in some way? Why has he done this to us?"

Alexa reached out and covered Sulía's hand with her own. "I cannot answer your question with utter certainty, sister. I can only tell you what I believe to be the reason we are here."

Marlí nodded and interrupted. "Milady, I believe his reasons are apparent. Once, after Sifiq persecution, you were the only anointed Valiria left alive in Turand. You faced them squarely, even after they destroyed your home and your family. Many Sifiq suffer more now than Turand did under occupation. More than understanding, you empathize with their suffering.

"As for the rest of us, we have always been faithful, always exceptionally strong. I won't deny that part of me is terrified, but part of me accepts this challenge almost as a reward. Through our combined strength and faith, we can present new ways to these people. By delving into the deepest recesses of our souls, we can anchor ourselves to the roots of our own faith—our own souls. We can light sparks of hope—fan flames for change."

"Marlí, you are indeed perceptive. This mission is dangerous. I do not know all we must endure. Neither can I say if we'll survive. However, I believe these people desperately need change. We must be patient and resilient. We must persevere. Most of all, we must believe that Val will not let us walk this path alone." Alexa's voice softly expressed the core of her belief.

"Milady, I believe that we, too, have lessons to learn. Last night, for just a moment, I was so afraid that…" Lisana's voice trailed off a moment. "I felt the encouragement of your words and gave myself back to Val and my faith in him. Within seconds, the Sifiq officer fell dead. I realized that, although we face much brutality here, Val will protect that which is most essential to us."

A quiet knock and gradual opening of the door interrupted their conversation. Oui-lest peeked in, her face tense and her eyes full of concern. "May I come in?" Receiving approval from the priestesses, Oui-lest tentatively entered and closed the door behind her. Sympathy shone from tear-glazed eyes as she looked down at Alexa's pale features. "I can't tell you how awful I feel…"

Alexa stretched out her hand. "Oui-lest, your caring means much to me. Thanks to the power of my god and the faithful love of my sisters, I am fine now. You are worried."

Oui-lest's curiosity concerning Alexa's startling recovery was secondary as she approached the window. Pushing the shade aside, she peered out at black heavens continuously split by blazing shafts of lightning. Trees bent far over, many losing battles for survival as their roots ripped from the ground.

"In my entire life, I've never seen such a storm. You cannot even stand against the wind to walk outside. From the hallway window, I saw buildings damaged by winds while water rises and rushes down the streets." She turned back to face the priestesses with wide eyes. "This storm came because they beat you, didn't it?"

Alexa adjusted her position and rose up on one elbow. "Why do you think so?"

Oui-lest shook her head. "I'm not sure. I suppose for the same reason Tal-Mon lies dead this morning. Our king may jest about your invisible god, but your god is real, isn't he?"

Alexa glanced up and around at her priestesses before smiling. Oui-lest's simple question provided welcome affirmation. Val's changes had already begun.

Chapter 13

W eeks later, the priestesses found themselves yet again in front of King Bin-Lot. This time, the Sifiq king was attired in formal court dress. Around his head circled the turban-like headpiece. From its side swung a cluster of braided silk tassels through which were drawn chains of gold studded with gemstones. His uniform had been fashioned of finely woven black fabric that flowed loosely around his body except where it was belted with a wide sash of red and gold. His trousers were also loose and flowing from beneath the hem of his tunic top.

Looking like some overly proud bird promenading in front of a prospective mate, he smiled at the Turandan women, whose faces were cast downward. "Ah, dear prisoners, it appears you finally display manners more appropriate in the court of your sovereign."

His voice sounded deliberately loud and pompous, eliciting snickers from officers and courtiers who provided a willing audience to their monarch. Glancing around to assure himself that he was the center of attention, the king initiated an arrogant strut around his captives. "Tell me, bitches, how do you feel now in the presence of a real king?"

Alexa glanced upward, recalling the stinging blows of past encounters when she had maintained silence in response. Hoping to avoid unnecessary distress for her sister priestesses, she replied to his question. "Sir, we have been taught well to show proper respect for the Sifiq ruler."

"Ahh!" he exclaimed, a falsely bright smile breaking his ruddy features. He feared his entertainment in taming the Turandans might be reaching a premature end. Still, the chance to exert final mastery over the leader of his captives was one he anticipated with relish. He sensed she would struggle to the end. "So, a few beatings have been sufficient to teach you how to behave. Good! I have several officers who deserve rewards, and I believe the lot of you will provide, shall we say, fresh diversion."

Alexa's eyes glittered with fresh warning. No longer did she fear that the king or any of his men would successfully violate her or any of her companions. Six attempts had been made. Six officers lay dead, each from what Sifiq physicians called failure of the heart. Alexa had endured vicious, bloody whippings after each incident. While her sisters had summoned Val's Healing Graces to close her wounds and relieve her pain, the heavens had unleashed furious torrents of rain and turbulent winds with increasingly destructive force upon the Sifiq capital of Atuliq. Would this king be ever so arrogant as to be unable to perceive a direct correlation between the beatings and the violent storms?

Bin-Lot approached Alexa and, with fat fingers, stroked the smoothness of her left cheek. "Since you have finally learned your place here, tonight, your companions are assigned to pleasure four of my finest officers who have come home after serving me in rebellious northern regions. And you, Alexa Maraná, will know the honor of offering pleasure to me." He turned and motioned toward two women kneeling just behind the throne. "Take her to my quarters. Prepare her for me."

Alexa cast her glance toward her sisters. Their eyes reflected anxiety; however, newfound strength had now replaced earlier fear. Each expected terrible punishment to follow. Under the guidance of their Valkana, each had explored new avenues of meditation to provide welcome relief and escape from the inevitable pain. They faced their tormentors with resolute courage, understanding their example provided the first source of hope ever to come before the Sifiq women they had encountered in Atuliq.

Alexa lifted her chin, giving her countenance an image of defiance. "Sir, I request permission to speak."

Bin-Lot's eyes opened wide and began to glitter. The expression gleaming in the eyes of the Turandan leader provided him great satisfaction. One glance told him she had not yet relinquished her defiance. Perversely, he welcomed the opportunity for continued sport with her. "Speak, woman."

"Sir, I suggested in the past that you consider the consequences of immoral actions against my sisters. Several attempts were made to violate us. Each time, you lost valuable officers, and your capital endured the punishing onslaught of terrible storms. We are prepared to show you respect due as ruler of the Sifiq Kingdom. We will willingly serve in whatever labor you ask of us. However, your intent to inflict unwelcome sexual assaults upon us violates not only our virtue, it violates sacred vows each of us is sworn to observe. Respectfully, sir, I request that you reconsider. To do otherwise will bring results not to your liking."

Fury sparkled in the depths of the king's blue irises. His lips drew into a thin, diabolical sneer. His intent to take her, to force her into surrender, showed plainly in his vulgar expression. Alexa met his expression of contempt with unyielding calm.

Abruptly, Bin-Lot sprang toward Alexa and grabbed her slender wrist in a vise-like grip. His voice dropped to a cutting whisper. "By tomorrow, bitch, you will understand that a woman never speaks to a Sifiq man as you just did—most especially not to the Sifiq king." He jerked his head toward a small group of officers who waited in front of the throne. Four approached, and each grabbed the Turandan priestess personally selected for him by Bin-Lot.

Alexa breathed in deeply as she watched uniformed soldiers forcefully lead her sisters away to private suites. Mentally, she issued reminders that sounded firmly in their minds. "Faith provides your strength. Val provides your protection. Remember and never doubt."

Later, she waited in the opulently appointed suite of the king. Clad only in a thin robe given to her by two silent women whose eyes had reflected both sadness and sympathy, Alexa studied the king's quarters with curiosity. Chairs and chaise lounges were upholstered in once richly colored velvets, oddly showing signs of wear. The bed was high, the mattress thick and plump. Headboard and bedposts had been carved into elegant scrollwork. Gold candleholders held candles that shone light upon worn carpets, hand-knotted into designs typical of Turand's western provinces. An enormous painting on the wall surprised her. Intricate brushstrokes and vivid colors depicted ocean vessels with sails unfurled at what looked very much like Fosan Province's main port.

She breathed in deeply. The Sifiq king surrounded himself with beautiful possessions, many of which had been crafted by hands native to her own homeland. Surrounded by reminders of Turand, Gregor's face filled Alexa's inner vision. His smile encouraged her. His eyes adored her. Her eyelids slowly closed. His love was powerful enough to span time and distance—strong enough to reach her even in this land of spiritual desolation. Desperately, she buried her longings, both spiritual and physical, for her beloved husband. Her lips moved silently. "I love you, Gregor."

"Do you pray again to that stupid, non-existent god of yours?" Bin-Lot's mouth was curved into a crooked, malicious grin as he strutted into the room and nonchalantly removed massive, jeweled rings from stubby fingers.

Alexa smiled benignly. "I wasn't praying. I thought of my husband. My heart remains faithful to him and the vows we made before Val. I couldn't help but wonder how empty an existence you must lead without love."

Bin-Lot lunged toward her, his fingers digging into the tender flesh of her upper arms. His face moved menacingly close to hers as he growled at her. "Never speak of another man while in my private quarters. You belong to me. I will tolerate no such disrespect." Jerking her sideways while maintaining his vicious grip on her right arm, he dragged her across the floor as he sat down on the edge of a chair. "Remove my shoes."

Alexa accepted his command without a word. Despite the throbbing ache where his fingers had pressed into her arm with bruising force, her face remained an emotionless mask, obscuring the fiery temper that threatened full eruption. Breathing deeply, she marshaled her thoughts into tightly controlled focus. One lesson she had learned well from her husband during the early months of their marriage: Never let the enemy know the exact nature of your thoughts. Play along carefully. Never let them see the true extent of your anger.

Bin-Lot roughly grasped her arms again and yanked her to her feet as he stood. "You will now undress me."

Alexa lifted defiant emerald eyes that began to glow eerily in golden candlelight. "Sir, I refuse to undress you. I am a married woman. I will not willingly participate in any action intended to betray my husband."

Bin-Lot grinned wickedly while he shed his garments. This Turandan woman was filled with spirit, and just as with a wild horse, he would achieve tremendous satisfaction by forcing her into submission. "Willingly or not, you will provide me the pleasure I seek."

Tightly grasping the flimsy fabric of her wrap with one hand, Bin-Lot tugged open the garment, and she jerked away from him. Maliciously appraising ivory skin and the fullness of her breasts, he smirked while pompously displaying his swelling arousal. When his hands reached to grab her, she surprised him by quickly stepping further back from him.

"I warn you, sir. Do not try to force yourself on me." Alexa's expression grew angrily defiant.

Her stubborn resistance served to arouse the king's sexual appetite to a higher plane. Unbridled desire to dominate her drove him forward as she backed up against a wall. His mouth curled into an ugly line. "I will now show you how to behave for your new master."

Alexa's breath caught for a moment. Val's words swept through her mind like breezes across Turand's central plains. She stiffened when Bin-Lot began to push his ample body closer to hers, thrusting his loins toward her hips.

Suddenly—violently—the entire room lurched sickeningly. Chairs tipped over, and a settee slid across the floor. Candelabras toppled. Flames extinguished beneath the swift flow of melted wax. Walls groaned. Windows cracked. Glass shattered. The world around them quaked as Bin-Lot stumbled away from Alexa and fell heavily to the floor. Already pressing her back against the wall, Alexa slid downward and drew herself into a tight ball.

After prolonged, furious shaking, darkness filled the room. Confused screams for help mingled with shouted commands echoing from the corridors outside. Cursing furiously, Bin-Lot dragged himself to his feet. Moonlight invaded through broken windows, revealing Alexa with her back still snugly pressed against the wall.

Incensed, Bin-Lot grabbed her and jerked her up against him. "Woman, what just happened? What have you done?"

Another powerful jolt rocked the floor and was followed by vibrating tremors. Both Bin-Lot and Alexa stumbled across the room. Alexa fell against the overstuffed mattress while Bin-Lot grabbed for a corner bedpost and held on tightly to avoid falling again. "Bitch! What are you doing? I command you to stop this insanity! Now!"

As the new tremors subsided, Alexa tugged her robe closed around her and stood up. Her chest rose and fell rapidly as she glared at the king with indescribable fury. His initial urge was to reach out and slap the insolence from her face. Something in her expression stopped him. Features that had earlier seemed to glow now appeared to float toward him. Unexpectedly, he felt the stab of pain in his stomach as nausea overwhelmed him. Between eruptions of vomit wrenched from the depths of his guts, he spewed searing strings of profanity at her. All the while, Alexa remained silent and motionless, showing no reaction whatsoever.

Bin-Lot finally straightened, spitting vile-tasting remnants onto the floor. Sweat slathered his forehead and cheeks as he held one fat forearm tightly against his revolting midsection. For several seconds, he stared in disbelief at his prisoner. The vision of her figure, now totally encased in a blue-white shimmer, prompted shivering shafts of fear along his spine. Then eerie light disappeared as quickly as he had noticed it, and the two were left to glare at one another.

Footsteps sounded in the hall as Sifiq soldiers and servant staff rushed through the corridors. Several officers pushed open the damaged door of the king's chambers as they sought to learn their ruler's fate. Two of them hurried to their king's side, shoving aside furniture and carefully avoiding the slick, glistening slime on the floor. Then, supporting him, they wrapped a blanket around their naked king and led him from the room. Another took Alexa's arm and dragged her along behind him.

Bin-Lot's expression grew increasingly enraged as he surveyed his well-ordered palace, now in chaos. Walls showed wide cracks. Shattered windows had sent sprays of slivered glass to cover floors in a carpet that reflected glints of moonlight. Paintings and sconces hung askew. Doors swung crookedly, many with hinges ripped from their anchors. Tall shelves and cabinets had crashed onto floors, creating massive obstacles to climb over.

Stunned soldiers turned to their officers for direction. Harsh commands rang through corridors, directing fearful soldiers to rescue hurt comrades. Women servants had already begun the task of clearing places where the injured could be carried for medical attention. Quickly, they had organized two distinct areas, one for men and the other for women. Men were to be treated first before any women could receive attention.

The officer who had led Alexa from Bin-Lot's chamber held tightly to her arm, although he ceased dragging her. His eyes scanned the damage around him. Unwelcome warning instinct had earlier twisted his insides upon watching his king send the prisoners from court to the pleasure suites. That young officer, Lieutenant Win-Das, had already mentally noted the chronology of events since King Bin-Lot began his campaign of subversion against the Turandan women. Win-Das had considered the unexpected deaths of fellow officers whose rewards were supposed to have been sexual pleasures with the foreign women. He had also noticed the severe storms following each beating inflicted upon the woman he now led through cluttered palace hallways. In charge of guards at the women's quarters, he was also keenly aware of Alexa's unusually rapid recovery from each beating. Mystified, he had decided to maintain silence regarding his observations.

An odd sensation sent tingling tremors through him as he stopped to push a heavy console out of his way. He glanced backward and gasped. Alexa's expression was tranquil. Faint light glimmered around her face. Win-Das released her arm, shocked by her glowing image that quickly reverted to normal. Lifting her eyebrows, shining eyes reflected inquiry. He felt her life force invade his being. With swift recognition, he realized his entire life had just transformed.

〜

A week after the catastrophic quake, Bin-Lot summoned Alexa back to his court. He drew on every ounce of self-restraint he possessed to avoid strangling her with his bare hands. Beyond the unrelenting abdominal pain that had assaulted him since the night of the quake, a crippling fear born during the violent tremors tempered any urge to retaliate. The memory of her light-encased figure tormented his sleep and rarely left his conscious mind. She was different—frighteningly different—from anyone he had ever encountered. Never could he admit the dread he felt as he stared at her erect figure. Neither did he dare exhibit weakness in her presence. To do so could precipitate his demise as Sifiq ruler. However, he also acknowledged that several of his best officers had experienced inexplicable deaths in the presence of these women. Worse, seemingly natural catastrophes had delivered widespread damage to his capital in the wake of his attempts to conquer them.

"Alexa Maraná," he snarled at her. She remained tranquil; however, her mere glance caused him deeper discomfiture. "I grow tired and bored with you and your companions. As king, I must rebuild my capital after the recent storms and quake. I have decided that you and your friends will be taken to the Talafaq Territory. There, you will work in the fields until I have time to decide what I wish to do with you."

Alexa smiled only slightly. She already knew what fieldwork meant. Prisoners were forced to endure filthy, squalid living conditions and to toil beneath the scrutiny of cruel guards. Still, she preferred the king's newest decision, feeling it better to work in the outdoors than remain constantly trapped within the palace's evil confines. She merely nodded her head in acknowledgment of the king's pronouncement before glancing directly at him. He shivered slightly when she smiled again.

Following seven days of exhausting travel, Alexa and her sister priestesses lay beneath the stars, anticipating the next day's arrival at the prison farm. The Valiria had survived the quake that had ravaged Atuliq and the surrounding countryside. Forced to work from sunrise to sunset, they had cleaned the palace and nursed the injured and dying. With Oui-lest's assistance, Alexa had directed the women's care. With cautious discretion, the priestesses summoned Val's healing powers, bringing conversion and recovery to many. Each priestess cherished the sense of satisfaction of restoring life to their sworn vows. Each displayed confidence meant to provide support for herself and her sisters.

Chapter 14

"Alexa?" Gregor's rich voice whispered to her from the doorway. She straightened the blanket covering the governor's daughter. The previous evening, Alexa had summoned Val's Healing Graces. Agonizingly blistered flesh was now smooth and pink with the healthy blush of youth. The girl and her brother had slept through the night. Following a light breakfast, they would sleep late into the afternoon. Val had healed them, and Alexa felt relieved that Nipala's kind governor could mourn his wife's death without watching his children suffer the excruciating pain of severe burns and broken bones.

Alexa rose from the bed and glided into her husband's waiting arms. He embraced her tightly before touching his lips to hers and gently leading her outside. "I promised Nikolai that we would visit Master Budrino today. Are you going?"

Early that afternoon, the king's party approached the Budrino farmhouse as the elderly gentleman swept his front porch. The old man's eyes grew wide with surprise at the appearance of the king's Royal Guard. Recognizing that King Gregor personally led the party and that a dark-haired, bright-eyed, little boy shared the king's saddle, the old man's face revealed shock at first, then unbridled delight.

Inside, Gregor clung tightly to Alexa's hand while Nikolai enthusiastically described Master Budrino's collection of carved wooden figurines. Conversation was cheerful and affable as Nikolai's elderly friend described the different varieties of wood and techniques he used for crafting his art. Gregor discovered himself as fascinated as Nikolai by the intricate details in the carvings.

When the grandfatherly Master Budrino finally sat back in a rocker with Nikolai perched on his knee, the discussion turned more serious. As a tired prince fell asleep, Master Budrino recalled stories his grandfather had told about another time when several explosions had occurred, much like the one that had destroyed the governor's home. Area elders had written accounts of the events, although he wasn't sure any had survived Sifiq occupation. Master Budrino remembered reading that, in each instance, ground swellings had occurred. In some cases, birds and small animals had been found dead near the bulges. Investigations following each explosion revealed fire had been introduced near the swollen mounds. When the ground swelled no more, the explosions ceased.

Clutching the hand of his wife nearly lost to such explosions, Gregor listened attentively. Perhaps nature provided signs of impending disasters. Perhaps gases as invisible as the air they breathed were escaping the ground, only to explode with violent force when ignited by some unwitting person starting a fire. Gregor expressed gratitude to Master Budrino, whose memories provided clues that Turand's scholars and scientific minds could study to predict sites of future explosions and, hopefully, avoid future loss of life.

Alexa's eyes squinted against hot, brilliant sunshine. Her hands, rough and calloused, gripped the handle of her hoe as she worked the fields. Her lips were parched, and she thirsted for a cool drink of water. A leather strap cracked against her hips. Harsh curses ordered her back to work. Her lips drew into a smile as her hands resumed their labor. However, her soul escaped back into the haven of the past. There, instead of holding an unfeeling wooden handle, her fingers entwined with Gregor's.

The Valiria priestesses lost track of time as they labored with the harvest yielded by fields too tired and overworked to satisfy the needs of the Sifiq military's swollen ranks. Men considered weak in character toiled under brutal conditions alongside women who had failed to meet their masters' expectations. Not enough food to meet the physical demands of such labor weakened many. When laborers grew too sick for work, they were often dragged into the woods, beaten, and left to die.

Alexa and her companions determined to improve things however possible. Knowing that poor yields spawned more violent punishment, Alexa sought permission to instruct fellow workers in farm techniques practiced in Turand. Alexa, native of Turand's most prosperous farming district, remembered her father's methods and taught how composting every shred of inedible vegetation or waste would enrich the soil for the next season's crops. While allowing any portion of the fields to lie fallow would be prohibited, at least the compost piles would provide fertilizers to encourage better growth.

With winter came bitter cold. The hut shared by Turand's priest-esses was small and drafty. A tiny stove provided heat so long as the women could comb nearby woods for branches and wood to keep flames burning. Often, two of the priestesses would venture out, wear-ing their sisters' garments over their clothes underneath blankets to fend off the cold so they could search for firewood and check traps set for small animals. Meanwhile, the others, clad only in thin under-garments, remained behind and huddled together on beds of straw, covering themselves with the last blanket. Without fail, they shared whatever they had.

As winter dragged on, other Sifiq slave laborers, men and women alike, were drawn toward the foreign women who faced hardship so courageously. With guards more interested in whiling away their time gambling or drinking in relative comfort inside their barracks, Alexa and her companions introduced Val, Turand's beloved god, to people barely able to conceive of hope, let alone a god who could love them–and save them.

⌒

"Gregor! You can't be serious!" Her face revealed incredulous reaction to his suggestion.

Dark eyes, more expressive than ever, glittered mischievously. Sensuously full lips approached hers and teased her with kisses that ignited irresistible fires. Long fingers, stroking through her hair before coming to rest alongside her cheek, began a tingling descent along her neck to a spot just above her breasts. His eyes shone with passionate promise when he lifted them back to hers.

"Why do you think I'm not serious, my love?" Even his voice, pitched low with undeniable sensuality, gently teased.

"Gregor," she pleaded, struggling to resist his deliberate assault on her senses, "don't ask me this. You have no idea what it's like."

Strong hands grasped her by the waist while he pressed against her body. Then, deliberately, he breathed into her ear, creating torrents of shivers that inundated her entire body with desire. "Would it really be so terrible? You always said you never felt better. Or happier. And never are you more beautiful."

"Gregor…" She gasped his name as she felt the moistness of his lips against the smooth column of her neck. During their years together, he had learned the most erotically sensitive spots of her body that could not possibly resist him. Drawing a deep, shuddering breath, she forced herself from his embrace. The startled disappointment on his face surprised her.

"Alexa, you know how much I love you," he whispered, reaching for her. "You also know how much I love making love to you. It's hard for me, too."

"Gregor, it's not that," she replied, moving back into his arms. "It's just that…"

"Just what?" he asked, his expression quietly pleading.

"Oh, Gregor, we already have four children. How many other Turandan families are so large? With so many responsibilities as it is, I fear another baby would take more time from you and the children we have already."

He slipped his hand around hers and guided her toward the inviting comfort of their bed. Settling into cushioned coziness, he watched her face intently. He saw her concern and listened to her thoughts as she voiced anxieties regarding his fervent request for more children. She agreed that she had loved being pregnant and that her deliveries had been relatively easy. He met her concerns with encouragement, insisting he had never once felt neglected and that no one could be a better mother than she.

So well did she know him. Still, she couldn't comprehend his obvious longing for another child. Together, they had anticipated the arrival of their four babies and shared the responsibilities of parenthood. How often had she laughed as he complimented the beauty of her pregnant figure? Patiently, he had endured with her the necessary abstinence from physical intimacies during the final stages of her pregnancies and preparation for the spiritual anointing of their babies. He had risen with her during nights while she nursed hungry infants or tended sick, fussy children. His rich voice had crooned sweet lullabies, coaxing all of them back to sleep. Although unable to imagine life without the precious family their love had created, she simply couldn't understand why he wasn't satisfied with all they had.

He saw her confusion—understood her unspoken questions. Reaching out, he placed his palm against her cheek. "Alexa, I love you and our children. You cannot know the sadness that all of you have driven from my life."

He paused, the thickness in his voice exposing deep, hidden emotions. "Alexa, for so long, I was alone. When Father died, I had no one left. No grandparents. No aunts. No uncles. No one. Yes, there was Stefan. And my godparents. I love them dearly, but it's not the same as having real family. I cannot explain that to you. Loving you—having babies with you—fills empty spots inside my soul. I suppose that's why I want more children. Please?"

Alexa gazed into his countenance. When her family had been murdered, she had not been left so alone. Cousins residing far from Zinzan had braved dangerous travel to come to her, to comfort her, to mourn with her. Bonds of family had been as essential to her recovery as Victor's and Adrina's love. That much she understood.

Turning her face, she kissed his palm. With adoring eyes, she smiled into his. Leaning forward, she placed her mouth against his and kissed him. How could she ever deny him? Moving slightly away, her eyes revealed the passion his touch had earlier awakened. Still, she wasn't prepared for total surrender. "Gregor, I realize how much this means to you. If I agree to another pregnancy, you must promise that you won't ask me to have any more children."

A frown drew his eyebrows together. His voice held a pleading note. "You know I want at least two more children."

She chuckled softly. "One more pregnancy. No more. If that isn't enough…" Moving over her, his body pressed hers down into the thick mattress. With his hands cupping her cheeks, his face hovered above hers. "Are you sure? Only one more?"

She parted her lips, inviting his kiss. With fires flaring hotly within her, she paused before responding. "Absolutely. Now promise you won't ask again."

Years of marriage had never diminished his passion for her. With his eyes, he beheld the woman who continuously inspired him. His hands began their practiced sweep of the feminine contours of her body. He breathed in subtle lilac fragrance as his lips traced passionately erotic lines along her neck and around the curves of her breasts. With fiery fingertips, he drew patterns across her shoulders and abdomen, stimulating her body into unrestrained desire. The surging power of his masculinity demanded its bond with the core of her femininity.

Physical restraint nearly escaped him. For a moment, with her body arching to meet the demands of his, he wondered if he could possibly find the ability to answer her. Just as he claimed her in physical love, he managed a hoarse whisper. "My beautiful Alexa, never again will I ask more than this."

Alexa awoke, the chilled stiffness in her body temporarily banished by memories of Gregor's heated touch. Pulling her thin blanket more tightly around her shoulders and tucking herself into a tighter ball, she escaped again into her haven of dreams.

"Alexa? Alexa? Please, beloved. Wake up. Alexa."

Far away, she heard the insistence in his voice. Struggling for consciousness, she attempted to respond. Unable to utter a sound, her lips formed his name.

Alertly, he leaned forward to kiss her forehead. "That's it, Alexa. You can do it. Come back to me. Alexa?"

Minutes later, heavy eyelids slowly opened to reveal dull, lackluster green eyes. "Gregor?"

Her whisper flooded him with relief. With each of her pregnancies, she had fainted once during the early weeks. With Anlía had come realization that the fainting spells resulted from the first time her spirit connected with the spirit of her unborn child. Each time, she had recovered quickly. Until now. Gregor had sat by her side throughout the afternoon and late into the evening, fearful of something seriously wrong this time.

"Alexa, are you all right?" Anxiety creased his brow. Fear darkened his eyes.

Gazing into his face, she responded weakly, "I'll be fine. Don't worry."

Drawing her close, he held her protectively. "Are you sure? It's been so long." Reluctantly, he lowered her back onto her pillow.

Somehow, she managed to grin shakily and then mumbled, "I cannot believe what you've done. I simply cannot!" With that, she eased his fears and began months of teasing as she kept from him the secret that his wish for six children would be fulfilled. Unlike before, she refused to tell him if they would have a son or a daughter. Sometimes impatiently, he begged her to explain cryptic remarks regarding her pregnancy and the accusation that he had somehow tricked her. Only sparkles of humor and lights of love shining in her eyes reassured him that all was fundamentally well.

On a lovely morning in summer, she crossed the square toward the palace. Carrying twins slowed her pace as Tirstan accompanied her from morning prayers at the temple. Suddenly, she stopped. Drawing in a sharp breath, she reached out to her favorite personal guard. "Tirstan, help me to that bench. I must sit."

Once she had lowered herself to the seat, Tirstan knelt before her and stared worriedly into her pale features. "Your Majesty, what's wrong? Are you all right?"

She shook her head. "Tirstan, quickly, bring Gregor."

Anxiously, Tirstan frowned. "The baby? Is it not too soon?"

Alexa nodded. "Six weeks too soon. Hurry, Tirstan. I'll be all right, but you must hurry."

A short while later, Alexa breathed through contractions that frightened her. Between contractions, she offered brief, intense prayers for the safe delivery of babies arriving prematurely. Adrina had already come and, along with the palace physician, carefully monitored the rapid progress of her labor.

All the while, Gregor refused to leave her side. He had been with her during the births of each of their children. Until this time, he had known no fear. Whispering words of love, he encouraged her with forced confidence. When she reclined backward and closed her eyes to rest a few moments, he silently begged Val to protect her and their unborn child.

After what seemed like hours, the birthing room filled with the sound of a newborn baby's cry. Alexa's eyes swiftly sought the source of the cry. Although very small, she sensed vitality in her tiny daughter. Glancing upward, she saw Gregor's worried face and squeezed his hand. When he looked down, he found welcome reassurance in her trembling smile. Focusing his attention on Adrina and the squirming infant she tended, relief and joy lit his features.

"Gregor!" Having started toward his new baby girl, the sudden urgency in his wife's voice reclaimed his attention, and he spun around in reaction.

"Alexa?" Immediately, he rushed back to her.

Managing a grin, she reached for his hand, and he leaned forward. Then, breathlessly, she whispered against his ear. "It seems   your wish— comes true, Your Majesty."

Shocked and confused, he stared when she was overwhelmed with the irresistible need to push a second child into the physician's waiting hands. When the second baby's cries joined those of the first, Gregor could only look from one baby to the other in sheer disbelief. Two perfect little girls! His dream family of six children! Months of Alexa's teasing accusations suddenly made sense.

When he finally looked back at her, tears shone on his cheeks as her tired, happy face told him all was well. His eyes alone told her how much he loved her before he allowed Adrina and the doctor to introduce him to the newest members of his family.

Hushed voices awakened Alexa from her dreams. Despite the gnawing, empty feeling in her stomach and cold that seemed unending, they could never steal from her the joy-filled years he had given her. Forcing herself to sit up to face a new day of captivity, she prayed thankfully for those years she had known his love.

Chapter 15

S pring rains gently washed cultivated fields. Alexa breathed a prayer of gratitude that the rains had not arrived until the soil had been plowed, fertilized, and sown with seeds. Such irony she perceived that seeds of faith had also been planted.

New prisoners had arrived to replace those who had perished during the winter. Among their numbers had been a young lieutenant whose face she recalled from the night of Atuliq's devastating quake. Mysteriously drawn to Alexa, he discreetly explained his fall from the king's graces. He had struck a guard guilty of raping a woman servant inside the women's quarters. Although men were forbidden inside the women's residence, the king had plunged into a fit of rage and ordered punishment for Win-Das. Disgusted by his king's irrational anger, the young officer welcomed exile. He had never genuinely believed in the way females were regarded and could no longer participate in the vile treatment to which they were subjected.

Throughout the early weeks of spring, he joined other field laborers. Under the guise of learning Turand's farming techniques, they also studied the ways of Turand's God Val. Men, once hopeless, took heart from the steadfast behavior of the foreign women. Women prisoners saw living examples that strength was not a matter of gender. When Sifiq prisoners spoke of revolt, the priestesses counseled patience. Obey the guards. Minimize the beatings. Make sure the fields were prepared to yield crops that would provide food. Conserve strength if they intended to confront their captors.

Leadership qualities emerged from the character of Sulía Kohira. The youngest Turandan priestess grew impassioned in the face of hardship. Sulía had inherited her father's determination and his analytical abilities. The challenges of captivity taught her lessons in perseverance and patience. She developed an uncanny knack for communicating with fellow prisoners without guards ever suspecting.

All the while, Alexa persisted in her mission. Without her sisters realizing, many weaker Sifiq prisoners found extra scraps of food in their bowls. Alexa always managed to work a little further than the person next to her, allowing others just a bit more rest. Secretly, she sacrificed of herself, affording them every possible chance to prepare. Her time for rest would come.

༄

Alexa huddled into the corner of the drafty, dirt-floored hut that she shared with her four Valiria companions. With legs drawn up close to her body, she hugged herself into a tight ball to conserve whatever body heat she could. The others sat as close as possible, her nearness comforting weary bodies and burdened spirits.

Alexa's voice enticed them into the meditative state that served as salvation through months of cruel, forced labor at the hands of Sifiq captors. Her melodious hum carried their spirits into Val's realm, where no pain existed. There was no penetrating chill to shake aching bodies. No hard ground prevented the rest of tired, aching muscles. There were no whips, no harsh curses determined to break their wills and, thus, their faith.

Instead, welcome freedom existed. Currents rushed around them initially, providing surprising warmth and soothing release from discomfort. Initial darkness faded into gray, then transformed into soft, cloud-like swirls colored in muted hues of blue, rose, and lavender. Alexa's voice receded as another spoke directly into the hearts and minds of the imprisoned priestesses. Val himself encouraged and praised them, promising relief and freedom from torment inflicted by bitter enslavers. But first, his priestesses must endure a little longer. Together, they must persevere. They must lose neither faith nor courage. There remained seeds to be sown, lessons to be taught, fruits to be harvested.

Val's words were like a heated tonic, penetrating their bodies and revitalizing their spirits. After seemingly immeasurable time spent in Val's protective cocoon, Alexa's voice once again became their beacon. Each focused upon the sweet sound, cleaving toward its source as they traversed the other world into which she had guided them. With growing awareness, the Valiria centered, finding themselves again locked inside the poorly heated hut that served as their prison.

Each Valiria cast her eyes around the tight circle. Bodies were warmed. Hunger had eased, and inner pains were relieved. Gratefully, spirits were restored. Yet this time, something was changed in this strange ritual that had continually sustained them throughout months of deplorable conditions in the evil Sifiq Kingdom.

The priestesses joined hands and edged closer to their Valkana. Alexa's hum had settled into a low, steady monotone. Although faint, her aura was ever-present. Her body appeared frozen. Her breathing had become so shallow that it appeared she breathed not at all. Her face had grown so pale that it seemed no blood flowed beneath the surface of her skin. She had not rejoined them. They reached out to her with only their senses, shielding with their bodies the shell that awaited return of the soul that breathed into it the fires of life.

Alexa hovered above Stefan and Adrina as they slept. She smiled at them, glad for their love that had grown through the years before drifting toward the remembered rhythm of Victor's breathing. Finding him, she first thanked Val that she could still rely on Victor's devotion. Then, reaching out, Alexa grasped his hands, connecting herself to his sensitivities and strength she would desperately need. He had turned, responding to her touch. Opening his eyes, Victor had seen only wisps of blue-white light. Enveloped by the softly sweet fragrance of lilac, he had heard her words and had promised that he would listen for her call to him.

Leaving Stefan's house, Alexa had gone directly to the palace, praying with deep gratitude that Val was allowing her precious moments with those she loved best. She understood that he gave her this time as both reward and fortification. Approaching each of her children, she showered them with her love as they slumbered. When she arrived at her husband's bedside, her heart ached at the exquisite sadness etched into his face even as he slept. She had been unable to resist her habit of running gentle fingers through his hair. Never had she wanted more to slip into the refuge of his arms as when he had reached out for her. Still, her time in Toraval approached its end. Her body already cried out from half a world away for the spirit that made it whole. Soft light swirled as the window to her own chambers slid noiselessly open.

Pausing, she felt Val gifting her with precious extra seconds. She smiled at the sight of her entire family asleep together. She floated once more toward Gregor. With love beyond comprehension, she allowed her spirit to brush his lips in loving farewell.

Dawn showed fingers of sunlight slicing through the thick of night. The Valiria maintained their vigil as Alexa slowly emerged from her heavy trance. They realized that she had gone far, far away. As her spirit flooded her body with returning life, they prayed their thanks. With her restored to them, they could face the new day and all they surely would have to endure.

Summer. The fair days and chilly nights of spring disappeared quickly. Sweltering heat, humid air, drenching cloudbursts, and stinging insects added misery to those laboring in the fields. Guards were always around with sharp words and sharper blows to encourage their charges to work harder and faster.

Collapsing one night onto the pile of straw that served as a bed, Alexa closed her eyes, unable to sleep. Why? Why must she face Sifiq evils again? Inner visions tortured her. She remembered the pressure, the sting of her chain snapping against her neck as she broke loose her crystal pyramid and tossed it aside when her horse had first stepped onto the bridge. Her hope had been that someone would find it and that it might provide a hint that something had gone terribly wrong.

Turning in her saddle as she waited for the others, Alexa had watched in abject horror as Sifiq soldiers shoved members of her guard over the bridge. Her mind was still haunted by screams of good men plummeting to their deaths. When the last of her guards had been murdered and all the Sifiq had crossed the bridge, the soldiers had laughed as they destroyed the supports, causing the structure to collapse into the canyon's depths.

Turning, she piled up some straw and then used her bent arm as a pillow. Tears escaped from her eyes. Yesterday, she had watched a man receive brutal lashes for helping an older woman who had stumbled in the field. Two days earlier, she had witnessed the collapse of a young woman who had not recovered from delivering a female child. Neither had she recovered from watching her baby die at the father's hands. The woman had not been seen since guards had dragged her limp body away.

Alexa's heart began to throb within her breast. Her body shook. She struggled to contain sobs threatening to overwhelm her. Questions! Angry questions! No! Furious questions! Why? Why? How long? When? When would the pain ever end? So many questions. Never any answers!

Exhausted and discouraged, how could she continue to stand as an example of her faith? Was she a fool to cling to faith in—how was it Bin-Lot had put it—some invisible god? Were pain and deprivation driving her to insanity? To believe all this could be happening with purpose? With the loss of everything and everyone most dear to her, could she be like that young woman? Was she approaching total collapse of faith, heart, and soul? Would she also disappear, becoming merely a faded memory for those oppressed into accepting bitter defeat?

Suddenly, anger rose anew as a boiling, churning tide, its wave crashing through her veins. Her hands tightened into fists, anxious to strike out at the tormentors who had dared to hurt her. As her fury grew, it turned toward Val. How much more could be expected of her? After the brutal, vicious deaths of her parents, had she not pursued her vocation with unwavering devotion? Had she not sacrificed the first great love of her life in blind trust given to her god? Had she not freely accepted the challenges of serving simultaneously as Valkana, mother, and wife without complaint? How much more could a loving god ask of any servant? How was it possible that Val could demand so much more of her after all she had striven to do in his name?

Tears flowed profusely from her eyes. Her throat ached with strangled sobs. Her stomach, empty and pinched, hurt. Overworked muscles burned with pain. Her body had grown thin. Physical weakness added to the spiritual void sucking away at the unwavering faith that had sustained her through a lifetime scarred by unspeakable tragedies. Utter despair stretched evil, nimble fingers to pluck away at threads of the Valkana's dwindling strength.

Tiny spots of light appeared in her line of vision. Strange, she thought. How could there be light when her eyes were squeezed so tightly shut in a room so dark? But surely those were lights. Soft. Glowing. Comforting. Then energy. Gentle. Soothing. Capturing her, cradling her, comforting her within a serene cocoon. Memories. Other sorrows. Other tragedies. Other questions. She had asked the questions before. Unlike now, she had not succumbed to anger. She had prayed. She had believed. She had driven away doubts. She had confronted fears. She had placed total faith in Val. She had received his blessings.

Acknowledging the need to conquer weakness that threatened complete dejection and subsequent defeat, Alexa directed her thoughts toward home. Her spirit journeyed afar, drawn by the power of another's meditations, another's prayers. Smiling at Anlía's beloved face, she saw the crystal pyramid sitting on her daughter's open palm. Faith—fresh and fervent. Alexa's wounded spirit remembered.

Drawing from strength generously shared by her daughter, Alexa recalled how to revive herself by partaking in the source of all power, succor, and strength—Val.

The words, "I love you, Mother," crossed Anlía's lips and traveled great distances to the prisoner's hut in the Sifiq Kingdom.

"I love you, too, my daughter." Alexa finally fell asleep as her lips formed sacred words that echoed into the night.

༄

The upcoming harvest season brought not only change in temperatures but also change in temperaments. Crop prospects were better than they had been in the last three years. Guards enjoyed boisterous spirits, confident they would be rewarded for the notable improvements. Buoyant spirits decreased vigilance. Decreased vigilance provided fresh opportunity.

The priestesses spoke in muted whispers inside their hut. Dissent had swollen outside the boundaries of the farm. Factions had surfaced, declaring themselves at odds with practices forced by government elite. Local people had grown weary of mistreatment and tired of surly soldiers. They sought means to implement change. Some prisoners had established covert communication with others beyond the limits of the vast prison farm. Time swiftly became a critical factor. Bin-Lot soon would send soldiers to guard food supplies for transport to key cities. With harvest ripe and experienced advice from foreigners, dissent began a transformation to action.

"Lady Valkana," Sulía spoke, her voice quietly intense, "all is ready."

Alexa, her expression solemn, nodded. How she detested the loss of life sure to come. Consolation appeared only in confidence that countless lives would be saved in the years ahead. "Sulía, you must never forget to pray. Always remember, too, that losing one's self to the path of war can be too easy. Guide these people toward Val. Always seek peace."

"Milady, you're here to remind us." Sulía began with a smile. Something in Alexa's eyes melted that smile. "I—I don't understand…"

Alexa did smile. "Sulía, this is now your direction, not mine. Val has another path for me to travel."

"But, Lady Valkana, we need you—your wisdom and your experience."

"Sulía, Kiralí has decided to go with you. I shall remain behind with Lisana and Marlí."

Sulía glanced at Kiralí in confusion. "I still don't understand. How can we leave you? You must know what they will do to you."

Lisana and Marlí sat close beside Alexa. Lisana said, "Sulía, our united stance has inspired these people to take control of their lives. Many came here because they tried but didn't know how. We have taught them a different approach and showed them the way to Val. They must travel that road. Your path lies with them."

Sulía shook her head. Brown eyes reflected the depth of her personal conflicts. "They'll take you back to the king! Who knows what may happen! I don't know how to leave you! I can't…"

Alexa leaned forward and took Sulía's trembling hands. "My sister, you know the path before you. You have many reasons for this new direction, including your love for Win-Das."

Sulía's expression showed surprise, unaware that her love for the former Sifiq officer had become so obvious. Still, she should have expected Alexa to know.

Alexa smiled again. "Sulía, I've seen love lighting your eyes as well as his. Val brought him to us for good reasons. Honor dwells within his soul. The two of you must help his people. As for us, we anticipate our return to Atuliq. We choose to follow Val's path for us just as you must follow his path for you."

Sulía dropped her face. She had never anticipated leaving them behind. Much like her father's, her nature was to protect those she loved, no matter the risk, no matter the sacrifice. "How can I just leave you?" she repeated in a distressed whisper.

Alexa squeezed Sulía's hands in reassurance. "Your plans are for tomorrow night. We expect Win-Das here a little later. He wishes to ask you to marry him according to Val's laws. Is that also your wish?"

Tears brimmed in Sulía's eyes when she looked up. "It is my dream, but how…?"

"Remember. Though not as well or as strong as when we arrived, I am still Valkana." Her words had barely escaped when a hushed voice requested permission to enter. All five priestesses turned as Alexa responded. "Come, Win-Das."

Glancing furtively behind him, Win-Das quickly entered and closed the door to the hut. Then, sighing his relief, he sat at Alexa's invitation. Having accepted Val into his heart, he had been trusted with the secret of

Alexa's role as High Priestess Valkana. "Lady Valkana," he began respectfully, glancing briefly at Sulía, "final plans are complete. There remains only one matter—a personal one that I wish to discuss."

Alexa smiled and nodded. "Win-Das, I know already. You and Sulía wish to unite in marriage."

Win-Das reacted without surprise. Ever since that night at the palace, when he had seen her engulfed in glowing light, nothing about her surprised him. He crouched down on the floor beside Sulía and wrapped his hand around hers. "Lady Valkana, I no longer have anything to offer her beyond myself. However, so long as I live, I promise to love her with all that is within me."

Two hours later, Sulía clung to him just before Win-Das sneaked back into the night. During those two hours, the Turandans and Win-Das discussed plans and prayed. Inside that dark, little hut, Alexa performed a whispered ceremony as Win-Das and Sulía exchanged vows of marriage. The path before them promised tremendous hardships. Recalling the beginning of her own marriage to Gregor, Alexa prayed that love would light their way.

Chapter 16

Lisana and Marlí shrank into the corner. Alexa courageously faced the angry Sifiq captain, who demanded information regarding the two missing priestesses. When Alexa repeated that she had no idea where they had gone, the officer struck her with such force that she staggered backward, falling into Lisana's arms. A junior officer jerked her from Lisana's grasp and dragged her back to face his commander. Again and again, the commander demanded to know how Sulía and Kiralí had escaped and where they had gone. Each time, Alexa declared she had no knowledge of their whereabouts. Each time, she received savage blows from the officer.

Finally, with Alexa unable to rise from the floor, the officer ordered the three women chained together pending his unit's return to Atuliq. He began preparing his report regarding the condition in which he had found the prison farm. He detailed the destroyed barracks, the number of dead soldiers, escaped prisoners, and missing priestesses. The army commander dreaded delivering his report and was grateful for the foreign women who would likely bear the brunt of Bin-Lot's fury. The king's reaction would be unpredictable once he learned the extent of the damages in Talafaq, especially the missing harvest and burned buildings.

Aside from shelter from the elements and an end to the harsh trip back, the Turandans felt little sense of relief upon being shoved into a filthy cell inside Atuliq's central prison. Lisana and Marlí grew extremely worried. Already thin and pale, Alexa had grown weaker and sicker after her brutal encounter with the Sifiq commander.

Meager prison fare provided little nutrition to promote healing. Then, unexpectedly, extra bread, dried fruits, and vegetables mysteriously appeared with their meals. The younger priestesses discreetly added some of their portions to Alexa's, hoping that even a little more would aid her recovery. Lisana heaped mounds of straw around Alexa to keep her warm and spent hours holding her head in her lap. Meanwhile, Marlí prayed constantly.

Days muddled together. Neither priestess knew how long they had spent in that dreadful cell when the door finally opened. Silently, four women, including Oui-lest Var, entered. Without speaking, they helped the Turandans up from the floor, wrapped them in blankets, and physically supported them until they reached the warmth of the women's quarters.

When Oui-lest helped Alexa step into hot bath water, her heart filled with anger. Not even false pride could justify the abuse to which the Turandan prisoners had been subjected. Oui-lest reaffirmed an earlier decision, accepting that she could no longer remain silent and submissive while others were treated so mercilessly. Momentarily, she envisioned the helplessness of her own infant daughter, deliberately murdered by an incensed father. Change must occur. While helping Alexa bathe, dry, and dress, Oui-lest silently vowed to become part of that change.

Once her charges had eaten and fallen asleep in clean beds, she began fervent discussions with those under her direction. Prior to the priestesses' exile to Talafaq, Oui-lest had accepted Turand's faith. Before their departure, she had helped nurse Alexa after severe beatings. Risking much, she had also sent extra clothing with the priestesses when they were taken from Atuliq. Learning of their return to the capital, Oui-lest had bribed guards into allowing her to prepare and deliver extra food to the prisoners.

Cruel punishment would certainly result should her actions be discovered. However, having chosen her course, she refused to look back. Instead, she encouraged others to join her.

Five days after being taken to the women's quarters, the priestesses were escorted to the palace. Oui-lest and a group of women chose to serve so they could be present when King Bin-Lot held court. Rumors had bubbled up from every corner. Sympathy, as well as fear, shone in the eyes of every Sifiq female. The king's fury had exploded, and many had already suffered his wrath. Unexpectedly, Bin-Lot ordered the women to leave. They dreaded whatever punishment he intended for the foreigners.

Hours before being led from the women's quarters, Alexa had requested time for private meditations. While in trance, she listened carefully to the voice of Val. His secret words bespoke love and pride that, despite enormous trials, she had remained faithful. His High Priestess Valkana understood his messages and prayed for the fortitude to face whatever lay ahead.

Inside the king's court, Alexa instructed Lisana and Marlí to stand behind her. Somewhat bolstered by decent food and rest, Alexa stood on her own and prayed quietly until King Bin-Lot approached them. The priestesses observed him curiously. His eyes were bloodshot, and his once florid complexion had grown sallow. His broad girth had reduced, and they were faintly aware of a foul, sick odor emanating from his person. However, his mouth remained an ugly line, and his eyes bore cruel, evil light. As he had done months before, he sauntered around them. Every aspect of his posture communicated hatred and contempt for the prisoners before him.

Caustically, he addressed Alexa. "I sent you and your companions to Talafaq hoping that field labor would convince you to acknowledge your place. I expected you to come to appreciate the relative comfort and benefit of returning here to personally serve me. Instead, our commander reports that you organized the destruction of my most productive farm and the murders of valuable soldiers. What I do not understand is why you did not escape with the others."

Alexa, mindful of past encounters, requested permission to speak. Nodding his head contemptuously, Bin-Lot granted her request. "Excellency, I did nothing to your soldiers. Neither did I participate in the destruction that occurred at the farm. It is obvious that my health has deteriorated since I left Atuliq."

Bin-Lot snorted his anger. In a snickering drawl, he found himself unable to resist a twisted barb. "Yes, I do see. You are now hardly fit for any useful purpose a man has for a woman. I rather imagine even that husband of whom you spoke so highly would find you totally repulsive."

Despite her physical weakness, emerald eyes blazed. "Excellency, I assure you that you are mistaken. If my husband were present, you would find his reaction absolutely opposite your expectations."

Bin-Lot, incensed, spat on the floor at her feet. Lifting his hand and snapping his fingers, he signaled to one of his guards and requested a whip. "You still insist on arguing! I have no more patience with such disrespect! It is time that I personally teach you how to behave in my presence."

Marlí and Lisana gasped and stepped forward until Alexa's sharp warning sounded inside their minds. Sifiq officers and soldiers inside the palace court straightened in their seats and leaned forward in anticipation of the king himself wielding the whip against the Turandan leader.

Defiantly, Alexa lifted her chin and glared directly into the king's eyes as he raised the whip. "Perhaps it is time for you to learn a lesson." Abruptly—and totally unexpectedly—her hand shot out as her fingers wrapped tightly around the wrist poised to strike her. Startled gasps and shocked cries echoed inside the court when brilliant blue-white lights pulsated and flashed around Alexa's figure.

"What?" Bin-Lot's eyes bulged as Alexa's aura intensified and expanded. Suddenly, a nauseating lurch assaulted his stomach as his feet lifted from the floor. No one in the hall moved as Alexa hovered nearly six feet above smooth stone tiles without releasing her grasp on the Sifiq king's wrist.

"I told you. Today's lesson is for you. We shall no longer be victims for your sordid behavior. We suggested many times that you release us—that you cease your abuse against us. We endured your punishment. In turn, Val dispatched lessons you ignored. Your abuse now ends. You will send us home."

Dizzily, Bin-Lot glanced toward the floor. Furious beyond anything he had ever experienced, he shut his eyes momentarily before staring at her rebellious expression. "I will do no such thing! The Sifiq king takes no orders from female bitches!"

Fires in Alexa's eyes began to glow so brightly that even her priestesses stared in fearful disbelief. Then, tightening her grasp around the king's wrist, she tilted her head even more defiantly. "The orders given to you come not from female bitches. The command I deliver comes directly from Val."

Bin-Lot again spat in her direction. "Set me down now! Your magic doesn't frighten me! Neither does your imaginary god!"

Light at Alexa's wrist began to fluctuate and broaden. What had been white transformed into vivid flashes of red. Bin-Lot shrieked in agony as steaming vapors rose from where her hand clamped around his arm. Twisting futilely, he cursed and screamed as the reek of his own burning flesh filled his nostrils.

Beneath them, soldiers running to his aid stumbled and fell as the floor tilted and swayed from shuddering tremors beneath Atuliq's palace. Long moments passed before the court grew eerily silent except for Bin-Lot's muffled, agonized groans and sobs.

Again, Alexa spoke, her voice stern. "Our God Val demands our freedom and our return home. What you see now is merely a warning. Your pain and the destruction already accomplished are nothing compared to the punishment you face if you continue your defiance."

Unable to bear the scorching heat transferred by her touch, Bin-Lot glanced toward his prostrate officers before raising enraged eyes to his prisoner. "Then tell your god that I cannot rid the Sifiq Kingdom fast enough of you and your cursed companions. You will be released."

Slowly, Bin-Lot and Alexa descended to the floor as her aura gradually dissipated. Before she released his scorched and blistered arm, she issued a warning. "A reminder, Excellency. None of your officers is to touch us with intent to harm. If they do, or if you reverse your order, you will suffer unimaginable consequences."

Days later, Bin-Lot again faced Alexa in his now deserted court. His lip curled scornfully, but he carefully marshaled his anger. His earlier disastrous confrontation remained fresh and frightening, especially considering the acute, unrelenting pain in his raw and blistered arm. Masking his disdain for her, he said, "A ship now prepares for the voyage to return you to Turand. You depart tomorrow. I have instructed Captain Raf-Zan that you and your companions are to be subjected to no further punishment."

Alexa nodded understanding. "You are aware that several Sifiq women wish to accompany us."

Exhaling heavily to control his reaction, he replied, "I have been informed. There is limited space aboard the warship. As such, only eight can be permitted to leave with you."

Alexa breathed out slowly, not thoroughly convinced that the voyage would occur without further hardship and deprivation. "Then I can only pray that you might learn to better appreciate those women who remain to labor on your behalf."

A bitter retort died before it was born when he once again saw the eerie glow in her eyes.

"And, Excellency, I pray for your sake that your Captain Raf-Zan heeds your command." When she turned to leave, she paused at the sound of his voice.

"I wish Captain Far-Ban had never brought you to set foot in the Sifiq Kingdom." Her response baffled him.

"King Bin-Lot, conversely, I am glad he did."

⌒

Oui-lest offered the tin cup to Alexa, who huddled into the threadbare blankets that did little to ward off the damp chill in the ship's hold. Nodding her thanks before sipping the tepid liquid, Alexa forced a smile. Despite thick shadows barely dispersed by two small oil lamps, this Sifiq woman's beauty was still evident. Her bright blue eyes were intelligent and kind. Golden blonde hair lay in a mass of curls, still very short per Sifiq laws for women. Beyond her gentleness toward Alexa, Oui-lest had demonstrated uncommon courage.

Alexa's eyes swept the confines of the hold. Her Valiria sisters had remained loyal companions and dedicated servants to Val. Along with Oui-lest, seven other Sifiq women had held firm to their decision to depart their homeland. They would accompany the Turandan priestesses who had been released by a king finally forced to confront the rapid erosion of his power in the face of a multitude of overwhelming calamities. Growing opposition from his own people had already jeopardized his rule. His power was further declining in the face of disasters that began with the arrival of those mysterious foreign women and growing more catastrophic each time punishment was meted out against them.

Lisana and Marlí smiled wearily at their Valkana as their thoughts wandered. Although they worried about the two friends left behind, they respected their reasons for staying. And although still apprehensive about this voyage, they were grateful to Val to be en route home.

From the beginning, Alexa had demonstrated steely strength and unshakable will in the face of her captors. After watching Sifiq soldiers murder her guards, Alexa had prayed fervently for the lost soldiers and their families, as well as Sifiq marauders who had violated Turand's shores for the first time in two decades. When moments of despair had driven her to question faith and purpose, Alexa had delved deep and recovered her direction. Now she appeared unspeakably weary and weak.

Not once had Lisana or Marlí witnessed any faltering sign in their Valkana. They had observed no hint of surrender to the constant privations inflicted by Sifiq soldiers. Never had their Valkana ceased efforts to encourage and console them, even when she had been weakest after wicked beatings and months of abuse. On the contrary, in response to their high priestess, their own spirits had continuously rekindled in the presence of her unswerving faith. They now concentrated their shared energies as Alexa's dwindled. Both prayed fervently that Val would bless them all with safe arrival in Turand following more than a year of brutal captivity.

Part 3

Wrath the storm pours upon raging sea.
Thunder exploding its unbridled fury.
Winds screaming and wailing the agony,
Waves crashing within the cacophony.

His heart swells, protesting tragedy.
His soul to hope clings desperately,
His tortured eyes searching endlessly,
His quest tormenting his soul so weary.

Then to the heavens, he lifts his eyes,
Perusing angry, fire-streaked skies.
With faith restored to make him wise,
Regrets ignored, forgiven his lies.

Within the tempest, he walks the shore.
His steps grow heavy, he can go no more,
Yet surrender he learned from long before
Must not win; its beck and call he must ignore.

His ears ring with sounds of crashing seas,
When in the dark, faint light he sees.
His voice calls out, "Dear God, Oh! Please!
With this light pray end my miseries."

His strength prevails 'gainst clutching sands.
He stumbles, falls, grasps those hands.
Humbled, he begs and no longer demands,
For light has returned to its waiting lands.

Yet, in dark of night, he confronts his fear.
Lifeless fingers; no sweet whispers does he hear.
For miracles from God he sends his prayer.
For this time, this loss, his heart cannot bear.

And the storm its great fury does expend,
As on his knees, entreaties he sends.
Fading light, his pleading heart does rend.
On wind-swept shores, his journey ends.

Tempest

Chapter 17

Trego offered Victor a mug of steaming tea. Victor smiled his thanks at the middle-aged fisherman before wrapping icy fingers around the heavy pottery cup. Gratefully, he sipped the sweetened brew while studying the horizon.

"Is it my imagination, or does that sky look odd?"

Trego shrugged. "The breezes hold a sharper chill than usual." Sharply observant blue eyes perused grayish skies with practiced intensity. "It looks like a storm is coming but not for another day or two. You've searched these shores every morning and every evening for almost two weeks now. Whatever you seek must be exceedingly important."

With hot liquid creating a soothing path of warmth from his throat to his stomach, Victor stared into the distance without responding. Alexa was out there. Somewhere. She needed him—his help.

Ever since arriving in Timeri, Victor had returned to the Karanan house in the early morning hours. Quietly tiptoeing up the staircase and sliding into bed, his body had trembled, shaking off damp chills that had invaded his bones during hours spent each night trudging across heavy, wet sands stretching along miles of beach.

Within easy sight of Timeri's towering lighthouse, he had located several cabins, all tightly shut against harsh, northern coastal winters.

Rocky shores boasted various rock outcroppings, several of which might have been Anlía's triangular formation.

What drove him so obsessively to continue his quest? Why did he trust the emotional pleadings of a teenage girl longing for her lost mother? Why could he not believe, as did her father, that she suffered denial of her mother's death? What possessed him to return night after night to search desolate shores?

Each night, discouraged and forlorn, Victor questioned his own sanity. Would he never rid himself of his obsession with Alexa? Had he deluded himself into seeing that momentary shimmer of blue-white light in her pendant? During the wee hours of morning, deep in exhausted sleep, Victor questioned if he had really seen those emerald eyes he loved so dearly. Had her spirit indeed called out to him for help? Or had it been only her ghost, reminding him of the precious love he had lost?

Abruptly, Victor tipped his head back and drained the cup. Then, pulling up the hood of his heavy overcoat, he glanced resolutely at the rugged fisherman he had paid handsomely to accompany him as he renewed his search of Timeri's deserted beaches.

⤶

Furious waves pounded the hull of the Sifiq vessel, tossing it to and fro across the broad Timeri Bay. Jagged bolts of lightning ripped through the skies and flashed like eerie spotlights, revealing powerfully built sailors manning the decks of the wildly bobbing warship. Captain Raf-Zan stood firmly planted at the helm, his dripping, livid face raging more than the storm battering his ship.

Finally, caught in a brief lull in the tempest, he shouted a command. "Bring them up!" He waited, jaw tight, fists clenched. Under his breath, he cursed Bin-Lot's weakness. Still, as a career officer, the captain had sworn himself to unswerving obedience.

When the women arrived on deck, the captain left his command post and strode arrogantly back and forth in front of them. His eyes shone with disgust. "If the decision were mine, every single one of you would be thrown overboard. You are disgusting creatures, not worthy of the effort to bring you to this place. However, our king decreed that you be put ashore here. May you rot in Turand, especially you traitorous trash who dare call yourselves Sifiq."

He gestured toward several burly sailors, indicating that they should place the prisoners into two lifeboats that would be lowered into rough seas. As the women found seats and gripped inside bars securely, the captain ordered a halt to the process.

"You!" he hissed at Alexa. "You stay!"

Tossing a wide noose over her head, he pulled the rope taut to prevent her from entering one of the lifeboats. Lisana and Marlí desperately called out her name and instantly rose from their benches. Losing their balance, they fell heavily when the lifeboat lurched into motion for its descent from the deck toward the roiling waters below.

Caught tight within the noose, Alexa watched in anxious, fearful shock as the boat lowered closer and closer to the water. Her stunned expression intensified when three Sifiq crewmen jumped overboard into the swaying craft just as the second boat cleared the deck. One called out loudly, "We, too, seek freedom! You would destroy us all with blind hatred!"

Infuriated more than ever by the deserters, the captain used the rope to jerk Alexa toward him. "You!" Raf-Zan pointed toward a young sailor and shouted, "Bring two ropes. Loop one around each of her wrists. Remember! Don't touch her. She's possessed!"

Alexa glared at the arrogant captain as the ropes tightly squeezed her wrists. Terror-stricken, she begged Val for delivery from whatever would come next. She desperately sought connection to her god in utter certainty that this captain was determined to inflict horrific punishment upon her.

Grinding his teeth and huffing his disapproval, he walked a slow circle around her. "You! You call yourself a priestess, sworn to good, yet you have nearly succeeded in destroying an entire society with your female deceptions and plotting."

"What do you intend to do with me?" Alexa demanded, her words nearly lost as buffeting winds again began to batter the ship. "Your king commanded that I be returned alive to my homeland."

"That he did, bitch. However, I decide the condition in which you are to arrive. Although our king may not have sufficient courage to deal with you, I do. You will pay for all the havoc and destruction you brought to the Sifiq Kingdom." Icy fury in his eyes made her shiver harder than the chill winds penetrating her thin clothing.

"I warn you, Captain! Don't do this!"

Raf-Zan glanced at the sailor who still held the ropes looped painfully around her slender wrists. "Drag her over there and tie her to the mast!"

Alexa struggled with every remaining bit of strength as the sailor grudgingly obeyed his captain. Within minutes, the front of her body was pressed against the cold, wet hardness of the wooden mast. Her arms had been stretched to encircle the mast's circumference and then tied securely. As she closed her eyes, her lips moved frantically in prayer, pleading for mercy. "Beloved Val, please! Please help me! I beseech you! How much more must I bear?"

White-hot lightning shot fresh, searing explosions across turbulent skies. Deafening roars of thunder drowned out her agonized screams as the captain himself wielded the leather whip that cracked through the air before it slashed against her back and shoulders.

Before he could strike her an eighth time, a massive wave slammed into the side of the ship, knocking everyone off his feet. Whirling winds shrieked and wailed around them. Turand's furiously foaming ocean sent stinging spray and slapping waves to punish the hands on deck. Many Sifiq sailors lost their bravado in the face of a storm that assumed a life of its own—a life seemingly intent on exacting vengeance for the brutal beating inflicted on their helpless prisoner.

The young sailor scrambled across the slippery surface of the deck and, with a razor-sharp knife, sliced through the ropes binding the woman to the post. The back of her simple sheath had been shredded. Flashes of lightning revealed bloody stripes ripped into her flesh.

As the ship leveled briefly, the captain forgot his earlier orders and grabbed her by one arm. "Bitch! I want you off my ship now! I deliver you to your precious Turand. May you be swallowed up by these demon waters!"

Suddenly, Alexa knew only vague awareness of falling—falling. Her mind and soul were captured within a swirling, velvety vacuum that drew her away from biting cold and the agony of the most vicious beating she had yet endured at their hands. A flash of clear awareness lasted no more than a split second. Turand. At last, she had returned home to Turand.

⌐

Since dawn, the storm Trego had predicted two days earlier had raged. Victor, accompanied by the sturdy fisherman, had been unable to walk the beaches for more than an hour that morning, so powerful had been the winds. The skies they saw were darker and more ominous than either had seen in his lifetime. Lightning struck brilliant blows against churning, boiling seas. Barely staying on their feet, the men returned to Trego's house. Totally disheartened, Victor finally surrendered. Then, defeated as much by the storm as by the futility of his search, he left for the Karanan home.

Victor had been poor company during supper with Gregor's godparents. Neither LeAndro nor his wife, Leila, had any idea of the true purpose behind Victor's trip or his stay. After a brief discussion regarding the unusually intense storm raging outside, they quietly finished their supper before retiring to the drawing room. Now, before the blazing warmth of the fireplace, Victor sat in brooding silence.

Leila silently stood and walked to a window facing the direction of the ocean. Pushing aside heavy brocade draperies, she scanned distant skies for any sign that the powerful storm might be waning. Suddenly, a particularly brilliant bolt of lightning ripped through the heavens and lit the horizon more brightly than if the sun were shining.

For a moment, Victor glanced up at Leila. Sighing quietly, she cast him a smile tinged with sadness. "I never used to pay much thought to storms. Now, they only succeed in reminding me of Alexa. Never in my life did I know anyone as fascinated by storms as she was."

Victor slowly lifted his head and stared blankly at Leila. What had she just said? What had he just heard? At first, his brain was too confused—too tired to register any significance in her comment. Still, something in her words bored insistently through the haze enveloping his mind. "Excuse me, Lady Leila. What did you just say?"

She shook her head. "Nothing really important. The storm—it just reminds me of Alexa."

Abruptly, Victor leapt to his feet, his heavy boots thumping loudly against the carpeted floor. "Storms!" he shouted. "Val be praised!"

LeAndro and Leila stared at each other in startled bewilderment as he careened out of the room. Completely baffled, they listened as their front doors slammed shut against the raging tempest outside their home.

"Trego!" Victor shouted, desperately pounding on the door and tugging his coat more tightly around him in useless attempts to ward off viciously whipping winds.

The door to the fisherman's modest home swung open, revealing Trego's shocked face. "Lord Garogan! What in Val's name are you…"

"Hurry, Trego! Grab your coat and get your horse! We haven't a minute to lose!"

Without protest, Trego snatched a wool jacket and a raincoat, dragging them on as he ran outside in a rush. Running down the steps from his front porch, he hurried toward the small barn for his horse. He shot a quick glance in the direction where Victor had already mounted.

With winds howling through the air and waves crashing against the shore, Victor leaned into his mount and rode across weighted sand that sucked at his horse's hooves. Forced to slow his pace, he fought for self-control as well as for breath. When they had ridden for fifteen minutes, Victor pulled back on the reins, slowing his horse to a stop. He raised alert eyes to the top of the lofty tower that was Turand's famous Timeri Lighthouse. Its light burned, steady and bright, defying violent forces of nature that had swept Turand's beaches into a state of frenzy.

Victor nudged his horse forward just as the lighthouse beacon circled around to illuminate the debris-littered beach stretching before him. That light bounced as it reflected off the windows of a small bungalow just a short distance from the shoreline. A craggy rock formation jutted out of the ground and reached past the shore into usually shallow waters.

Victor halted, his breath catching in his throat. The Timeri beacon continued its slow rotation, leaving the beach before him in darkness. Vigilant eyes scanned the distance. For a stunned moment, he was sure his heart stopped beating. Just beyond the top of the rocks, he glimpsed the faintest shimmer of light—no more than a barely visible bluish-white mist that, to him, was as brilliant as summer sunshine.

"Alexa!" Her name escaped his lips in a desperate cry as he jumped from his horse and ran in the direction of the light, slipping and sliding as he scrambled over piles of slick rocks. As he stumbled around the edge of the rock formation, his heart felt ready to explode. His boots sank into thick, wet sand that slowed his headlong rush toward the motionless body lying on the beach.

"Alexa!" he cried out, falling to his knees. "Alexa! Sweetest! I'm here! I came!" As he leaned forward, her face turned to him, and her eyelids lifted. For a moment, her gaze was blank, nearly lifeless. Then, with lips blue from cold, she weakly smiled.

Conscious thought escaped Victor as he wrapped his arms around her frail body. He clutched her close against him. Huge sobs wrenched from the depths of his being, shaking him violently as he held her.

"Lord Garogan!"

Victor's eyes flew open, seeking the voice that had burst through the night and penetrated his brain.

"Lord Garogan! She's freezing! We must get her out of this cold!"

Trego shouted to be heard above the storm while ripping off his rain-coat and peeling away the dry, warmer coat he wore beneath. Tossing the coat to Victor, Trego turned to run toward the deserted cabin and kicked the front door open.

Victor moved feverishly to wrap Alexa in the fisherman's coat. Then, as he lifted her from the sand, her agonized scream pierced his heart as surely as a dagger's thrust. Carefully, he cradled her in his arms and rushed toward the cabin, confident that she would die if she remained outside much longer.

Inside the cabin, Trego had already lit a lantern and immediately bus-ied himself with shoving a meager stock of wood into a stove and building a fire to ward off damp, penetrating cold. Victor stood in the center of the room for only moments, quickly assessing the dim interior. There was a small cot to the left of the stove where he carried Alexa. Taking great care, he laid her down at the end of the bed and then shed his dripping overcoat to allow more freedom of movement.

Trego, familiar with the cabin belonging to one of his fishing companions, made sure the fire had started in the belly of the iron stove. Quickly clanking the door shut, he then hurried toward a large cabinet. Jerking open the doors, Trego removed several blankets, rushing to cover the bed with one clean blanket while Victor held the woman.

Stacking the remaining covers on the end of the bed, Trego ignored baffling questions racing through his mind. This mystery woman must surely be the reason behind Lord Garogan's strange traipses along Timeri's extensive beaches. With no idea of the woman's identity, the fisherman could only wonder how Lord Garogan had known they would eventually succeed in such a bizarre quest. Trego's gruff voice finally broke the silence. "Lord Garogan, I'll go for my wagon. You stay with her until I return."

Victor looked up from the bed where he had so gently placed Alexa's limp body. "Trego, hurry," he urged. "Hurry with all that is in you. Bring more blankets. And pillows, too."

"I will, my lord. Whoever she is, she's extremely fortunate that we found her when we did."

Victor's eyelids dropped closed, unsuccessfully battling scorching tears. "Trego, you must hurry. Your mission is now sacred. You go to save the life of your queen."

Trego's mouth dropped open in disbelief. "What?" Without another word, the fisherman turned and bolted from the cabin, stopping only long enough to secure the door against invasion of cold, whistling winds.

With Trego gone, Victor turned complete attention to Alexa. He spoke to her, his voice low and intense. "Alexa? Sweetest, listen to me. Alexa, can you hear me?"

Almost as if the task exceeded every possibility, she lifted heavy eyelids. The image in front of her face was fuzzy and unclear in the dim lamplight. Breathing hurt almost as much as the searing agony on her back. She resisted waking, desiring only escape and return to the dark void that held no pain. However, the insistence in that vaguely familiar voice refused to allow her retreat.

Desperately, Victor chafed her hands between his own, coaxing blood to circulate into icy fingers. "Alexa, it's Victor. I came, Alexa. I came for you, Sweetest." His voice vibrated, fear woven into every word. "Alexa, please! Don't leave me again, Sweetest! I cannot bear it! Alexa!"

Reluctantly, she opened her eyes. Pleading desperation in that voice insinuated itself beyond the hazy borders of her mind and pierced into her receding consciousness, calling her back. Emerald green eyes that had been dull and lifeless sparked with sudden recognition and near disbelief. "Victor?"

She reached out to him, seeking reassurance that she had not awakened from yet another empty dream. Pressing her face snugly against his chest, she weakly sobbed his name again and again. Although he clutched her tightly, even the pain in her back faded from immediate awareness. Within the circle of Victor's arms, her entire being was swept with flooding relief that she was no longer a prisoner.

Victor fought tears, feeling how very much she needed his strength. Never in all the years he had known her could he have imagined Alexa as she was now. More appalling than her terrible thinness was the weakness of the energy he had always associated with her presence. Victor felt himself filling up with the almost tangible hurt pouring from her. His heart throbbed, trapped between his joy of finding her and the terrible fear generated by the fragility of the shivering woman he held so lovingly.

Without conscious thought, his hands moved up to her cheeks, tilting her face until he could kiss lips that, despite her condition, still held power to move all that existed within him. The part of her that had known so much loneliness and despair responded. Neither was capable of conscious question. Victor sought reconnection to the single love of his life, while Alexa discovered confirmation in his kiss that her delivery from the Sifiq was indeed reality.

Regaining his senses, Victor became suddenly aware of how hard her body trembled. Dragging his lips from hers, he struggled to speak. "Sweetest, you're soaked. We must get you out of these wet clothes."

With tears streaking through salty, sandy grit on her face, she only nodded, sensing her strength diminishing. She allowed Victor to help her slide to the edge of the bed. With his hands firmly grasping her upper arms, he helped her to sit. After gently removing the fisherman's coat from her shoulders, he began pulling her drenched sheath up her legs. He waited patiently as she weakly shifted her weight so they could pull the fabric above her hips. He stopped abruptly when she screamed out and jerked forward just as he had begun to slide the dress upward to remove it.

His face instantly transformed into a frightened grimace. "Sweetest, what? I'm sorry. What?"

With her teeth chattering violently against cold and excruciatingly sharp pain, she could barely answer. "Victor, my back… My back…"

He shifted his position and pulled her closer to discover what had prompted her cries. His stomach lurched in horrified, sickened dismay upon seeing her back, covered with wet sand stained crimson by blood oozing from open slashes in her flesh. "Oh, holy Val! My sweet Alexa," he gasped before forcing himself to speak to her in a soothing voice.

Quickly, he straightened and fumbled in his pocket until he pulled out the sharp knife he always carried. "Sweetest, lean forward and hold me tight. I promise to be as gentle as I can." With her head pressed tightly against his stomach, Victor began loosening the strips of shredded fabric that clung tightly to her skin. Swiftly, he worked at slipping his knife beneath the strips, slicing through them and flicking away clinging sand. With each flick of his knife and with each pitiful sob that escaped her, he battled swelling, ferocious anger.

Finally, he succeeded in removing the wet fabric and cleaned whatever he could from her back. Standing, he quickly shed his bulky knit sweater and removed the smoothly woven linen shirt beneath. Gently pulling his shirt over her head, Victor wrapped her once again in the fisherman's jacket. After putting his sweater back on, he shoved the ragged remains of her dress along with the sand-covered blanket onto the floor at her feet.

With swift efficiency, he laid out a fresh blanket and sat on the bed, his back against the cold wall. Carefully positioning Alexa on his lap and then holding her snugly, Victor covered them with the last clean blanket. Praying silently, he begged Val to bring Trego swiftly back.

Time crawled. Victor pushed from his mind everything except Alexa's presence in his arms. Her uncontrollable shaking finally slowed, as did the chattering of her teeth. As she rested against his warmth, he felt her body slowly begin to relax. He lowered his face, allowing his cheek to rest against the top of her head.

Part of Victor pleaded unceasingly with Val to expedite Trego's return. Another part of him almost wished never to move from this spot, this moment. Alexa, his dearest love, had returned. For those few moments, Victor submerged himself, diving through waters of time to another place that existed in the long ago—a time and place where she again belonged to him just as he would always belong to her.

When the door finally opened, Victor tucked his fingers gently beneath her chin and lifted her face. Feeling safe and warmer in the secure haven of his presence, she had drifted into light sleep. When her eyelids fluttered and finally opened, evergreen irises were glazed, reflecting intense pain and the critical nature of her weakened condition.

"Lord Garogan, how is she?" Trego inquired quietly, his sun-wizened face drawn into worried lines. He was much like other loyal Turandans. His king and queen had earned special places of esteem within the hearts of their people. Hardly a Turandan citizen lived who could not find some way their lives had been impacted by their monarchs.

Victor shook his head slowly. "Trego, she's very sick. Worse than that, someone has beaten her. Viciously." His voice choked as a fresh wave of tears burned his eyes.

"Let me help you. My wife and daughter wait for us. They'll know best what to do."

With exceptional care, the two men managed to move her from Victor's lap until he could stand. Alexa, thoroughly exhausted, could do little more than whimper when Victor lifted her into his arms. He kept her snugly wrapped in Trego's coat and then carried her from the cabin, jostling her as little as possible. Trego had already climbed into the back of the box-shaped wagon and carefully removed Alexa from Victor's arms, settling her into a mound of blankets warmed by a pan of hot coals.

Victor climbed in with her for the trip back to Trego's home. He leaned back against the wagon's sidewall. Alexa lay on her side and rested her head on his thigh. He held her shoulder as firmly as he dared when the wagon lurched forward into motion.

Victor breathed a prayer of gratitude that the storm's fury had finally abated. The trip back would certainly proceed more quickly without pummeling rains and whipping winds to delay their progress. His thankfulness grew to encompass the blessing of having found people as reliable and decent as Trego and his family. Their help would be crucial in preventing Alexa's condition from worsening.

Again, his attention focused on the woman nestled within the mountain of blankets Trego had brought. Beneath the light of a small lantern suspended from the wagon's roof, he stared downward at her. For the first time, he noticed that her once long hair now barely reached past her jawline. Lovingly, he combed his fingers in and out of wet curls that clung to her cheeks and forehead. For no more than a second, she turned her face upward and smiled. His heart contracted. Her smile was still as beautiful as he remembered.

After a trip that seemed to have lasted a lifetime, the wagon rolled to a stop. Alexa's mind struggled, awash in a seemingly infinite sea of confusion. She was aware of Victor and another man carefully sliding her, still nestled within her blankets, to the end of the wagon. She heard women's voices as the men carried her in from the cold.

Inside, she wondered for a moment if she might have died. Her body reacted to velvet warmth she had not known in a very long time. Lights were bright, almost blinding to sensitive eyes. Colorful, cheery mementos of a loving family created an inviting and appealing ambiance. Wonderful aromas of typical Turandan foods drifted in the air, making her mouth water. Hands were everywhere, stroking hair from her face, holding her hands, tucking blankets around her, or supporting her head so she could drink from a cup filled with hot tea. Unaccustomed comfort surrounded her, and her head nodded as she drifted toward beckoning unconsciousness.

"Alexa? Alexa, please. You must stay awake. Alexa?"

Exerting extreme effort, Alexa forced her eyes to stay open. Focusing, she saw Victor's face close to hers as he knelt by her side. Golden-brown eyes held so much fear. She stretched out a hand and stroked his cheek. "Please don't worry so."

Victor's head dropped, his lips pressed tightly together as he sought to control his emotions. No matter what she had endured or how sick she was, his sweet Alexa never changed. Finally trusting himself to look back into her eyes, he smiled. "Alexa, listen. We're in the home of Trego Sochino. His wife and daughter have prepared a warm bath for you. You must be strong, Sweetest. Right now, more than ever. We must cleanse your back to avoid infection."

Squeezing her eyes tightly shut, she grimaced. After several anxious seconds, she nodded. Even as he spoke, she felt salt burning and sand grinding inside her torn flesh. Preparing herself for this newest ordeal, Alexa took solace in the fact that the hands now ready to bring her pain were loving hands seeking to begin the process of healing. Supporting herself on one elbow, she smiled shakily at Victor. "I understand. It's all right." She breathed heavily, her lungs feeling full and congested. "Victor, first, you must listen."

His voice was tender as he reached out to rest his palm against her face. "What is it, Sweetest?"

She swallowed with difficulty, her throat sore and scratchy. "Victor, the others. They need help, too."

"Others? What others?" he asked in surprise.

"Lisana and Marlí. And the Sifiq women who came home with us." Her eyes grew intense, shining with a reviving sense of purpose.

"Sifiq women? Alexa, what in Val's name are you saying?"

She whimpered softly, biting at her lower lip. "Where do you think I've been all this time? Anyway, that doesn't matter right now. The others were put off the ship in two lifeboats. Please, Victor, help them. Please."

Closing his eyes against an unwelcome invasion of remembered hatred, Victor sucked in a deep breath. Rising to his feet, he turned to Trego. "You must get help. Go back to the beaches. Search for any sign of the others. Trego, I promise compensation to you and any of your neighbors who go with you."

As Trego disappeared again into the dark, stormy night, Victor returned to Alexa's side, helping her sit up. Fearful of the grating pain in her back, she refused to let him carry her again. Instead, she leaned heavily against his sturdy body as he slowly led her into the bath where Lizia Sochino awaited her.

Left in the care of Lizia and her teenage daughter, Alexa sat on a padded stool as the women removed Victor's shirt. Lizia gasped at the sight of gashes encrusted with sand where Alexa had apparently collapsed onto her back on the beach. Immediately recognizing the daunting task at hand, Lizia left Alexa in her daughter's care and went to bring in a metal tub usually used for laundry.

Out in the kitchen, Victor waited. Lizia gently touched his shoulder. When he turned to face her, she was instantly struck by the solemnity reflected in his eyes. Deep worry obviously swelled from the depths of his soul. "Lord Garogan, we need your help. It will take both my daughter and me to clean her back. As weak as she is, we need someone to hold her up and support her."

Fresh concern crossed Victor's face. "What do you want me to do?"

"I just took in a large washtub. We can help her get into it. I already put in a stool so she can sit. As soon as we cover her with towels, I would like for you to come in so she can lean against you. Lord Garogan, this won't be easy for her. We'll have to pour water over her back to flush away the sand."

Victor nodded, dreading the need to subject her to this newest torture. Still, he recognized the necessity of cleansing her wounds. Wordlessly, he proceeded to shed his sweater, leaving him in his woolen undershirt.

Once Victor arrived inside the bath, Alexa gazed into his face, her eyes clearly reflecting intense anxiety. Victor leaned slightly forward over the edge of the tub, letting Alexa wrap her arms tightly around his waist as she braced herself. When the first pitcher of warm water flowed down her back, carrying with it sand and grit, she stiffened, unable to check the tears that surged forth with the pain.

Victor had never felt so completely helpless, knowing there was nothing he could do to ease her suffering. Without conscious thought, he raised his hands to press her cheek tightly against his chest. Meanwhile, Alexa's muffled sobs sliced into his heart. Quietly, he initiated a soothing, continuous monologue, intent on diverting her attention from the excruciating process so gently tended by the Sochino women.

"Alexa, Sweetest, I know it hurts. Think of something else. Alexa, keep your eyes closed." Victor squeezed his own eyes tightly shut and swallowed hard. "Alexa, try to picture Gregor. Remember how he looks. Tomorrow, I'll send for him. You know he'll come the instant he knows you're here. Just think about Gregor coming for you. Before you know it, he'll be here, and then we can take you home—home to Toraval to be with your children."

He felt her stiffen sharply, crying out as Lizia plucked a sharp sliver of broken shell that had lodged into one of the gashes. The intensity in his voice swelled. "Alexa! Think of Gregor. Think of all the good that's coming. You can't imagine how much he still loves you. We all do, Sweetest. Please." Victor began to cry even as he continued his non-stop words meant to draw her attention from the pain.

For a time, it seemed the cleansing would never end. Lizia and her daughter patiently worked at their task, drawing fresh water and pouring it down her back so that its flow carried away salt, dirt, and debris embedded in open wounds. They gently dabbed and wiped, plucking tiny shards of shell stuck into her flesh. Finally, when they worried she might collapse, the streams of water flowed clear, although still tinted red with blood.

The women then prepared a warm, shallow bath. With Victor's assistance, they helped her step into the tub. Alexa, weak and nearly drained of energy, sat motionless as the two women bathed her, washing salt and grit from her face, her hair, and the rest of her body. When they finished, they wrapped her hair in a towel and supported her firmly as she stepped out onto a colorful, loomed rug.

With tender attentiveness, the women bandaged her back with large pads cut and formed from clean sheets. When Alexa sat on the stool again, Lizia pulled a soft, flannel gown over her head and wrapped her in a thick robe while her daughter slipped woolen socks onto their patient's feet.

Very slowly, the three emerged from the bath. When Victor glanced up, he smiled through a film of tears. Although deathly pale and frightfully thin, her eyes held a faint glow, and her lips spread into a feeble smile. Drawing in a shaky breath, she reached out to him. As he pulled her into a cautious embrace, Victor praised Val yet again.

Later, after convincing her to take some broth and drink a little hot milk, Victor helped her lie down to rest. Alexa had begged to be allowed to sleep on the floor in front of the hearth. She had complained that the very core of her bones remained half-frozen. Lizia, honored by the unique opportunity to nurse Turand's beloved Valkana in her own home, obligingly dragged a mattress from a spare room and prepared the bed where Alexa would sleep.

Unable to bring himself to leave her side, Victor stayed with Alexa. He dozed on and off with his back against the couch they had dragged closer to the fire. Victor frequently woke through the night to check on the woman who now slept quietly, once again using his lap for her pillow.

Chapter 18

Reluctantly arousing from a deep sleep, Alexa's mind was disoriented as she attempted to remember where she was. Warmth surrounding her was deliciously comforting. The sensation curled itself around her and invited her to resist the need to awaken. With a start, she realized she wasn't alone. Too quickly, she tried to sit up, crying out against what felt like thousands of needles jabbing all at once into her back. Instantly, Victor's eyes flew open. Carefully supporting her head while he moved away from her, he then slid a pillow beneath her face.

Involuntary tears swam in her eyes when she saw him, illuminated by early morning sunshine that peeked through the windows. Smiling at the same time she tried not to cry, Alexa whispered, "I thought I only dreamed of you last night."

Kneeling by her side and stroking her cheek, he returned her smile. "I'm too big to be a dream, but since we're talking about dreams, I think you look like a dream come true."

She pressed her lips tightly together and, unable to repress the silly little smile that escaped, tried to joke despite the burning pain in her back. "I imagine I look more like a nightmare."

As the Sochino household stirred to the life of a new day, Alexa found herself immersed in a rush of feelings that vividly reminded her why she had missed her people so much. Even in the home of strangers, she had been received with loving compassion and the natural, deep-rooted desire to alleviate her obvious suffering. She sincerely believed it would have made no difference had she been someone other than queen and Valkana. The hearts and souls of these people were filled with decency and kindness.

Through the blur of tears and pain, Alexa perched on the edge of a chair while she sipped the honey-sweetened richness of freshly brewed Raija tea. Slowly, she ate from a bowl of hot cereal flavored with preserved fruits. Each taste reinforced the growing sense of reality that Val had finally brought her home to Turand. Finishing as much breakfast as she could, she gazed over to where Victor stood across the room in earnest conversation with Trego, who had just come home.

When he glanced in her direction and saw her watching him, Victor quickly approached and sat beside her. Curling his fingers around her hands, Victor bent his head and kissed her fingertips. He hardly knew what to say, so great was his happiness at simply being in her presence.

Finally looking up at her, Victor smiled. "You'll be happy to know that Trego and his friends found your companions and some Sifiq sailors. All seem very anxious to begin new lives here. They're safe now."

Alexa closed her eyes and whispered a fervent prayer of thanksgiving. There was powerful solace in the knowledge that her suffering had not been in vain and that her example had inspired and touched other lives. Weakly, she nodded.

"Alexa, Trego has his wagon ready. LeAndro and Leila are in winter residence here in Timeri. We're going to take you to their house." Expecting happiness in her reaction, he frowned at shadows crossing her face. Her face mirrored worry that only mushroomed as he noted the dark circles beneath her eyes and the pallor dulling her complexion.

"How far?" How long will it take?" She obviously dreaded another bumpy ride in the wagon.

Gently, he tucked hair from one side of her face behind her ear. "In the wagon, less than an hour. Sweetest, we must go. There are good physicians in the city who can better treat your injuries. Plus, I must dispatch a courier to a certain king I know."

The mere thought of her husband prompted silent tears that crept down her cheeks. "Gregor," she whispered softly. "Oh, Victor, I've missed him so much."

Victor nodded without reply. For that moment at the very least, every shred of hatred and antagonism he had ever felt for Gregor vanished. Alexa was finally safe, and if Gregor was the one she needed to ensure her recovery, Victor vowed to do everything in his power to summon her husband to her side.

Taking her outside and lifting her into the wagon proved an exhausting and agonizing effort for them all. Her body's weakened defenses had already permitted the first signs of infection to appear around the seeping slits across her back. Every time someone touched her back, she cried out in agony, involuntary floods streaming forth no matter how hard she tried to check her tears. Finally settling her inside the wagon, Victor climbed inside with her and Lizia, making themselves as comfortable as possible. Then, with his daughter beside him on the driver's seat, Trego began the trip toward the outskirts of Timeri and the Karanan manor.

Alexa slipped into the kind of deep sleep known only to the very sick. Victor felt grateful that yesterday's storm had drifted back out to sea, allowing the trip to progress faster than it would have otherwise. When they arrived, he climbed out and raced up wide front steps to the brick manor house, bursting through the front doors.

"Lord LeAndro! Lady Leila!" he shouted out, his voice urgent. "Where are you? I need help!"

Lady Leila hurried out of the kitchen and through a corridor into the foyer, where Victor breathlessly waited. Seeing him, she was startled more by the desperate expression on his face than by the breathless, pleading tone in his voice. "Victor, calm yourself! Whatever is wrong?"

LeAndro appeared from upstairs just as Victor plunged into a rapid stream of instructions. "Lady Leila, have someone start brewing Raija. And get a room ready—one attached to a bath. We need pillows and blankets. Lots of them. And bandages, too. Big ones. And hurry! Send for the nearest physician!"

"Victor," Leila repeated, deliberately keeping her voice quiet. "Calm yourself. What are you talking about?"

Victor stopped abruptly and stared at her long enough to heave a deep breath into his lungs. An enormous sob burst forth, wrenched from the very core of his being. "Lady Leila, hurry! Please! It's Alexa! I found her! She's outside."

The Karanan household exploded into a whirlwind of activity. Within seconds, the entire household staff knew that Lord Garogan had found their queen alive. Once everyone had launched into tasks to swiftly prepare for their injured queen, the Karanans hurriedly followed Victor outside. With painstaking care and aid from the Sochino family, Victor soon held Alexa securely in his arms.

Disturbed from sleep by a sense of motion and the sounds of anxious voices, Alexa opened her eyes. She saw the softly lined face of Gregor's godmother. "Mamina?" she whispered faintly. "Is it really you?"

With tears sparkling in her darkened blue eyes, Lady Leila forced a smile as she began stroking her fingers through Alexa's hair. "Yes, child, I'm really here."

Lord LeAndro, standing close by his wife's side, grasped Alexa's frail hand. "We're both here, Alexa, and we'll all take care of you until Gregor comes." His words shook, not from advancing age but from overwhelming emotions.

Alexa responded with a feeble smile, pulling LeAndro closer to her. "Tell Gregor to hurry," she mumbled, her eyelids drooping as she drifted back into the welcoming void of sleep.

Thunderous pounding jolted Stefan from deep sleep. Waking sufficiently to realize that the demanding racket echoed from downstairs, he slid out of bed and tugged on his robe. Rushing from his bedchamber with Adrina following close at his heels, he arrived at the spacious entrance of his private home just as a drowsy servant dragged open the front door.

"I must speak with Sir Stefan immediately," the voice outside insisted. "The matter is of extreme urgency."

"Pravano? What in the world?" Adrina called out, recognizing the voice of a man who had spent years in service to the Garogan family.

"Lady Adrina!" he responded, his voice strident despite near-exhaustion following a five-day ride that he had made in four. "Lord Garogan has sent a dispatch. He said to deliver it with utmost haste directly to Sir Stefan."

Leaving Pravano with the servant, Adrina hurried into the family parlor and lit two lamps. Stefan swiftly followed her, breaking the wax seal and sliding his finger beneath the envelope flap. Adrina watched her husband's face closely, her heart beginning to pound as she observed his changing expression as he read the letter.

Shaking his head back and forth, Stefan exclaimed in disbelief. "Almighty Val, I don't believe it. I don't believe it!"

Adrina grabbed Stefan's arm and shook him impatiently. "Stefan, tell me. Victor? Is he all right?"

When Stefan finally looked up at her, his astonishment was apparent. He opened his mouth as if to say something but only shook his head instead, looking completely bewildered.

"Stefan!" Adrina almost shouted at him. "What does it say?"

Recovering his senses, Stefan folded the letter and shoved it back into its envelope. He then threw his arms around Adrina in an excited hug, pausing to kiss her briefly. Pulling away and seeing her startled reaction, he grinned before planting a swift second kiss on her lips. "Quickly, Adrina! I must go to the palace. Help me get dressed."

"Stefan, tell me! What's going on?" she begged, following as he ran up the staircase.

Pausing only a moment, he turned slightly to look at his wife. "Alexa! Victor found her. She's alive!"

⌣

Gregor rolled over in bed, trying to ignore the insistent rap at his door. In a sleepy daze, he finally tossed his blankets aside, dragged himself from bed, and stumbled toward the door of his suite. The sight of Stefan in the doorway shocked him awake. "Stefan! What in Val's name? What time is it?"

Stefan pushed past Gregor and strode straight to a private secretary, where he lit a lamp. "One thirty in the morning, and I dare say you'll sleep no more tonight. This dispatch just arrived. Read it."

Baffled by the expression on Stefan's face, Gregor took the proffered envelope and sat down at the desk. Then, blinking away sleep, he removed the letter within, unfolded the paper, and began to read.

Stefan, my brother,

This letter bears with it great reason to rejoice. You must immediately take it and go to the palace. Tell Gregor that I am in Timeri and reside as guest at the manor of Lord Karanan.

Timeri was struck yesterday morning with a frightfully tremendous storm that raged well into the night. Heeding the voices of memory and of our cherished Anlía, I found myself searching deserted beaches. I thank Val with all my being that I listened to those voices.

Tell Gregor that, lying on the sand, I discovered the woman we both love more than our own lives. Stefan, tell him she needs her husband now more than ever before. Tell him to come without delay. Her condition is dreadful, Stefan, and I fear for her life. Tell Gregor to send Valiria at once.

Stefan, you must also dispatch an additional regiment of the king's soldiers. I am unsure what may lie ahead. It was our old enemy, the Sifiq, who took Alexa from us yet, oddly enough, have brought her back home.

You must also tell Adrina, the children, and everyone else to pray for Alexa's recovery. Her condition is indeed most grave. And, my brother, pray in thanksgiving that Val has already listened to the prayers of our people. Our Alexa has finally come home to us.

Victor

Stefan observed as Gregor read and reread the letter. His breathing grew more rapid with each line. The paper shook violently in his hands as Gregor stared at words that shattered the icy block of grief he had carried with him for more than a year. His eyelids blinked slowly and then closed as he drew in a shuddering breath, only to expel it in prayerful exclamation. "Dearest Val above, be praised!"

Gregor rose quickly, joyfully accepting the embrace Stefan offered. Their arms contracted tightly as both men exchanged the brotherly love that bound them so closely.

"Stefan, I must leave immediately," Gregor announced, striding toward an enormous armoire for clothes.

"I already sent word to the captain of your guard to assemble a small escort to accompany you. I also issued instructions to begin preparations to dispatch soldiers immediately."

Gregor glanced up at Stefan with an expression of intense appreciation. For the moment, he found speech too difficult, so great was the onslaught of joy mixed with a fresh kind of fear. Then, at last, he managed to find words. "Will you also summon Tirstan?" Hurrying to dress, he lifted eyes that shone with renewed admiration. He could only marvel at how well Stefan knew him upon being informed that Tirstan should be waiting downstairs to lead the king's escort.

Nikolai, a light sleeper, had awakened at the sound of knocking at his father's door. Arising in time to watch Stefan hurriedly disappear from the corridor, Nikolai stepped just inside his father's suite, dark eyes full of questions. "Father, why was Stefan here? It's almost two in the morning. Is something wrong?"

Gregor looked up, his face serious. "Nikolai, come in. Close the door, my son." Once Nikolai had entered, Gregor continued, "I'm leaving for Timeri as soon as I pack a few things." Hardly trusting himself to speak, Gregor pointed toward Victor's letter. "Read for yourself."

Nikolai glanced at the page lying open on the secretary. As the prince read Victor's message, he felt tears prick his own eyes. "Mother," he whispered. "Alive." Turning to his father, it was impossible to conceal the smile that transformed his handsome, young face. "I'm going with you, Father."

Gregor looked up from his task without stopping. He shook his head. "No, Nikolai, I need you here."

"But, Father..." Nikolai began to protest, still clutching Victor's letter.

"Listen to me, Nikolai. I need you here. I'm departing with only a small escort. Your godfather's messenger made the trip in four days. I intend to make better time going. I want you to pack clothing for your mother and me and then send them with soldiers preparing to leave later today. You must also dispatch a message to Zinzan requesting Valiria to leave at once for Timeri."

"Father, Tirani is already here. She arrived yesterday. Shall I send her?"

Gregor's head shot up. "Tirani? With General Council, I didn't expect her until next month."

Nikolai's index finger touched his sister's name where Victor had written it. "Anlía sent for her. Two weeks ago."

Gregor glanced up for only a second. "That child." Pausing for only a matter of seconds, he continued, "Nikolai, work closely with Stefan until I send word. According to Victor's letter, your mother's condition is critical." He stumbled over the words. "Depending on how I find her, I may want you to lead an escort to bring your brothers and sisters. I don't know yet. As you read, there may also be a threat from the Sifiq." Gregor's hands never slowed as he rapidly folded enough clothing to last for no more than a week.

"Father, may I ask a question?" Nikolai's voice took on a different note, momentarily drawing Gregor's attention from his packing.

"Of course."

"Father, something has always puzzled me but now more so than ever."

Gregor's left eyebrow lifted in question at the slight tremor he detected in Nikolai's comment. "Explain," he said, resuming his task.

"I always wondered why Victor never married and why he always seemed so blindly devoted to Mother. Exactly what did he mean when he wrote that he had found the one woman that you both love more than life?"

Gregor's head shot up again, and he abruptly stopped packing. Sucking in his breath, he recalled Victor's words and recognized the folly of allowing Nikolai to read the letter. The moment had come for him to face past shame that he would have preferred to forget. Walking toward Nikolai, he gripped his son's upper arms. Gazing into dark, inquiring eyes, Gregor realized there was no way to avoid the truth.

"Before I say a word, I want you to remember when we talked before your birthday. I told you then that there were many truths you would need to know one day. I ask your confidence regarding what I'm going to tell you until we have more time to discuss the matter in detail."

Nikolai studied his father's worried countenance, concerned by the anxiety etched into every feature. "I promise to keep confidential anything you say."

Gregor swallowed and gazed deeply into his son's eyes. "Nikolai, the times just before your mother and I married were extremely complicated. The Sifiq were tightening their grip of cruelty on our people. Complicating matters even further, many believed I was cooperating with the Sifiq, unaware that Stefan and I were plotting our own strategy to end their bloody scourge. At the same time, a revolutionary movement had gained momentum. The movement centered primarily in the south. I haven't time to go into all the details right now, but Victor was one of the rebel leaders."

"Father, I know all that, but..."

"Nikolai, how I hope your mother will live to help me explain this."

Gregor's expression clouded, and tears overflowed as he spoke aloud his greatest fear—that he might not reach her in time. Thrusting the thought from his mind, he continued, "Nikolai, what I am going to tell you is, in one way, the greatest personal shame I have ever known. However, in saying that and knowing what I now know, I would do nothing differently if I had it to do over again."

"What are you trying to say?" Nikolai sensed his father's distress and felt uneasy in the face of the confidence his father was preparing to share.

Gregor turned away from his son and walked toward the window. Pushing aside the curtains, he looked out over the square where his escort was assembling. He closed his eyes against the rush of memories. "When I met your mother, she was betrothed to Victor Garogan."

"What!" Nikolai's startled exclamation held undeniable shock. "Mother? Betrothed to Victor? Father! That can't be true!"

Gregor turned back to face Nikolai. "I haven't enough time to explain everything now. Briefly, Victor was imprisoned at Zenox, awaiting execution. In short, your mother came to Toraval as a Valiria priestess to plead for clemency."

Nikolai shuffled over to a chair and sat down, visibly shaken.

"I granted your mother's request." Gregor paused, going over to close the travel bag where he had placed his garments. "In exchange for Victor's freedom, your mother agreed to marry me."

Nikolai stared in outright disbelief at his father, certain he must have misunderstood. "Father, are you saying that you forced Mother to marry you? I—I don't understand. I always thought you two were so happy together."

Gregor walked to his son's side and rested a large hand on his shoulder. "Nikolai, I love your mother. Beyond everything else in this world, I love her. If I survived this past year, it's only because of the years of love she gave me and because of you and your brothers and sisters. Your mother always insisted that Val brought us together in the strangest of ways. We shall discuss this further when I return. Please, Nikolai, I can only ask for your trust and that you not judge me too harshly until you know the whole truth. I want to say goodbye to the others so I can go to her. She needs me—just as I have always needed her."

Stunned, Nikolai gazed into his father's face, seeing both lines of worry and fear creasing his brow. Confusion stemming from his father's unexpected revelation exploded into myriad questions he felt desperate to ask. Still, his mother lay suffering far away. Only one clear thought came to the forefront of his mind. His parents loved one another. That much he believed.

Nikolai stood and removed the travel pack from his father's hands. "I'll carry this down for you."

Gregor's face reflected terrible concern. "Nikolai, if you feel the need, speak with Stefan and Adrina. For now, just know that I love you."

Nikolai forced a smile. "Father, go. Don't worry about me. Mother needs you."

Leaving his suite, Gregor stopped for a matter of seconds to pray for the blessing of returning to this private refuge with Alexa. His steps then carried him straight to Anlía's room. Carefully, so as not to startle her, he sat on the edge of her bed. Fresh tears tracked down his cheeks as he caressed his daughter's face.

She turned toward him and lifted sleep-heavy eyelids, smiling drowsily. "Father? Do you need something?"

Gregor leaned forward and drew her into his arms, holding her tightly.

Slowly, she returned his embrace, her sleepy brain confused by her father's unexpected gesture. Suddenly, her mind awoke, and Anlía leaned away from him. A slow smile spread her mouth as she sensed confirmation of her dreams. She discovered validation in the sparkling tears and unsteady smile on her father's face.

"Mother? Victor found her?"

Gregor nodded, speaking in a trembling voice. "I'm leaving now, Anlía. Victor wrote that she's... Your mother's..."

Anlía grasped her father's hand and held it to her lips. "It's all right, Father. I know already. Let me get up." She climbed out of bed and hurried to an armoire in her dressing room. When she returned, she carried a travel pack. "Here are some things Mother may need."

She placed the pack beside him and turned to the night table beside her bed. She picked up the carved wooden box her father had given her and removed her mother's crystal pyramid pendant, now suspended from a heavy, braided, gold chain. She turned back to him and lifted the chain over his head before tucking it beneath his uniform jacket.

"Take this to her, Father. And don't take it off until you get there. As long as you wear it, she'll feel you coming. It will help her until you arrive."

Speechless, Gregor embraced Anlía yet again, marveling anew at the blessing of this daughter he had deeply longed for so many years earlier.

A short while later, following tearful explanations to his younger children, Gregor hurried down the broad marble staircase to where his escort waited with Stefan, Nikolai, and Tirstan. Gregor approached Tirstan first, understanding from the brief shake of Stefan's head that no one in the escort had been informed of the reason for the mission they prepared to undertake in the early morning hours preceding dawn.

"Your Majesty," Tirstan greeted, inclining his head respectfully.

"Captain," Gregor began, recalling Tirstan's anguish following the funeral for Alexa's guards, "are you ready for an extremely arduous ride?"

Tirstan looked at him without comprehension before responding firmly. "Sire, I am sworn to serve. I undertake my duty without reservation."

"Very well, Captain. Our journey will be trying. I can assure you that I shall permit little time for rest and no slacking in our pace. Upon reaching our destination, I shall expect you to resume your assignment as Captain of the Queen's Royal Guard."

Tirstan shook his head quickly, not quite understanding the king. "Excuse me, Sire?"

"We leave immediately for Timeri. My wife has been found there. Alive."

With no further discussion, Tirstan immediately assumed command of the king's escort and ran outside to the waiting horses, carrying the king's travel packs himself.

Gregor turned back toward Stefan and Nikolai. "Pray that our trip goes swiftly and unimpeded. Most importantly, pray for Alexa." He then gazed into Nikolai's somber brown eyes. "I leave you to fulfill my duties during my absence. Stefan will assist you. And, Nikolai, remember. Your father loves you."

Gregor then spun toward the front doors of the palace, the heels of his boots clicking in rapid rhythm against polished marble floors. Outside, he quickly adjusted his horse's bridle and saddle before mounting. For a brief moment, he placed his right hand over the two crystal pyramids now tucked against his chest. "Alexa, my beloved, wait. Please wait for me. I'm coming."

He then glanced quickly around at Tirstan and the four others in his escort. "Gentlemen, we ride."

Chapter 19

Oui-lest carried a cup of tea and offered it to Victor, who had spent the night in a chair by Alexa's side. Too weary to say much, he only smiled his thanks. He sipped from the cup before setting it aside on the night table. Slowly, he dragged himself out of the chair, taking time to stretch uncomfortable kinks from his muscles.

Gently, he took Oui-lest's arm and guided her from the room where Alexa now dozed. He wanted to avoid disturbing her with conversation. Outside in the corridor, Victor said in a low voice, "She had a terrible night. I think the infection is worsening. She finally fell asleep only an hour ago."

Oui-lest's face reflected grim sadness. "She doesn't deserve this." Looking into Victor's hazel eyes, she tried to smile reassuringly. "You also need to rest. Why don't you go to bed? I'll stay with her."

Victor gazed at Oui-lest's lovely face, framed by short, golden curls. Such an odd feeling he had, entrusting Alexa to the care of this Sifiq woman. Still, he was tired to the bone, and Alexa had confided how much Oui-lest had risked by helping her and the other Valiria. Sighing, Victor reluctantly surrendered to exhaustion. "You'll come for me immediately if she gets worse or if she asks for me?"

Oui-lest nodded in response. "Of course."

Later, just before midday, Victor awoke with a start. Leaping from bed, he tugged on shirt and trousers and ran barefooted into Alexa's room. Her screams had awakened him. As he arrived in her room, he saw that Lady Leila and Oui-lest were trying to calm her as the Karanan's physician attempted to gently wipe away thick, yellow pus seeping from several ugly, infected stripes on Alexa's back.

Victor rushed to her bedside as the women moved aside. Dropping heavily onto his knees, he gazed into Alexa's dark green eyes filled with tears as she lay face-down while her back was cleaned and covered with fresh dressings. "Sweetest, you must believe me," he soothed, his voice still shaking following his frightening awakening. "You must be strong for just a little longer. You'll see. Gregor's coming, and I've asked him to send Valiria to help you."

She wept so hard she could barely speak. "Victor, I hurt so much. I don't think this pain will ever go away." She bit into her lower lip, trying to stop crying.

Victor stroked damp hair from her forehead. Sensitive fingertips registered the heat of raging fever. "Alexa, the doctor is almost finished. After that, you can rest."

"You won't leave me, will you?" she whispered.

"Of course not. When have I ever left when you needed me?" He continued stroking his fingers across her forehead, his caresses soothing her.

"Victor, how long?" she whispered, her eyes begging something from him that he could not give.

"Alexa, the messenger left five days ago. It can't be much longer. I expect no more than five days. Pravano is one of the best horsemen I know. And you know better than I that Gregor will push with all his might to come to you."

She trembled and drew in a shaky breath. "I'm so afraid, Victor."

"Of what, Sweetest? Tell me." Victor spoke to her tenderly, as if she were a small, frightened child.

"I'm afraid I won't live to see him again. Or my children."

Victor exchanged anxious glances with Lady Leila. He closed his eyes for mere seconds, suppressing tears that sprang forth so readily. When he spoke again, his voice conveyed confidence he did not feel. "Alexa, listen to me. You are stronger than any one of us here right now. Sweetest, draw from that incredible faith of yours. You cannot think about dying. You must believe that you will live. We need you, Alexa. I need you. Lord LeAndro and Lady Leila need you. Your children, too. Alexa, no one needs you more than Gregor does. You must live for Gregor. Fight, Alexa, as you've never fought before. Pray, Sweetest, and I'll pray with you."

Then, just as he had done many years earlier when she had lain in his arms, pregnant and suffering heat sickness, he prayed Val's ancient prayer for the sick. For the first time in his life, he fervently wished that Gregor could be with them, joining them in the prayer now being whispered by every person in the room.

At supper that evening, the atmosphere filled with gloom. Victor had left her under the watchful care of a maid so he could join the Karanans at the dinner table. He ate mechanically, his mind so concentrated on Alexa's deteriorating condition that he barely tasted his food.

"You're not really thinking of taking her out, are you?" Lord Karanan asked, worried that Victor might relinquish and give in to Alexa's pleas to be taken to Timeri's sacred chapel.

Victor lifted his gaze to meet LeAndro's. "I don't know," he sighed. "I'd give anything that Gregor could be here. That kind of decision is one he should make."

Leila nodded in agreement, her face somber and sad. "Just as I would give anything that the Valiria General Council weren't taking place right now. Lisana and Marlí are much too sick to help."

Victor's face was grim. "Lady Leila, you've done a remarkable job turning your guest house into a temporary hospital. The Sifiq women are all nearly recovered. The Valiria have simply been mistreated too long to recover as quickly."

Oui-lest squeezed her eyes tightly shut, ashamed by what her people had inflicted on the Turandan priestesses. Victor saw her pained expression and reached out his hand to cover hers. "You mustn't blame yourself. Alexa said none of them would have survived had it not been for you. For that, we are all grateful."

Unaccustomed to receiving praise from a man, her lips quivered in a shy smile. "She helped me in ways I cannot begin to explain. When I see how much all of you …" she stammered, unable to complete her thought.

Leila rose and, going to Oui-lest, placed her arms around the young woman's shoulders. "We all love her for the same reasons you do. When our lives were dark and desperate, she inspired us to rely on our faith in Val. She taught us how to open ourselves to receive his strength. Alexa never let us forget, and she always encouraged us. The time has come for us to do the same for her. Personally, I'm glad you're here, Oui-lest. You are living reminder that Val's light can come from any darkness if only we let it."

Once supper ended, Victor spoke quietly to LeAndro. "If she sleeps no better than last night or today, I intend to ask the doctor to administer a sedative in the morning. She needs rest if she's ever going to recover."

LeAndro agreed. "I'll speak with him as soon as he arrives tomorrow. I think you should try to sleep a while now."

Victor lifted his eyes heavenward, glad for the four hours of sleep he had managed earlier in the day. "I will. When Gregor comes. Until then, I don't know how I can leave her."

Well aware of the past, LeAndro had developed newfound respect for his godson's former enemy. He hoped his pity didn't show too plainly. "This must be torture for you."

Victor clenched his teeth and swallowed before allowing himself to speak. "Torture or not, I can't let her give up. With all my heart, I believe she'll start to improve once Gregor arrives. I've already lost her too many times in my lifetime. To lose her this time—like this…" He strangled on words he couldn't finish.

LeAndro patted his back and then watched as Victor, determined to maintain another nightlong vigil, turned to climb the stairs.

Upstairs, Victor reclined into the chair where he had spent several nights watching over her. Sometimes, when Alexa had been awake and lucid, they quietly conversed. Discussing anything and everything, they attempted to distract her from the burning pain created by the brutal flogging and the biting bits of sand and salt that continued to grind agonizingly into raw, infected flesh. Other times, when she cried or grew delirious with pain and fever, he sat on the edge of the bed, stroking her hair or holding her hands while maintaining fervent monologues of encouraging words. During those rare periods when exhaustion claimed her in fitful sleep, he pulled the chair close enough to hold onto her hand while he snatched a few moments of rest for himself.

The following morning, Victor wearily descended the stairs, weighed down by the burden of heavy spirits and growing apprehension. He had left Lady Leila and Oui-lest with Alexa, the two women begging and pleading as they coaxed Alexa to eat a little and sip spoonfuls of fortifying Raija tea. He joined LeAndro and Doctor Zilondo in the foyer.

The elderly doctor's solemn face showed that he, too, was growing more concerned. "Lord Garogan," he greeted.

Victor only nodded his head in response. "She had another terrible night. That damned fever is draining every ounce of her strength. We can barely convince her to drink, let alone eat." His voice trailed off, his mind too weary to continue.

"That is what Lord Karanan and I were just discussing. After I check her back, I intend to administer a heavy sedative. Hopefully, that will help her sleep through the rest of the day and most of the night. Someone should stay with her."

"Someone is with her day and night," LeAndro informed him.

Victor left them and went to the kitchen, staying only long enough to gobble down some cheese and fruit before returning upstairs. When he arrived, Alexa lay sideways against a mountain of pillows and cushions. Lady Leila patiently wiped tears from her face. Victor's heart felt ready to break for the thousandth time. Alexa's face was deathly pale, and her eyes were dull and sunken. Upon seeing him, she feebly reached for him.

"Victor," she whispered fearfully, "the doctor wants to sedate me. I'm afraid. Gregor—I feel him coming closer. What if I go to sleep and don't wake up?"

As Leila moved away, Victor sat on the edge of the bed and, taking a fresh cloth, tenderly stroked more tears from her face. He breathed in deeply, searching for ways to console her. "Alexa, you'll never get better if you don't rest. The sedative will only help you sleep so that your body can begin to heal."

"But, Victor…"

He understood her fears. Compounding those fears were infection and pain. The subsequent deprivation of sleep created a combination rendering her nearly incapable of rational thought. Somehow, he knew he needed to allay her anxieties. "Alexa, do you trust me? Do you really trust me?"

She barely managed to nod her head once.

"Then you know I would rather die than let anyone do anything that might hurt you. Please let the doctor give you the sedative."

Beginning to weep piteously, she stopped pushing away the medicine the doctor had tried to give her. Once the medicine worked its wonders and her eyelids grew heavy, she squeezed Victor's hand. In a voice so hushed that those around her strained to hear, she begged them, "If something happens—tell Gregor—tell him—I tried. If I die—tell him—how much I love him."

Victor watched as she finally drifted off to sleep. Slowly rising, he arranged the blankets around her. Bending over, he kissed her forehead. Then, except for a servant who would stay with her, they all left so that she could rest undisturbed.

Outside the room, Victor clutched the doctor's arm, preventing him from leaving. "How long can we expect her to sleep?"

The doctor looked directly into Victor's tired, blood-shot eyes. "I gave her enough to make her sleep through the afternoon and well into the night. However, considering her condition…"

Victor released the doctor's arm and shook his hand.

"You must summon me immediately if anything changes. But, for now, I suggest you try to get some sleep while you can. You're exhausted."

Victor half-smiled into the doctor's kind eyes. He would try to sleep a little. He knew, however, that he would never truly rest unless Alexa started to recover.

⌒

Winter sunshine spilled into the room through brocade drapes opened at arched windows on either side of the enormous oak-trimmed fireplace. Warmly finished wood floors showed beyond the fringed edges of a burgundy carpet. A sofa covered with cream-colored brocade faced the fireplace and was flanked on both ends by matching easy chairs.

After sleeping several hours, Victor checked in on Alexa before descending to the first floor to join the others for midday. Oui-lest, who was staying in the main house, sat on the sofa beside Victor. Her face was lowered as she stared at her hands folded in her lap. When she glanced up at him, her expression was plaintive. "I wonder how I will ever grow accustomed to the way you Turandan men treat your women."

Victor had listened for nearly half an hour as the Sifiq woman shared some of her thoughts and impressions following a week in Turand. His smile was sympathetic. "I have little doubt you will find that kindness and respect will soon alleviate your concerns."

Looking at him, her hands trembled ever-so-slightly. She felt amazed already by the ease with which she conversed with him. Still, she wondered how she could ever free herself from a lifetime of subservience. "You say that," she responded at last, "but you haven't spent your entire life being drilled never to look at a man directly in the eyes. Or never to speak without permission."

Victor smiled again, his features kind and thoughtful. "You seem comfortable enough talking with me."

It was her turn to smile, a reaction so easy that it quite surprised her. Breathing in, she nodded slightly. "I have no idea why. Perhaps it's because of the way you are with Alexa. Until this week, I swear to you that part of me never really believed men could ever treat women the way Alexa described. Seeing you with her exceeds my comprehension."

"Turandan character and beliefs aside, you must understand that I've known Alexa all her life. We've always been very close."

Oui-lest rose and walked toward a window. Her hands shook more noticeably. "Lord Garogan, before we arrived here, all I knew was that she was a priestess. None of us ever knew. You cannot imagine my shock when I learned that she is also Turand's queen."

"Does that change the way you feel about her?"

Oui-lest turned slowly toward him. Large blue eyes were luminous as they thoughtfully gazed at him. "I'm not certain. I think I respect her more, knowing that she never behaved as I might have expected from royalty. Men in the Sifiq Kingdom are arrogant enough. Nobility is especially obnoxious."

Victor studied her face, perceiving fearful uncertainty lying just beneath the surface. "I believe more than that troubles you."

She dropped her face and stared at the floor. "After all that happened and, considering how badly Alexa has been mistreated, I'm terrified."

Victor arose and went to stand by her. "Terrified? Of what?"

"Not what. Whom. If her husband loves her as much as I have heard, how do I face him? What will he think of me? And the others? How can he not blame us for the terrible way she was treated considering that, no matter what, we are Sifiq?"

Victor resisted his natural inclination to take her hands, knowing how she still struggled with physical touch so natural among Turandans. "Oui-lest, when our king learns all you did to help Alexa and the others, I promise you'll find such fears are completely without foundation."

Suddenly, the clatter of horses' hooves on the brick drive outside drew Victor's attention. Peering out the window, he observed riders rapidly approaching the house. "Praise Val!" He spun on his heel, pausing long enough to give Oui-lest a reassuring smile. "You will see very shortly that your worries are groundless. Our king is arriving. Excuse me."

Victor called out to his hosts as he bolted from the drawing room and through the foyer. Not even bothering to don a coat, he rushed outside. Gregor had already dismounted and turned his reins over to one of the Karanan's stable hands.

"Praise Val that you've arrived so quickly!" Victor greeted, extending his hand. "How in the world did you get here so fast?"

With hands still clad in black leather gauntlets, Gregor firmly grasped Victor's proffered hand with both of his. "Nothing less than sheer determination." He stopped and inhaled to calm himself. "Victor, how is she?"

Victor's eyes darkened, and he closed them for a tense moment before forcing himself to meet Gregor's waiting gaze. Then, shaking his head, he replied, "Her condition has worsened. I've been terribly afraid that—that she might not live long enough for you to arrive."

Gregor's face blanched. Burgeoning tension drew his features taut. "Take me to her."

Turning toward the house, they saw LeAndro and Leila already waited for them in the doorway. Gregor rapidly climbed the steps leading to the entrance, stopping to embrace both of his godparents before they entered together. Standing inside the foyer, Leila grasped Gregor's arm while Victor attempted to prepare Gregor for impending shock. With each detail regarding Alexa's condition, Gregor's brow furrowed more deeply, his dark eyes mirroring sorrow far worse than he had anticipated.

Abruptly, their discussion was interrupted by frantic calls from the servant who had been watching over Alexa. "Lady Karanan! Lord Garogan! Hurry! Summon the doctor at once! The queen is suffering a seizure!"

Side by side, Gregor and Victor bounded up the broad staircase, leaving the Karanans behind to send for the physician. Bursting into the bedchamber, both men's hearts pounded with near panic. Oui-lest, who had come to check on Alexa after Victor went outside, shot them a desperate look. Her efforts were utterly ineffective as she struggled with Alexa's wildly flailing arms and legs. Then, quickly, she stepped away from the bed as Gregor ran to his wife's side.

"Gregor! Quickly!" Victor barked out. "Grab her hands while I hold her legs! Those wounds on her back are going to open even more if she doesn't stop!"

Gregor sank heavily onto the bed, his hands swiftly grasping Alexa's within a firm grip. From the moment he touched her, she began to quiet. Instantly recognizing the effect of his presence, he slid closer to her, grasping her upper arms and pulling her upward against his chest. In response to his touch, her legs ceased their erratic kicking, and her arms relaxed, falling limply to her sides.

Holding her now fragile body for the first time in more than a year, Gregor's head dropped, and he placed quivering lips against her soaking wet hair. His whispering voice seemed to penetrate far into the depths of her drugged, unconscious mind.

"Shush, my love. Shush. Alexa, I'm here now. I won't leave you, beloved. I've come..." Amid a string of loving endearments, he began to weep so hard that he could scarcely avoid choking on words meant to reach and calm her heart. Without conscious thought, he began rocking her back and forth, slowly, rhythmically.

He lost any concept of how much time elapsed before a hand on his shoulder drew him back into awareness. He glanced up, seeing his godmother's gentle face. "Mamina." He choked back a single sob.

"Gregor, hold her until we rearrange the pillows. Then I want you to carefully settle her on her side."

Only his expression indicated his comprehension. Leila and Oui-lest rapidly put the pillows back in order and straightened blankets that her thrashing had twisted into knots.

Carefully lowering her onto the pillows, Gregor saw her clearly for the first time since entering the room. His heart ached abominably. He could scarcely believe that the frail, waif-like being before him was the same vibrant woman with whom he had shared so many years of his life.

Reaching out with his right hand, he caressed her cheek, flushed scarlet by the fever ravaging her body. He tucked a strand of her hair between his middle and index fingers, sliding them down along the entire length of the damp tress that stopped just past her jawline. Leaning forward, he planted tender kisses upon eyelids that had not yet opened to him and against fever-hot lips that remained still and silent. Straightening, he lifted her hands to his lips. As he touched kisses against her fingers, cherished images of those hands filled his mind. Gregor remembered their gentleness as they had cared for his children, their strength as they had applied themselves to aiding others, and their fiery touch as they had always delivered such intimate pleasures. For long minutes, it seemed his very soul began to revive in an ocean of memories, dreams, and fresh hope, the heart of which was formed by his love for this woman, his wife.

Disturbing his momentary lapse, he felt someone touch his wrist. Looking sideways, he saw yet again his godmother's kind face. "Gregor, the doctor has arrived. You must move aside so he can examine Alexa."

Reluctantly, Gregor released her hands, gently laying them on the bed. When he rose to his feet, Leila grasped his arm and guided him out of the doctor's way. Victor and Oui-lest had also remained in the room. All held silent their thoughts while they watched the doctor complete his examination.

Once finished, the doctor led them all outside into the wide hallway. His face showed sympathy for those who waited so impatiently. Grimly, he shook his head. "Obviously, her condition is critical. Still, her heartbeat is relatively strong. I cannot say exactly what triggered this apparent seizure, but I believe fever to be the cause."

"Doctor, is there nothing we can do?" Gregor inquired desperately, his trembling voice revealing the intensity of his anxiety.

"Spoon feed her tiny amounts of water. Keep cool towels on her head. Pray."

Solemnly watching LeAndro and Leila accompany the doctor back downstairs, Victor laid a firm hand on Gregor's upper arm. "He's wrong. I know Alexa too well. That was no simple seizure."

Gregor spun to stare at him. "What do you think it was?"

Victor gazed directly into the blackness of Gregor's eyes, wondering for a fleeting moment what it was that Alexa saw when she looked into them. "You."

Seeing his startled reaction, Victor continued, "She sensed your presence. She was fighting the sedative, trying to reach you."

"Do you honestly believe that?" Gregor asked incredulously.

"I know it. You saw as well as I how she quieted the instant you touched her. She was reacting to your presence. I told you when I wrote. She needs you."

Gregor's eyes fluttered closed, and he inhaled deeply. "I came as quickly as I could." In truth, he had pushed himself and his escort to the very limits of their endurance. An unfathomable love had driven him relentlessly as he struggled to subdue guilt and near resentment that he had not been in Timeri when she first came ashore.

Victor's voice interrupted Gregor's private thoughts. "For a week now, I've watched Alexa deteriorate. When we left that room, her face was peaceful for the first time since I found her." Victor paused, unable to restrain the voicing of his next thought. "No matter what frictions have ever existed between us, I am forever grateful that you came so quickly. She can now find the will to live."

Still resting on Gregor's arm, Victor's hand squeezed tightly for a moment. Then, without another word, he strode through the corridor, down the stairs, and outside.

～

Hours later, Leila entered the room where Alexa still lay peacefully asleep. Gregor dozed in the armchair positioned close beside her bedside so he could hold her hand within his. Affectionately, Leila brushed his hair back from the side of his face with fingers still elegant despite her advanced years. "Gregor?" she whispered.

Tired eyes opened slowly. Seeing his godmother's face, he arched his brow in unspoken question.

263

"Gregor," she repeated quietly, "supper will be ready in about an hour. Alexa has slept since the doctor left. I brought Olga, our housekeeper, to stay with her. I want you to come downstairs long enough to eat a decent meal."

Gregor ran a hand across his eyes in a weary gesture. Part of him resisted leaving Alexa's side. However, he had eaten nothing since a light breakfast. Now, his head was beginning to throb. Besides that, he wanted to wash quickly and change from travel clothes he had worn the past two days. Finally responding to his godmother's gentle insistence, he forced a smile and tiredly pushed himself from the chair. Pausing, he leaned over and kissed his wife's forehead. "I love you, Alexa. I won't be far away."

In the drawing room downstairs, Gregor stood by the ornately carved mantle and gazed into dancing, golden flames. Bathing and changing into clean clothing had refreshed him. He now waited for supper in the company of Victor, Oui-lest, and his godparents. Feeling heartbroken and as if his soul remained still upstairs, he spoke little.

Conversation centered on some of what was known of the priestesses' captivity. Victor discussed a few of the experiences Alexa had shared with him before her condition had worsened. Oui-lest confirmed some of the incidents, adding details from her own perspective. Gregor's stance alone revealed how heavily his worries weighed on him. Still, anxious to learn everything possible related to Alexa's abduction, he managed to listen attentively.

Upstairs, a single lamp shed soft light. Alexa breathed in deeply several times, focusing her spiritual energies, directing them into limbs preferring to remain in their drug-induced state of rest. Her eyelids fluttered several times before she was able to force them to remain open. She saw Leila's housekeeper seated near the light and bent over a large hoop holding colorful needlework.

"Olga?" Her voice was hoarse, barely loud enough to be heard.

"Your Majesty!" Olga exclaimed quietly, laying aside her needlework. "Olga, please help me up. I need to go into the bathroom."

"Your Majesty, let me…"

Alexa shook her head firmly, her mind clearing enough to let her perceive the older woman's thoughts even before they were voiced. "No, I don't want you to call for help. I want you to help me."

Moments later, Alexa leaned heavily against the stout woman as they made their way into the adjoining bath. With personal needs addressed, Alexa shuffled to the marble basin of an ornate vanity stand with Olga's aid. Waiting for Olga to fill the colorfully painted porcelain bowl with cool water, Alexa washed her hands and face. She then took a crystal cup and, with shaking hands, waited for the housekeeper to fill it with fresh water and add a few drops of clean-tasting mouthwash. After rinsing her mouth, Alexa felt better just ridding herself of the dry, bitter taste left by the sedative she had drunk that morning. Seeing a brush, her feeble fingers wrapped around its carved, wooden handle. Barely able to lift her arm, Alexa found herself too weak even to brush her own hair.

"Here, Milady," Olga said kindly, pulling a vanity chair up so Alexa could sit. Then, carefully, the woman used the brush to bring order to the queen's waving tresses. Meanwhile, Alexa closed her eyes, relishing the simple pleasure of the woman's attentive touch. When the task was complete, Alexa felt stronger despite painful, needle-sharp prickles burning inside the stripes marring her back.

Returning to the bedroom, Alexa breathed in slowly and smiled, suddenly certain she had felt his touch—that she had heard the muffled sound of his voice. Now, with every breath, she detected faint traces of his presence lingering in the room. "Olga, my husband was here, wasn't he?"

A sweet smile softened the older woman's round face. "He stayed with you most of the afternoon. He's gone downstairs to dine with the others. Let me get him for you."

"No, Olga." Alexa shook her head emphatically. "Fetch me a robe. I wish to go downstairs."

"Oh, no, Milady! You mustn't! You're much too weak!"

Alexa interrupted her. "Olga, I wish to go to my husband. Are you refusing to offer assistance to your queen?"

Olga stammered, appraising the queen's expression. She saw a face rosy with fever as yet unbroken. However, she also observed the steely resolve and single-minded determination that all Turand associated with its priestess-queen. Instantly recognizing the uselessness of arguing, Olga yielded.

By the time they reached the bottom of the stairs, Olga marveled at the queen's unexpected strength that increased with each step closer to voices drifting through open double doors leading to the front drawing room. She watched as the queen paused, lifting her head to listen more carefully.

Alexa expelled a shuddering sigh when the cherished resonance of her husband's voice reached her ears. She rejoiced in the glorious sound that she once believed she would never live to hear again. With energy reserves she never knew existed, Alexa straightened her back and approached the parlor on unsteady legs.

"I can only believe her faith in Val sustained her all this time." Victor's voice was hushed and reflectively serious.

"I never saw anyone suffer the way she did without losing all hope. What amazes me most is that she never surrendered to anything my people did to her. Not the intimidation. Not forced labor. Especially not the beatings. She always sought good in things around her. She always encouraged the rest of us." Oui-lest's eyes held a faraway look, her voice a slight tremor.

Without shifting his attention from the flames, Gregor pensively remarked, "My wife always taught us that if we search for good because we believe it exists, we will surely find that good. I can honestly say that, for me, Alexa is the greatest good I have ever known. At this moment, there's nothing I would not give just to be able to look into her eyes and tell her how much I believe that."

"Gregor." Victor's voice was quiet but just sharp enough to garner Gregor's attention, causing him to look up and around.

Just inside the doorway, Alexa stood, open hands slightly outstretched. Her lips curved into a trembling, slightly hesitant smile. Emerald eyes, filled with love flowing from her soul, spilled rivers of tears down flushed cheeks. "Gregor?"

Losing all sense of the others' presence, Gregor quickly sidestepped around furniture and rushed toward his wife. Making no effort to check his emotions, he cried with her, his tears freely mingling with hers. Having never forgotten their special place, his huge hands lifted to cradle her cheeks between their gentle strength. Lips that had been lonely too long sought to touch every part of that beloved face he had missed with physical pain.

Words poured forth in a voice saturated by a flood of powerful feelings. "Alexa," he murmured. "Alexa, my love, I've missed you so much. Alexa. My beloved Alexa. How can I ever tell you how lonely I've been? Alexa, I love you. Alexa…" Almost frantically, he kissed her between every uttered phrase of love that escaped his lips.

Her lips trembled as she closed her eyes to fully savor the warmth of his touch. She covered his hands with her own, turning her face to place delicate kisses against his palms. Swallowing against a sob, she whispered fervently, "Hold me, Gregor. Please hold me."

He pressed his forehead firmly downward against hers. "Beloved, I can't. Your back…"

"Please, Gregor. I never thought to—I've dreamed of this for so long. All I want is to feel myself wrapped in your arms again. Please, Gregor," she began sobbing piteously. "Please, my love."

Unable to find it within himself to deny her anything, Gregor carefully reached around her, enfolding her as gently as he could within arms aching to press her snugly and securely against the entire length of his powerful, protective body.

"Tighter, Gregor. Hold me tighter. Let me feel you close," she begged.

He responded to her request, feeling her face press tightly against his chest. Her body began to quake against his as she finally surrendered to the intense agonies she had borne over the past year. Locked within the protective haven of his embrace, she no longer needed to be an example for those reliant on her. No need existed for her to provide a living symbol of her god. Just as she had been at the beach with Victor, she was simply a woman, tired and suffering great pain. Reunited with Gregor, she had rediscovered the solace and refuge of her husband's presence. Safe in his arms, she sobbed out months of intense agony, bitter loneliness, and wretched sadness. Simultaneously, she reveled in the fulfillment of her most precious dream.

Time seemingly stood still as he whispered to her of love that had never dimmed and of inexpressible joy at having her restored to his life. She listened intently to his voice, clinging to every word that penetrated her with healing effect. The familiar beat of his heart soothed and reassured her. Lights, sounds, the room, and even the people in that room existed on a plane far removed from their consciousness as the boundaries of their private world were formed by Gregor's body while he held her securely within his embrace.

Leila moved closer to her own husband, leaning against him as tears filled her eyes. LeAndro gripped his wife's hand tightly and raised it to his lips. They both loved Gregor as if he were one of their own sons. To see him regain the happiness lost with Alexa's disappearance brought them unimaginable joy.

Oui-lest's eyes grew wider than ever as she gazed toward Gregor and Alexa. Never could she have imagined the existence of such a bond between a man and woman. Neither had she ever dreamed of witnessing such an uninhibited demonstration of love unfolding before her eyes. She felt like laughing and crying at the same time. Yet she remained motionless, transfixed by the living image of the love Turand considered legendary.

Oui-lest's attention shifted toward Victor as he rose from the end of the sofa. Momentarily, she wondered if she had only imagined the fleeting expression of bleak desolation that was quickly replaced by what she could only describe as solemn, resolute acceptance. Comprehension of Turandans' open display of emotion was challenging enough for her. Victor, especially, perplexed her with his unparalleled devotion to Alexa. Her confusion deepened with her vague perception of a tightly managed barrier between Victor and the king. She studied Victor intently as he approached the reunited couple and placed a hand on Gregor's shoulder.

Wordlessly, Victor turned and inclined his head toward Oui-lest, then to the Karanans. As they all rose to leave, Leila's quiet voice interrupted for only a moment as she whispered to Gregor that she would hold supper a little longer.

Hearing the glass-paned double doors click shut, Gregor struggled for some semblance of composure. Cautiously keeping his elbow bent to avoid pressure against her back, he gingerly rested his hand at the side of Alexa's waist. His tall body provided necessary support as, with her slight weight leaning against his side, they slowly walked toward the sofa. When he began to help her lower onto the couch, he felt her fingers loosely grip his wrist. Looking down into emerald eyes still glistening with teardrops, he smiled tenderly. "What is it you want, my love?"

She blinked once, a tiny smile playing at the corners of her mouth as she relished one of so many precious moments when their love allowed them to communicate with few words. In a quiet voice, she answered, "May I sit on your lap—the way I used to?"

Smiling tenderly, Gregor settled his enormous frame into a corner of the sofa before holding Alexa as she lowered herself onto his legs. Patiently, he waited while she adjusted her body and gingerly rested her back against his arm and the padded side of the sofa. Then, closing his eyes, he breathed in and savored her closeness with each of his senses as she finally relaxed against him.

Only crackling flames inside the fireplace disturbed the peaceful quiet. Alexa's cheek rested against her husband's broad chest. She listened contentedly to the unfaltering rhythm of his heartbeat. Her right hand lay open upon his chest, satisfying her desire to touch as much of him as possible all at once. Gregor's hand cupped the side of her face, the tips of his long fingers repeatedly caressing her temple. His full lips rested against the crown of her head. Over and over, he murmured her name and how very much he loved her.

"Gregor." LeAndro's voice was hushed when he finally drew their attention from each other back into the present. "Supper is ready. You should eat something."

Gregor tucked his fingertips beneath Alexa's chin and tilted her face upward. His expression revealed intense adoration. "Do you feel up to joining us? I would feel so much better if you would try to eat a little."

The gentle pleading in his voice trickled through her spirit, caressing chords of her soul into life as fresh and tender as the first buds of spring peeking at the sun through a late winter dusting of snowflakes. Swallowing and unable to speak, she only nodded. Gregor was here— now—with her. For him, no matter how acute the pain, she would strive for recovery. With him by her side, life once again held promises of laughter and happiness.

With LeAndro's assistance, Gregor placed his hands securely around Alexa's waist and lifted her to her feet, taking great care with her back. Both men braced her as she swayed dizzily. Patiently, they walked slowly as tiny, halting steps carried her toward the dining room. Everyone stood and waited until Gregor guided his wife to the nearest chair.

"Alexa, sit, and we shall pray."

Firmly, she shook her head. She stretched her arms out to each side, joining hands with Gregor on her left and Lady Leila on her right. Although still sunken and lackluster, her eyes revealed the return of her fierce determination. "I shall pray with you all in our tradition that I have sorely missed."

With snowy white eyebrows arched and a slight dip of his head, LeAndro invited his godson to offer grace.

Gregor's voice quavered at first. Then, with eyes shut tightly and Alexa's hand securely within his grasp, he lifted his prayer of thanksgiving. "Beloved Val, we approach you to offer thanks for your generosity in providing food to nourish our bodies and for this loving home that shelters us. Dearest Val, my heart begs your acceptance of my gratitude this night for those gathered to share this meal. I thank you for our new friend, Ouilest Var, who risked much to help our priestesses during their captivity. Thank you for my godparents, who opened their home to care for our returned priestesses and Sifiq refugees seeking freedom in Turand."

He squeezed Alexa's hand more firmly. "Loving Val, I can never thank you enough for the unyielding faith and perseverance that inspired Victor Garogan to pursue what seemed a hopeless search. Beyond all else, I praise you, Lord Val, for bringing my beloved Alexa home to us. I pray you will heal her quickly."

Not a single face remained dry as Alexa leaned her face against Gregor's arm. Gregor's right hand still held hers, but his left rose and crossed over his chest to press against her cheek. With enormous effort,

Alexa faced those at the table. Though faint and weak, her voice infused them with the power of her unbroken spirit. "I love you all. Shall we dine?"

As supper neared completion, Alexa's energy waned. Tempting aromas had enticed her to lift small bites to her lips. Tender, roasted fowl and fluffy, smooth soufflé practically melted in her mouth. Once familiar flavors teased her palate with exotic effect. Still, her stomach filled quickly, the hot food inside creating delicious warmth that successfully coaxed her into such a state of drowsiness that she rested sideways against her husband's arm.

"Alexa, my love," he murmured gently, "would you like some dessert, or should I take you upstairs to bed now?"

His voice was a blessed caress stirring her from the fuzzy, relaxed haze into which she had slipped. Eyelids, heavy with sleep, barely lifted. A feeble grin lit her face. "I'm sorry. I'm so sleepy. The sedative. I think maybe I might manage to share a bit of custard with you."

Gregor's smile glowed indulgently as he spooned some of the creamy dessert to her lips. As Alexa's mouth closed to savor the smooth cream, Oui-lest found herself suddenly overwhelmed, unexpectedly sobbing aloud. All eyes turned toward her and filled instantly with compassion.

Alexa pushed her chair back from the table and motioned for Oui-lest to come to her. Oui-lest immediately rose from her seat and rushed around the table. Falling to her knees, she rested her head in Alexa's lap as Alexa's fingers comfortingly stroked her hair.

"Milady," the younger woman wept, "I never imagined it this way. I remember all you said. I wanted so much to believe—but—seeing love expressed as I've witnessed tonight..." Her voice broke off in a strangled sob.

"Oui-lest. Dear Oui-lest. For you, tonight is only the beginning. You now have a lifetime ahead in which to love and be loved."

"If only that could be true. Oh, Milady, I so regret troubling you. Especially now. I'm so sorry."

The smile on Alexa's face was full of kindness. "You mustn't be sorry, Oui-lest. Your heart overflows with good things. Your tears remind me that everything happened with purpose—even the suffering. Be joyful, dear one, for Val gives you a new chance at life."

Victor gazed across the table, deeply absorbed in the vision of Alexa in the weakest, most fragile condition he had ever seen. Her heart never wavered. Her spirit never failed. Her soul never turned away. Teardrops dripped from his eyes, creating tiny puddles on his plate. His lips mouthed a simple prayer as he praised Val yet again for returning her home to them all.

Chapter 20

S hifting her position ever-so-slightly, Alexa's eyes flashed open as she emitted an involuntary cry of pain. Instantly, Gregor awoke and rolled over, reaching out to stroke her cheek. Her skin felt taut, still hot and parched with fever.

"Beloved, are you all right? Did I hurt you?" His voice was hushed, fearful. The night before, he had carried her upstairs and cautiously lowered her onto the bed. He had been so afraid when she had pleaded with him to sleep beside her. With her insisting that rest would come more peacefully if she could just feel him next to her, he had finally relented. He was uncertain how long he had managed to stay awake. At first, he had caressed her face and hair. All the while, he had offered silent, earnest prayers to Val. Then, feeling so exhausted from the journey to Timeri, sleep had proven a formidable foe and overtaken him shortly before midnight.

Her eyelids slid shut a moment, and she swallowed several times. When she finally gazed back at him, her lips formed a weak smile. "You're really here. I thought I might have been dreaming again."

"Alexa," he whispered, barely able to control swelling emotions so thick that he feared he might choke. "I was afraid I had hurt you in my sleep."

She rolled her head slightly from side to side. Trembling fingers slowly traveled upward to rest against his bearded face. "You didn't hurt me. I just moved the wrong way." Pausing, her eyes glazed with pain. "Oh, Gregor, it hurts so much."

Barely able to restrain tears stinging the backs of his eyelids, he forced a smile. "I know, my love. I promise. We'll make you better soon. Tirani is already on her way."

Again, Alexa gestured no with a bare shake of her head and breathed in shakily. "Do you really still love me? The way I remember?"

Gregor placed his lips against her forehead, his heart aching at the mere idea that she had asked the question. "How can you imagine I wouldn't? I've felt barely half-alive without you." His voice cracked. "Alexa, not an hour has passed since you left that I haven't thought of you or longed for you."

"Gregor, I need you to love me enough to help me. I begged Victor, but he refused."

He smiled tenderly, but his forehead wrinkled into a puzzled expression. "I can hardly believe Victor would deny you anything. What are you wanting me to do that Victor wouldn't?"

Her eyelids drifted closed. Gregor almost wondered if she had fallen asleep until she looked at him again, glistening tears beading at the corners of her eyes. Her hand found his, and their fingers intertwined.

"Gregor, please say you love me enough to take me to the chapel."

"Alexa," he responded gently, "as soon as you're better, I promise I'll take you."

"No, Gregor, you don't understand. Now. Today. Please say you'll take me today."

Propping himself up on one elbow, he stared down into her almost colorless features. Only her eyes seemed alive as they begged him to fulfill her request. "Alexa, how can I? You're too sick. The fever…"

Her intensely insistent whisper interrupted him. "That's exactly why I need to go. Trust me, my love. Say you'll take me. Please."

Even with his eyes closed, the image of unrelenting agony reflected from the emerald depths of her eyes burned into his soul. Air filled his chest already uncomfortably tight with grief for her suffering—suffering he was helpless to alleviate. Her fingers had fallen from his. Even her hand, now resting limply over his wrist, felt hot. "Alexa, is it really so important for you to go?"

"Gregor," she answered, "if you don't understand, no one will. I must. I need to be there. Trust me. Please?"

Thoughts blurred. Vague memories echoed somewhere in his mind. The past year without her spurred renewed terror of losing her again. Forcing himself to speak above the choking knot in his throat, Gregor answered, "Beloved, if that is truly what you want, I'll take you to the chapel later today." He responded to the hopeful gleam that sparked in her eyes, "However, you must first promise to do something for me."

Her lips pressed tightly together, and she nodded. "Anything."

Lying down again, Gregor edged closer to her. "Alexa, I want you to promise that you'll try to eat a decent breakfast. Then, after the doctor comes to change your bandages this morning, we'll get you ready, and I'll take you to the chapel. Agreed?"

Dreading the necessary agony of the doctor's visit, she nodded. "May I eat after the doctor leaves? I—I… Eating will do no good if I only lose my breakfast."

Later, Gregor clenched his jaw and pressed her hand tightly against his lips. His will was no match against the sight of the hideous, infected wounds crisscrossing her back. Bitter, scalding tears rolled down his face as he attempted to console and encourage her through the doctor's procedure. With every excruciating sob wrenched from her, scorching fury flared from the very core of his being. How could anyone be so cruel as to inflict such savagery on another person? How could any man so brutalize a woman, already sick, and still call himself a man? Consciously thrusting rage aside, Gregor forced himself to concentrate on helping Alexa endure this newest ordeal.

Thankfully, she had slept the night before. Even so, the morning's procedure left her drained, and she now dozed. The doctor had left while sternly expressing dismay and disapproval over intentions to take her out. Gregor then sat beside his wife, stretching his arm out and around her. Carefully positioning herself, she had leaned against him. Leila sat on the edge of the bed next to Gregor, feeding Alexa until she could eat no more. Gregor had then eased Alexa onto her side, leaving her asleep under Oui-lest's watchful eye while he organized details for the short trip he prayed desperately he would not live to regret.

The Karanan's spacious coach slowed and eased to a gradual stop. Victor sat in the driver's seat, concentrating on making the trip as smooth and comfortable as possible. Aroused when Gregor shifted slightly, Alexa lifted her face from his shoulder. Words were unnecessary. Her expression reflected both gratitude and anticipation. She snuggled back into the warmth of blankets wrapped around her.

The coach door opened. Cautiously leaning forward, Gregor supported her firmly as he transferred her into Victor's waiting arms. The two men hurried, intent on carrying their precious burden out of winter's cold and into Timeri's hallowed Chapel of Val. Inside, LeAndro, Leila, and Oui-lest already waited. Captain Fratino, accompanied by the Royal Guards who had escorted Gregor, held the chapel doors open until Victor and Gregor passed through.

Gregor strode rapidly to the front of the chapel. Nearly a hundred votive candles had been placed on steps leading up to the altar. Dancing flames flickered brightly. Uncertain what to expect, cushions and blankets had been arranged in front of the steps. Gregor turned and faced

Victor. Together, exercising extreme care, they lowered her until Alexa's feet touched the floor. Allowing her to guide them, they held her securely until she could kneel on one of the thick cushions.

Slowly, reluctantly, Victor backed away. Despite everything that had happened since that night on Timeri's beach, he could never remember being more afraid.

"Victor," she had whispered quietly into his ear while waiting for Gregor to disembark from the carriage, "don't worry. Even if I die here, I die peacefully—in Val's holy presence. And remember. I do love you."

Beside her on bended knees, Gregor grasped her arms to prevent her from collapsing sideways. Watching her as she silently mouthed words meant to be chanted, he questioned how anyone so frail could have possibly managed to walk downstairs the night before. A distinctly sweet hum began emanating from the crystal pyramid suspended above the altar. The sound was one he had not heard for more than a year. Despite the fever and sickness racking her body, she had come before the altar of Val. Gregor closed his eyes and prayed his thanks. Acknowledging her effort, Val had come to comfort his Priestess Valkana.

Pausing for a moment, past events swept through Gregor's memory. Twice before in his life, he had confronted terrifying possibilities of losing her. The first time, circumstances had been very different. He had known then that she was alive, snatched from his presence and taken back to the place she had called home after her parents' murders. Searching his soul and discovering that his love exceeded any selfish desire to keep her for his own, he had realized how readily he would have sacrificed his own happiness for hers. Soon afterward, he watched over her after she nearly died from injuries in her desperate act of saving his life.

Now, fear twisted knots into every muscle of his body as he faced this newest threat of losing her. This third time, the finality of death again hovered over her. Frightening questions confronted him. Was he strong enough? Could he bear the pain? Would his grief be too great?

From the core of all that he had ever been and ever would be, he drew strength to begin a new prayer. Never had any prayer required so much effort. Spilling from the soul of a man who loved his wife more than himself or any other living being, words flowed fervently. Yet, even as those words expressed how much he wanted and needed her with him, Gregor surrendered her into Val's care, pleading only that she be freed from her suffering, even if it meant that Val should will an end to her life within the confines of this sacred chapel.

Suddenly, brilliant light shone through tightly closed eyelids. Anxiously—gradually—Gregor opened his eyes. Blue-white light shimmered. Flowing from the crystal pyramid above, liquid light encased her body. Unwillingly, his hands loosed their grasp on her. He watched as her body shifted and rose from the floor. Musical waves swelled, filling the chapel with penetrating crescendos and decrescendos.

Oui-lest stared. Suspended high in the air, Alexa's figure relaxed and began a slow, continual rotation. The light enveloping her radiated a steady, intense glow. Sounds, melodic and exquisitely beautiful, penetrated not only her mind but also her body. No Sifiq women had been present during Alexa's momentous confrontation with King Bin-Lot. Officers and soldiers who had witnessed the event had been terrified. None had openly discussed the incident. Their muted whispers had concealed something shocking—mystifying. Mesmerized, she wondered if what they had observed could have been nearly as spectacular as the vision before her. Fascinated, Oui-lest praised the God of Turand for allowing her into a world she could never have imagined.

Victor gazed steadily upward. Listening to Anlía's pleas, he had initiated his frantic search. His soul had believed he would eventually find Alexa. His troubled heart had not permitted the surrender of hope. When his eyes had first fallen upon her body, lying on that deserted, wind-swept beach, panic he had not thought possible had staggered him. For fleeting seconds, he had feared his arrival too late, that she was already dead. Realizing that she still clung to life, he had sworn to do everything within his power to save her.

Watching the mind-boggling spectacle of Alexa hovering within a cocoon of glowing light, he felt the resurrection of his own soul. His breathing quickened, and his heart throbbed. Her words echoed inside his mind. Although he knew she would never love him as she once had, he had not lost her completely. No conscious prayer formed in his mind. Instead, his entire being transformed into supplication that projected into an atmosphere of vigilant hope.

Without anyone's conscious realization, hours passed. Gregor was called from his meditative state by words meant for his mind only. Raising black-brown eyes upward, he watched as Alexa's body slowed its rotation and descended toward him. Without stiffness despite the hours spent kneeling beneath her, Gregor rose to receive his wife into waiting arms. Cradling her close against his chest, he knelt once again. Gazing into her face, he praised Val. Faint rose colored her cheeks. Touching sensitive lips to her forehead, he noted that her skin was cool, her fever broken. Her chest rose and fell in quiet, even rhythm. Val's Healing Graces had come as blessing to his faithful priestess.

Gregor heard his own name. Looking up, he saw the frightened expression that clouded Victor's eyes. Smiling at his one-time enemy, Gregor spoke softly, "Victor, will you help me carry her back to the carriage? We need to take her back and get her into bed."

Unashamed, Victor choked on a sob. "All thanks and praises be to Val," he uttered as he knelt down on one knee and gathered Alexa into his arms.

Slowly rising to his feet, he turned to carry Alexa from the chapel. Gregor had preceded him in order to reach the carriage first. Exiting the chapel's front doors, they were greeted by brilliant winter sunshine and the apprehensive faces of hundreds of Timeri's citizens who had maintained their own vigil in the frigid cold. Gregor paused only long enough to smile and wave before hurriedly entering the waiting carriage.

Inside, he quickly seated himself on cushions arranged on the floor, making it easier to transfer Alexa into and out of the vehicle. Leaning forward, he removed his wife from Victor's arms. Holding her on his lap, he leaned back.

Comfortably nestled against her husband's body, she gazed into his face with eyes barely open.

"Alexa?"

A faint smile brightened her sleepy face. "Gregor," she whispered, "My back doesn't hurt anymore."

Blinking back tears, he sucked in deep breaths of air. Words stuck in his throat, and he only nodded in response.

With slender, delicate fingers, she lovingly stroked his face. Pausing frequently, she whispered, "I love you, Gregor. Thank you for trusting me—for understanding. I promise. I'll get better now. You will stay with me, won't you, my husband? My beloved Gregor."

"Shush, Alexa." He finally managed a whisper. "I'll stay very close, my love. You need to rest."

Her head nodded slightly. "I will. Gregor?"

"What now, my love?" he asked indulgently.

Emerald eyes closed to him. Despite the velvet haze of sleep that beckoned, her lips slowly formed quiet words. "I never once stopped loving you either."

Chapter 21

Alexa flexed her shoulders and stretched stiff muscles in her arms and legs. Eyelids, weighted with slumber, slowly lifted. Twisting her head from side to side on the pillow, she responded to growing wakefulness as her mind registered the luxurious softness enveloping her body. When her eyes finally opened, mere wisps of morning's first light sneaked inside beneath the edges of velvet draperies covering the window. Large, shadowy forms gradually materialized into recognizable shapes. An armoire. A dresser. A chair. Dark squares on walls that must be paintings.

Breathing in deeply, air filled lungs no longer congested following her plummet into icy ocean waters. Lying on her back, grating sand and salt no longer scraped or burned inside torn flesh. However, there was an irritating, scratching sensation. Besides that, she really felt a pressing need to relieve herself. Alexa drew herself into a sitting position and, carefully turning sideways, slid her legs off the bed.

Grasping the spiral-carved bedpost, she steadied weak legs. A fleeting sense of imbalance struck, then eased. Blinking several times against the heavy cloak of sleep that lingered after her encounter with Val's Healing Graces, she concentrated on each step toward the bathroom. Emerging, she felt more alert after splashing her face with cool water. Suddenly stopping close to the bed, she realized she was alone in the room.

For an instant, blinding panic struck her. What had happened? Where was everyone? Hadn't Victor brought her to the Karanan house in Timeri? Had she not snuggled against the warmth of Gregor's body? Was her mind failing, causing her to succumb to hallucinations? Shaking her head hard, she determinedly dismissed the abrupt onslaught of fearful doubts.

Closing her eyes and reaching out with her senses, she sighed with invading relief. Alexa felt Gregor's life force very close. He was likely asleep in another bedchamber, allowing her time for undisturbed rest. She reached for a faceted crystal doorknob, turned it, and opened the door. Leaving her bedchamber, she walked through the deserted corridor without opening her eyes. Trusting her senses, she stopped at the door of the bedchamber next to hers. As she inhaled deeply, her mind reached beyond carved wood to where her husband lay asleep.

Within moments, she had silently entered the room. Opening her eyes, she gazed down at Gregor's sleeping face. Throughout the years of their marriage, most cherished were the private moments after dawn when she had quietly observed him before leaving for morning prayers. Most often, she returned before he awakened to arouse him from slumber with the indescribably tender caress of her fingers stroking through his hair. As if their favorite morning ritual had never been interrupted, her fingers stretched out. Delicately, they combed through sleep-tumbled locks.

Sighing heavily, Gregor turned over and reached for the hand that had so gently awakened him. Abruptly, his eyes flew open, and he jerked upright. "Alexa! Dearest Val, what are you doing out of bed?"

Shaking her head admonishingly, she grinned. "Searching for my husband. I'm starving, and I thought he might be willing to feed me. But first, I need his help." She then sat on the bed next to him and luxuriated in the feel of strong arms winding tightly around her. Burying her face against his neck, her lips pressed tiny kisses against warm, smooth skin.

Her hand swept across the firm expanse of his chest. Touching him reconnected her to life itself.

Without releasing her, he eased back onto the bed. He released her long enough to tug up the edge of the thick comforter that had fallen aside when he sat up. Tucking it around them, he then allowed his hand to caress her hair. "My God, how much I've missed waking up with you beside me."

Heated tears brimmed behind closed eyelids. Her lips formed tremulous smiles while his touched tickling kisses against the sensitive skin of her forehead. If only her back weren't so irritated, Alexa thought, she could spend forever there without moving. Reluctant to end her morning magic, she whispered, "Your Majesty, I must ask your assistance."

"For you, beloved, anything." His rich voice vibrated slightly as he spoke. "Tell me."

"Can we go to the other room? The bandages are hurting, and I can't remove them without help."

Gregor saw no need to question her. Instead, he got out of bed and put on a thick, warm robe. Walking around to the side of the bed where she now sat, he took her hands and gently helped her get up. He then held one side of the robe wide open while he tucked it and his arm around her. Their awkward closeness caused them to shuffle slowly toward her bedchamber while attempting to control giggles that threatened to erupt into laughter any minute.

Gregor lit a lamp, then waited for her to sit on the edge of the bed. Gregor carefully removed her gown, grateful for the warmth inside chambers Alexa had occupied since Victor had brought her to the Karanan house. After she lay down on her stomach, he gingerly worked at the edges of the bandages covering her back. When they were sufficiently loosened, he began to peel the fabric from her skin. The underneath side bore dark stains formed by bloody pus that had seeped from infected wounds. With her back uncovered, Gregor angrily clenched his teeth upon seeing red stripes that evidenced the necessity for the divine healing powers Val had sent to her. Touching her skin, he felt dried residue from the infection and grit that must have chafed tender, healing skin beneath the pressure of the bandage.

"Alexa," he said as he covered her with a blanket, "I want you to wait here while I prepare a warm bath. You'll feel much better once we cleanse your back."

When Gregor helped her step into the spacious tub, she swayed slightly. Painfully vivid memories of the bath at the Sochino house shafted into her mind. Braced by her husband's arms, she balanced before lowering herself into the tub.

Few words passed between them. Gentle hands foamed large puffs of fragrant soap over her back. Cupping together his large palms, he scooped water up and allowed it to roll down her back in a cascade that washed away the offending grit that had been so irritating to delicate skin. While she washed her body, he shampooed her hair and rinsed it until it squeaked when he slid his fingers along the shortened tresses.

With his continued help, she stood and stepped out onto the floor. With large towels warmed over the ornate coils of a steam radiator, he wrapped first her body, then her hair. While she sat on a vanity chair, he vigorously dried her hair and then combed through the shining waves.

Meanwhile, Alexa rejoiced in Gregor's attentions despite a vague sense of something remote and suppressed within him. She would choose to explore that another time. For the moment, she wished only to immerse herself in the abundant love with which he tended her. Pain had disappeared entirely. Months of sadness and loneliness were banished. Constant fears had fled, replaced by the security of her husband's presence.

A little later, wrapped in a robe and standing at the top of the stairs, she glanced down and experienced a nauseating wave of vertigo. Whether it was lingering weakness or the haunting recollection of her plunge over the rail of the Sifiq ship, she wasn't sure. However, Gregor alertly observed her hesitation, and before realizing it, she found herself lifted into his arms for the trip down the staircase.

Luckily, a quick trip to the kitchen found the cook already removing fresh loaves of bread from stone ovens for the day. Shooing the king and queen into the drawing room, the cook immediately began beating eggs for fluffy omelets for their breakfast. Meanwhile, Gregor guided his wife to the sofa in the parlor before adding wood to a low fire in the fireplace to build a blazing fire to chase away morning's chill.

Seating themselves on plump cushions dragged onto the floor, Gregor and Alexa uncovered plates bearing their beautifully prepared breakfast. Alexa's eyes sparkled with humor. Tasting her first bite of herb-sauced omelet, she wondered aloud how she could ever eat the generous portions set before her. Then, giggling like an adolescent, she commented that she would soon become as round as winter snowmen if such delicious foods continued to appear before her.

When both had eaten their fill, Alexa glanced over to a side table and spied a book. Fetching it for her, Gregor then lay down on his side on the carpeted floor, tucking a small cushion beneath his head. Alexa sat next to him and opened the leather-bound tome. Ivory pages, filled with poetry, met eyes that had not read from a book since before her captivity. Affectionately smiling into his face, her eyes then returned to flowing print as she began to read aloud poems that spoke of both faith and love.

Arriving just outside the double doors of the drawing room, Leila glanced over her shoulder when her own husband approached. Holding one finger against her lips and bidding him remain silent, she pointed. Looking inside, LeAndro's eyes fell upon an image that, days earlier, he would not have dared to dream. His godson's hand affectionately ran up and down Alexa's arm. Gregor's eyes openly adored the woman whose beautifully modulated voice pronounced exquisite phrases expressing enduring truths. Deeply moved, the Karanans watched until the sounds of a waking household reached their ears and beckoned them into the life of a new day.

Nightfall. Staring out through frost-edged windowpanes, Alexa pensively gazed at the shimmering white corona circling the winter moon hovering against ebony sky. Casting its light upon the darkened breast of her beloved Turand, that brilliant orb appeared much more beautiful compared to memories that had comforted her throughout her imprisonment in the Sifiq Kingdom.

Leaning backward, her eyes closed. She had spent most of the day resting in bed. Still, for the first time in what seemed to have been longer than eternity, Alexa had spent an entire day with her Gregor. Drawing in a deep breath, she delighted in the firmness of her husband's body as his hands locked together in front of her waist.

"So very strange." She spoke her thoughts aloud.

With his arms wrapped snugly around her disturbingly thin figure, Gregor rested his chin on the crown of her head. Thoughtfully, he studied her tranquil expression reflected by spotless glass. "Tell me, beloved. What seems so strange?" Feeling her expel a heavy sigh, he placed a kiss on her hair and awaited her response.

A softly subdued voice expressed her answer. "It's so difficult to comprehend that the beautiful moon shining outside there is the same moon that appeared so stark and cold while..." Fleeting tremors traveled along her spine as words faded into silence.

Turning within his embrace, her face tilted upward. Gazing into dark eyes that had filled months of dreadfully lonely dreams, her eyes glazed with fresh tears. "How do I explain? Simply being with you again makes everything that happened seem so far away, yet..."

Tenderly, his fingertips brushed glistening streaks from pale cheeks. Full lips lightly grazed her forehead. "Alexa," he spoke quietly, "I cannot begin to imagine all you faced or all you must feel. We both need to talk about it, and we will. I promise. However, for the moment, nothing is more important than your recovery. It's getting late, and you need to sleep."

Her lips curved slightly as she allowed him to guide her back to bed. How many times over the years had he tucked her in at night? Until now, she had never consciously realized that this task held its own rhythm or that he always performed each motion the same way. The way he straightened her pillow as her head sank into feathered fullness. The angle of his body as he leaned across her with his hands grasping the blanket's edge. The slight tautness of the blanket as he pulled it into a straight line before sliding it up to cover her shoulders. Months of nostalgic longing were now transformed back into the reality of her life with him.

Observing the changing play of emotion crossing her face, Gregor could not ignore the sudden grimace that wrinkled her forehead. Before he could halt the question, it was already spoken. "Alexa? What?"

So few words, yet so great was their understanding of one another. Her lips pursed tightly together, and, for a moment, she looked ready to cry. Instead, she swallowed and hid her face in the downy depths of her pillow.

Gently, he stretched out his fingertips to coax her face from its cushioned hiding place. "You know there's nothing you can't tell me." Black-brown eyes that studied every nuance of her expression also promised compassionate understanding.

Tremulous lips slowly and deliberately formed hesitant words. "Gregor, they tried so many times to—to force themselves on me. I would have preferred death to being raped by any one of them. Thankfully, Val saved me each time. However, one thing they did broke my heart."

Several times, as he had relentlessly pressed himself and his guard during the trip to Timeri, that horrible thought had taunted him. Not for a moment had he doubted that he would want her back, no matter what. Mostly, he had feared the undeserved guilt and torment she would have inflicted upon herself. Profound relief settled in his heart as his lips pulled into a tender smile. "How did they break your heart, my love?"

The scene replayed itself behind closed eyelids. The stinging jerk on her arm. Squeezing pressure painfully compressing the fine bones in her hand. The gloating sparks in Bin-Lot's eyes when he realized he had triumphed in at least one battle over his obstinate prisoner. Her intense disgust that such a man had defiled something that, to her, held sacred significance.

Slipping her hand from beneath the blanket, she grasped his hand and pulled it toward her lips. Reverently, she kissed the wide band that gleamed softly with aged patina. Finally, green eyes opened, revealing a different kind of sorrow. Sadness suffused her voice. "Gregor, he took my wedding ring."

Dropping his face and closing his eyes, Gregor breathed in and out several times. Then, after letting several moments pass, he leaned forward and kissed her. Straightening, his countenance reflected more than just sympathy. "Alexa, we'll get you another ring."

Sparkling tears slid from the corners of her eyes, and she shook her head. "No. You don't understand. It would never be the same. I had worn that ring since we married, Gregor. Only one time did I ever think of removing it." She paused as she considered her confession. "Only once. That first time Victor took me back to Garogan. I discovered I couldn't. Although I didn't fully understand at the time, deep in my soul, I knew it belonged on my finger. In some ways, that ring helped me discover my path to you because it felt so wrong when I tried to take it off. Now…"

Wordlessly, Gregor rose and walked around the bed. Stepping out of supple leather slippers and letting his flannel robe fall to the floor, he then lay down and held her in his arms. "Alexa," he whispered comfortingly, "the ring was a symbol. Nothing more. Nothing less. You must remember that the promises we exchanged are what matter most."

Choking against the knot in her throat, she replied, "My ring was so precious to me, Gregor. Now it's gone."

"The ring is gone, Alexa," he told her soothingly. "That is something I cannot change, but what truly matters is that you are not. I have you back, and I hope never again to let you be far from me. And though you may have lost your ring, the man who gave it to you still loves you more than anything else."

Closed eyelids prevented visual distraction. At that moment, her world existed only within her other senses of him. The familiar, masculine scent of his body. The remembered pattern of his breathing. The secure feeling of his arm holding her. The comforting touch of his face against hers. Sadness for her stolen ring abated. Gregor had reminded her that he still loved her, and after all, their promises lay in their hearts and souls, not within metal rings circling their fingers. Listening to the constant rhythm of his heart, Alexa drifted off to sleep.

⌒

Two days later, a smiling Alexa reached out to embrace her former lady-in-waiting. "Dear Tirani, you mustn't scold me. Lisana and Marlí never once failed me. I must go to them."

Tirani Tarandá, respected Valiria in her own right, had arrived the day before. Within minutes of arriving in Timeri, she had lifted prayers to Val upon checking in on her sleeping queen. Turand's prolonged, apprehensive months without the presence of Valkana had ended.

Turandans had maintained their way of life without relinquishing their faith. Tirani recognized that the people of Turand had been subjected to a test while members of the Order of Val had faced different trials altogether. Later, there would be time to bring questions directly to the Valkana. But, first, two sister priestesses needed her ability to summon Val's Healing Graces.

"Milady," Tirani countered, "your own recovery only begins. Allow yourself a few more days. Lisana and Marlí know your spirit is with them. They do not expect you to venture into the cold to see them."

"Beloved, are you ready?" Gregor, barely able to conceal his reluctance for this outing, appeared in the Karanan drawing room with a warm woolen cloak in his hands. He smiled apprehensively at Tirani. However, Alexa had decided, and they both knew that no one would change her mind.

Nearly two hours had passed when, with Gregor's huge hand firmly at her waist, Alexa paused along the curving brick pathway leading from the Karanan guest house to the nearby manor. Wintry breezes gently nipped, coaxing pink color into her cheeks. Skies the color of aquamarine glowed with the caress of late morning sunshine.

Cold, fresh air tingled with a cleansing effect as Alexa inhaled deeply. Strange. Again, that word penetrated her mind. In the Sifiq Kingdom, winter's chill carried threats of frozen death. In Turand, the cold of winter felt alive and invigorating. Bold contrasts, she thought, born of starkly different perceptions created by circumstance.

When Alexa looked up, Gregor gazed into eyes as dark as the towering evergreens lining the front of his godparents' estate. Stepping directly in front of her, his hands rose to cup her face. Her adoring smile brought flashing sparkles to brown irises. The glow surrounding her conveyed the pensive, spiritual mood of her thoughts. Words need not be said, for they could never satisfactorily express the love that bound them. Dropping his bearded face, his lips sought connection to hers.

⌣

Drawing in a deep breath, she hesitated, still lacking in confidence. However, something in his posture struck her as so somber—so sad. As he silently stared out the window, Oui-lest looked over Victor's shoulder and saw King Gregor standing outside on the brick walkway, holding Alexa in a tight embrace. Suddenly, though quiet, the sound of her own voice caught her by surprise. "Has she any idea how much you love her?"

Slowly, Victor turned. Hazel eyes revealed the undeniable truth inherent in her question. "Oui-lest, I thought you were at the guest house."

Ignoring his evasive comment, Oui-lest moved closer to the window and noted that Turand's king and queen appeared oblivious to the day's wintry cold. "You didn't answer my question. Does she know?"

Victor stared into the ivory features of the shy Sifiq woman who had uncharacteristically initiated conversation involving a very personal subject. Clenching his jaw for several moments, he finally produced a reluctant smile and nodded. "She knows."

Somewhat unnerved, Oui-lest crossed the room and sat, her back straight, on the edge of the sofa. Turquoise eyes studied the man whose attention was no longer fixed on the lovers outside. Eyes that reflected intelligence and sensitivity guarded inner sorrows rarely revealed. Darkly rose lips, narrow without losing sensuality, pressed together. Brown hair, neatly combed, curved in a soft line across his forehead. He had shown her kindness such as she had never known from any man. Somehow, his sadness touched her heart, prompting a wish to comfort him.

He glanced once more through the window. Gregor and Alexa had moved from sight. In resignation, he sighed heavily and sat on the chair closest to where Oui-lest perched on the couch. What to say? How to say it? Hazel eyes were drawn to blue. "You mustn't look so concerned, Oui-lest. Everyone here loves Alexa."

Nervously, Oui-lest wet her lips with the tip of tongue. "Not as you do."

Too much had transpired over the past weeks. Unable to maintain his normal façade, Victor smiled ruefully. "Truth cannot be denied. I have loved her since the moment I first saw her. Unfortunately, some things can never change."

Blonde curls bounced as she shook her head. "I don't think I understand. You searched until you found her. You rescued her and then watched over her night and day while she was so sick. You sent for the king to come to her. How can a man so love a woman who belongs to another?"

"Oui-lest." Victor stopped. The front doors opened and closed. Thankfully, he heard Gregor insist on taking Alexa upstairs to bed. Turning his attention once again to Oui-lest, Victor's bow-shaped mouth curved into a smile. "I watched Alexa grow from a tiny baby into womanhood. Along the way, I fell deeply in love with her."

Perplexing questions clouded Oui-lest's eyes. "You said she knows how much you love her. Can that be true? I mean, you both seem so close, yet…"

"Yet her love for Gregor exceeds anything else you've ever seen?" Although laden with emotion, his words fell short of bitterness. Instead, he recalled his many prayerful promises if only Val would bring Gregor in time to save Alexa.

Nodding in confusion, Oui-lest cast her glance toward floral patterns woven into the carpet. Unbidden words continued to spill from her lips. "Alexa has always been so caring, so thoughtful. Yet, somehow, her relationship with you seems almost cruel if she really knows how much you love her. It makes no sense to me."

Feeling her distress, Victor joined Oui-lest on the sofa. Tentatively, he wrapped strong hands around hers as their eyes met. "Cruelty exists, but I must admit that it was self-inflicted. Years ago, Alexa and I were betrothed."

"Betrothed?" Unfamiliarity with the term, let alone the concept, further clouded her eyes.

"Betrothed," Victor repeated. "Alexa and I once planned to marry."

The revelation spawned even greater confusion. "Marry? You and Alexa? What happened?"

Releasing her hands and searching for words, Victor ran his right hand across his cheek. He needed time to sort out the deluge of memories and new, disconcerting feelings that swelled in response to Oui-lest's innocent, concerned inquiries. "There is no easy or quick explanation. Perhaps you feel up to a walk outside?"

Fresh air served to clear his mind as they ambled across the vast, brownish-green lawn. Victor felt less inhibited outside, where little chance existed for others to listen to his private thoughts. Sympathetic to Oui-lest's feelings, he slowly described Turand as it had been under Sifiq occupation. For the first time in years, he would listen to his own voice as it unraveled for her the drama of times that had led him to personal tragedy.

Light winds grew cooler as afternoon waned. His voice carried different dimension as he spoke of the days when he and Alexa had been in love. Regrets and guilt vibrated within his voice when he described leaving Alexa, wed to their enemy, in Toraval. Oui-lest could almost feel his joy when Alexa returned to Garogan and his subsequent despair upon learning of her newfound love for Gregor. Finally, in Alexa's defense, Victor tried to explain and justify the relationship they continued to share.

Long moments of silence passed as she absorbed the import of his tale. Intelligent comprehension was elusive. Too much of what she had observed since coming to Turand remained thoroughly bewildering. Her heart, however, perceived matters on a different plane. Despite having never known love as it existed between Gregor and Alexa or even as it had once been between Victor and Alexa, she sensed an awakening in her own soul. Possessed of a sympathetic nature that had found a place to grow, Oui-lest felt Victor's grief and acknowledged it with compassion.

After supper, Oui-lest retired early. She needed to think—to ponder Victor's story and how strong her desire had been to provide him some measure of comfort. It seemed he had been responsive. Tormented eyes had appeared less solemn and his smile more relaxed. In the quiet solitude of her room, she instinctively understood that he trusted few with his feelings. However, he had trusted her and even confided in her. For the first time in her life, she wondered what it might be like to love a man—a man like Victor Garogan.

~

Four days later, Oui-lest sat beside Victor inside the parlor after supper. Alexa's expression could only be described as resolute. Oui-lest had seen similar expressions several times in her own homeland. Each time she had observed that staunch determination, the Sifiq king had inevitably encountered daunting consequences. Victor's face showed little surprise. Gregor, who stood on the opposite side of the room, was obviously disturbed.

"Alexa," Gregor spoke patiently despite understandable aggravation, "it is absolutely too soon. You are much too fragile to even consider such a thing."

Sighing, she continued, "Gregor, I intend to go home. I need to go home." She pronounced the word *need* with heavy emphasis. "After being away so long, I want to see my children, to hold my babies again. Is that so impossible to understand?"

Drawing a sustaining breath, Gregor briefly rolled his eyes toward the ceiling and impatiently shook his head. "Alexa, we're discussing a week of travel in cold weather. You're simply in no condition to make such a journey right now."

Her shoulders lifted, then dropped with the deep breath she took and released. She understood well that everyone gathered around agreed with her husband. Unable to argue the point, she lapsed into silence. Persuasion would require another tactic. Praying her fatigue wasn't too obvious as she stood, she smiled graciously. "I suppose I must say an early goodnight then. I think only rest will speed my recovery enough that I might convince my husband to take me home—where I belong."

Gregor stared as she swiftly left the room. Then, surprised, he listened to her footsteps as she started up the stairs. Until tonight, he had carried her up to bed each evening. Shaking his head in consternation, he also excused himself and followed his wife.

Leaving everyone else inside, Victor and DiLeno decided to go for a brief walk. "Well, what do you think he'll do?"

Victor glanced around at DiLeno's inquisitive expression. "Our good king has my complete sympathy. Did you see the look in her eyes?"

DiLeno suppressed a laugh. "The same look I've seen dozens of times. This time, though, Gregor seems more adamant than I've ever seen before."

Nodding, Victor stopped to stare at the sky. Far in the distance could be heard the soft rush of ocean waters rolling onto Timeri's frosty beaches. "Adamant, yes. Right? Without a doubt. Will he prevail? Probably not. I completely understand his worry. I know how I felt when she begged me to take her to the chapel. For the first time I can remember, I refused her because I thought it was too dangerous. Dearest Val, how wrong I was. How glad I am he had the courage to listen to her. DiLeno, she was dying, and I almost let her. And most assuredly, I prolonged her suffering. There is no doubt, and I must live with that. She is alive now because he loved her enough to listen. As crazy as it sounds, I hope he'll give in. She does need to go home."

"Do you honestly believe so?" DiLeno asked incredulously.

"I do," Victor responded. Thoughtfully, he continued, "You didn't see her the way I found her. If she survived that, a trip home, even now, would be nothing in comparison. Her journey back to Turand will not be complete until she goes home and reunites with the children."

"Aren't you afraid she'll suffer a relapse?"

Victor shrugged his shoulders. "I expect the journey won't be easy. She knows that, but this isn't a simple matter of just wanting to go home. Toraval is much like a magnet drawing her spirit. Years ago, she accepted that Val's destiny for her lies in Toraval. She needs to return."

In silence, they walked while puffs of light, powdery snow swirled around their feet. Pensively, DiLeno mulled over Victor's words. Knowing Alexa so well, Victor was probably right. On the other hand, despite a mood tinged with regret, DiLeno perceived a subtle change in his cousin. He could only wonder.

⤳

Concern creased Gregor's brow as he sipped hot tea. Shaking his head, he quietly told Victor, "After all her pleading last night about going home, she slept so badly. She tossed and turned and whimpered constantly."

Victor hardly knew what to say. "She misses her children."

Gregor cocked his left eyebrow. "I know, but this was something more. I can't quite explain. The fact that she decided to stay in bed convinces me she isn't up to traveling so far."

LeAndro joined the conversation. "Have you considered that she might recover faster at home? Alexa thrives on being home."

As Gregor reached out to set his half-full cup of tea on the table, terrified screams from upstairs startled him so badly that the cup tipped and spilled onto the table. In unison, both he and Victor leapt to their feet and raced through the house and up the main staircase. Heavily falling onto the bed, Gregor swiftly grasped his wife's trembling hands and pulled her into a tight embrace.

"Alexa!" he breathed out. "Alexa, beloved, calm down! What is it?"

"They're here! Sifiq! I feel them! They've come back! Don't let them hurt me again!"

Firmly grasping her shoulders, Gregor held her. Terror-stricken features were streaked with tears. Her vision appeared far-removed from the bedchamber. "Alexa," he soothed, "it was a dream. Just a dream. No one can harm you here."

"No!" she wailed. "You don't understand. I saw them! They're here! Please, Gregor! You must stop them! They'll hurt someone else if they can't get to me!"

"Alexa, I'm with you now. Please, beloved, you must calm yourself. How can you imagine I would let anyone hurt you? Especially Sifiq."

Dropping to his knees beside the bed, Victor reached across Gregor's thighs to take one of Alexa's hands. "Alexa, Sweetest, Gregor's right. The Sifiq are far away. You've just had a nightmare."

Sharply shaking her head, she opened eyes filled with tears that spilled down pale cheeks. "Victor, they're here! I saw them!"

"No, Alexa, you only saw a dream…"

"It was no dream!" she shouted. "You have to believe me! I saw them! On the shore. Near the lighthouse!" Pushing them away and jerking her hands free, she covered her face. Her chest heaved as her entire body shook. "Why can you not believe me? I know what I saw!" Weakly, she collapsed forward against her husband.

Again, Victor clasped her hand. "Alexa, look at me," he commanded gently. Once he received her attention, he continued, "Alexa, listen carefully. You're in Turand. Tirstan is just outside the house with loyal Turandan soldiers. Even if someone got past the guards, they would have DiLeno, me, and Gregor in the middle. No one will hurt you. I swear it."

Sobbing, she pressed her face back against her husband's shoulder. Although tension stiffened her body, she valiantly mastered her emotions. Finally, she gazed up into Gregor's fearful eyes. Desperation clearly showed in the depths of hers. In a hushed voice, she insisted, "Gregor, they are here. You must send the soldiers. Please, Gregor, please believe me."

Glancing up for just a moment, Gregor watched Tirani, who had been summoned from the guesthouse, appear at the door. The petite priestess had begun to approach the bed but stopped abruptly. Her brown eyes met Alexa's. Inside the crowded bedroom, their unspoken connection crackled with energy. Tirani turned stunned eyes toward Gregor. "DiLeno told me as I came up. Have you not yet sent soldiers?"

Gregor's expression was one of speechless surprise as Victor's voice cut through the tension. "Tirani, she had a nightmare."

In a strong voice that belied her tiny stature, Tirani shook her head impatiently. Then, approaching Alexa from the side opposite Gregor, she reached out and stroked Alexa's mussed hair. "Our queen is still Valkana. I recommend that you heed her warning."

Gregor and Victor exchanged appraising looks as Victor rose from the floor. "Are you certain?" Receiving a curt nod and a stern frown in response, he inclined his head slightly. "I shall go then and take soldiers with me. If Sifiq have indeed come ashore, then I personally intend to see they do no harm."

Striding toward the door, he paused and turned back to gaze into Alexa's ashen features. "Near the lighthouse?" When she nodded yes, he smiled reassuringly. "Alexa, here, you remain safe with your husband. I swear to you. Neither of us will ever let the Sifiq hurt you again."

⌇

Tugging back sharply on the reins, the bay gelding halted with a jerk as Victor leapt from the saddle. Flanked by Captain Fratino and DiLeno, he ran toward an obviously infuriated throng of fishermen. "Trego!" Victor shouted out, "What's going on?"

The sturdy companion, who had helped search for Alexa, turned upon hearing the familiar voice. "Filthy Sifiq sailors!" he spat out. "Probably the same ones who tried to murder our Lady Valkana. We kept them here until someone could come. Didn't expect our messenger to reach you so soon!"

"We encountered no messenger," Victor responded with a shake of his head. "Our Lady Valkana sent us."

Soldiers who had accompanied Victor swiftly dispersed the fishermen surrounding the stranded sailors and took charge of huddled prisoners who had been unable to fight their burly captors. At Fratino's command, guards carefully began to separate and count the shipwrecked Sifiq, several of whom were either injured or too sick to stand.

"Remove your hands from me!" A caustic voice grated out the command as two guards grappled with a tall man who struggled violently against them despite clutching one arm tightly against his body.

A silent nod sent two additional guards toward the troublemaker. "Sir!" Fratino's voice rang out clearly. "I am Captain Tirstan Fratino. Cease your resistance, or my men will bind you and gag you."

Pain that drew ugly lines in the man's face failed to erase the hateful sneer that curled his wide mouth. Contemptuous blue eyes snapped angrily. Realizing he had little choice, the surly captive straightened and cynically inclined his head toward the fishermen who had withdrawn and waited in case their help might be necessary.

"Captain Fratino, as you can well see, we have arrived on your shores as victims of a shipwreck. Instead of offering assistance, this rabble actually threatened us. I leave their punishment in your hands. In the meantime, I require that you see to the welfare of my crew."

Fratino's brows lifted angrily, although he remained calmly at attention. "And who are you that you presume the right to command here?"

Glancing around, the man again inclined his head with sardonic politeness. "I have forgotten to introduce myself. My name is Captain Raf-Zan."

The words had barely been spoken when Victor lunged forward and cried out furiously. "You savage, cowardly bastard!" His clenched fist landed against the captain's squared jaw, jolting Raf-Zan from his feet and hurling him backward onto the sand, with Victor landing on top of him.

Reacting swiftly, DiLeno ran forward and, with Fratino's help, forcefully dragged Victor off Raf-Zan. Driven by rage, Victor's strength required assistance from two additional soldiers before he could be restrained. The stunned Sifiq officer groaned as he rose to his knees before doubling over in agony.

"Lord Garogan! Stop it now! These men are prisoners! We will deal with their crimes later! Control yourself!" Captain Fratino shouted.

"You don't understand! That bastard is the one who hurt her! He tried to kill her!"

"Victor!" DiLeno hissed into his ear. "Look at him! He can't fight back! We'll deal with him later! According to the laws of Turand! Laws you helped write! Control yourself!"

Heaving one furious breath after another, Victor closed his eyes, which only made matters worse. Images flooded his mind. Her limp body—lying on that storm-swept beach. Hideously infected slashes across her back. Eyes fearing not death but instead that she would not live long enough to see her family again. Victor's rage-filled eyes flew open. "Raf-Zan, I swear! You will pay for what you did! You will pay!"

As DiLeno attempted to reason with Victor, Fratino approached Raf-Zan, still swaying drunkenly on his knees. Disregarding the captain's wounded arm, Tirstan grabbed him roughly and jerked him to his feet.

"Captain Raf-Zan," Fratino ground out, "you are a prisoner of Turand's Royal Guard, and I command here. Understand well. I, not you, issue all orders, and I require that you obey all directions issued by members of this Guard. As you can see, your presence is less than welcome and, for you especially, exceedingly dangerous."

Captain Fratino turned his attention to his own soldiers. "Gentlemen, secure your prisoners and await my orders. Remember. They are Sifiq soldiers, meaning they are experts at murderous deception."

⌐

Alexa nervously paced from the drawing room to the dining room and back again. Clutching her shawl more tightly around her, she frequently returned to the window to peer outside. Watching her only served to increase Gregor's anxiety regarding her emotional state and her health. Finally, he stood and embraced her. "Alexa, you wear yourself out. Let me take you upstairs to rest until they return."

Walking with him toward the staircase, she suddenly whirled out of his arms and rushed toward the front doors. Flinging them open, she ran down the steps and across the walkway. Breathless from her short run, she stopped to wait for Victor, who, along with two soldiers, had just ridden through the gates.

Inside, Gregor paused only long enough to snatch a cloak for his wife. Arriving outside just as Victor dismounted, he draped the coat around Alexa's shoulders while noting the riders' grim expressions. "Well?"

Victor stretched out gloved hands to receive Alexa's. Meeting Gregor's waiting gaze, he nodded. "We should know never to doubt our Valkana. Shall we go inside from the cold?"

Seated on the drawing room couch, Alexa's slim fingers nervously clutched the porcelain cup of hot tea. "I can hardly believe it! How many did you say? What did they tell you?"

"Fourteen, including three officers. Plus, of course, Raf-Zan. Apparently, half the crew was lost overboard during the storm. They told of a stationary whirlwind that caught their ship and claimed that, after several days, horrendous gusts of wind ran the ship aground. Considering the wreckage just offshore, I can hardly believe anyone escaped with his life."

"Where are they now?" Harsh, furious notes infused Gregor's voice. Listening attentively as Victor recounted details of finding the enemy crew, he found it impossible to feel compassion for the ragged condition of Sifiq sailors who had returned to desecrate the shores of his kingdom. His primary responsibility was to protect his people from any renewed Sifiq threat. His first goal was to prevent their presence from adversely affecting Alexa's recovery.

"We took them to a small storehouse near the center of Timeri. It's sturdy and easily secured. Fratino is getting them properly received. I left DiLeno with the mayor to arrange for clothing, bedding, and food. Some also need medical attention."

Suddenly, Alexa's eyes shot up and locked onto Victor's. Setting aside her half-empty cup, she rose from her seat and crossed the room to where he had just wearily lowered himself into a chair. Curling her fingers around his right hand, she gazed into his surprised eyes. "Why did you not tell me you were hurt?" Without waiting for his reply, she concentrated on broken skin across his knuckles. Within seconds, his injured hand was healed.

"Alexa, you mustn't waste energy on a small hurt like that," he gently scolded. Actually, he had taken an almost perverse pleasure in the bruised soreness. Had DiLeno not stopped him, he would have taken even greater satisfaction in pounding his fists into pulp against the arrogant, abrasive officer who had turned out to be Captain Raf-Zan. Quickly, to avoid distressing her unnecessarily, he redirected his thoughts.

The clock chimed one o'clock before Gregor finally headed up to bed that night. He had first awaited Fratino's return to report on the status of the Sifiq prisoners. Quietly, he had then discussed plans with DiLeno and Victor to personally inspect the prisoners the following day.

Later, Turand's king had remained alone in the parlor. Staring at glowing embers in the fireplace, he had taken time for personal reflection. So many events packed into such a short span of time. So many emotions stirring within his soul. Stefan's midnight visit. News that Alexa was alive. His dreadful, unanticipated confession to Nikolai. The anxiety-plagued journey to Timeri. His decision to take her to the chapel. Sifiq returning to Turand. Unexpected celebration. Shameful remorse. Crippling fear. Jealous resentment. Blazing wrath. The past two weeks had delivered an astounding array of life's complexities that he must face as both king and as man.

As a man of faith, Gregor had failed not a single day to pray thankfully for Alexa's return. During her absence, he had coped with grief and loss by devoting himself to his children and to his people. Few times had his composure cracked in the presence of others. Lonely nights had been much different. She had been part of him for so long. That first night at the Karanan manor—holding her for the first time in more than a year—he had finally comprehended exactly how empty he was without her. Unconsciously, he smiled. He felt whole again.

His broad chest rose and fell. Sooner or later, he must tell her about Nikolai. His heart ached at how his son had learned the circumstances under which he and Alexa had married. He had lamented the lack of time to explain adequately. Yet, somehow, Gregor was convinced that Alexa had already sensed something amiss. Occasionally, he had felt her eyes upon him, her expression holding silent questions and promising reassurance. Each time, he had smiled and told her how much he loved her.

Thinking of Nikolai and his questions about Victor reminded Gregor of years spent suppressing feelings for his one-time adversary. Gregor often pondered the irony that the love his wife once felt for Victor had brought her into his life. He had never forgotten the tragically disconsolate expression in her eyes the night she had agreed to marriage in exchange for Victor's life. Months later, he had despised Victor for releasing the arrow that had nearly slain her. Then hatred mushroomed with the escalation of violence and his near-fatal encounter with Garogan on the battlefield. During the years following the war, Lord Garogan had striven for personal redemption. His efforts had also earned grudging respect from Turand's king. Now, Gregor failed to quell resentment that Victor had been the one who had rescued Alexa in Timeri. Chastising himself in silent frustration, he reminded himself that nothing mattered beyond the fact that Alexa was safely asleep upstairs because of Victor.

With his mind turning to the Sifiq, righteous anger seethed throughout his being. Their scourge had been eradicated once from Turand. That they had dared return to murder and take defenseless hostages incensed Gregor. Mere thought of what he knew of Alexa's captivity sent blood boiling through his veins. He dreaded the personal challenge that the following day would bring. He would meet the Sifiq captain who had so brutalized Alexa. As Turand's king, he must display the integrity inherent in the core beliefs of his nation. As a man, Gregor questioned the true face of justice and his personal abilities to administer that justice.

Chapter 22

"In Val's great name! Now what?" Gregor abruptly stopped with one foot in the stirrup and the other inches above brick pathways. Quickly stepping down, he shot a look of utter frustration at Victor, who only nodded mutely. The king then hurried toward a small carriage that had rolled to a stop in front of the entrance to his godparents' house.

Alexa, covered from head to toe with a hooded winter cloak, had just appeared outside in the morning sunshine. She smiled charmingly and raised emerald eyes to meet her husband's angry brown ones. "I made it!"

"You made it? Meaning exactly what?"

"Meaning that I came out just in time to accompany you."

From remote corners of his mind surfaced amusing memories of that wide-eyed, innocent expression. Placing leather-clad hands firmly on her shoulders, he leveled a stern, intimidating glare at her. "You, my love, are going nowhere except back inside the house."

One nod challenged him. "I am not going back inside. With or without your approval, I intend to follow you today."

"Alexa!" Clenching his jaw for a moment, he struggled to control his temper. "We are leaving to review Sifiq prisoners."

"That is precisely my reason for going. As I recall, I am your queen. My place is at your side during such times."

With rising frustration, he inhaled sharply. "Ordinarily, I would agree with you; however, only days ago, you lay near death after what those men did to you. Just yesterday, you were hysterical about their return. What makes you think I would allow you to go today under such circumstances?"

Pressing her lips together, Alexa gazed into her husband's scowling face. "Gregor, I am also still Valkana. If Val saved my life, it is because he wills resumption of my responsibilities as Turand's High Priestess."

"Alexa, I do not believe for a single minute that Val expects you to see these prisoners right now—not after everything you suffered at their hands." Pausing, his voice lost its sharp tone as his worried eyes scanned her face. "I love you, Alexa. Don't do this to yourself. Please."

Her eyes glazed. Her voice grew quietly intense. "I must, Gregor. I must face them. The sooner I confront them, the sooner I really begin to heal. Besides, I want them to witness their failure to destroy me."

Black-brown eyes gentled as they seemingly caressed every precious detail of her face. "Beloved, I fear it's too much too soon."

Intensity flared in the eyes that gazed back at him. "Fear, Gregor— my own fear is what frightens me most of all. I cannot live the same kind of fear that kept me from Zinzan all those years. I need to confront my fears if I am to conquer them. This is the only way I know how. As long as you're with me, I know I can do it. Help me, Gregor. Please?"

As she moved into his arms, Gregor closed his eyes. Even through heavy clothes, the fragility of her body was starkly, painfully evident. However, he also sensed her revitalized resolve. Reluctantly, he admitted that even her stubbornness commanded his respect. Turning to help her into the coach, he silently rebuked himself. Stubbornness? Hardly. Though she spoke openly of being afraid, never had he known anyone as courageous as she.

Raised canvas shades let bright sunshine filter hazily through dusty film on the windows. Steam running through coiled radiators heated open space. Mattresses with clean sheets and blankets were arranged in two rows on the floors. Several tables with benches provided eating space. Three officers sat at one table while subordinates sat on their beds. Several sailors lay ill in beds positioned aside from the rest.

"Prisoners, except for the sick, you will rise," Tirstan Fratino announced in a commanding voice. Nodding his satisfaction when all stood, he continued, "You will show respect to the King and Queen of Turand."

Victor preceded his monarchs through a side entrance and approached the prisoners. Conceding to Gregor's wishes, Alexa stepped back and was instantly flanked by the captain of her Guard and another soldier. She stood quietly without removing her hood.

Silently, Gregor paced from end to end of the line of prisoners. His stature emanated intimidating authority. His eyes were darkly ominous, his olive-bronze countenance daunting.

"I am King Gregor." Even his voice, powerful and echoing, commanded the attention of startled prisoners who had never seen anyone so tall. Finally, he stopped before an officer who had stepped forward slightly. "You are?"

Thrusting out his chest, the blond officer said, "I am Lieutenant Fen-Gaf, in service to the Sifiq Kingdom and first mate to Captain Raf-Zan."

"Lieutenant, you stand corrected. You find yourself in Turand. Therefore, you are removed from service to the Sifiq Kingdom. Why are you here?"

"Our ship ran aground during a storm." Fen-Gaf stared at the Turandan king, wondering about his unusual appearance.

"I heard about the shipwreck. What I want to know is why your ship violated my territorial waters."

Warily, the lieutenant chose his words. "We were on a mission commanded by our king."

"And that mission was?" Gregor's curt tone only accentuated tightly suppressed fury.

Fen-Gaf paused. "King Bin-Lot ordered the return of Turandans who were living in the Sifiq Kingdom."

Dark eyes bore the icy sheen of polished obsidian. "Living there? Or taken captive?"

The Sifiq officer bristled at the tone in Gregor's voice. Ingrained arrogance saturated his voice. "Such details hold little importance. They were in the Sifiq Kingdom, and they were transported here by royal command. That is all."

Swallowing rising bile born of fury, the king felt a hand come to rest against the small of his back. "Lieutenant, according to Turandan custom, you and your men will kneel to show respect to my wife, Queen Alexa."

Emerald irises sparkled as Alexa slid back the hood, revealing her face. No hint of malice marred her expression. However, the collective gasp from former captors clearly satisfied part of her purpose for coming.

"Sailors, stay as you are!" Fen-Gaf then snarled venomously, "As a Sifiq officer, I will never kneel before a woman!"

Before the man could draw another breath, Victor jumped forward, grabbing Fen-Gaf 's arm. Within seconds, the Sifiq officer's arm was twisted painfully behind his back as Victor hissed into his ear, "You are in Turand now. Your disrespectful insolence will not be tolerated."

Gregor's arm shot out to his side to restrain Alexa. Turning his head, he quietly reminded her that she had promised no interference as he dealt with the Sifiq on whatever terms they established. Reluctantly acquiescing, she stepped backward. Gregor advanced to hover above the officer resisting Victor's grip. Powerful hands landed on Fen-Gaf 's shoulders and closed with painful, vise-like pressure on each side of the younger man's neck. With deliberate slowness, he pushed downward, forcing the Sifiq lieutenant to his knees.

Through clenched teeth, Gregor addressed Fen-Gaf. "As Lord Garogan has stated, you are now in Turand. You will conduct yourself accordingly, especially in the presence of my wife."

Fen-Gaf jerked his head sideways and spat in Alexa's direction. "Damn your wife!" His exclamation was followed by a loud snap and an agonized groan.

Again, Victor hissed into the officer's ear. "I will happily break your other arm if you persist."

Alexa stood with her eyes closed. She listened as Sifiq soldiers, disobeying their lieutenant, fell to their knees. She sincerely desired no more violence, not even against these men who would have gladly killed her. Gregor, however, had insisted on her heeding his judgment. Years of dealing with Sifiq occupiers had taught him many harsh lessons, one of which was that communication with them had to be established in terms they could understand. In the case of the Sifiq military, that translated to superior strength and the will to use it.

Gregor backed away as Victor released Fen-Gaf, who broke his forward fall with his good arm. Victor directed a look into the king's eyes. "Your Majesty, I apologize if my actions offended you."

"Lord Garogan, you have done only what was necessary." Shifting his gaze toward the other prisoners, the king's voice rang out loudly. "I suspect many of you have heard old tales that Turandans fear the use of force. We have given you concise orders and instructions. As honorable people, we will continue to do so for you to know what is expected. You can be assured, however, that we will not hesitate to utilize whatever force is necessary to persuade you to follow directions.

"Also, I have long known of your ridiculous attitudes toward women. Such attitudes have no place in Turand. Respect and courtesy will be shown to men and women alike. This is my royal command." He paused, shifting his eyes from man to man. "Especially with regard to our Queen and High Priestess Valkana, you are required to kneel in her presence until instructed otherwise. I believe her very presence before you today proves that she is inferior to no man and merits respect."

Gregor turned toward Alexa and, taking her hand, pulled her close. His voice softened in response to the distress in her eyes. "For you to remember is that he made his choice. None of these men will be deliberately mistreated, but they must learn acceptable behavior."

Nodding, she lifted her hand to touch her husband's bearded face. She then turned toward kneeling Sifiq soldiers and said, "Gentlemen, you may rise."

While members of the Royal Guard resumed supervision of the prisoners, Alexa approached the sailors who remained sick in bed. All had been injured during the storm. Two had grown critically ill. Looking down into one young man's face, she saw silver light glinting from a steel blade raised high in the air. That knife had slashed downward into ropes binding her to the mast of the Sifiq ship. Blinking against terrible images accompanied by distinct sensations of dismay and regret, she remembered.

Despite abject fear of punishment, this one sailor had demonstrated signs of compassion and had dared to try to help. Kneeling, Alexa slowly extended her right arm and passed it over the youth she thought was close to Nikolai's age.

Fevered eyes opened. Sudden shock faded into a hesitant smile. "I— am glad—you survived," he murmured in a low, hoarse whisper.

"I remember. You are Per-Tuk?" In response to his weak smile, she continued, "Per-Tuk, you are more than very sick. You are dying. You know that. I can ask my God Val to help you, but only if you acknowledge him." Leaning forward, she listened to his faint, broken reply.

"I tried, but—I could not—save you. If your God saved you—perhaps he—will save me?"

"Alexa?" Her husband's hand gently clasped her shoulder. The sympathy glowing on her face both frightened and heartened him. "Are you sure you have the strength?" Receiving reassurance in the form of a serene smile, Gregor nodded. Giving her time to perform sacred duties, he would concentrate on another matter still awaiting his attention. Bending over, he kissed her cheek before leaving her under Fratino's watchful protection.

Despite baleful Sifiq attention directed toward her, Alexa sat on the floor by young Per-Tuk's bedside. Feeling safe in the presence of Turandan guards, she closed her eyes and initiated a quietly melodic, prayerful chant. Within moments, an orb of blue-white light appeared, expanded, and enveloped her and the Sifiq sailor whose hands she now held in her own.

⤳

Just before he exited the warehouse area for the attached office wing, Gregor hesitated and paused to glance backward. Lights of Val danced off the globe of light surrounding his wife. Trusting Val to watch over her, he strode quickly toward a heavily guarded door and entered the office now converted to quarters isolating Raf-Zan from his men. Only Victor accompanied the king.

Sitting on the edge of the cot that had replaced an old desk, the Sifiq captain cast his visitors a steely gaze. Holding his right arm tightly against his body, he rose to his feet. Recognizing Victor and seeing him poised to strike, Raf-Zan took a precautionary step backward and widened his stance in wary anticipation. Noting the fearsome glare from the other man's black eyes, Raf-Zan's face remained a frozen mask as he waited for someone to speak.

Hostile indignation flared in Gregor's eyes. Muscles in his tall body contracted tensely. Then, with calculated, measured motions, he removed leather gloves from hands that clenched and unclenched. Breathing deeply, he took one stride forward. "You will identify yourself."

For an instant, Raf-Zan appeared puzzled. Quickly, he recovered his usual, haughty manner. "I am Captain Raf-Zan of the Royal Sifiq Navy."

The solid thud into Raf-Zan's midsection was followed by the sickening sound of the king's fist crashing into the man's jaw. Stepping back, Gregor stared in quiet fury at the stunned man, now fallen backward onto his bed.

"Stand up," Gregor snarled.

Swallowing hard, Raf-Zan gathered his wits and slowly stood. Excruciating pain plainly marred his features. Blood trickled from the corner of his mouth, and his already bruised face showed signs of renewed swelling. Then, bringing himself to stiff attention, he faced the tall stranger. Grateful that his jaw remained amazingly intact, he spoke. "I seem to provoke a most unusual reaction in you Turandans."

Victor addressed the prisoner. "Captain Raf-Zan, may I introduce you to King Gregor?"

Surprise registered in the captive officer's eyes as he inclined his head to acknowledge Gregor's position. "Perhaps you will overlook my ignorance. I would never have expected to be honored with personal attention from Turand's king."

Rage still painted its dark mask on Gregor's face. His deep voice sounded uncharacteristically abrasive. "You receive no honor from Turand's king. You merit naught but my absolute contempt considering the cowardly violence you inflicted upon those unable to defend themselves."

"Ah," sighed Raf-Zan, thinking he finally understood. "Perhaps you refer to those troublesome women I put off my ship in lifeboats. You must understand. I only followed orders from my king. I am a man sworn to obey orders."

"You dare call yourself a man?" Menacingly, the king advanced toward the prisoner. "Neither courage nor honor exists in a man who would commit such despicable deeds as you have." Gregor abruptly stopped upon hearing the door open. Turning, he met Fratino's worried countenance.

"Sire, our Lady Valkana has finished tending to the sick and wishes to join her husband." Solemn eyes revealed personal anxiety regarding his queen.

Gregor's eyelids closed momentarily, and he exhaled sharply before instructing his captain to wait a moment. Pivoting on his heel, Gregor glared once again at the Sifiq captain. "My wife will now join me. She is not only my queen. As High Priestess Valkana, she is also the spiritual leader of this nation. For your sake, I highly recommend that you demonstrate no disrespect."

Anxiety gnawed at his stomach as he paused in the doorway. Eyes that had spewed fury only seconds earlier now gentled. Her face was exceptionally ashen. Lips quivered. Thankfully, emerald eyes glittered with resolve. He had no need to ask. She would do this, no matter how difficult. Lightly cupping her elbow, Gregor guided her into the room to face Captain Raf-Zan.

"You! How…? What kind of demon bitch are you?"

The captain's eyes widened as shocked disbelief disintegrated any memory of Gregor's stern warning. The result startled both Victor and Alexa. Grabbing Raf-Zan tightly around the throat, Gregor jerked the Sifiq captain off his feet. Raf-Zan's face turned purplish-red, and his eyes bulged as he stared into the king's livid features.

Gregor's voice conveyed razor-sharp menace. "If you ever dare speak to my wife like that again, I shall personally rip you apart, piece by piece. Do you understand me, Captain?"

Unable even to gasp for air and resisting unconsciousness, Raf-Zan barely nodded in response. Then, abruptly freed from Gregor's brutal stranglehold, he stumbled backward and collapsed onto his bed.

Never had Alexa observed such unbridled rage in her husband. Suddenly, despite her quaking insides, she felt grateful she had come. So powerful was Gregor's fury that her presence alone prevented him from using his bare hands to kill Raf-Zan. Eventually, he would have regretted his actions.

The eerie tone in her voice commanded the Sifiq's attention. "Captain, my Lord Val wills that we should meet again."

Overcoming nauseating dizziness, the captain caught his breath and dragged himself to his feet. His painful jaw and throat were nothing compared to the searing agony in his arm. And, for the first time in his life, Raf-Zan faced a woman in fear. The very thought that she might touch him again spawned abject terror.

Receiving no reply, Alexa continued, "You defied your king's orders. In doing so, you invited disaster upon yourself, your command, and your comrades at home. I warned Bin-Lot. Why? Why did you disobey him?"

Nearly paralyzed with fright, Raf-Zan swallowed against the choking knot in his throat. Resorting to bravado, he forced a hoarse, sneering whisper. "You brought destruction to the Sifiq Kingdom. Our king may have feared you, but I did not. You deserved punishment."

Alexa jumped at the captain's agonized scream as Victor grabbed the man's arm. "Victor, please." Without hesitation, she approached the prisoner. "What is wrong with your arm?"

Dropping his face, he attempted to slow his erratic breathing. His heartbeat raced, and blood throbbed like ice in his veins. Finally, he looked up. "You should know better than I. You inflicted this curse upon me."

Advancing menacingly, Gregor's face held a warning expression. "I warn you, Raf-Zan."

Gritting his teeth against unceasing agony, the captain straightened. "My arm burns as if covered with flames. See for yourself." Extending his arm, he rolled back his sleeve. The flesh appeared raw and blistered from just beneath his elbow to his fingertips. "Since the night you left my ship, this has spread from my hand upward. My arm grows useless."

Alexa lifted shocked eyes to her husband before moving closer to Raf-Zan, whose entire body trembled as she reached toward him. Victor prevented him from backing away.

"Don't touch me!" he shouted desperately. "Not again!"

"You have no need to fear me, Captain," she scolded. "Be still. I will not touch you." Instead, she closed her eyes and allowed her energies to focus. Smoothly sweeping open hands over the length of his arm, she sensed horrific agony and gasped. Lifting her eyelids, she stared boldly into blue eyes. "This I have not done. You brought this upon yourself by disobeying your king's command. After you beat me, you used this arm to throw me overboard into the ocean. What you endure is the wrath of our God Val."

"You. Your god. What does it matter? I suffer, and my arm dies. A Sifiq officer is better dead than left to live with a useless arm."

"Alexa," Victor quietly addressed her. Already he observed sympathy welling inside her despite atrocities suffered at Raf-Zan's hands. "What should we do?"

Craving reassurance from his closeness, she moved closer to Gregor. "Little can be done. Immobilize the limb. Call a physician to administer medication to deaden the pain. He faces death without amputation."

Heavily, the Sifiq captain collapsed onto the bed. Amputation. Worse than a death sentence. Raising his head to face Gregor, Raf-Zan said, "I request immediate execution."

Remembered images. Life. Death. So little time elapsed since he and Nikolai had discussed the tribunal following civil war in Turand. Gregor

317

had believed those lessons in justice would never be forgotten. In truth, they were not. In fact, they now returned as explosive reminders of exactly how vulnerable the substance of those lessons could be. Violence itself provided the most fertile ground for cultivating new violence.

On a different plane, he suddenly comprehended all Victor had faced after leaving Alexa in Toraval those many years ago. Gregor's personal desire to punish Raf-Zan was the mirror image of Victor's pursuit of vengeance. Another truth struck Gregor. Alexa had once again delivered him from destruction.

"Your request is denied. And not because your pain gives me pleasure. My wife reminds me that our laws require you to face appropriate judgment for your actions. You will be provided proper medical care until that time."

Then Gregor gazed thoughtfully into her face. "Without you, my love, I am lost," he whispered before issuing orders for the Sifiq captain's care and taking Alexa home to rest.

Chapter 23

"Gregor, please. Just one day."

Huffing an exasperated sigh, he had shaken his head. "I warned you it was too soon."

"We've traveled three days straight already. I only need one day to rest. Then we can resume the trip."

His fingertip had gently brushed away the single tear rolling down her cheek. Recalling how she had nearly fallen still troubled him. Luckily, he had been by her side, alertly catching her. "You are very fortunate we were so close to Taprina today."

Sheepishly, she smiled. "You'll see. We can stay here tomorrow and start again the next day. Don't be upset."

Leaning forward, he kissed her forehead and pulled the covers up around her. "Rest. We can discuss it later." Soon, the warmth inside one of Turand's busiest inns had seeped into her bones, coaxing her to sleep.

Downstairs, Gregor strode toward the massive stone fireplace dominating the inn's lounge. Accepting a tankard of Taca from the jovial innkeeper and dropping into a leather chair, the king joined Victor. "She's asleep already. Why did I let her talk me into this insanity?"

Victor chuckled. "Don't deride yourself too much. I honestly think you made the right decision."

Consternation creased Gregor's brow. "How so?"

Victor shook his head. "We both know how she is. She would be just as likely to attempt the trip on her own if you had refused. As it is, we can at least watch over her. What amazes me is that she admits to needing a day to rest. She can hardly wait to return home."

Nodding thoughtfully, Gregor agreed, then looked up as Tirstan Fratino approached. "Captain?"

"Sire, the Sifiq prisoners are settled in at the Taprina garrison. This is the ideal location if you intend to stay an extra day. Taprina provides all the necessary accommodations and security."

"Convenient," Gregor remarked vaguely. "Very well, Captain. Organize arrangements as you deem appropriate. In the meantime, accommodate your men and plan to remain through tomorrow." Then, turning to Victor, he asked, "What about the other ladies?"

"I think the priestesses also welcome the respite. Oui-lest and Mei-sat Tan say little but haven't complained once."

DiLeno and Tirani had remained behind in Timeri. Later, they would escort the remaining Sifiq refugees to Toraval. However, Lisana and Marlí, plus Oui-lest and another Sifiq woman, had chosen to travel with Alexa's party. Oui-lest preferred braving the wintry trip to stay close to Alexa, while the priestesses longed to reunite with their husbands.

"I cannot dismiss the feeling that Alexa is stopping here for some other purpose."

Victor raised his eyebrows inquisitively, then shrugged. "One can never quite tell with her. However, as anxious as she is to be home, I can think of no other obvious reason."

Hours later, Alexa tightly grasped the handrail and descended to the first floor. Her heartbeat quickened, and butterflies fluttered in her stomach. Anticipation of life's pleasures was returning with a rush. Entering the cozy atmosphere of the inn's lounge, she smiled tentatively, expecting her husband's chastisement.

"Alexa! Dearest Val! You weren't supposed to come down!"

Approaching him and standing on her tiptoes to lightly kiss his lips, she said brightly, "I knew you wouldn't disappoint me. You scold so sweetly." Amused laughter instantly escaped their companions.

Closing his eyes, Gregor drew in a frustrated breath. "My sweet Alexa, you are completely impossible!" he exclaimed. Yet again, memories swept through his mind. How many times through the years had he told her that? Thanks be to Val that he could do so again. His expression grew gentle. "We were just going in for supper. Will you join us?"

Starting to sit after grace, Alexa suddenly stopped. "Gregor," she said quietly, "please go ahead. I'll be right back." Giving him no chance to respond, she hurried from the dining room toward the inn's reception desk. Finding the innkeeper's teenage daughter, she requested use of the girl's cloak. Then, donning the garment, she went outside.

Velvety blue hues created a dramatic canvas for emerging diamond-like points of light. Shimmering silver transformed the crescent moon into a bedazzling jeweled brooch fixed to expansive night skies. Cold air smelled cleanly stimulating as light breezes swished through towering evergreens. Taprina snuggled into wintry white blankets while its inhabitants cast golden lights into nighttime darkness.

With eyes closed, she directed her senses outward into the night. Almost. Almost. Hooves plodded along roads covered with compacted snow. Closer. Closer. Looking up, she watched the group of riders round the corner. Carefully, she made her way down snowy steps to the street. The riders stopped. Swiftly, one dismounted and ran toward her.

"Mother!" Nikolai cried out as he swept her into his arms and lifted her off her feet. "Oh, Mother!"

"Nikolai," she sobbed against his shoulder. By bits and pieces, Val was returning her life. Her maternal spirit recognized every aspect of his embrace as if he still remained a little boy. "My dear Nikolai! How much I've missed you!"

Reluctantly, he released her. Tears shone on olive cheeks as he lifted a gloved hand to stroke her hair beneath the edge of her hood. Nervously, he smiled. "Father may be angry, but I could wait no longer." Thickly lashed eyelids fell for seconds before he gazed at her again. "I needed to see you for myself." Only a mother's smile could convey such reassurance as hers did.

Nikolai proceeded to explain how, upon receiving Gregor's last dispatch, he had personally visited the families of Lisana and Marlí. Learning of their wives' safe return, two elated husbands immediately prepared to leave Toraval. Nikolai had offered to lead their escort.

Scarcely able to suppress growing excitement, the prince's travel companions respectfully greeted their Valkana. After instructing accompanying guards to take charge of horses, Nikolai escorted his mother and the others into the inn.

Returning the borrowed cloak to its owner, Alexa turned and looked up into her eldest son's face. Observing his expression, she touched her hair self-consciously. "It was even shorter than this. It's finally growing back."

Unable to mask his surprise, he stroked a long finger across her cheek. "It doesn't matter. You're as beautiful as I remembered. Having you home again is most important."

She smiled past him at two very anxious men. "An entourage awaits us in the dining room, including two ladies who'll be ecstatic to see you." Clinging to her son's arm with both hands, she proceeded inside toward the sounds of voices and aromas whetting the appetites of three young men who had ridden many hours in winter's cold.

When the new arrivals entered the dining room, conversational din ceased instantly. With expressions frozen, Lisana and Marlí looked up in tearful astonishment at the unexpected appearance of their husbands, who crossed the room with blinding speed.

Meanwhile, Gregor stared at Nikolai. Stormy brown eyes held questions more than anger. Tentatively, father embraced son. "Your arrival surprises me."

Although cautious, Nikolai's gaze remained steady as he faced his father. "Since there was no immediate Sifiq threat and you were bringing Mother home, I decided to ride to meet you."

"You were to wait in Toraval."

Despite the softness of Gregor's voice, Nikolai heard the reproach but stood his ground. "Father, you left me in charge. My absence from the palace presents little risk, so I decided to lead the escort for Masters Faradón and Gotrano."

Observant green eyes studied the exchange between father and son. Although there were no discernible hostilities, strain definitely showed in both their faces and their stances. Smiling brilliantly, Alexa interceded by stepping between them. "Gentlemen, we mustn't be rude. Shall we introduce Nikolai and then have supper? I, for one, am quite hungry."

Turning, Alexa saw the Sifiq ladies had already risen to their feet. "Oui-lest and Mei-sat, I finally have the pleasure of introducing you to my son, Prince Nikolai."

Nikolai warmly greeted the foreign women with the same courtly elegance as his father. He laughed aloud when Oui-lest delightfully expressed agreement with the many times Alexa had spoken of how handsome her eldest son was. Showing no embarrassment whatsoever, Nikolai leaned over to kiss his mother's cheek while winking at Oui-lest. "The compliment is accepted with appreciation—from you both."

Dinner proceeded amiably, with Alexa seated between Gregor and Nikolai. Animated by Nikolai's presence, Alexa chattered endlessly, expressing amazement that he now stood even taller than his father and indulging herself in memories from his childhood. Following dinner, she requested that Gregor escort her upstairs before leaving for his nightly inspection of Sifiq prisoners.

Reaching their chambers, Alexa waited while Gregor lit lamps on each end of a polished wooden dresser. Crossing her arms in front of her, she glanced around. Recently covered with fresh coats of ivory paint, the walls displayed small paintings depicting life in Turand's countryside. An enormous bed invited her to slide beneath plump comforters of velvety green and gold fabrics. An array of pillows teased her with their promise of a soft place to cradle her head. First, however, she knew the time had come to address the suppressed waves of anxiety she had detected from her husband.

"Gregor," she said quietly, "may I ask you something before you go back downstairs?"

The line of her mouth softened without creating the beautiful smile he adored. Observing the grave expression in her eyes and approaching her, he cradled her face between open palms. His left brow lifted questioningly. "I don't like that worried look in your eyes. What is your question?"

"What matter divides you and Nikolai?"

Sliding his hand down along her arms until he could enfold her hands within his, he gazed into emerald eyes that would forever hold him captive. Forcing a smile, he replied, "There is no matter dividing us."

"Perhaps I asked the wrong question. Nevertheless, I know what I have sensed in you. Tonight, I saw both of your reactions in the dining room. You know better than to try to deny that something isn't right between you. Will you tell me, or do I ask Nikolai instead?"

Gregor's face paled. Her senses proved as keen as ever. Sighing, he turned away and walked toward the window. Pushing aside striped velvet draperies matching the comforter, he gazed blindly at silver flurries swirling through the air. His vision held only the memory of Nikolai's bewildered expression the night Victor's dispatch had arrived.

Her footsteps barely sounded on the carpet. Her face rested against his broad back, and her arms reached around his waist. His hidden sadness seeped into her being. Alexa's unique sensitivity to his emotions remained intact. "You mustn't lock this inside, Gregor. Whatever it is, you cannot resolve or reconcile the problem until you face it."

Icy cold from the windowpane penetrated his skin as his forehead rested against frosty glass. He berated himself for the inability to obscure his feelings concerning Nikolai. She needed no additional burden to complicate her recovery. His breathing labored as he found it nearly impossible to draw in sufficient air to satisfy his body's needs.

"Gregor?"

He recalled other terrible times, now threatening the relationship with his firstborn child. With a mighty heave, he dragged in a breath that shuddered throughout his body. Dropping his head backward, he stared at the ceiling and clasped his hands over hers. Then, without a word, he turned and led her to a sofa where they sat together.

Lifting sorrowful eyes, he smiled uneasily as her fingers floated through shining waves in his hair. "I feel such guilt about troubling you with this now."

She leaned forward and kissed a warm tear from his cheek. Straightening, she sighed. "Just tell me what happened."

His throat contracted, and he swallowed hard. His words trembled. "Alexa, you know that Victor wrote a letter to Stefan when he found you. When Stefan brought me that letter, it was well past midnight. I was dumbstruck. All I could think about was how fast I could reach you.

Victor had written how critical your condition was. Nikolai heard Stefan knocking at my door to wake me."

Tension drew Gregor's face into a taut mask. Alexa gracefully rose to her feet and went around behind the sofa. With skillful fingers, she began kneading the tightening muscles in her husband's neck. "Will you tell me the rest?"

Gregor lowered his face. He had nearly forgotten her talent for massaging away stress when he had faced past crises. "When Nikolai asked me what was going on, I was too overcome to speak. Instead, I let him read Victor's letter."

Sensing growing distress, Alexa moved to kneel in front of her husband. "And?"

Taking her thin hands into his, he winced at calluses that testified to the labor she had been forced to perform. No matter how rough, those hands still held power to bring him great comfort. "In my shock, I had forgotten that Victor had written about having found the woman we both love."

Freeing one hand so she could caress his lined brow, Alexa nodded thoughtfully. "Knowing Nikolai, I assume he questioned Victor's meaning. What then?"

Agitated, Gregor jerkily stood up and strode across the room. "What could I do? I told him the truth."

"And?"

"Alexa! I told him the truth! You should have seen the look on his face! You know how close he and Victor are. He was stunned! Shocked! I was desperate to get to you, so all I could do was beg my own son to be patient and not pass judgment on me until I could return! Alexa…"

This time, Alexa led him to the sofa. Firmly, she held his shaking hands. "Gregor, we both know that what happened with us was Val's will."

"Alexa," he interrupted her, "you and I understand that, but how do I tell that to our son? How do I explain to him that his father, who spent years striving to provide an example of integrity to a whole nation, actually forced his mother into marriage against her will? How do I face him? How can I ever expect Nikolai to respect me or believe in me again?"

"Listen to me, Gregor," Alexa commanded sternly. "Listen carefully. I know that Nikolai loves you. We will work this out. Together. You don't have to face this alone, and you won't."

Utterly frustrated, Gregor covered his face with his hands. "Alexa, beloved, this is so unfair. We should be concentrating on making you well again. Instead, I draw you into a personal crisis of my own making. Now is not the time to worry you with a problem of this magnitude."

A film of tears glistened in her eyes. "Gregor, would you deny me the fulfillment of a most precious dream?"

He sighed, drawing her into his arms. Even her unshed tears stung him. "What precious dream?"

Freeing herself from his embrace, she breathed out heavily. "Gregor, ever since the Sifiq captured me, I dreamed of coming home, of resuming a life I cherished. I can only imagine what you must feel regarding Nikolai. With me home, though, you don't have to face him alone. I'll be with you. Together, we can help him understand. And, at long last, I can again be mother to my children and wife to my husband. Don't deny me that."

As always, her intensity penetrated every fiber of his being. Solace poured into his soul as her mouth opened to receive the kiss he bestowed. "Alexa," he gasped, growing fearful of the unbidden tide of passion swelling within him. "How I've missed you, Alexa." His eyelids dropped, and he breathed in deeply. "Nikolai is waiting downstairs for me. Go to bed now. I won't be too late." Then, lovingly, he kissed her goodnight.

Just as he started to leave, she called out to him, "Gregor, my love, remember. We're together again. Everything will work out. I promise."

Heels of leather boots crunched through brittle snow and ice. Reaching the barracks where Sifiq prisoners were housed, father and son conversed quietly with the officer on duty. Prisoners had immediately risen to attention upon noting the entrance of Turand's impressive king and the young man who was obviously his son. Silently, Gregor strode past Sifiq prisoners startled by the appearance of two men so tall. Both Turandans wore severe expressions as they inspected the captives.

In separate quarters, Captain Raf-Zan dragged himself to his feet to acknowledge Gregor's arrival. The Sifiq captain's eyes quickly assessed Nikolai. "This is your son, Your Majesty?"

Gregor's voice sounded starkly cold. "This is Prince Nikolai, my eldest child."

"Prince Nikolai," Raf-Zan acknowledged. "No wonder your father favors your mother. A woman who breeds such fine-looking sons is quite a valuable asset."

Nikolai's large hands instantly shot out and twisted into the fabric of the captain's shirt, jerking him forward. "Never speak of my mother in such derogatory terms. She is not breeding stock."

"I meant no disrespect," Raf-Zan ground out. Swaying slightly when Nikolai abruptly released him, the Sifiq captain grimaced and gritted his teeth against pain shafting through his arm. "You must understand that my nation grants high esteem to those females who produce sons. We need strong males to make brave soldiers."

"Why? To torment and murder those weaker than you? How brave and strong must a so-called man be to whip a woman already sick from malnutrition and multiple beatings and then throw her into the ocean? You have the audacity to call yourself a man?" Infuriated by what Victor had told him while they waited for Gregor, Nikolai glared at the Sifiq captain. "Physical strength doesn't translate to courage. Cruel cowards don't deserve to live."

Raf-Zan cocked an eyebrow as he glanced at Gregor. "King Gregor, the prince shares your basic philosophy. Commendable."

Gregor remained composed. "Captain, I do not disagree with my son; however, if you intend to incite violence in order to get yourself killed, you will be disappointed."

Raf-Zan's jaw twitched from side to side. "I told you. A Sifiq officer without an arm is useless. The two of you agree that I don't deserve to live. Why not simplify matters? Execute me."

"Because I once traveled a similar road. My son will learn the lessons I learned without having to partake in the violence and bloodshed upon which the Sifiq military thrives."

Quickly glancing sideways, Nikolai wondered how his father could remain so calm before such a despicable, loathsome man. Forgetting the discussion in Gregor's suite months earlier, he pondered his father's true feelings yet again. Ever since that last night in his parents' chambers, the prince had grappled with questions that haunted him day and night. He recalled times when Victor had dismissed inquiries regarding why he had never married or sometimes looked so haunted and sad. He also wanted to know why Anlía had sent Victor to Timeri instead of Father. A veritable parade of questions had assaulted him. He hated them but had been unable to ask Stefan or Adrina.

Without noticing his son's lapse into silence, Gregor said, "Nikolai, I wanted you to meet Captain Raf-Zan. He is living example of those who once tried to destroy our nation. Your responsibility and mine is to ensure that even he receives justice according to our laws."

Casting frigid eyes upon Raf-Zan, Gregor continued, "My wife's character is so good she would advise that even you have options. Unfortunately, I am not so inclined. I abhor what you did, and I will never forget seeing the results of what you inflicted on her. May Val forgive me for saying this in my son's presence. While I never deliberately wish suffering upon anyone, you certainly deserve every second of your agony."

⌣

Alexa rose hours before dawn. In her sleep, she had heard the distant voice of a woman. Mournfully, that voice had beckoned her. Inconsolable weeping. Sorrow curling tremulous tendrils into her soul—begging relief, begging succor, begging compassion. Such echoes sounded vaguely familiar. Where had she heard them before?

Silently, she dressed in darkness, sensing everything in the suite as if she had always lived there. Lightly padding to the bed's side where Gregor slept, she gazed down upon his shadowed face. Pressing fingertips to her lips, she transferred the kiss to his mussed hair. Lips formed silent words. "Sleep well, and do not worry, my husband. I love you."

Descending the stairs, she was oblivious to the inn's hushed, pre-dawn quiet. Instead, keen hearing locked on pitiful weeping that neared with each step she took. Glancing toward the reception desk, a lamp glowed as the desk clerk dozed with his head resting on his arms. His sleep deepened as waves of tranquil energy projected from the mist-encased figure leaving swiftly through the door.

Outside, Alexa quickly tugged her hood over her head and clutched her cloak more tightly about her. She lifted her eyes to blackened heavens bearing glittering stars. "My dearest Lord Val," she prayed aloud, "carry me to the source of those cries and help me assuage that terrible grief."

Once again, she looked around. Fading moonlight glinted off fresh, glittering, crystalline snow. She knew no fear when she stepped into the center of the shadowy, deserted street. Valkana again, enrobed in light, she pursued the sounds that had awakened her. Her heartbeat quickened. Beginning to recognize the cause of sorrow, her mother's heart connected with another mother's heart. Her spirit responded to another mother's misery. Needing to better understand and to share her blessings, she hurried faster. Finally, she stopped. Opening her eyes, she noted her location with dismay. The voice had led her directly to the compound sheltering Sifiq prisoners.

Alexa's breath caught painfully in her chest. The weeping inside her head grew louder, more insistent. Her hands began to shake violently. Hot tears stung her eyes. Biting into her lips, she tasted salt in her own blood. What power had carried her here? Who expected her to enter this place where, in humane captivity, slept one-time captors who had viciously tormented her?

Loosening the grasp on her cloak, she fearfully stretched out her arms. With palms upward, the Valkana prayed. Val did not speak. However, she felt his spirit enfold her. She must trust as she had always trusted. She must follow his path as she had always followed. While the weeping continued, Alexa heard the echo of other words, her own vows pronounced the day she had become a Valiria priestess. Drawing on battered faith, she entered the compound gate.

Two guards immediately met her at the entrance. Shocked by her appearance, they led her inside from the cold. One left to summon Captain Fratino while the other allowed her to link her arm with his. Instantly, he felt pulsating energy in her touch. Wordlessly, he escorted her through barracks where the only sounds were their footsteps accompanied by snorts and snores from sleeping prisoners. An odd thought crossed his mind. He acted as escort, but she, with eyes closed, guided their course. Finally stopping, the guard's face reflected fresh concern.

"Lady Valkana." Tirstan Fratino's voice was low when he arrived and worriedly faced his queen. Years in her service had led him to automatic changes in the way he addressed her. Misty blue-white light surrounding her presence represented the will of God, not of man. Not even a hundred years in her service could ever diminish the shivers that shafted along his backbone whenever he saw that light. "Why have you come at such an hour?"

"Tirstan, I come, summoned by sorrowful crying."

"Lady Valkana, no one here is crying. Everyone is asleep, as you should be." The tranquility of her smile never failed to inspire him. "You know who sleeps behind this locked door."

Nodding in response, she stared at the door, illuminated by her aura's light. "I do. The weeping lies behind it."

Her captain breathed in deeply. Earlier in the evening, he had checked a final time on Captain Raf-Zan. Despondent and thoroughly dispirited, the Sifiq captain had spoken to Tirstan regarding the king's visit. Something mentioned by the king had struck a repetitive note. Raf-Zan openly asked Tirstan's opinion of the king's meaning. He had somehow expected Tirstan to understand. What had surprised him was the time afforded to answer. Tirstan left behind an exceptionally contemplative prisoner.

"Shall I get the key and unlock the door?"

Alexa shook her head. "There is no need." Firmly grasping the door handle, metallic clicking was followed by the smooth opening of the door. Alexa breathed in several times, fortifying herself to face whatever lay beyond. Deriving security from knowledge that Tirstan waited merely steps away, she slowly entered. The stench of burned, deteriorating flesh stung her nostrils.

Raf-Zan sat on the bed with his back against the wall. Fever-glazed, pain-stricken eyes met hers. Once, he had dismissed the recollections of palace officers in Atuliq as ridiculous hallucinations. The light that moved with her now came as no shock.

"Why have you come?" His voice held not a hint of malice.

"I heard her crying. Who is she?"

Pain medications administered by a Turandan physician had drugged him into sleep. Rarely did he ever dream. Tonight had been different. He watched a little boy clinging to his mother as she ran through the forest, clutching him tightly to her breast. The crashing, cracking sounds of pursuit came faster than she could run. Suddenly, she dropped to her knees and crawled beneath some bushes.

Barely able to breathe, she struggled to keep her whispers quiet. "You mustn't cry in front of them, or they will hurt you. Never truly believe what they tell you, my son. What they teach is wrong. I love you. I always will. Hold that in your heart and never forget."

Abruptly, he felt powerful hands grab and roughly tug him through scratching brambles and thorns. The officer who held him stood him off to one side. Two other soldiers then dragged the terror-stricken woman from the thicket.

Frightened by his mother's terrified sobs, the child was puzzled by the anger contorting his father's face.

"Son," his father said in a mighty voice, "this is your first real lesson in manhood. A woman never defies a Sifiq man and never, ever denies him his son." The boy's father then rammed a sword through the woman's heart.

Raf-Zan stared into Alexa's face. Unable to resist, he felt the power of her mind reaching into his, observing the dream and the small boy choking back tears, fearing his father would do to him as he had done to his mother. Subjected shortly afterward to austere military instruction, she watched that same boy bury fear and submit to the warrior demands of the father. To please his father, the boy became a Sifiq soldier, earning a reputation for fearlessness and ruthlessness. However, in a faraway corner of his heart lived the final words his mother had spoken.

"Your mother was a courageous woman. She did not lie when she said she would always love you. Even now, after all you have done, her spirit begs that you be saved."

Raf-Zan's face fell forward. "I followed orders. I knew no other life. Tonight, I dreamed of her for the first time since my father sent me away to military school."

"You forgot what she told you."

Emotion choked his voice. "I didn't dare remember! He would have killed me the same heartless way!"

"And so you became your father."

Unexpectedly, Raf-Zan sobbed aloud. "Yes, I did! What choice did I have? I needed his approval! No one else cared about me! I turned fear and anger into glory, recognition, and wealth until you came along and ruined what little life I did have!" He waved his dying arm in the air to emphasize his point.

Surrendering to instinct, she approached and sat on the edge of his cot. Noting that he did not shrink away from her, Alexa grasped his bandaged hand.

Unexpectedly, he leaned toward her and squeezed her hand with his good one. "You think this arm is agony? You can't imagine how a five-year-old child feels, watching his father murder his mother."

Suddenly, repulsed by his touch, Alexa jerked from his grasp and dashed out the door. Racing through the corridors, her heart threatened to burst from her chest as she sought the cleansing air of freedom. Once outside, she stumbled, falling to her knees in the snow. Strangling on body-wrenching sobs, Alexa gasped for breath. Hot tears drew red, chapped stains along her cheeks. With resolve failing, she questioned how she could ever bring herself to accomplish this task as she rocked back and forth in overwhelming distress.

Slamming the door to Raf-Zan's room, Tirstan chased after his queen. Outside, he hit the ground at a run, sliding on his knees across snow and ice. Upon reaching Alexa and embracing her, he held her while she cried.

"How? Tell me, Tirstan! How do I do it? I don't know how! Not anymore! Not after all they did to me—all they took from me! How can Val ask this of me?"

"Lady Valkana, no one expects this of you."

"Never have I denied Val's will!" she wailed. "I made every sacrifice he asked of me. But not this! Oh, Tirstan, not this!"

Time crawled until Alexa finally raised her face. In prayer, she had always sought strength from God. With prayer, she beseeched understanding. Sacred, illuminating prayer. Eternal source of revelation. Her weeping subsided. Her breathing slowed. Her shivering ceased.

In truth, Val had delivered and healed her. He had brought her back to Gregor. Again surrounded by friends, she was going home. Val's gifts had always waited at the end of every hardship she had faced in his name. Delving into the depths of her faith and bracing her resolve, she banished memories of Raf-Zan's hateful savagery.

Minutes later, she returned to the presence of the man she had fled. Her aura glowed more brightly than ever. Softly spoken words were clear and tranquil. "Raf-Zan, life leads you away from the violence. In Turand, you have new options, new choices. The decision is yours. Your mother's spirit awakened me and brought me here. You are still her son. My question is this. Do you have her courage?"

Weakly, the Sifiq captain struggled back into a sitting position. He hardly dared believe she had returned. Involuntary tears streaked a face contorted by pain. "Your husband said last night that you could offer options. I asked your Captain Fratino. He says you have powers to heal."

Alexa shook her head. "Not I, Raf-Zan. Only my God Val can heal. My faith allows me to be his tool to channel healing into those who believe."

Confused and distraught, Raf-Zan wasn't sure he understood. "I know nothing of your god, so how am I to believe?"

"I stand before you when you know that I should be dead. I live because Val saved me. Have you forgotten how your ship was trapped within a whirlwind for days, only to be driven aground on Turand's shores? These events occurred and not without reason."

"What is it your husband called you?"

"I am Valkana, Turand's High Priestess."

Pressing his arm tightly to his chest, Raf-Zan considered all the events in the Sifiq Kingdom following the arrival of the Turandan priestesses. No rational explanation existed within his realm of experience. Then, sighing heavily, he said, "If your Val is truly the god you say, he knows that I am nothing if not a man true to his word. He can reveal himself by healing my arm. To you, Valkana, I pledge this. If he heals me, I vow to serve your Val and the throne of Turand for so long as I live."

Mulling over his comments as well as his pledge, she finally decided and climbed onto the bed, reclining into a pillow against the wall. Instructing him to lie down with his head on her lap, she rested her hand on his dying arm and chanted sacred prayers, beseeching Val's protection. Despite blessed communion with Val, exposing her soul for the healing of this man would be among the most trying tasks Alexa would ever undertake.

Turning in his sleep, Gregor's arm snaked out beneath the covers to draw his wife close. Sweeping his hand along the mattress, his brain registered the fact that she was missing from bed. He sat up. Sleepy eyes opened, fully expecting to see her engrossed in morning prayers. The room was dark, silent. Instantly, he realized she was gone.

Pushing away the blankets, he rose quickly and lit a lamp. Still groggy, he checked her things. She had dressed and left the room. Quickly, he drew on warm clothing. Passing the window, he stopped to look outside and gasped. Bursts of brightly colored lights streaked across the still-dark night sky.

'Almighty Val! No! Alexa!"

Rushing down the hallway, he didn't hesitate to knock at the door where Nikolai had been forced to share a room with Victor. That necessity had been another thorn in Gregor's wounded spirit, but there had been little choice. The royal travel party had filled Taprina's large inn to capacity. Thankfully, Victor slept soundly, but Nikolai had responded to his father's light rap.

"Nikolai, hurry! Get dressed and meet me downstairs."

Within minutes, both men raced through Taprina's streets. Their breaths created frosty, fluttering clouds in frigid air. Their arms pumped as their legs stretched out. Sliding occasionally on icy patches, sheer stubbornness kept them on their feet. Their boots pounded up the steps to the barracks, where they were met by guards who had resumed their duty.

Throwing open the doors with a loud bang, Gregor and Nikolai thought nothing of the prisoners sleeping inside. Having seen the Lights of Val, Nikolai knew that his mother was nearby. Instinctively, he trusted his father and followed him as they made their way through the corridors leading to the isolated room occupied by the Sifiq captain.

Careening around a corner, Gregor nearly collided with Tirstan. Forcefully, Tirstan restrained his king. "Your Majesty," he whispered tersely, "there was no stopping her. You mustn't go in. Not yet."

Drunkenly staggering backward, Gregor pressed his head and back against the wall. The corridor's dim light revealed his bitter anguish. His broad chest expanded and fell rapidly. Clenching his hands, he pounded his fists rhythmically against the wall. He knew how and why. If only he could reconcile himself to Val's will as she did.

"Father?" Nikolai grasped his father's muscular upper arms. "Father!"

Swallowing several times, Gregor met his son's gaze. Helplessly, he uttered brokenly, "I—can't—even—help her."

Since the night Nikolai learned how his parents had married, one part of his father's words had resounded in his mind. How had he phrased it? "Nikolai, I love your mother. Beyond everything else in this world, I love her."

Those echoing words drew Nikolai closer until he embraced his father, whose powerful body shuddered. That same trembling began to strip away layers of doubt born the night Gregor had departed for Timeri. Although full comprehension would remain elusive, Nikolai could at least offer comfort to the man he now tightly embraced.

"Sire?" Tirstan's subdued voice aroused Gregor, who sat on the floor with his face and arms resting on knees drawn to his chest. "I believe you can go to her now."

Stiffly straightening his tall frame, Gregor gratefully accepted Tirstan's offer of assistance from the floor. Nikolai also stood and, observing Tirstan's approving nod, followed his father into Raf-Zan's quarters. A lantern lit the room. Silently, Gregor approached the cot and knelt before his wife, who weakly moved Raf-Zan's sleeping head from her lap so she could edge forward into her husband's waiting arms.

Rising to his feet, Gregor lifted her against his chest. Outside, Alexa drew delicate fingers along the line of her husband's cheek. "My beloved husband," she whispered. "You always believe in me, and you always come when I need you most. Your love never fails me."

Nearing the inn, Nikolai noticed that his father's gait and posture showed signs of fatigue. Nikolai firmly grasped Gregor's arm, stopping him. "Father, you're tired. Let me carry her the rest of the way."

Gregor resisted, desperately needing to hold her, not wanting to let go of her. Alexa opened heavy eyelids. "My husband, I have given you a strong firstborn son. Let Nikolai help."

Reluctantly, Gregor transferred her body into his son's waiting arms. "Steady. Be careful with her."

Nikolai smiled compassionately. "Have no fear, Father. I love her, too. Go ahead and get her bed ready."

Reaching the foot of the inn's main staircase, Alexa asked her son to pause a moment. Wearily, she smiled. "Nikolai, I must tell you something—something very important that you must never doubt."

Inquisitively, Nikolai smiled, looking more than ever like Gregor. "What is it wish to tell me, Mother?"

Wrapped in the uniquely quiet blanket of a winter night, Alexa gazed into her son's expectant face. "Nikolai, I love your father as I have loved no one else. No man alive could ever have given me the love or the happiness he does. Know that, my son."

Unable to speak, Nikolai swallowed hard. Dumbly, he stared at the blissful expression on her face.

Weakly, she stroked his cheek. "Now. Now you can take me to your father."

∻

Golden sunshine chased away winter shadows. Carillon bells pealed glorious welcome. Drawn by melodious summons, people spilled into Toraval's streets. Tossing its head regally, the king's horse strutted proudly along city avenues. Upon its back, clad in lavender robes, rode Queen Alexa. Seated behind his wife, King Gregor held her securely as he led his party toward the palace. He had understood her desire to return home outside in the open air, beneath the light of day.

Arriving at the front steps of the palace, Nikolai dismounted first so he could lower Alexa to the ground. Amid a flurry of flying hats, flowing hair, and shouts of joy, she found herself surrounded by her four youngest children. Frantic kisses mingled with tears. Arms were everywhere, reaching out in enthusiastic hugs. Dropping to his knees, Gregor joined the fray, joyfully embracing his brood and his wife, wherever she was in the tangle of Toscano children.

Finally, with her husband's help, Alexa rose to her feet. Casting her eyes upward, she glimpsed Anlía. Stretching her arms outward, she drew her eldest daughter into a tight embrace. Alexa kissed that lovely face upon which tears flowed freely from sparkling eyes. "My beautiful Anlía. How blessed I am to have such a daughter as you."

Meanwhile, cheers from Toraval's citizenry carried in waves, filling the afternoon with revelry. Stefan and Adrina joyfully welcomed Victor with excited, tearful embraces. Oui-lest and Mei-sat marveled at the sights and sounds in this shining city they had once doubted could possibly exist.

Disturbed from indulgent memories, Alexa glanced up as Gregor approached, carrying two glasses of sparkling wine. The remembered sensuality of his smile enchanted her once again. Gleaming brown eyes promised loving satisfaction that only he could give her. Snuggled close and sipping their wine, her mind wandered anew.

Her return to Toraval had initiated weeks of celebration. Today, that celebration had culminated in a final ceremony and gala in the observance of her wedding anniversary to Gregor. Wearing the same gown she had worn those many long years ago and carrying sweetly fragrant lilacs delivered that morning from Lindaval, her step was evermore firm, evermore confident, as she walked down the chapel's carpeted aisle. As matron of honor, Adrina finally fulfilled another promise made between the two. Accompanied by dark-haired bridesmaids, this exchange of sacred vows promised naught but happiness.

Having spent days in giggles as Gregor teased her about a mysterious surprise to be revealed at the ceremony, Alexa had waited in excited anticipation of the event. Before the chapel altar, after they had renewed their commitments to one another, he solemnly announced the secret for which she was totally unprepared.

Dark eyes had beheld her tenderly. "Alexa, my love, not a day has passed that I haven't seriously contemplated a sorrowful lament that deeply troubled my heart. Knowing how you felt about the loss of your wedding ring, I searched for a solution that might ease your hurt."

She had looked perplexed as Nikolai instantly stepped forward to present a lace-covered pillow. Stefan and Adrina carefully lifted the edges of lace, exposing two rings gleaming in light yielded by hundreds of candles.

Earnestly, Gregor took her hand in his. "Alexa, I cannot return your original ring to you. However, I offer these as testament to the original vows that bound us as husband and wife and to new promises for our future together. I hope you can accept them because they have been crafted from new metal into which I had melted my own wedding ring. The melded metals of these rings signify our past, our present, and our future."

The intensity woven into his words and the emotion suffusing his voice collapsed her composure into tears of pure joy. How her hand had shaken when he slid her new ring into place. Then, with pride, he had watched as she placed the other on his finger.

Candlelight now cast a mellow glow on the ring as she glanced downward. Her emerald eyes then sought his. Setting aside her glass, she reached out to encircle his neck. Smiling lips parted to invite and taste his intoxicating, wine-flavored kiss. The pressure of his body against hers hampered the removal of her gown. How she ached for the connection so long denied them. Finally, feeling the heat of his skin against hers, she sighed.

While her exploring hands remembered the paths that had always best delighted him, her body's velvety smooth, cushioned curves inspired his. Her lips spawned burning passions he had once believed lost forever. Fleeting thoughts echoed through his mind. Was life no more than mere moments of reality transformed into chains of memories? Was reality indeed the substance of memory? Or did memories combine to comprise complex, faceted reality? Was one as the other? If there was a difference, he decided he didn't care. It only mattered that they were together again.

A final, coherent thought flitted through his mind. No mere memory compared to the overwhelming sensations beginning to inundate his entire being at that moment. Responding with surging power to fervently sweet pleas breathlessly whispered into his ear, Gregor reconnected himself, body and soul, to the greatest reality that could ever be—his love—his very life—his beloved Alexa.

Epilogue

Song of Turand
(Gregor's Song...Reprise)

Your gift of grace from me sadly gone.
My heart cried out its lonely refrain
Into darkness, my soul drifted alone.
Then your spirit returned to ease my pain.

Of Love and of Light, you were born for this land.
Sing the sweet song, the Song of Turand.

Home to your children, their mother needing.
Home to this land, you finally returned.
Home to your people, their hearts rejoicing.
Home to this heart that for you yearned.
To God, I had prayed, cast off my despair!
It was you who led me, extolling Your promise
To banish my sorrow through love we would share.
Thankful, my soul renders this new song of bliss.

Return to Turand

Of Love and of Light, you were born for this land.
Sing the sweet song, the Song of Turand.

Though trials persisted, by faith we were shielded
By sorrow nor anguish could we be conquered.
Through courage sustained, we neither yielded
Inspired by our love, we never surrendered

Of Love and of Light, you were born for this land.
Sing the sweet song, our Song of Turand.

Again, my voice lifts in joyous refrain,
To heaven, my soul soars gloriously free,
Infinite boundaries extend once again
For your light, my love, has come back to me.

Together again, your hand held in mine
Precious this gift, truth I now realize
For now I know merely one lifetime
With you, my love, will never suffice.

Of Love and of Light, born for more than this land,
Born to bring life to this solitary man.
Again, so sweet this song do I sing,
Two hearts rejoined, eternally one,
United in joy beneath golden sun,
Again, so sweet this song do I sing,
For you, my love, my own sweet Song of Turand.